BLUE

BLUE

A NOVEL

BENJAMIN ZUCKER

THE OVERLOOK PRESS
WOODSTOCK & NEW YORK

First published in the United States in 2000 by
The Overlook Press, Peter Mayer Publishers, Inc.
Lewis Hollow Road
Woodstock, New York 12498
www.overlookpress.com

Library of Congress Cataloging-in-Publication Data

Zucker, Benjamin.
Blue / Benjamin Zucker.
p.   cm.
1. Diamond industry and trade—New York (State)—New York—
Fiction. 2. Jewish men—New York (State)—New York—
Fiction. 3. Jews—New York (State)—New York—
Fiction. 4. New York (N.Y.)—Fiction. I. Title.
PS3576.U2259B58   2000   99-058821   813'.54—dc21

Book design and type formatting by Bernard Schleifer

Manufactured in Hong Kong
First Edition
1 3 5 7 9 8 6 4 2
ISBN 1-58567-000-6

Blue is dedicated with all my heart to
(in order of their appearance in my life):

LOTTY JOHANNA GUTWIRTH ZUCKER: an eternal blessing.

BARBARA BESSIN ZUCKER: ever changing, ever beautiful.

RACHEL ZUCKER: a radiant jewel.

THIS NOVEL MAY BE READ AND UNDERSTOOD IN VARIOUS WAYS. I would suggest reading the central text of Chapter 1 first and then returning to the first page and reading the commentaries together with each page's central text. After reading Chapter 1 thusly, the reader should read the central text of Chapter 2 and then return to the beginning of the chapter to read the commentaries along with each page of Chapter 2. And then, by Joyce's slow "commodious vicus of recirculation," finish the remainder of the book, chapter by chapter.

The commentaries may be read starting from the upper left-hand corner of the page, clockwise around the page until one arrives—or, in Joycean, "rearrives"—at the upper left-hand corner. Each commentator takes a tag line from the central text and muses on it. The pictures offer further commentary on the text. And yet the central text and the commentary itself may also be seen as commentary on the pictures.

The order in which to read is ultimately your choice. To the extent that all of us accept commentary on our lives, welcome it or don't listen to it; to the extent that we feel the central text of our lives is of interest to others or not, still we persevere; to the extent that we feel our lives move forward chronologically, or that although Gatsby's green light "recedes before us . . . we beat on, boats against the current, borne back ceaselessly into the past"—so, too, can one read this novel forward or backward, circularly or in a linear vector.

◆ RACHEL ABENDANA TAL, ABRAHAM TAL'S MOTHER: Advice—My husband used to come home and sit down. And before he would kiss me he would start to talk. And it would always be the same thing. Every single thing that happened to him during the day he would mention. If I would say a word or ask a question, he would grab my hand, squeeze it tightly, and talk faster. "Let me finish, let me talk," he would say quickly. And then he would talk about what didn't happen during the day. How Pollack didn't call or a stone hadn't been sold or a cutter had gone to a competitor. And suddenly he would get upset and start to talk about Tuviah. He always started with Tuviah—defending and explaining how his mistakes would teach him, how small mistakes were so important. But he never mentioned Abraham. And then I would mention something of Abraham's and he would sigh and say, "Who knows what the boy thinks?" And abruptly he would get up and kiss me and say, "From you I get the best advice." And he would go upstairs and change in our room and then come down for dinner.

■ JAMES JOYCE: Blue—Is it Tal's blue or Dosha's blue? Green to her and blue to him. Like the color of the cover of *Ulysses*, too white, too light to me. How should my printer have known that I see with my memory? And Tal, asking this "dimber wapping dell" question of color that rest on the sight of his youth and then forgetting the question before she can answer. Raffaelo's Angels dancing before him on earth in the sandbox of life. Blue and white, Bloom's Day, hortensias, my harmonic colors. Tal's blue and Dosha's green and all your pasts and futures swathed in white.

■ FRANZ KAFKA: Two-dollar advice—Why does advice for two dollars involve change that is not change? This Dosha, is she not Milena? For Dosha is looking directly at Tal. And Tal, is he not me? For could I gaze directly at Milena? Dosha should be the giver of advice and Tal and I the humble recipients. Money changing hands is always an illusion. The more you spend the less you have.

In my apartment on Zeltnergasse abutting the Tyn Cathedral I would stare for hours, waiting for something to happen, transfixed by the people who went in and out. I was absorbed. I couldn't move. And the room was rent-free, as I lodged with Father and Mother. When I lived in the Schonberg palace complex on Marktgasse, I paid a lot. And I sat and I sat. And nothing happened, because all I did was write about people waiting. And I knew that my manuscripts would be burned by my friend Brod. But the truth is that the money is irrelevant. Whatever you pay, you still wait, and there is no change. But people have been trained to concentrate on the payment and forget about the reward.

C H A P T E R I

"BLUE IS WONDERFUL," Dosha said, "but this blue is more green than blue." Her clear blue eyes with not a hint of green in them stared intently at the stucco walls of a large room on the ground floor of a Hudson and Perry Street apartment house.

"Who is giving advice to whom?" said Abraham Tal, leaning toward her, dressed in a dark blue suit and white shirt that glowed against the azure walls and the pure white ceiling of the Greenwich Village apartment.

Holding her right hand in his left, he mumbled, "For one dollar I can give you advice that will change your life. For two dollars I can give you advice that will change it back again." With flecks of white in his hair, Tal appeared to Dosha angelically floating above her, Chagall-like, still grasping his would-be Bella.

"For three dollars will you let go of my hand, you dear, sweet old man?" said Dosha, her long eyelashes quivering with laughter.

"I am not too old. You are too young!" Abraham replied, absentmindedly picking at the already and always peeling wall to his right.

"Listen, Abraham. Give me the two-dollar advice. And make it about Raphael Fisher. My angel."

◆ ISAAC TAL, ABRAHAM TAL'S FATHER: This blue is more green than blue—How does she know green from blue! She looks more like a fortune-teller than a Jew, with her red scarf and those red shoes. When I studied in the yeshiva, I remember green and blue. "*From when do we recite the Shema? From the time we cannot tell a green thread from a blue thread.*" This is Abraham's Talmud. Learning with a woman half his age as a partner. He not married and she a half-Gypsy. And he asking what color her apartment walls are painted—a short step from asking himself in. He spoiled his life in Antwerp, walking through the park when he should have been studying, and studying in an empty classroom when he should have been in the park with friends. I would fetch him at night on Sundays, and he was always alone. Why did he close the door? He's not married to her. He'll never marry. And he doesn't even sit by the window. Always hiding—from passersby, from his neighbors, from me.

● RACHEL BELLER, ABRAHAM TAL'S GIRLFRIEND: Old man—Dosha, she is exactly like me, exactly as I wished to be, with her matching scarf and shoes. Abraham is in love with her. He'll never forget me, and he'll never be able to love her because she isn't me. But he doesn't even see himself—an old man now—with a young woman. He waited too long, too long. He could have had me: scarf, shoes, and me. But he's always waiting. And now it's too late.

■ JOHANNES VERMEER: Blue—Blue is a color I can remember when I was three years old. We had visited my grandmother's house in The Hague. The kitchen faced the garden by the river. I was thirsty. I came into the kitchen in the middle of the night. But it wasn't the middle of the night. It was morning. Grandmother was very old. She had lifted a pitcher of milk and was pouring it into a flat silver tray to soak the bread for egg bread. Before I could ask for milk, she had ladled out a beakerful for me. Her right hand was extended, and I came over to the window to reach for the beaker. I took the cold metal in my hands when suddenly her face turned blue. I burst out crying and dropped the beaker on the floor. The milk, running over my feet and onto the floor, was blue. "It's blue, you're blue," I cried. Grandmother gathered me into her apron and whispered, "It's the light of The Hague. Everything looks blue in the morning here, my little darling." She gave me another cup of milk and heated it. I sat in my room with her and drank it, but it turned back to white.

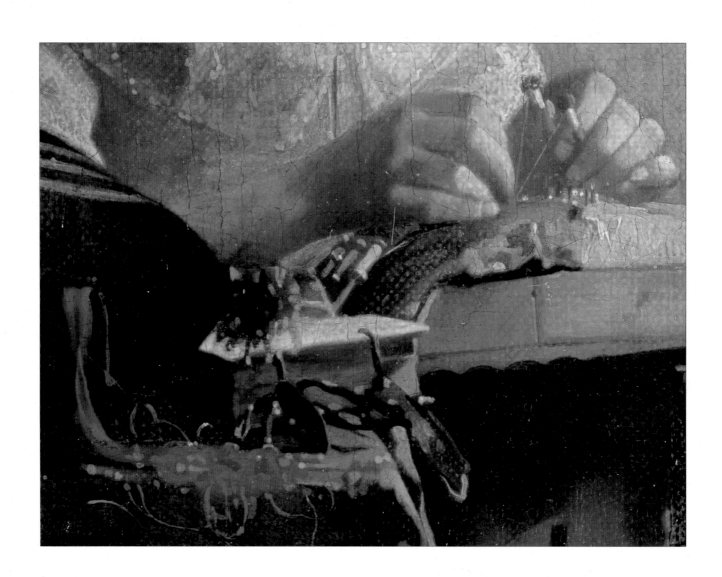

◆ RACHEL, TAL'S MOTHER: Dreamboat—When he was young I always put him to sleep with a story. Without one he would cry, but Father would never come down. Tuviah wanted only true stories, but Abraham wanted my stories, especially the ones my father had told me when I was a girl. One night, as I closed my eyes by his bedside, the same story I had heard only once, twenty four years before, came out:

There was a country whose only product was dreams. And in that land all the wise children wouldn't go to school. They would sit around all day and manufacture dreams with their hearts and their hands. Once they created enough dreams in thin rice paper, they would roll the paper into tiny curled-up scrolls and take them down to the river. There the angel Raziel would sit in a boat and softly sing, "Dreams, dreams, six pennies each." And all the dreams he liked he would take into his boat, although an occasional nightmare or two might also enter his stock. Finally, when the boat would be almost too heavy to push off from land, he would, with a sigh, move the boat off and glide downstream. He would float down the golden Sambatyon, guided only by the moon and the bright eyes of mothers putting their children to sleep. And Raziel would deliver each dream to the child who needed it. In the morning, when the child woke up, a bit of rice paper would be stuck, almost dissolved, in the corner of the child's eye. But Raziel's dream boat would have silently disappeared back downstream to pick up the next day's dreams.

■ BOBBY FISCHER: Dreamboat—My sister and I would play chess in Brooklyn while my mother was out. She played a pretty good game until I was seven, and then it was no contest. Boys, movies, going down to the beach was all she thought of. I'd stay at home and play both sides of the board. As soon as Mom came in I'd complain about my sister. And Mom would say, "She has her friends but one thing I can tell you, Bobby, is she loves you more than you love yourself."

"Why do you want the two-dollar advice about Fisher? The one-dollar advice would be better," parried Tal.

"The customer is always right," said Dosha.

"Not only here in this ninety-year-old building—551 Hudson Street—but also in Venice, Bukhara, and Troyes," Tal answered, even as she spoke.

"Make it about Dreamboat, Abraham," Dosha insisted.

"Fisher?" Tal whispered, leaning conspiratorially toward Dosha.

"Yes. Dreamboat is the name he calls himself late at night, alone with me, as we watch the light on our red and white walls."

Dosha's eyes fixed on Tal for the longest of minutes and only relented when he intoned, "Fisher. Advice about Fisher for you. Fisher. What to say? I've lived on Hudson Street for seven years. He's lived on Hudson Street for seven years. I'm looking. He's looking. He thinks I'm old and ridiculous. I know he's young and ridiculous. I write about Jews. He doesn't write about Jews."

"From what I hear you don't write about anything, Abraham," said Dosha softly.

◆ TAL'S FATHER: Venice—Abraham always had everything backwards. Rashi was our ancestor a thousand years ago. I must have told him this at least once every Sabbath from the time he was two years old. He must have heard from me hundreds of times, before he left my house, of Rashi and of the holy yeshivot of Troyes. But he has to mention Venice first because of the ring. It's not the ring that is special, but study. But he wanted it all at once. And Bukhara. He knew it only through my partner, Suleimani. And after all, it's only Suleimani's word that Maimonides' blood flowed in Suleimani's veins. I think Abraham learned more from the Indian in Suleimani's office than from Suleimani's sermons on the Rambam. But Venice definitely should be last. At least Abraham is consistent. He always exaggerates. And then he belittles.

● RACHEL BELLER, TAL'S GIRLFRIEND: Dreamboat—My darling Tal. My poor Tal. Always looking for someone to take you in her arms and float you down the warm waters in her boat, gliding you softly down the glistening shores, shining in the moonlight and warm, still, from the sun just barely set. I would have been the boat of your dreams, if only you had been able to push off from your shore. For no one can be both boat and river. But you were afraid to close your eyes gently and lie on your back. And oh, oh, I could have kissed your eyelids and you would have been my floating, dream-laden cargo, if only you had dared.

■ VERMEER: Red—When I was a young painter, I was mad for red. Father had just died, and the shock of his last words to me made my world a pool of red, with oranges and yellows swimming inside. I would stretch a canvas for days and cover and recover it, but it would always appear red. I had to paint around the color red, fill in the canvas. If I didn't I would just sit for hours staring at the canvas, thinking it was dripping with blood. I realized I should go mad if I didn't remove part of the "red" from the canvas. This young girl should repaint her walls. Imagine red walls to stare at each morning. What will she ever paint?

◆ RACHEL, TAL'S MOTHER: How can I get him to marry me?—Of course, the question came up. I admit it freely. And, of course, it is true that Gabriel sits on high before we are born and not only arranges marriages but also writes out the invitations. As I told Abraham one night, the reason that marriages of poor people are more numerous than rich people's is that Gabriel is a bit lazy. The angel knows that the guest list for a rich wedding is infinitely long and often refuses to fill out the invitations before the child is born. That leads to those "last-minute" broken engagements that the rich have so often. But the poor marriages have few invitations, and those Gabriel finishes with ease. And as the last invitation is being written, the child descends to earth. And it is the last guest that the fight is always about. Not enough room. And so the last guest is uninvited. The mother-in-law puts her foot down. The bride or groom cries. That is why all babies enter the world with a cry. They have just been protesting the last disinvited guest.

■ KAFKA: How can I get him to marry me?— The price of the *kvittel* was tiny. Here I had sat for two months writing every possible reason that Dora Dymant, the girl I was so terribly, desperately, and unswervingly in love with, be allowed to marry me. She had had me. We fulfilled at least one Talmudic injunction. But no, that was not enough. Her father must agree. He didn't disagree. How could he? I came from a fine Prague family. He didn't agree either. How could he? I came from a "fine" Prague family. It was simple. I would write out my request on a piece of paper and he would present the paper to the Gerer Rebbe. Whatever the rabbi decided would be final. I liked the simplicity of it very much. When I presented Mr. Dymant with my one-hundred-twenty-page apologia, he mumbled "a Prague *kvittel*" and immediately, with my manuscript, he went to the Gerer Rebbe's court. As he was leaving I asked him how much it would cost to have the manuscript read, and her father said, "Only one groschen." And I thought, If that is all my work is worth, it is better not to publish anything. The next night she came to my room and wept through the night. The Gerer Rebbe, after reading my work, answered— simply, clearly, and with finality—with only one word, "*No.*"

"If you know so much, how come I'm not paying *you* the two dollars?" asked Tal, gazing directly into Dosha's eyes.

"Abraham, get to the point. How can I get him to marry me?" Dosha lowered her head.

The question caught Tal off guard. As Dosha always did. Whenever and wherever she was and most of all when she was not in his sight. But she had come to his advice shop. And he was duty-bound to answer her, a valued client.

"Dosha, I can tell you, but then you must pay me only one dollar. Go home tonight. Before you hear him leave his room to greet you at the front door, burst in crying. Go to bed with him, but not in the way of the last several months. When he comes to you, sob uncontrollably. Sit down on your overstuffed maroon sofa facing east and tell him you have just seen your father— your mad father who has come to New York to take you home to Chicago."

"Are you crazy, Tal? My father died three years ago."

"Listen, Dosha. I am telling you how to marry him. If that's what you want." And if she couldn't hear him because he was shouting, he whispered, "If that's what you want."

◆ TAL'S FATHER: How can I get him to marry me?—One way is to give the bride a ring "equal to a penny," that is to say, not gem-encrusted. As the rabbis teach, it should not look as though she is being bought. The ring is a symbol that she will be *kadosh*— set aside for her husband as he is set aside for her. Set aside. Alone. Apart. Unmixed. Sole. Unmistakably the property of another. The other way is to make love to a woman. But the rabbis don't favor this method, for it is the manner of "the nations of the world." Why doesn't Abraham tell her of the ring? When talk about the ring is irrelevant, he speaks of it. When it is relevant, he forgets about it. He and this Gypsy are suited for each other.

● RACHEL, TAL'S GIRLFRIEND: How can I get him to marry me?—Yes, that is the question. That is the question and always will be. One waits for the other to end the wait. Abraham should leave the room and weep forever, for he caused me to weep forever. And not for my children. How can he have the effrontery to answer? And if he knows that answer, why didn't he answer me?

In Antwerp, when I was her age, I asked him the exact same question, clearly and evenly. But he didn't answer. He was crude enough to take the question to his mother and, worse, to his brother. Some treasures are so heavy they should not be moved from place to place. And, of course, the brother pontificated. "Such questions are not for the woman to ask." And the mother pontificated. "Such questions are not for the woman to ask aloud." But did they give him the answer? I pity the woman who must be desperate enough to come to Abraham with such a question. But I do hope he is able to help her. I can feel her tears on my cheeks already. As for Abraham, he will not sleep tonight.

■ VERMEER: How can I get him to marry me?— The question is so weak, so faint. I can hardly hear it. But I can read it from the creases around her mouth. The question that more properly should be asked, however, is, "How can I make it impossible for him to refuse to marry me?" Simple. So simple. The kernel of simplicity. But not by words. Never by words. Simply by looking. There are two ways of looking: one that will get the man to ask the question and the other that will keep the man forever enchanted. If she will look directly at him without gazing away—simply look directly at his eyes—if her eyes will make contact with his so he knows she will look at him, both by day and by night, through the dark, it will be impossible for him to resist asking for her hand in marriage. Words, however, will sour vision quicker than a summer day will turn milk to cream. If she really wants to keep him, not only wed him but keep him, she should look directly at him, but with her eyes gazing gently downward. Through her lowered eyelids, she can see him in any case. But if she casts her eyes down and freezes her glance, his eyes will widen and his vision will encompass her in a light that will never end. And he and she will be wed forever.

5

◆ RACHEL, TAL'S MOTHER: He and your mother separated—It is not only in America that so many men leave their women and so many women suddenly don't finish washing the coffee cups and move across the street, so that every day their husbands can see them and not touch them. We had that in Europe even before the war. In Antwerp, Schreiber's daughter left and no one talked about it for twenty years. It happened, no matter how we try to distort the picture of our past to our children. What is happening here that didn't happen before is that here the parents use the children to separate. They can't leave by themselves. They need someone to carry their burden of guilt. And thus, children are created. And when the child is old enough, the parents enter his room and, with a coldness that blows only here, announce evenly, "We are separating. We are divorcing. We love each other, but, you know, it's too much. It's too little." And the child is in charge of retelling the legend to every old man and woman and of hearing those magic words, "It wasn't your fault." How can Abraham put such a curse in this girl's mouth? Does he hate me so much? He wasn't in our bedroom. It wasn't like that at all.

■ KAFKA: America—"How can you write of Amerika," my father asked, "when you have never been there?"

"I would like to write about Prague, but I never lived there, either, Father." I did not tell him of my walks through the old city with Milena. That was my first visit to the old city. She told me her mother's bedtime stories. And we played hopscotch in Czech and stayed up until dawn.

"If you don't like Prague, you should leave, Franz," my father said. "I, myself, regret having come to Prague."

"I've never come to Prague," I repeated stubbornly.

"I don't understand your lawyer's German, son." And he didn't.

So I finished *Amerika*, Brod's title for my work. I finished it in a country in which I had never arrived. And before we Jews truly come to America, we will leave to go to the Holy Land.

"Then cry some more and finally, by and by, tell him of your cruel father, a Gypsy who was born in the town of Ceneda, just north of Venice. Speak of your Gypsy father and how he and your mother separated when you were seven. Tell Fisher slowly how your father met your mother after he had come to America, hoping to live in his uncle's house in Chicago, only to find he had to marry his cousin. That he refused to do so because he had seen your mother, who lived just across the garden in front of his uncle's house.

"They ran off together, lived together, loved together. You arrived. Your mother left. Your father drank. You cried. He wept. And when you were eighteen you moved to New York to become a painter. And now Dad would like to take you back to his once-removed Chicago home."

■ VERMEER: Only to find he had to marry his cousin—They, too, wanted me to marry my cousin in The Hague. My mother had been so eager for me to live in my uncle's house. Uncle thought he was a painter and Mother was mad for painting and family. And I wanted my cousin also. But my father came and told me that I had to return to Delft for a year and think, reflect, decide coolly. And I did. And since that day I can see my cousin still in every canvas I have painted. If she had waited for me, perhaps it would have been different. But she told me simply on my last day with her, "You will never show your face, Johannes." And I haven't. Seven daughters I've had, but none can compare to her.

◆ TAL'S FATHER: Come to America—At first, when Rachel said we should come to America and not to Israel, it sounded wonderful. Wasn't the Babylonian Talmud superior to the Jerusalem one? But there are intermediate categories here that I never understood. What is separation? Is it marriage? Is it unmarriage? It's nothing. Nothing. But it's worse. It's all the obligations of the *ketubbah*. The husband brings the food. The husband brings the clothing. And the husband brings the roof. But he can't live with her as Jewish men live with their wives. And because Rabbi Gershon forbids two wives at once, he can't marry anew. So he must find another person in this kingdom of madness. Four entered America. One went mad: those who never married. One died: those who divorced. One cut down the roots: those who are separated. Only Akiva was left unchanged; he remained married.

● RACHEL, TAL'S GIRLFRIEND: Mother—Don't take my life, Abraham, and mold it into a clay idol for this woman. As G-d is my witness, my mother died when I was seven. And my father never, never, never mentioned her name to me without saying, "And her memory is a blessing." Jacob longed for Rachel and worked for her for seven years. And they were as a day. After your seven-year courtship, you could have had me, but you left, and you didn't even take Leah. And here you would put this girl as her father's Rachel. But a daughter is not a wife, and your Rachel was not more than a mother and not less. This distinction you could never understand.

Passport photograph of Franz Kafka at the time of his working for the Worker's Accident Insurance Company.

♦ RACHEL, TAL'S MOTHER: Mean and cunning ways—Abraham, my darling son, when I held you, as a boy of four, in my arms and kissed your eyes, did you think I would ask for those kisses back? All your life you've been trading. First you give and then you wait for the gift in return. You have no right to give to this woman and then tell her to despise your gift. Love given is given forever and beyond. And now you would have her take her father's heart and throw that away, too. Fisher is no fool. One day he also will expect to be cast off by her. But that is your mean and cunning way. You never could accept because you never truly gave.

■ JOHNNY APPLESEED: Violence—I could see from Cambridge, Massachusetts, to the Ohio River. For every tree I planted, there grew a mirror tree in heaven. A tiny seed on the ground looks so narrow, but if you look the branches are wide and, at night, the leaves kiss the stars. You've got to look up through them. The weight of violence is what towers over our heads and blocks us from the rainbow that stretches across America in all weather. If Fisher sees the connection between violence and nearsightedness, he is a fine man for her. Not a bad Swedenborgian sermon. Reminds me of my own. Could be the echo.

Dosha had sensed what Tal would tell her before he spoke. Not the names, not the cities, but certainly the tears. She asked: "And why, Tal, should Fisher suddenly find this the cure to his marital insecurities?"

Dosha took her right hand and rested it softly on Tal's. The touch of his skin was cool. And the movement, not more than three-quarters of an inch, totally silenced him. A voice not his own emerged from Tal's throat: "Because of what you do next. You tell him you hate your father. You hate the violence and the narrowness of his vision. You hate the smallness of the rooms you grew up in. You will never return. And then, with an incredible sigh, throw yourself on your bed. Suddenly, take off the locket you've been wearing around your neck and lift up the window sash and throw it out the window, screaming, 'Father gave this to me. I hate him, and I hate his mean and cunning ways!'"

"Tal, you gave me that locket!" exclaimed Dosha, jumping up and removing her hand from his.

"I gave you that locket and I'll be downstairs to retrieve it. Don't worry," Tal responded, without a trace of emotion in his voice.

■ CLAUDE MONET: The smallness of the rooms—Don't be a fool. The size of the room doesn't count. It's the position of the window. At Giverny I built my room so small that I could hardly lie down on my bed. But the window faced the lily pond. And my life was prolonged for forty years while I gazed on the lily pads as they picked up the light, slowly swaying in the blue-violet spiral forms, and expanded concentrically beyond the days and years and miles of my vision.

♦ TAL'S FATHER: The locket you've been wearing around your neck—Abraham, honor thy father and thy mother. First you teach this girl to lie. Then you teach her to despise her father. And on this foundation you'll build her marriage? She should tell this to Fisher: "Here is my father's locket. He gave it to me. It has never left my neck since he placed it there years ago. Now it is yours. And you must give it to our child in the years to come." Then this woman could build.

But maybe you're right. The Breslover says that before the Messiah comes, the summers will be cold and the winters will be hot. Men will dress like women and women will dress like men. Rabbis will be crooks and crooks will be rabbis. So your sermon for this jeaned lady on a cold summer day is just what will fish him out of the water.

■ JAMES JOYCE: Mean—"All me life I have been lived among them but now they are becoming lothed to me. And I am lothing their little warm tricks. And lothing their mean cosy turns." "Silence, cunning and exile." For me and for her. Molly Bloom with a brush. How fine this Bloomenthal seems to me. And he misquoting me. At least she will misread my lines. They all do it nowadays. Just as I knew that for the next thousand years I'll be misquoted. "Finn, again! Take. Bussoftlhee, mememoree! Till thousendsthee."

◆ RACHEL, TAL'S MOTHER: Love—Abraham, Abraham, you are pushing her. And she is young. And she doesn't see the bottom of the hill any more than you can remember the top. Fisher won't ask if she's Jewish first. No, first he will sleep with her. And you will call it love. He doesn't want to know about her any more than you really wanted to know. You relied on Father and me to guide you, and when we did you turned on us. But Fisher wants it both ways. Don't all men? He wants to sleep with her, to hold her, and then he wants to find out if she's Jewish. And once he finds out she's not, it can't be for him. So he will leave her—not right away, but eventually. So if you are to be the matchmaker, make a match for him with a Jewish girl. And if you're not a matchmaker, let them be. They will find their own way in the new world. But don't be a modern matchmaker, as you won't be modern and you won't be a matchmaker.

■ BOB DYLAN: Nothing—
Oh the time will come up
When the winds will stop
And the breeze will cease to be breathin'
Like the stillness in the wind
'Fore the hurricane begins,
The hour when the ship comes in.

Who's Goliath and who's David here?

All this sobbing and grabbing and moaning and, most of all, telling this Fisher he's different, is fine. This is just the way to do it. But the nothing is the key to it all. The harmonica is what carries the words. Songs go straight to heaven. But songs without words go to the highest of heavens. But once the hurricane begins, she can't hold back. Six minutes sound awful short to me.

No one knew the circumstance
But they say that it happened pretty quick.

So maybe she can pull him in double time. Happened to me in Sault Sainte Marie not so long ago.

"Then what, Abraham Tal?" said Dosha, with equal coldness.

"Then what? Then what? Then you burst out sobbing and grab Fisher and scream and moan and tell him he's different. Tell him he's honest and tell him that he's all you have. Then say nothing. Within two minutes Fisher will be stroking your long dark hair, and within four minutes he will be talking softly to you, and within six minutes you will be making love and then you will be close, a hair's breadth, a whisper away from success. But if you don't listen carefully you will lose your chance, which won't come easily again."

"Are you proposing a permanent change in my sexual technique too, Tal? All for two dollars?" Dosha asked, without the slightest hint of a smile.

"Listen, Dosha. I've got it." Tal started to pace forward and backward in the advice shop. "Follow me clearly. After you've made love, he will say to you, 'It can't be. You told me you were Jewish.' Then you burst out crying again.

■ JOAN BAEZ: Nothing—Dylan's right, of course. Bobby was and is and always will be a genius. But of song. Of music. The words mean nothing. Even if Dosha says something she'll be saying nothing. *"When I first met Dylan in Gerde's Folk City, he seemed tiny, just tiny, with that goofy hat on. He came over that night and there wasn't anything I could say. I said 'far out' or 'beautiful' and Bobby mumbled, 'Hey, hey, too much.' I don't know what he said. Something equally dumb, and that was all."*

◆ TAL'S FATHER: Jewish—America is a country where you have to ask, "Are you Jewish?" In the Talmud we learn that the Jews stayed Jewish for four hundred years in Egypt because of three things: They wore different clothes from the Egyptians, they spoke their own language, and they had different names. But here in America, the clothes are the same, the language is no longer Yiddish or Hebrew or Judeo-Persian or Ladino, and the names are becoming the same.

What is this girl's name anyway? Abraham never calls her by her family name. So, to know if a person is Jewish, you have to ask. And what do they answer? "Oh, my parents are Jewish," or "Do I look Jewish?" or "Why do you ask?" It's the promised land. But to whom?

● RACHEL, TAL'S GIRLFRIEND: Different—I would gladly have taken him in my arms. I would have even if my father and one hundred rabbis had forbidden it. I would have lain with him in Antwerp, on the boat to Portugal, on a ship to Palestine, or in a narrow bed in a kibbutz in the Holy Land. Anywhere. And not for his technique or his beauty, or even for his eyes, but for his silences. When he said nothing, my heart opened to him and I felt my blood surge toward him. Tal was different from anyone I had ever met. But I couldn't give myself to him because without a ring, without a *ketubbah*, without the blessing, he would have been forever at sea, unable to reach any green island. If he couldn't marry me, he wouldn't stay with me. And if he couldn't stay with me, he would have been unable to go through life making love to another. I couldn't consign him to a loveless life. That much I knew from his silences.

■ ISAAC LURIA (1534–1572): Nothing—The Torah's true meaning is not in its words. These give the simple meaning. The true meaning lies in the spaces between the words. When the Messiah comes, the nothing between the something will be revealed. Do not read as n-o-t-h-i-n-g, but as "no thing." For if she says the name of G-d—Ain Sof, no thing—he will be hers forever without end.

◆ RACHEL, TAL'S MOTHER: The ceiling, the glass, and the window—If you suggest a proper wedding, then they would have a good chance, Abraham. You have stayed so long in America that you have forgotten what a proper Jewish wedding is like. The main thing is no ceiling, no glass, and no window. Everything here is so denaturalized. You place five hundred people in a suburban amphitheater with air-conditioning. The glass is wrapped in cloth so, G-d forbid, the industrial carpeting isn't damaged, and the windows are lit up from behind with the names of the parents of all the wealthy Ashkenazim. And from this you expect a wedding that will last through all the couple's moonlit nights?

Abraham, in Antwerp it was different. The ceiling was silk, and wind would flutter the *huppah* in a methodical flapping that would echo in the rustling of the bridal sheets hours and years later. The glass would be uncovered and glisten against the bridegroom's polished shoes. And the crack of the glass would echo in the crack of the bride's body hours and years later. And windows were raised open to heaven as the stars twinkled like assenting witnesses.

■ KAFKA: The glass—My apartment was reached by walking up a circular staircase. Above the staircase was an immense ceiling skylight that flooded my vision as I went up to my room, so much that I studiously avoided looking up until I had arrived safely. I would go past the dank bedroom of my parents, place a ream of paper on my desk, which I had moved to the window that gave out onto the Tyn Cathedral. Then, instead of writing, I would fix my vision upon the glass window directly in front of the square table.

Person after person would file by the priest and meekly accept the wafer and the blessing after kneeling before him. The priest would then walk silently toward the shaft of light that illumines downward from the window and walk out through the tiny door, just beyond my vision. Oftentimes, I thought of abandoning my desire to write and going down to the church. I was curious about whether they could see me as well as I could see them. But I was fearful of leaving my parents' house once I entered it. And I couldn't bear taking my eyes away from the glass, hoping as I was literally to see a miracle. I repeated this pattern so often that the images of ceiling, glass, and window have become a childhood nursery rhyme that I hear still.

"If you can't cry, at least throw a glass at the ceiling. Or break some dish on your knee. Then throw the pieces out the window again. The main things are the ceiling, the glass, and the window. Then he will tell you that you're mad. And after a while, perhaps around three o'clock in the morning, he will ask you again, somewhat tentatively, 'You're really not Jewish?' And suddenly you will turn toward him and, with an incredibly sharp blow, hit him hard on his hand and in one gasping breath say, 'I met you walking on the street. You picked me up, Fisher, fished me from the deep streams of New York. And I knew that if I told you I was a Gypsy's daughter, you would never, ever marry me. And I loved you from that first glance in the same way that my cheeks reddened when you spoke.

◆ TAL'S FATHER: Picked—You are a Cohen. And your mother's father is a Cohen. And we are all Cohanim descended from Cohanim. And this Fisher. Is he not a Cohen also? And did he not pick her out from all the women of New York? And now you would have his bride despise the hands that give her the blessing? The echo of this slap will last much longer than you might imagine, Abraham. Much, much longer.

● RACHEL, TAL'S GIRLFRIEND: Picked me up—You too, Abraham, picked me up. It is true that I spoke to you first. But you had followed me from my house to school every morning for many months, always a block behind me, never closer, never farther. All my friends teased me about it. "Tal's treasure," they called me, because your father was so rich and your mother was even richer.

After all those months I finally turned around and said to you, "Abraham Tal, it's my birthday." And you said, "I know." And how did you know? Unless you could see my past, as you claimed. And could you see my future, too? As you claimed. When you could not walk with me. Women on the Right line, men to the Left. My death day. Did you know that all you said was, "May I walk you to school, Rachel?" And I let you. And you shook my hand, and on that day you gave me a golden locket as a gift that I wear still. It will be many generations before women can first choose the man, Abraham. But it will never be that the man can choose without the woman waiting to be chosen.

■ VERMEER: The ceiling, the glass, and the window—Or, more precisely, the knowledge and the sense that there is a ceiling, there is glass, and there is a window. Everything on earth has a ceiling except one thing, light. In my painting of a woman in blue with a water jug, I view her from the top of the room and peer downward at her. She is unaware of my staring at her. It is not that she is indifferent to me; no, far from it. She is gazing down, also. She is looking at me, as when I was in her house in Antwerp when she would pour me a glass of milk in the morning. She was always up before me. She would take her jewels over to the window, open up the window to model her pearls and stones. When she would hear me coming from my room, she would place her hand on the milk jug and pour me my morning milk. She would kiss me on my eyelids and call me her blue jewel. And I would nestle in the blue folds of her dress, wishing to hide there forever.

● Tuviah Gutman Gutwirth, Fisher's grandfather: Lied—My father would quote the Talmud Yevamot: "*The liar can lie with impunity by telling tales of far-off lands. He will say that in the far-off land of Media he saw a camel dancing on stilts.*" And all my life I never heard my father tell an untruth. And if he didn't know, he didn't speak.

● Rachel, Tal's girlfriend: Lie—And if she didn't lie, if she never lied and if she would never lie, would she have kept him? I don't know. I honestly don't know. I could have told Tal I was pregnant by him. No matter that we never made love. He was so sick with love. And he would have married me. Impossible to believe? Conceptis Immaculis! But I didn't claim it. And I didn't lie. And we didn't wed. So perhaps she's right, after all.

■ Kafka: The judge—Our idea of justice is not to make ourselves innocent but rather to convict ourselves. How else would Joseph K. awake in the morning and accept the fact that he was on trial? No, we are all two years old, and our father holds us on the balcony. We see the infinite stars, and only Father's arms prevent us from crashing to our deaths.

And then come the petty and senseless wrongs we do. But no one really cares, for no one knows. And then we forget our petty sins—almost, but not quite. And we spend our lives searching for the judge who can convict us and punish us. But our father has abandoned us, and G-d is elusive. So we seek temporal justice. And so it is that the justice of the peace is an admirable choice. Naturally, we must pretend to fear and simulate innocence. Therefore, we choose women to push us into the judge's room.

■ Bob Dylan: Gypsy—Robert Johnson. He was the one. Not the first, not the only, but certainly the source. A guitar Gypsy who wandered the Delta and poison didn't finish him. He was two bodies in one: one body playing his guitar and another body singing. And his soul gypsying from his hands to his mouth and back again. And right into my bloodstream too—I just gotta make sure to watch those free drinks that poison pen pal of Robert Johnson also might have in store for me.

"'And so it was that I lied, Fisher, for I had to have you. And still do. And always will. Will you accept my fire as it is?' Then turn on him and love him until morning. And keep after him. If he tries to breathe, stop him. Don't give him an inch of space. As soon as it is eight o'clock, get him into a cab. Wear your fiery red dress with the lace collar and go to Twenty-two Center Street. Push him into the judge's chamber, hand twelve dollars to the judge, and he will be breathless, fascinated, overcome, and weary enough to marry you." Now exhausted, Tal collapsed into his seat.

"Tal, impossible," said Dosha evenly. "A tall Tal tale, told by an idiot. How can it be? It's a lie. All of it. My grandmother would turn over in her Kiev grave. To spurn all those Cossacks and now be adopted by a Gypsy?

◆ Rachel, Tal's mother: Grandmother—A grandmother is a better matchmaker than a mother, a mother a better matchmaker than a father, and a father a better matchmaker than a neighbor. Why? Because a grandmother knows the story of her grandparents and has seen her children and grandchildren born. Dosha's grandmother is already turning in her grave, but not because of this tale. No matchmaker's tale is accepted at face value. And let's admit it. Every Jew in Europe has had to claim Gypsy blood once in each generation. Kol Nidre. We are pardoned. Within the year. And what will be the result? Fisher seems fine. The reason her grandmother spins in her grave is America. In Europe you invented rabbinic ancestors to close the *shidduch*. Here, one invents Gypsy parentage. The ground is so loose here that one spins in one's grave.

■ Isaac Luria: Had to have—I would walk down the hill with Hayyim Vital and talk softly to him. And I would awaken him to *kavanah*—the desire and intent, the preparation, that must precede prayer. And on these walks he would whisper to me of his fears, which would melt away as the sun went down. And gradually, he knew that he had to have the One, the Only One.

Alkabetz was on a higher rung of the ladder. He had to have been. But he was lost in the present. And I would sing to him the prayer, "Come to me, my Sabbath bride," and he would place his hand on my shoulder, and as the sun would set in Safed, he knew he still needed the One, the Only One.

Vital's son was born knowing, for he came from Simon Bar Yohai's time. And Gabriel did not blow his trumpet too loudly, so Simon's teaching remained intact in his mind. A child knows the present need. But he was frightened of the future. After we had sung "Lecha Dodi," I would take young Vital's hand in mine, and we would walk down the narrow path. He was so tiny. We would pass the cemetery on the right side of the ravine, and his hand would clutch mine tightly. And I would whisper in his ear as gently as my wife would whisper in mine later that evening, "This is where I will be soon, and also your father. But the One, the Only One, will always be with you."

◆ RACHEL, TAL'S MOTHER: A Gypsy from Ceneda—When my father took out my *Yihus* brief—my list of ancestors—and showed my fiancé, Isaac, who we were, Isaac's eyes shone and never stopped shining. I never entered the room when Isaac wouldn't rise before me. When my father died on the day before Tisha B'av, Isaac cried all night and said, "What will I do without your father now?" And I said, "We will name a son after him." And we did. Isaac never went to Italy without visiting the small graveyard across the Lido lagoon from Venice, where my ancestor, the father of Moses Hayyim Luzzato, was buried in the shadow of the Ceneda synagogue. And when Isaac was most happy with me, he would hold me in his arms and rock me back and forth and call me his "little Ceneda Gypsy."

■ JOAN BAEZ: And he, a writer—*I invited Bob to sing in August 1963 in my concerts. I was getting audiences of up to ten thousand at that point, and dragging my little vagabond onto a stage was a grand experience and a gamble.... The people who had not heard of Bob were often infuriated and sometimes even booed him when he would interrupt the lilting melodies of the world's most nubile songstress with his tunes of raw images, outrage, and humor....*

One afternoon on tour I drove us into a hotel parking lot and asked Bob if he would go and check us in. When I got to the desk I was greeted warmly, but the management was eyeing Bob most unenthusiastically. 'And do you have a room for my friend?' I asked. No, they did not.... Dylan, looking to the artistic eye, like a poet, but to the untrained eye, more like a bum. I was in an impetuous, protective rage. I told management I would go elsewhere if they didn't find a really nice room for Mister Dylan. They did. I apologized to Bob, who said it didn't bother him none. But that evening, by the time my concert was over, he had written an entire song, 'When the Ship Comes In.'

Oh, the foes will rise
With the sleep still in their eyes
And they'll jerk from their bed
And think they're dreamin'.
But they'll pinch themselves and squeal
And know that it's for real
The hour when the ship comes in.

Oh, he was the writer. But Dosha should be careful. For Fisher is a writer, too. Two Davids, Bob and Fisher. What are Goliaths for? First to protect and then to be slain?

"You're a lecherous, evil man. But how do you know it will work?" she asked with a smile.

"Because Fisher is an American. And he's a Jew. When you tell him you're a Chicago Gypsy's daughter—a Gypsy from Ceneda, no less—who could resist? Just what he always nightmared to bring home to Mom. And he, a writer. And wishing to be different. And the speed of it, the sudden twist of plot—he can't resist."

"And when he finds out, what then?" said Dosha.

"Well, he won't find out," parried Tal. "In seven years, if you're still married, you burst out crying in the middle of the night and hit him as hard as you can, again, on the same hand, and when he awakes you tell him you lied.

■ BOB DYLAN: A writer—
Oh, baby, baby, baby blue
You'll change your last name, too.

I wanted to be a writer, and I wanted to be different from everyone I knew—from my father, from my neighbors. But I knew everybody had to have a name and everybody had to have a father. So I figured I would write my own name. And I figured I'd go east and see Woody and get me a father. But when I had a son, I didn't want him to do the same. So I called him Abraham. And now it's his choice.

◆ TAL'S FATHER: Ceneda—"Honor thy father and thy mother." It doesn't mean merely standing up when they enter the room, or even kissing them on both cheeks, although these would be a minimum. It means learning their story and knowing it is important. Here in America a Jew doesn't know even the name of the town in Europe from where his grandfather came. Everyone is an American here. Fisher has no first name and this girl has no last name. A good match: one hundred percent American. Funny how Abraham should bless her with Ceneda. Not a country but a city. Not even a city but a village. Not only a village but an edict. Rachel's ancestors couldn't settle in Venice, so they slept in Ceneda at night and then were permitted to trade and learn in Venice's ghetto during the day. Even the ghetto was too good for them. But she doesn't ask about Ceneda, and Fisher won't either. Maybe Abraham will tell her later.

■ KAFKA: A writer—My father was a writer also. But he was able to write only one fairly good short story, which he forced me to memorize at an early stage. It involved a superman who was born in the small Czech town of Wossek in South Bohemia. This superman arrived in Prague with very little money but, through miraculous intelligence, founded one of the greatest companies in the world. With great treasures, all honestly earned, he dutifully fed my sisters and me exactly the proper amount of bird food every day. He also made sure no predatory hunters—for at the time there were many menacing hunters circling about our castle, both Jews and Gentiles—would threaten to rob, kill, maim, or kidnap us while he was managing his mercantile kingdom.

In addition, another miracle occurred to Father. Father had time to learn everything worth knowing in the world. (This he did by studiously avoiding stupid gossip and foolish wastes of time that my mother and sisters and I seemed to concentrate on during the day.) It always astonished my father that I, too, wished to be a writer, for he had already written the only important story in the world.

Joan Baez (second from left) and Bob Dylan (at right).

● SIMHA PADAWER, DOSHA'S GRANDFATHER: In fact he was Jewish, very Jewish—After Reb Abraham Weinberg left the Slonim yeshiva to go to the Holy Land in 1935, I was chosen. For what? Certainly not to be the factotum, the Gabbai, running the synagogue. And even more certainly not to be the Rebbe—for as my dear Rickele would always say, I would have made the best combination of Rabbi and Gabbai—but the worst Rebbe or the worst Gabbai that Slonim had ever seen. No, Reb Weinberg told me, you will be my eyes. And you will write me when I am in Tiberias and tell me everything that happens here in Slonim.

So of course when "the man with the box" as they called him entered the yeshiva, everyone came running to me. Simha, is he Jewish? I had seen him wandering in Slonim: barrel-chested, looking everywhere, with a large box camera. Heavy it was, but he was a Samson, so strong he carried it over his shoulder like a two-year-old child. I asked him, after seeing him wander the streets for two days, *Fin ven kimt a yid?* (From where does a Jew come?). And he answered, without a smile, *Fin gehenna* (Hell—Berlin). And he asked me what I did and I said, "Do I look like a Rothschild? I am Reb Weinberg's eyes in the Slonim yeshiva.

Then he said, "I will be Reb Weinberg's eyes for the next generation. And he introduced himself simply: "I'm Vishniac." And added: "I will be at the yeshiva tomorrow at noon." And when the yeshiva boys asked me, "Is he Jewish?" I said that in fact he was Jewish. Very Jewish. For I understood from his eyes what he was doing.

● RACHEL, TAL'S GIRLFRIEND: The door—We lived on a narrow street, more an alley than a street. The make-believe lions that guarded the staircase leading down the alley to the main thoroughfare looked more like sleeping stray dogs than royal animals. Before my father would go to the synagogue, I would have the house all shining, and he would stand by the door as I lit the candles. He, too, would be shining, and he would say softly, thinking of Mother who had long since passed away, "I am in the presence of the Sabbath Queen and my Sabbath Princess." The only time I saw him angry on Shabbes was when I had left Tal at my doorstep in front of my house—he was with his expensive camera—and I realized it was not meant to be. I cursed our poverty and said to my father, "I may be a princess, but no prince will come to get me in this alleyway." He burst out crying and after a long time held me in his arms and told me this:

"If a man loves a woman who lives in a street of tanners, if she were not there he would never go into it, but because she is there it seems to him like a street of spice makers, where all the sweet scents of the world are to be found. So even when my people are in the land of their enemies, which is the street of tanners, I will not abhor or reject them, because of that bride in their midst, the beloved of my soul who abides there."

"It's true your father came from Ceneda, north of Venice, but, in fact, he was Jewish, very Jewish. Two thousand years Jewish. More Jewish than anyone. Sephardic Jewish. A descendant of Moses Hayyim Luzzato. A Sephardic princess, you. And all for him. And if that won't keep him yours forever, I'll return your two dollars."

"Tal, you're shrewder than you look and I love you, but I'd like my money-back guarantee in writing." And with that she left the shop, closing the door behind her, leaving Tal alone with his past.

◆ RACHEL, TAL'S MOTHER: Princess—I was the only daughter of an only daughter. My father would always look at me after he returned from synagogue on Friday night and place his hand on my forehead and bless me: "All Jewish women are princesses. May your eyes reflect the light of Rachel, our Queen." But between his hands and my forehead I could feel a slight breeze. When he was on his deathbed, I asked him where this breeze came from. He sighed such a deep sigh that I shuddered, and he said to me, "It comes from the grave of Rachel, our mother, and it travels from the Holy Land to all who live in exile and Rachel's sighs will only cease when we all return to the Holy Land." And then, Father quoted the Holy Zohar: *"Open to me an opening no bigger than the eye of a needle and I will open to thee the heavenly gates"* (Zohar III 95a). And then I knew his end was near. But it didn't matter for I knew I would be buried close to him.

◆ TAL'S FATHER: Two thousand years—When I was in yeshiva, on my first night, I was sleeping in the dormitory with the other students and I had a dream. In the dream all the books from the library were piled up in the courtyard where we would sit and study on hot days. But they were piled up in an inverted pyramid. There was one book on the bottom of the pile. On it rested two books, perfectly balanced. And on those two sat four more books. There must have been thousands, all told. Some had frayed spines. And not all were in Hebrew; some were in Dutch. Some that I saw were in a script I could not decipher but appeared to be Arabic. The whole pile seemed to dwarf the three-story wooden yeshiva building. The pile seemed to sway in the slightest wind, and I was afraid those books would topple onto the ground. On the edge a page or two would fly off from one of the coverless frayed leather bindings.

I walked to class late after this dream and as soon as I came in the classroom, Reb Yakov asked me where I had been. I told him I been dreaming. And he asked with a sigh, "What were you dreaming, Isaac?" I told him. He explained that the Talmud is like an ocean continually eddying, swaying, and shifting. Two thousand years and we still haven't charted its waters. "It's a good dream, Isaac Tal." And he sat down next to me and we began to learn: "From what time do we recite Shema?"

■ KAFKA: Jewish—In the Holy Land it was easy. "For I will give you a land . . . and make you as numerous as the stars in the sky and the sand on the beach." And Abraham went to Canaan. And that was that. Abraham answered G-d with *"the promptness of a waiter."* But now the skies are clouded over and the sands are no longer accessible. So our connection, that once was crystal clear, now has an overlay of the patina of centuries: Aramaic, Latin, Greek, Arabic, Yiddish, German, so-called English. And to keep the vision clear we try to cleanse the rust—a full-time occupation. And whoever can do it after two thousand years, is he not more Jewish than anyone?

◆ RACHEL, TAL'S MOTHER: Burst— Abraham would sit in his room for hours. Books would be open on his desk, but I never saw him read. I think he could hear me coming and he would look up as soon as I entered the room. He was the only child I ever saw who needed no other children to play with. When I asked him what he was doing, he would say pompously, "I am mastering silence." It was absolutely maddening to Tuviah. He could not stand to be alone for a moment. He was always pacing, peering, poking or looking to play with me, with Father, or, best still, with Abraham. He would tiptoe up the stairs and suddenly burst into Abraham's room. But Abraham was always ready for him. After a long time of Tuviah's begging, they would go out for a walk or to play. But Abraham never asked Tuviah to play. No, Abraham was always the prince.

■ BOB DYLAN: Father—
Come mothers and fathers
Throughout the land
And don't criticize
What you can't understand
Your sons and your daughters
Are beyond your command
Your old road is
Rapidly agin'.
Please get out of the new one
If you can't lend your hand
For the times they are a-changin'.

And not only mothers and fathers but sisters and brothers. And kings and bus drivers. To criticize you have to hear. And to hear you have to listen. To listen you have to respect. To respect you have to care. And Tuviah is no more a brother to Abraham than I was Joan's brother. Two stars streaking across the sky; they seem close from a billion miles away.

■ ROBERT JOHNSON: Between his thumb and index finger—Willie noticed him first. He was tall and no fatter than Willie's father's dowsing stick. "He's the devil," says Willie to me, when I was in Robinsonville one night. "He's looking at your hands, Robert, and he's gonna steal the way you play from you. And you're gonna go back to nothing."

"Willie, how you know he's the devil?"

"'Cause he don't blink. He just stares at your thumb and your little pinky finger." And from that night on when any man—or even any friend girl— looked too close at my thumb or my index finger, I just turned my back on the audience so they couldn't steal my moves. Simple thing, I told Willie, for the devil to turn himself into a friend girl or any damn shape person.

C H A P T E R   2

OUT OF THE BLUE you burst in," said Tuviah, a slender man with a bookish air, giving the impression of a rabbinical student who took a summer job in a diamond merchant's office and stayed for thirty years.

"Well put, Reb Tuviah," said Tal to his brother, pausing between each word.

"I'm serious, Bram. You never call, you never write. You just burst." Tiny beads of perspiration fogged the upper part of Tuviah's eyeglasses, betraying a sense of exasperation.

"We're brothers, Tuviah. With brothers you burst. Jews don't write their relatives." Tal smiled boyishly at his own joke, but Tuviah didn't blink.

"Father used to write us," said Tuviah evenly.

"And Mother used to burst." Abraham picked up the diamond crystal lying in front of his brother. Fingering it and rolling it between his thumb and index finger, he suddenly walked over to the window and held up the crystal to the light.

◆ TAL'S FATHER: Between his thumb—I would take a diamond crystal between my thumb and index finger and roll it around slowly. The light would hit the inclusions within the rough. The piqué marks would be visible immediately if I held the crystal close to my left eye. It was as though I could use the crystal as a monocle. I would play with the crystal for hours, turning it first on one side, then the other. Then I would put it upside down on another side. From each angle the crystal seemed to be a different creation. It was like Bava Metziah—just a simple tale of two people clutching at one tallis. Here, two figures are clutching one crystal. Only after days would I mark the crystal with ink where it should be cut. I always marked my own stones. Others used black ink for this. I used blue. But I never told my cutters why.

■ MONET: Out of the blue you burst in—"It's disgusting. I see everything in blue," I said. I was eighty-five years old, and Professor Mawas thought I was gaga. He laboriously wrote out a prescription to Meyrowitz for me. Just to check if I was all there he asked me, as one would speak to a child, "How do you know you are painting in blue?" I thought I would crack the canvas stand over his head. He was two inches away from my face. I had stood for sixty-eight years on my feet outdoors in scorching sunlight and the drenching cold of Giverny, and this fool was asking me how I knew I was painting in blue. From the day my stepdaughter brought me the second, third, and fourth canvases as I was painting the haystacks, I knew that it all came from one source, absolutely one. And that source was time. But I didn't know where time came from. Only at the end did I come to know it: Out of the blue you burst in. But to that fool Mawas, I simply said, "By the tubes of paint I choose."

Claude Monet in his garden in Giverny.

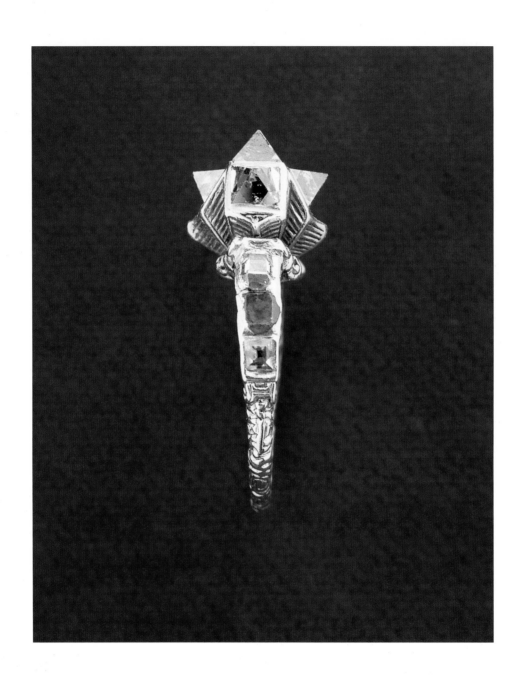

◆ RACHEL, TAL'S MOTHER: Diamonds leave me cool and I'm not about to drop something I'm quite indifferent to—In the early twenties my father made a trip to America, although the America he visited was one of distant relatives' homes and was more like Europe. When he returned to Antwerp, the rumor spread in the market that Father was going to settle in America. With a twinkle in his eye he would reply to everyone, "I'm not going to America because you can get rich there but it's impossible to make a living there." And he stayed in Europe. But when I told him that we were leaving for America, he didn't mention that but instead sighed and said, "Don't go. The real reason I didn't settle there is that the people had all their blood koshered out. They were all cool and indifferent." He thought that because America was surrounded by water, the temperature of the land was cooler than that of Europe. Even when I showed him that the United States wasn't an island, he still said, "The streets may be gold but they're still cold."

● SHABBETAI SULEIMANI, SULEIMANI'S FATHER: Old—When Suleimani was ten, after his mother's death, I used to go to my office on Zaveri Street in Jaipur very early on Sundays. And Suleimani would be left with Batchubai, the family servant. He must have been young then, maybe twenty-five, thirty, but to Suleimani he seemed like an old man.

As soon as I would leave, Batchubai would take out the leather case from under his bed and play his sitar. For hour after hour he and Suleimani would sit in the garden in the courtyard of our house. And Batchubai would say that when he played, he could imagine his own house in a small village near Jaipur. The music, he said, had wings that lifted him back to his mother.

When they heard my car return, Batchubai would rush to his room and hide his sitar in its case. He would then say, "One day I will return to my native place." "Take me with you," Suleimani pleaded. "Yes, of course. I will adopt you, Suleimani." And Abraham Tal and Tuviah Tal, both sons of my son's partner. Each looking to be adopted by a new father. Each generation, so little change.

"Abraham, put that back on my table. You're making me nervous. It's worth twenty thousand dollars." Tuviah spoke with the authority of an older brother, though, in fact, he was younger than Abraham by two and a half years. Tuviah continued. "If you drop it, it's worth two hundred dollars."

"Tuviah," said Abraham, "there are ten reasons why I shouldn't listen to you. First of all, if you're so sure I'm going to drop it, don't get so excited about losing a two-hundred-dollar stone, then you could make me even more nervous. Second, it's also my stone—we're partners. Third, I was in the stone business before you. Fourth, diamonds leave me cool and I'm not about to drop something I'm quite indifferent to. And reasons five through ten, I forget, because I'm getting old."

"You are not my partner, Bram, you are my brother," Tuviah said sternly.

"I am your partner. Adopt Suleimani as your brother," insisted Tal.

◆ TAL'S FATHER: Diamonds leave me cool—Suleimani used to tell me that a stone dealer must have "a heart of stone." It sounded foolish coming from him. To verify his stories about prices received, he generally used his children's lives as oaths. If I criticized anything to do with his cutting, he would swear on his mother's life. He always said that Abraham was a born stone dealer. "Precious stones flow through his veins," he would say. "He's absolutely cool." But I think it was because he couldn't talk to Tuviah. Tuviah was the cool one.

● RACHEL, TAL'S GIRLFRIEND: Ten reasons—My father used to tell me a story which went like this. A poor Polish Jew (were any rich?) had a horse and wagon that he wanted to sell. He went to market and approached a merchant, who told him, "I have ten reasons why I can't buy your wagon and horse." "What's the tenth?" asked the driver. "I don't have the money," replied the merchant. "Forget about telling me the other nine," replied the driver. Poor Abraham. He always has ten reasons for everything, but it always amounts to the same answer.

Sixteenth century Venetian ring set with uncut diamond crystals.

◆ RACHEL, TAL'S MOTHER: Blood—Tuviah would sit at night and look at Abraham's school exercises. He would do his math table for him. He would fill out all the capitals in his geography homework. He would conjugate all those Flemish verb endings. Tuviah would stay up late into the night when they were teenagers and read the books that Abraham was assigned to read and report on in class. And in the morning at breakfast Abraham nonchalantly would ask Tuviah what the books were about. Then Abraham would go into class and repeat what his brother had told him. And, of course, Tuviah would throw it up to Abraham. But Abraham would accept his brother's efforts as normal, and he never acknowledged a debt to him.

■ KAFKA: In the office—Dreams are reality and reality is a dream. A dream becomes a reality. And a person who has no dream never can come into reality. I wrote *The Trial* as a dream, for Joseph K. never really awoke. And then the dream, having been created, ushered forth the reality of the West and all the big office buildings with the endless files and the numbers and the microfiches. And, finally, the endless loops of inventory breakout sheets that Tuviah keeps. If only Brod had destroyed my writings as I told him to. We wouldn't have this reality of the madness of bureaucracy.

"Work with me in the office and you'll be my partner," said Tuviah, without any disingenuous hesitation.

"You mean, Tuviah, work *for* you in the office and I'll be your partner. No, thank you. Pay me what you owe me and buy me out." Abraham pronounced each word slowly in such a fashion that it was certain he had offered this proposition many times before to his unyielding yet enthralled brother.

"I don't owe you, Bram. You owe me. I've paid your rent for the last ten years. I've paid for all your food. I've honored every charitable commitment you've made. And I've never refused any one of your holdups of me in my office. What do you want now?"

"One percent of Suleimani's business with us. Any simple Satmar broker would ask for two percent for such a dream customer. And I'll settle for one percent. See how blood is? With a relative, you can talk." Again, Tal smiled boyishly.

"Why do you always come back to Suleimani? If I lost money on my transactions with Suleimani, would you reimburse me?" asked Tuviah, with an exasperated air.

■ JAMES JOYCE: Blood—Bloom adopted Dedalus. It took me 936 pages but I was the G-dfather. Of course, we Irish are Jews. Did not the Ten Tribes wander across Europe and settle in Ireland? And we, lost Hebrews? And now they claim we're Copts. Bober's *bubbe-mysehs*. Down to our last Donlevy, we're the tribes of Dan and Levy.

◆ TAL'S FATHER: Work—Abraham had one trait that made money. As my grandfather said to me, "If you work so hard when do you have time to make money?" Abraham never interrupted anyone in the middle of a story. He always waited for a person to finish speaking. If Tuviah had that quality he would be better off. Abraham could have "worked" and never shown up in the office.

● RACHEL, TAL'S GIRLFRIEND: One percent—My father, may his memory be a blessing, would say of the Klausenburger that a rich Hasid would take the Rebbe around and say to him, "Is this home good? Is that property good?" The Rebbe would just look and nod. And the Hasid got richer. But one day the Klausenburger stopped in front of a yeshiva and said, "This will vanish, for it was built with money earned on Shabbes." The two percent paid to a person who keeps Shabbes is a blessing. People forget that money is given as a blessing, so that good deeds can be done with it. Abraham deserves the one percent, not because of business reasons but because he would use it to do good.

◆ RACHEL, TAL'S MOTHER: The man— When my husband brought him home in the middle of the day without warning, I thought, What could I serve him? You never know with him. I offered coffee or tea (They like that, I thought) or hot milk. And when I mentioned hot milk, he threw himself on the ground and started to wail. I had never seen a man scream and weep at the same time. He kept sobbing that I looked like his mother and only she had ever given him hot milk. He went on and on, sobbing when I put honey in his milk, which he swallowed without stirring and all in one gulp. And he didn't stop mumbling to himself in Hindi.

Through the years my husband would bring him to our home in the middle of the day because Suleimani wouldn't drink in their office. He said the milk was sour there. I don't know what he did at night, with his wife dead and his son out of the house. He seemed more woman than man to me.

■ SIR ERNEST OPPENHEIMER: Sight—They never, never understood. Not the directors, not the dealers. I knew as soon as I arrived and started sorting. I would lay the crystals on the table and grade them for color, shape, and purity. I could spend ten hours at a time without ever being tired. When I told them we preferred the word "sight" to "allocate" or "shipment," they accepted but they didn't understand. Even when I had the directors in my home and they saw my collection of colored diamonds lying flat on my night table next to the window, they didn't understand the meaning of the word "sight."

● SHABBETAI SULEIMANI, SULEIMANI'S FATHER: The man—They would sit my son down in the office and make him tell the same stories over and over again, the stories I told him as a boy walking toward the Shaar Shamayim synagogue in Bombay. First, Tal would ask whether my son was my favorite son. And then they would ask me about the panic of 1932 in Bombay, and the riots, and how we escaped with our fortune intact because I could sense, by a change in the morning air, that trouble was coming. And then Tal would ask him over and over to describe the first time he saw sapphires and diamonds being sorted on my table in Bukhara, before we came to India. Then my son had to visit his mother. And if I didn't talk about my mother, she would be insulted. Mrs. Tal never talked, but I think she held the power in the family. It wasn't enough that I made their fortune. They needed the stories over and over, my stories, sometimes beyond my recognition, as a starving man needs bread.

"Tuviah, twenty years ago I told you that Shlomo Suleimani was the man. For you. For me. For our family. And you listened despite yourself, and now I have come to collect," said Tal, with a self-satisfied smile.

"Let's not get melodramatic," Tuviah said dismissively, not looking at Abraham but at the stones shimmering on the white blotter in front of him on his desk. "Suleimani comes to us because we have a sight from DeBeers. He needs our rough and my financing. He's desperate to have us buy his remarkable Moghul treasure— the Taj Mahal emerald—an amazing gemstone but also an amazing price. I have spent fifteen hours a week for the last twenty years listening to his infinite stock of stories, anecdotes and bubbe-mysehs. All of which have one punch line—he's the only honest Bukharan Jew in the world."

"And how did you find him?" pressed Abraham, sensing some movement.

"Abraham, tell me what you want. We go over the same story each time you come to the office."

◆ TAL'S FATHER: The man—Suleimani was the man because he knew one simple thing. It was so simple that Tuviah and Abraham together couldn't understand it. He knew about time. I would give him a stone to cut, marking it for him as to where to place the facets. He would stare at it for a long time. Then he would say, "I will take it to the factory." And Abraham and especially Tuviah would want to walk over with him to get it back more quickly. But he always refused. Then he would go with me to our house and eat a full meal. He was so stingy. I don't think he spent any money on food. He would even take the leftovers back to his Indian servant. A few days later he would return with a cut gem. He never rushed and he never spoiled a stone, even when we started to get those enormous sights. And when he sold stones for us, he also never paid on time.

● RACHEL, TAL'S GIRLFRIEND: The man— Abraham was always talking about his father, or his mother or his grandfather, whose grave he would visit with me and mumble questions to. He would always ask me to ask my father to ask the Rebbe questions. One day, my father got angry at Abraham and went to the back of the house. He returned with a Sefer Torah, which he placed in front of Abraham, and whispered to him, "Enough of asking indirectly. Ask directly." And Abraham broke down like a baby and said, "I'm afraid." My father rested his hands on Abraham's shoulders and said softly, "If you're afraid, no one else can help you. Be a man."

◆ RACHEL, TAL'S MOTHER: In all of his nine languages—My husband would always say he spoke nine languages. Each left its mark on whatever language he was speaking at the moment. His Flemish, Yiddish, French, Hebrew, Aramaic, Spanish, Ladino, and Hindi coalesced into an English that could never pass into an independent tongue. I told him that there was only one language and it had no vowels. It was the language of the eyes. You looked into the eyes and you saw the heart. Only Americans were foolish enough to speak on the phone. Sound means nothing, vision, everything. And even if he spoke eighteen languages, he would still be poorer than a clear-sighted man. He sighed, but at least he never talked to Suleimani on the phone.

■ ELIE WIESEL: Words—Words of a Hasid of Breslov in the kingdom of the night: *"He repeated to anyone willing to listen the words of his Rebbe, the only Rebbe to survive himself: 'For the love of Heaven, Jews, do not despair.'*

"Two men separated by space and time can nevertheless take part in an exchange. One asks a question and the other elsewhere later asks another, unaware that his question is an answer to the first."

● SHABBETAI SULEIMANI, SULEIMANI'S FATHER: No tie . . . no jacket—I knew those Ashkenazim couldn't take the heat. Even in Bukhara, a cool day was hotter than a Forty-seventh Street scorcher. And those fools wore ties and jackets. They should have just hanged themselves in their office. They would have been cooler. I guess if they hadn't had ties on, they would have been afraid that the banks would come by unexpectedly and cut their credit because they weren't serious American businessmen. And, of course, with their air conditioners vibrating like mad, they hoped to stay sane.

Suleimani put an end to that when he said he couldn't look at stones with an overhead light on or with the air conditioner making waves in the air. They gave him that Ashkenazic look of pity that he didn't know optics and turned off the machine. After that they left, so desperate those Ashkenazim

"Tuviah, twenty years ago I came to Father and you. I remember it like yesterday. It was a hot summer's afternoon. We were in the office on Forty-sixth Street then. I rushed into the room and Father had his jacket off and was sweating. You had no tie, not to mention any jacket. I ran in and said I'd found the solution to our problems. All we had to do was walk around the block, go to Suleimani's office, and escort him, royally, personally, to our office on an imaginary howdah—Suleimani would never deign to come alone. Five, ten minutes' work maximum. I remember Father's words: 'Abraham, five, ten minutes, that sounds like just about your maximum.'

Disregarding Father's—shall I call it—wry but strangely inaccurate sense of vocabulary, in all of his nine languages, I proposed my plan: we treat Suleimani with the respect he deserved and get a life-long customer in the process. Five minutes later, in we walked and escorted Suleimani from his office on Forty-seventh Street to our office: Father holding Suleimani's arm, I in front clearing the way for the great man, you walking behind, securing our flank—"

◆ TAL'S FATHER: Five, ten minutes—Abraham was such a fool. It was more than just being young. He was negligent to an unbelievable degree. I asked him about Suleimani. Who is Suleimani, and what will we do with him? And Abraham, my son, talks time. I didn't come to America to get an engineer for a son. Abraham said to me, "Father, did the Blessed one tell Abraham, 'Go to Mount Moriah? It will only take you two hours, round trip'?" Time is so stupid a measure, it is unbelievable. Abraham, Abraham. And he said, "Here I am. Of course, it was quick. If you decide it takes only a minute. An absolute minute. Less." My son reduced the decision to time or money: that obscene expression they use: Time is money. That is why Abraham never had either time for me or money to deal with Suleimani.

● RACHEL, TAL'S GIRLFRIEND: Five, ten—In other words, seven on the average. That is what he always told me. He would convince his father and mother that I was the one for him, and then our prenuptial wait would be like the seven-year wait for Rachel. And those seven years were as a day. I told him that they would be as a day but that he must speak to my father. He was afraid. I told him that seven days with me would be like seven years to him, and he cried. But he was afraid. And now the wait will be forever. And beyond.

Rabbi Ezra Dangoor with his family in Iraqi dress.

◆ RACHEL, TAL'S MOTHER: This prince of Bukhara—Personally, I doubt if he really was from Bukhara. Perhaps he was born there. But he couldn't have been there for many years because he used to describe being a four-year-old in Bombay. And as to being a descendant of Maimonides, this claim I doubt too. He didn't really seem to be able to read. Sometimes he gave me a note with a telephone number and address on it and seemed relieved when I would take him there in the afternoon, when he would get drowsy after overeating my lunch. He may have been a prince in his mother's eyes, however. She certainly was a queen in his, if you count all that weeping and wailing he did as honoring thy mother.

■ SIR ERNEST OPPENHEIMER: Piqué—When I was in the sorting office preparing my goods for England, I noticed that Dunkelsbuhler was more relaxed if he saw me wearing my glasses. He was always afraid of my missing the piqué in the goods. The truth was that my eyes in those days were perfectly fine for close vision. But the glasses reassured him that I was sorting correctly for his account. Later I realized that any fool could sell a flawless diamond. The real skill was in marketing the flawed goods. From that day on I always described the flawed stones as worse than they were. "Heavily spotted" is what I called the nearly clean goods. And pretty soon I had a clientele of sight-holders. They thought my vision was poor. Once they had confidence, they specialized in those goods. Suleimani was smart enough to claim that he was astigmatic, and the Tals thought they had an edge. Very Eastern. Interesting man. I would have enjoyed dealing with him.

"I remember it, Bram," interrupted Tuviah. "And even if I didn't, I've heard the story enough times. Let me tell it to you, slightly correcting your version. Yes, you were breathless and full of hopes, absolutely radiant about this prince of Bukhara, Rabbi Shlomo Suleimani, a descendant of Maimonides, a parnas of the Shaar Shamayim synagogue in Bombay. Suleimani was a man of honor, who had ten rabbis in his courtyard in Bombay, all supported by him only to join him, the Prince of Bukhara, in grace after meals. What a picture. In addition to all that, he was astigmatic and an easy mark for our piqué goods. You hardly knew him. I think later it turned out that the two of you had met only twice."

"Tuviah, to you, meeting is seeing. That's you. To me, meeting is understanding. I understood the whole picture," said Tal, pointing his index finger at himself.

◆ TAL'S FATHER: Ten rabbis—He needed the ten to pray for him. If Suleimani knew more than ten words in Hebrew, I would be surprised. And he was so primitive that he thought their prayers would fulfill his obligations. He never understood that to hire another to pray was never Jewish. How his ancestor Maimonides would have laughed, had he been at the table.

● RACHEL, TAL'S GIRLFRIEND: Maimonides—Rachman, our upstairs' neighbor, like Abraham, couldn't stop talking about how Maimonides' blood flowed through his veins directly from his mother. He would take hold of my hand and tell me how our children would be blessed because the blessing came through the mother's name. The oldest would be Ezekiel ben Rachel, after me. He had the name picked out. But not the ring.

● SHABBETAI SULEIMANI, SULEIMANI'S FATHER: Ten rabbis—Of course I had ten rabbis in my courtyard to accompany me while I ate lunch. And I had the heart to feed them and I had the heart to marry off their daughters. In the heat of the afternoon, they would say grace after our cook, Batchubai's, meals. And on the roof, Batchubai would play the sitar. And as hot as it was I always managed to stay awake through most of the chanting.

After the Depression the prayers seemed to go on for hours. They must have thought I paid by the hour. They and Batchubai thought each other mad. And when I awoke from my afternoon nap and went back to the office in the cool of the afternoon, I felt young again. My son listened more to the strumming of Batchubai than to the prayers of the rabbis. But that is a different story.

◆ RACHEL, TAL'S MOTHER: But you, too, are lucky to have me as a brother— I would place a challah on the table and both would grab at the heel. I would offer an egg and both would want the yolk. I would walk in the park and even when they were only two and four, each would grab my right hand. My father would laughingly call them, in Hebrew, "two grabbing at one tallis." And then, one day, I saw the rash on Abraham's body and I called the doctor, who hurried to the house and took him to the General Hospital. For two weeks his temperature mounted. And Tuviah would go to the courtyard in front of the hospital and shout up and wave, as he wasn't allowed inside. I came down and said, "Tuviah, go home. Now is your chance to have your room to yourself and your games to yourself and the whole house to yourself." But Tuviah stayed in the courtyard until Abraham was finally released. And I told them both, "You are, indeed, lucky each to have such a brother."

■ ALBERT EINSTEIN: One big thing—I was asked by Rabbi Goldstein: Do I believe in G-d? I replied, "I believe in Spinoza's G-d, who reveals himself in the orderly harmony of what exists." Details, details. G-d is in the details. But then the red shift. And the galaxies that are shifting away from us. And then the unmistakable proof that the universe is expanding, that it did not exist forever in the past. But the one big thing: Where, where, where did it all start from?

■ ARCHILOCHUS, c. 680 B.C.E.: One big thing— "The fox knows many things, but the hedgehog knows one big one." Abraham knows one big thing. And Tuviah knows many things. But Tuviah knows that Abraham knows one big thing. And that is why I would rather be his partner. But I would rather have Abraham as a brother.

"You were lucky," interjected Tuviah. "Mother called and told Father what to do and that a Bukharan Jew would never steal if any mention of one's mother figured in the story. That's the long and the short of it. When Father later understood the feebleness of your acquaintance with Suleimani, I thought he would kill you. I've never seen a seventy-year-old man race back to the office so fast."

"And didn't it work? Tuviah, why can't you admit I've always been right about the important thing? You're often right, Tuviah. You're a genius about everything, every little detail, every item in your inventory, every figure on your balance sheet. I'm right about one thing, one big thing: where it all comes from. You're right I'm lucky. *Hakol talui b'mazal.* 'Everything depends on luck.' I am indeed lucky to have you as my brother. But you, too, are lucky to have *me* as a brother.

◆ TAL'S FATHER: *Hakol talui b'mazal.* "Everything depends on luck"—I asked my father on the eve of my bar mitzvah where my name came from, but he didn't answer. That Saturday morning, however, he went to the *bimah* and said, "When I was of bar mitzvah age, my father stood before the congregation and said, 'Everything depends on luck: your birthplace, the softness of your bed, the warmth of your garden, the length of your journey, and even your ability to learn. If you have a good partner in yeshiva, you dialogically learn how to study life. If you have a good partner in life, you learn how to be good. *Hakol talui b'mazal,* even the Talmud. The blessings from heaven come down as the dew of life. Tal, the Dew of Life.'"

■ VERMEER: Every little detail—In the morning my father awakened me and took me to the small room in the back of the Red Fox Inn. There, on an oak table, were mounds of coins. My father had me stack the coins in piles of twenty. Then he carefully balanced a book on top of them to make sure they were all level. I counted the rows, and he noted the number of guilders and the date of the counting was noted in a large black book in which he kept his records. Once he had the sum, he swept his hand across the pile and poured all the coins into a large box that he kept open on the edge of the table.

"What is the point of it all?" I asked him one morning. "All you do is give the box to Mother every day to buy food with. Why do you care about the counting?" Father did not answer, or could not answer, or would not answer. But I saw his answer in his eyes. For Father thought with his eyes and spoke with his eyes. And the vision of my stacks of his coins was his pleasure. And from him I learned to think with my eyes. Silently. Father was fascinated by every little detail. Then and there, I knew that I would never be a merchant. I was interested only in the one thing: that there would be enough in the box for dinner.

◆ RACHEL, TAL'S MOTHER: He was charitable—My father used to go to the synagogue early with me on Friday night. He would hold my hand in his and take me to Etz Hayyim Synagogue near the exchange. Sometimes I would try to run ahead, but I couldn't free my hand from his grip. When we got to the synagogue, he would reach into his pocket and give me a coin. Then he would loosen his grip and I would place the coin into the charity box. A sigh and smile would appear on his face. He told me that when he was a boy, the angel Raziel had told him in a dream that charity was like apple seeds. If planted, the fruits would eventually come back to the table of the giver. And I was told to place the coin in the box marked "for dowries of orphaned girls." On the way home, my father would tell me that I would marry and my daughters would marry, even to the tenth generation. And because he believed so firmly, I believed too.

■ VERMEER: Face—Even then we were frightened. The Spanish could always come again. And they were burning Jews upside down in the Plaza Real in Madrid, my grandmother said. She would speak only after she had closed the doors and each window in the house and had drawn the curtains. Then she would whisper, If they come here, may their feet be frozen, better to kill yourself than surrender, for to them a Jew is a canteen of blood. And she would use a phrase in the old Spanish of her grandmother. Then she would take my hands in hers and gaze at me long and deep. "Your eyes are the eyes of my father. You and he are as alike as two drops of white water." Then she would open the curtains and look at my features by the window light and mumble, "Never, never paint your face. They will come and find you and all of your children and even your grandchildren. And they will burn all of you." She was mad, but her words have haunted me until now. And I never, never painted my self-portrait.

"I knew, Tuviah," continued Abraham, "when I invited Suleimani that sweltering New York summer day, that he was our salvation. And I knew what had to be done. When I suggested to you to offer Suleimani tea as soon as he walked in, you laughed. You wanted to talk about 'business conditions' and 'interest rates' and how much the rupee was worth. And when I casually mentioned to him we had heard of him in New York, and even in Antwerp his name was gold, and we trusted him, not because he was rich but because he was charitable, he listened. You can remember his face when I told him that we had to leave to get Mother, who had just arrived at the airport back from Israel, and that Suleimani should go through our stock and see if there was anything he thought he could purchase. And that we would return in two hours.

◆ TAL'S FATHER: To offer [him] tea—My G-d, it was ridiculous. This overweight carpet dealer sitting in our office and Abraham asking him what kind of tea he wanted, black tea from Ceylon or a Lipton mixture from Manchester. And Tuviah trying to change the subject to mortgage rates, interest rates, the prime rate and interbank loans. The man couldn't read, much less understand fine print. How could these two brothers, Abraham and Tuviah, have come from the same mother? It was so embarassing—my two grown sons fighting over him like suitors over an eighteen-year-old bride, two men fighting over one tallis. I finally got them both out of the office and let Suleimani study the diamonds and sapphires in peace. And all the while we walked around the block, Abraham ranted about how important the choice of tea was, and Tuviah bragged about how we had Suleimani off balance. I don't think the two brothers listened to each other once in their lives.

● SHABBETAI SULEIMANI, SULEIMANI'S FATHER: Sweltering day—To them it was always sweltering because of all their layers of clothes and the dark colors of their suits. They tried to look like bankers. All the air-conditioning in the world couldn't help them. And then there was the cigar smoke they filled their lungs with. Maybe in Antwerp, with all the breeziness, it didn't make much of a difference, but in America, on 47th Street, it was a deadly combination. They dressed like that every day—winter, spring, summer, and fall. I wonder if they will be buried in those suits. They probably took their credit lines to the grave with them.

But I knew how to wait. I came up at two o'clock and made them serve me hot tea, just to see their faces sweat as I drank it. I ignored their idiotic questions about interest rates. If they knew so much, why didn't they just open a bank themselves? Bombay taught me at least one lesson I was able to pass along to my son—how to think on a hot July afternoon in New York.

◆ Rachel, Tal's mother: G-d created angels—When Abraham was six years old, he suddenly couldn't sleep at night. He kept complaining of his bed moving and the walls shifting, and nothing could comfort him—not hot milk, not honey, not cake. The thing that worked was a story of how, at the beginning of the world, on the fifth day, G-d created the angels Raphael, Gabriel, Uriel, and Michael. Even angels get tired, and after they had soared through all the blackness and the white, throughout the waters and the land, they became restless. Then G-d created Adam and Eve. During the day the angels continued to frolic through the universe, but at night they stood at the four corners of Adam and Eve's bed. And today they still stand there until morning, protecting us while we sleep. After hearing about the angels, Abraham would whisper, "Raphael, Gabriel, Uriel, and Michael, good night," and slip into a deep sleep.

● Shabbetai Suleimani, Suleimani's father: I told him the Bukharan proverb—To hear my son's partner's son Abraham Tal tell it, he was born, raised, and died in Bukhara, only to be reborn again on 47th Street. Oh, how he knew our proverbs. He would quote me ones that my mother's mother had never heard. What could I do but smile and sigh politely?

One time he took me to an old Ashkenazi's house that was made into a museum. They had a show of Bukharan art, with so many old Indian stones, barely cut from diamond rough crystals, and so much jewelry that it reminded me of Zaveri Street in Jaipur. In fact, most of the jewelry was made in India. But why tell them? And what if I said what I thought? All I'd be is an old man with a faulty memory. And if I told them that if every Bukharan jewel now in a Jewish museum was once worn in Bukhara, we would have been so rich we never would have left, all they would have said was, You don't remember because you're a half-eaten apple. Why they must lie about our tradition after forgetting theirs, I'll never know.

"The expression on Suleimani's face as he protested that he didn't wish to be alone in our office with an open safe. Even if we had to honor our mother by all going to greet her. How he lingered over the word *mother*, the tears in his eyes. I told him the Bukharan proverb, 'G-d created angels before man,' and that we could recognize an angel even in human form. Suleimani wept as we left him totally alone in our office."

"Abraham," protested Tuviah, "Suleimani didn't buy anything that day. He didn't have any money at all at that time—"

"Tuviah," Tal interrupted didactically, "you forget that our stock was close to zero. We had goods on consignment from Ellman and from old man Schneider. When we came back Suleimani bowed low, almost touching our industrial carpet, to Father and took Father's hand into his and said from then on his money was our money, his sons were our father's sons. Suleimani raved how no one in America trusted anyone, and to leave a safe full of diamonds open to a man we had never done business with was more than he had ever heard of throughout the East. And he said he would tell our story. And our name would be a blessing in the Gates. And—"

■ Rabbi Nachman of Breslov: Money—"*Money is an illusion.*" Here for a few years. A rich man famous in his village, town, city, sometimes country. Then lost. Maybe regained. Occasionally passed on to a child. Maybe for two generations. Sometimes taken from one country to another. Rarely salvaged across an ocean by a refugee.

◆ Tal's father: Money—Money always was, is, and will be nothing. A good name, on the other hand, always was, is, and always will be everything. Suleimani, in my opinion, never had any money, even later on in the boom times. Either he had stock or loaned money to a cutter, or he'd given money to a relative. But Suleimani was a man without shame. He didn't thank you when you gave him credit or money. He expected these. In a way, it was a gift. Not that I was any different. Old man Schneider practically begged me to take his stones to sell. He kept ranting and raving about the new elements coming into the business and how there would be a day of reckoning and the new elements would go bankrupt. The banks would sink. Even the old-timers would suffer. If Schneider had known that I gave his goods to Suleimani, he would have had a heart attack on the spot.

● Rachel, Tal's girlfriend: An angel—"An angel" is what Abraham would always call me. Not "his" angel or "my" angel but "an" angel. He would stare into my eyes. I could see his right eye focusing in and out, like a telescope on a distant vessel. Then suddenly he would pronounce, as though making out the ship's flags, "An angel, that's what you are." It was touching, but he wasn't touching. He would just stare at me for hours.

One day, when we were in the park at sunset, just before he was about to say it to me for the one hundred eightieth time, I grabbed his ears hard and shook him and screamed, "If I'm an angel, it's a curse! Because you can't marry an angel. And you can't love an angel. And an angel can't make children. And an angel on this planet, on this continent, in this city, is shorter-lived than a rainbow." And I pulled his ears as hard as I could. It scared him, but he could never accept me as I was. Only He could ever have thought of creating humans after angels came into being. Abraham wouldn't have had the imagination.

■ SHLOMO CARLEBACH: And when he said his money was our money, he meant our money was his money—And why then was Suleimani calm? There was a wealthy Hasid of the Tsadi Ger who got two letters one morning. The first letter told him that in two weeks he would owe such a vast amount of money that all his wealth would disappear. The Hasid decided that he would spend all his time on his business and would be able, with an incredible concentration of effort, to pay off the note and maintain his wealth. There was, however, a second letter, from the Rebbe himself. In those days, before reading a letter from the Rebbe, a Hasid first would wash himself, put on his *bekeshe*, and prepare himself spiritually. These things the Hasid did and went back to the *mikvah* to prepare himself to open the second letter. When he opened the second letter, he was shocked to read that the Tsadi Ger told him to spend the next few weeks gathering two thousand rubles in the villages for a poor bride's dowry. The Hasid thought to himself, I will do what my Rebbe tells me and when I am finished, I'm sure that my business will have taken care of itself.

After two weeks the Hasid was able to collect the two thousand rubles. When he returned home, however, he found that not only had things not improved in his business, he was, in fact, completely bankrupt. Still hopeful, he went to the Tsadi Ger and handed the Rebbe the two thousand rubles. "Thank you," said the Rebbe, perfunctorily, and waved the Hasid away. "Rebbe, I just gave you two thousand rubles." "I see," said the Rebbe impatiently. The Hasid was so overcome that he left thinking what a fool he was to have had such faith in his Rebbe. He was angry for having wasted his life and spoiled his fortune in the service of the Rebbe. At the door, however, he turned and started screaming at the Rebbe, "You fake! You fraud! You don't know what I went through to get this money. You are an animal. You don't have the least spirit of G-d in you, Rebbe."

The Rebbe looked up and told him the same thing that his late grandfather, the Rizhiner, had once said to one of his followers. The Rizhiner, too, had told a rich Hasid to get him money for a bride-to-be, and the man became bankrupt while spending two weeks gathering the money. The Hasid had screamed at his grandfather, may his memory be a blessing. . . . And his grandfather proceeded to tell him this story, which the Tsadi Ger proceeded to repeat:

"Once there was a man who was extremely wealthy. He used to go to the fair in Leipzig twice a year. He was a very honest man and would always take two million marks with him in cash. When he bought merchandise, being honest, he would pay cash immediately. Because it was dangerous to carry so much cash, he would always go to the fair with his secretary. And because guarding such a vast sum was so dangerous and exhausting, he would keep the cash in a box. One day he would guard the box and the next day the secretary would watch it. At night, either the rich man would sleep with the box under his head or the secretary would. One night after an especially hot day, the rich man and the secretary went to sleep under a tree. The rich man put the box under his head. When they awoke, they continued on their journey. When they reached the fair, the rich man discovered, to his horror, that he didn't have the box.

"And, and," Tuviah interrupted. "And, Bram. He didn't buy. Pure and simple. He was broke. And when he said his money was our money, he meant our money was his money. I had to struggle with Schneider for years to get goods on memorandum to give to Suleimani. And when Suleimani sold, he wouldn't pay anyway. Not for months. Every sale was sweated out. It wasn't the way you like to pretend, that because of his connections with Jews in Bombay and Calcutta, he would be our salvation. It was my efforts, not yours."

"Tuviah, he sat in the Shaar Shamayim synagogue directly opposite the rabbi. The synagogue was the biggest one in all of India."

"'Where is the money?' he screamed at the secretary. 'You have it,' said the secretary. 'No, you have it. It's your day.' Suddenly, the secretary said, 'It must be at the place under the tree. Let us go back there and maybe, miracle of all miracles, it will still be there.'

"Of course because thousands passed en route to the fair it seemed impossible that the box would still be there. But when they returned to the place amazingly enough, the box was still there. The rich man looked at the secretary and said, 'I've had enough of you. You go your way and I'll go mine. Here, take one million marks and I don't want to see you again.' The secretary was shocked, but he took the money and left.

"Shortly thereafter, the rich man bought merchandise that declined so in value that, within months, he lost all his money. He became a *schnorrer* and wandered from town to town, begging. Even begging is a craft. You have to know how to do it well. And being formerly rich, the man couldn't make a living by begging. He covered his face, bowed low, and asked for charity. But he got hardly anything.

"One day, the former rich man came to a house and, covering his face and bowing low, he asked the wealthy master of the house for money, which he got. Every week thereafter, before Shabbes, he returned to the house and got more charity. On the third week, he went to the *mikvah* before Shabbes. There, partly out of malice, other poor people stole all of his clothes. Having not even his filthy garments, he could not go to the rich house.

"Meanwhile, the wealthy man was saying to his children, 'Something must be wrong with the *schnorrer*. Go find him.' The children searched and questioned and came upon one of the poor townspeople, who said, 'Oh, him. He's in the *mikvah* without any clothes.'

"The children went to the *mikvah* and, outside, under a tree, was the former rich man, naked and laughing. They gave him a coat and some clothing and brought him to their father's house.

"'My children found you naked under a tree near the *mikvah*,' said the rich man (who, although unrecognizable, was in fact the former secretary). 'Why were you laughing when you have nothing?'

"'When I started to lose my fortune—' the former rich man began to answer with remarkable calm. Suddenly, the former rich man recognized his secretary, and they both embraced each other with a love that only survivors can feel. The former rich man added, 'I knew that I was on top of the wheel going down. And I knew that I would soon lose all my money. But when your children found me under the tree, I had lost everything, so that I was on the bottom of the wheel and this time on the way up.'

"My grandfather, the Rizhiner, then said to the Hasid, 'I tell you that raising money will bring its own blessing to you. But, now, I bless you to be outside the wheel and not to spend your life going up and down.'

And the Tsadi Ger ended by saying, "I bless you to be outside the wheel."

■ ERNEST HEMINGWAY: Would take . . . and hand it to . . . And we got part of the Brachah—When I was in Paris in 1922 I would walk to the Pont de Tournelle and wait until noon. And that old rascal, La Farge the valet, would stagger out from the Tour d'Argent Restaurant/Hotel with a dozen books. He would take them from the boarders' rooms and sell them to Marie Fournier for whatever she would offer. Sweet Marie, she couldn't read a sentence of English. For two francs we (Hadley and I) got part of the blessing. I would race back to my apartment and read aloud all day and night to Hadley until I had finished every line. And then and only then would I start writing again. After the war I returned to the Tour d'Argent. When I saw La Farge—he had survived the Germans but could barely walk with his gout—I asked him if he remembered me. "Oh, yes, Monsieur Hemingway," he answered. "Le Grand Ecrivain, you were too proud to try to buy those books from me. I always saw you staring at me across the Pont de Tournelle. I certainly would have given them to you, rather than sell them to Madame Fournier." We laughed together and later that night, I got him so drunk on Veuve Cliquot at Brasserie Lippe that I had to carry him home.

■ HARRY CROSBY: Maybe they are millionaires, only you can't count their money—Harry Davison, whose sole regret in life was that he was not J. P. Morgan himself, had a fit when I arrived in the office: in water-stained trousers from Caresse horsing around and sprinkling the waters of the Seine on me. "I am the pope," my wife Caresse playfully announced. "And you, my husband, are twice baptized and thrice blessed." She kissed me and, dressed in her blue bathing suit, tried to lure me back upstream for what she laughingly called brunch.

"Did you swim here, Mr. Crosby?" asked Morgan's senior partner. "No, Mr. Davison, I am boated to work by my devoted wife." "So I see," said Davison, staring at me with that Morgan partner's look. "Mr. Crosby, perhaps the bank is not your proper home. Perhaps you would be better suited to living on the Left Bank with your coterie of Parisian beggars." I answered, "Mr. Davison, maybe they are millionaires, only you can't count their money. Come to my house this evening and we shall dine and ponder on this." He blanched and said, "Not if I value my Morgan partnership." I calmly riposted, "Suit yourself. But you can be assured Mr. Morgan would have accepted my invitation." "I am not Mr. Morgan, Mr. Crosby," he quipped. "Nor shall you ever be," I retorted.

"Rabbi Ben Zaken would take the Torah from the Ark and hand it to Suleimani. From Ben Zaken came the Brachah. Direct. And we got part of the Brachah."

"To hear you tell it, Bram, every Orthodox Bukharan beggar in Jerusalem should be a millionaire diamond dealer on Forty-seventh Street today."

"And then, by definition, they would be beggars. But they wouldn't be in Jerusalem either. Maybe they are millionaires, only you can't count their money. I can."

"Good, Bram. Go to them to finance your activities."

The two brothers suddenly stopped talking, each holding on to the table separating them. And slowly, with the sun going down outside, Abraham reached across the table and touched Tuviah's hand. "Tuviah, stop already. Admit that Suleimani is your best customer. Admit that I brought him in. Admit you can see far but I can see farther."

"And I can see you need money. How much, Bram?"

■ F. SCOTT FITZGERALD TO ERNEST HEMINGWAY AT THE CAFÉ LE SELECT: Millionaire—I was in the wrong country at the wrong time, trying to look like a millionaire but dreading the appearance of having earned the money. "Ernest," I said. "The rich are different from you and me." "Yes," Hemingway said. "They have more money, Scott." Ernest was a beggar financed by the air of Paris and fed by the chestnut trees on the rue Descartes. The right country at the right time. And then the war came.

■ CARESSE POLLY PHELPS JACOB PEABODY CROSBY: Beggars . . . millionaires—When I was a debutante in Philadelphia, I invented the wireless bra and sold the patent to the Warner Brothers Corset Company. The president, Corliss Jenkins IV, smiled at me when he handed me the check, put his hand on my hand, and asked me in a fatherly way, "And where are you going to live, young lady, now that you've become a millionaire?" And I looked straight at him, and a tiny voice came out of somewhere deep inside me and said, "Paris. Here in Philadelphia millionaires live like beggars. But in Paris a beggar lives like a millionaire. That's where I'm going. I'll be a beggar living like a millionaire but I'll hold on to my money like a good Philadelphia girl." "Take me with you," Jenkins said with a smile. And I answered, only half joking, "I'll ask Harry tonight."

■ SARA MURPHY: Maybe they are millionaires, only you can't count their money—23 quai des Grandes Augustines. "*Paris was like a great fair and everybody was young.*" I would look out of the window on the quai des Grandes Augustines and, while I couldn't make out their faces, I could tell by their strides how many Parisians walked with a sense of joy. They were young even when they weren't young. And they remained young. And I told Scott that, but he could never understand it even for a minute. He adored Gerald and me but I always knew that if we lost or spent or didn't have or bequeathed or squandered our fortune, our friendship would be over.

◆ RACHEL, TAL'S MOTHER: Soon—What does it mean, soon? It means they are living together. He answers the phone so that if his parents call they won't know. Or she answers the phone so that if her parents call they won't know. Or they both don't answer the phone without a prearranged signal. Or they both answer and the parents of the girl want to meet the parents of the boy but they can't. After all, they will soon be married. And then of course they can get together, the in-laws. Abraham looks for the dowry of $1,800—just like my father's father, Benjamin, who founded the dowry society for poor orphaned girls in Antwerp. His memory is a blessing. But Abraham would be better off to give them a plane ticket together. At least then "soon" would come.

■ KAFKA: Soon—I was always frozen as a child. I could never answer soon enough. I wrote *The Judgement* in one sitting during the night of the twenty-second to the twenty-third from twelve o'clock at night until six in the morning. My legs were so stiff from sitting that I could hardly pull them out from my desk. The horrible strain and joy as the story began to unfold before me. Several times during the night I doubled over with pain, with my knees held to my chest. Soon can be instantly. The quickness of Abraham to bind Isaac. Grete grabbed my feet, weeping, and said, "Franz, soon. I am to have your child soon. We must wed now." And the word froze in my ear— I could not be both Abraham and Isaac at once. I could not bind myself. And had I? Had I? She and I would have gone to Palestine. She and I. And later she was murdered en route from Florence to Auschwitz.

With Milena it was easy. I wrote her to answer me soon with the words, "*I expect one of two things, either continued silence, meaning Don't worry, I am quite well, or else a few lines.*" Even no answer can be a timely answer. Dora, a Gerer Hasid's daughter, knew that *soon* did not exist. For did her father not expect the Messiah soon? And though the Rebbe said no to the marriage proposal, though the trip to Palestine proved impossible, though the trip to Berlin proved unaffordable, my legacy to her—"*Only he who knows Dora can know the meaning of love*" was her *soon*. As I was laid gently in the grave, Dora tried to leap in.

"Eighteen hundred dollars," said Tal, lowering his eyes with a surprising delicacy.

"And for what?" demanded Tuviah.

"For a friend of mine, Fisher, a young boy who is soon to get married. He needs money."

"A Jewish girl?" queried Tuviah, surprised.

■ MILENA JESENSKA, KAFKA'S LOVE: Soon— "*I knew his fear before I ever knew him. And I armed myself against it by grasping it. Franz will never get well. Franz will die soon. Life for him is entirely different than it is for the rest of us. . . . His books are amazing. He himself is much more amazing.*"

■ BOB DYLAN: Soon—Soon is late. Late is soon.

Sooner or later, one of us must know
You just did what you're supposed to do.
Sooner or later, one of us must know
That I really did try to get close to you.

◆ TAL'S FATHER: Soon—Soon to get married. Soon to get pregnant. Soon to die. Soon to get reborn. Soon to pay back. Everything in America is soon. There are two parts to "getting married," the *Erusin* and the *Nisuyin*. There is no soon. All the man and woman need to do is have their parents make an agreement. A concrete passing of the handkerchief can do. That's an intention. They are then engaged. And afterward under a *huppah* they get married. A thousand years ago couples at thirteen or fourteen would be engaged. And only married four or five years later. That soon was sooner than this soon.

● RACHEL, TAL'S GIRLFRIEND: Soon to get married—I used to ask Abraham when would we get married. And he would stare down at his shoes and always say quietly and steadily, "soon." I am still waiting and the echo of that word is still in his mouth, as though Fisher's marriage could be an atonement for his waiting. When I would ask, When is soon? and press Abraham, he would say that we were young. The very same word used here to describe Fisher. What is young? I would say. At seventeen can't I bear your child? At seventeen can't you teach your child? There is no young, I would tell him. There is only "old." And perhaps, just perhaps, all Abraham wished for is for me to say nothing. Nothing. Simply to act. Simply to carry me off, elope, wed me.

One day my father saw us sitting on the steps in front of our house. And he called out, "Abraham, Abraham." And Abraham said, in a voice so distant, "Here I am." And my father took my young bridegroom into the house and Abraham emerged half an hour later pale as a lamb. And he was quivering the way a child did during the summer swims at Scheveningen. "He asked me when and I said soon," Abraham whispered. Later my father looked at me and said, "Your *soon*, your *here I am*— your words are correct, but you will never be Abraham. You will always be Isaac until the end of your days. And my Rachel is to be the ram."

Franz Kafka at the time he received a doctorate of law, c. 1906.

43

● ZEVI HIRSCH BEN JACOB, FISHER'S ANCESTOR: An Ashkenazi who has to be a Gypsy before she can be a Sephardi— Even when we fled Vilna from the Cossacks, my grandfather, Ephraim Katz, my light and the light of the Exile, taught me each night. Wherever we were. If we ate, or if there was no food. "Travel is study," he would say. "If the Torah does not leave your mouth, bread will surely follow." I was afraid. But I trusted in my grandfather, and G-d be praised we were saved. When we were comfortable in Moravia, suddenly my grandfather said, "You should travel again to Salonika to study, learn how the other world thinks, the universe of Maimonides." I jokingly asked my blessed grandfather, "Do you wish me, G-d forbid, to become a traveling Gypsy?" Grandfather answered simply that I was an Ashkenazi who has to be a Gypsy before I could become a Sephardi. And travel I did. Haham, thanks to be G-d, I also became.

■ REMBRANDT: Jewish bride—I lived on the street of Jews. Mostly among the wealthy Sephardim. Ephraim Bonas descending a staircase in black. They were austere. I asked him to dress in a turban and he laughed. The same laugh that mad da Costa would give when I asked him to pose as Aristotle. Only their foreheads show the biblical light trapped in orange crevices above their sad eyes. Their women would never come to my house to pose. Extraordinary to find a Jewish bride.

■ ELIE WIESEL: Gypsy—In Auschwitz the Gypsies were rounded up from the Carpathian hills of Romania and Hungary to the distant mountains of Spain. Transported in closed cars to Auschwitz they were placed in a separate *lager*. From the moment they arrived in the camp the men and women Gypsies began to howl. They screamed day and night for weeks on end. They were not chosen for work detail by the *Sonderkommandants*. The howling did not cease until they were herded, pushed, dragged, and thrown into the crematoria. Their pulverized bodies thrown into mass graves, only the echo of their tragic last song remains.

"A Jewish girl who can't say she's Jewish or else she won't be a Jewish bride. An Ashkenazi who has to be a Gypsy before she can be a Sephardi.

"What's with you, Bram? The more obscure the case, the more irresistible to you. Why can't you be straight, normal, like Father? Like me? Open?"

"Tuviah, in this generation in America, everyone is Marrano."

"Abraham, get the check from Samuel. I've got work to do." Tuviah got up from his chair and started putting each stone into its own tiny diamond paper.

"Tuviah, may your children's children receive this blessing," Tal said to his brother, who still did not raise his eyes from the desk.

Suddenly, Tuviah Tal arose and went to the rear room of his office, leaving his brother alone with his past.

◆ TAL'S FATHER: An Ashkenazi— Abraham wanted to know who was Ashkenazi and who was Sephardi. Suddenly in America he has a new distinction: Gypsy. In Antwerp, our next door neighbors, the Tedescos, were renting from Rachel's father. They were Italian Jews who had been living in Italy for hundreds of years. Abraham told them they were not Sephardi but Ashkenazi, as their name meant German in Italian. I will never forget the look of disdain they gave Abraham before bursting out laughing, believing my son to be totally mad. Tuviah is so right that the more obscure the case the more Abraham loves the complication. Those Tedescos remained in Antwerp in 1940. When Ephraim Tedesco came to New York after the war, having survived Auschwitz, he came to my office. Abraham didn't ask him his origins then. Abraham sat and stared at Ephraim. Afraid and terrified. Ephraim's German identity paper stated it simply: Ephraim Israelite Tedesco. We were all Israelites.

◆ RACHEL, TAL'S MOTHER: Jewish girl—- Abraham would have this girl deny her Judaism. My father, Benjamin, always told me of our ancestors, the Almanzas, who had been Marranos and returned to our faith. My father quoted Maimonides who said that a forced conversion was null and void. Religion is not a novel. And then poor Abraham thinks that Gypsies can give birth to Sephardim. These Ashkenazim can become Gypsies all right. But they will never become Sephardim. And we will never become Gypsies.

■ MAIMONIDES: Who has to be—And that is the *ikkar*, the core. If she has to be, she has to be. She can become a Gypsy, a Gentile, a Sufi, an apostate, an Aristotelian. And when her time of coercion is over, she may return. I wrote the Yemenites and told them that their forced conversion was null and of no account. But to become a pure Sephardi, that is something one can become only by study and practice.

NATVS IN NOVA ANGLIA
E. GOSTELMAN PINXIT IVNII

◆ RACHEL, TAL'S MOTHER: Get married—Absolutely crazy. In Antwerp, my father told me that his grandfather used to be the head of the Venetian Society to raise dowries for orphaned Jewish girls. This was the greatest honor: to enable a poor girl to get married, not only changing her life but how many lives afterward, ripples without end. Of course, in America they make fun of dowries. A man is difficult enough to live with, without having him lord it over the woman, she having brought the dowry in any case. Abraham remembers the stories I told him but he gets the ends of the tales confused. Perhaps he fell asleep before the finale of those bedtime stories. He should give the girl the $1,800 as a dowry. That would be as my ancestor Don Isaac used to do in Ceneda. And Dosha should give it to Fisher.

■ BOB DYLAN: Seven years ago I graduated—Twenty years of schooling and they put you on the day shift. Take the money.

Oh baby, baby, baby blue
You'll change your last name, too.

It's already taken Fisher. Bobby made the move. So switch. Don't fight it. Or you'll spend the next seven years buying pens and paper, choosing inks and apartments. Telling girl-friends about your coming masterpieces. Take the money. But change your name. And quick. And never tell anyone where you come from. And never tell anyone where you're going or all you'll ever be is an Old Blue.

◆ EMIL FISHER, FISHER'S FATHER: Walk-up—I came to America from France, a feather dealer selling ostrich feathers, goose satinettes, peacock flue for women's hats. When I was thirty-six years old, I remember pulling into the harbor and thinking: I will change America. A few years went by and I thought, I will change the feather line. A few years later all I could think of was to give my kids a college education. My son, a scholar, eating books, not reading them. And then in his last year of college telling me, Dad, I have bad news. I want to become a nov-elist. I didn't know what he was talking about. I never read a novel in my life. But what is the point of his whole set-up? The police lock—the sixth-floor walk-up. Even in Poland we had it better.

■ ELIHU YALE: An Old Blue—I sent the books and they called the college after my name. Which is just and proper. And the blue part makes sense. I spent twelve years buying indigo in Madras, living on Prospect Street. The summer heat was blinding me. I thought to myself, My skin is flaking. My books are crack-ing. Blue ink is turning black before my eyes. I am faint. I will die in this mis-begotten Indian land. Thank the lord I escaped to Queen's Square in London, and in the fullness of time I packed my books and sent them via Salvador to that crackpot preacher Stiles, in the Americas. And he started that scheme about a college for the propagation of the true faith of the Bible. At least he got the indigo blue right. And true.

Enoch Zeeman, *Governor Elihu Yale*.

CHAPTER 3

AN OLD BLUE, that's what I am today," said Fisher to Tal as he opened the police lock to let Tal into the top floor of his walk-up apartment on Hudson Street, six flights above Tal's advice shop.

"What's an Old Blue?" asked Tal, puzzled, looking over Fisher's shoulder at the desk, piled high with books and fountain pens and pencils and ballpoints all stacked and fastened together in a coffee can with rubber bands like huddled troops standing together, awaiting the general's orders.

"An Old Blue is a Yale man seven years out. Seven years ago I gradu-ated, Tal. And here I am not writing it. The. The only. The Great. The Great American—"

Tal was running out of patience. "You're neither old nor blue. I brought money for you, Fisher. Eighteen hundred dollars."

"For what?"

"So you can get married." Tal's eyes narrowed as though they were peer-ing at Fisher through a microscope.

"To my knowledge, Tal, it still costs only twelve bucks."

"Eighteen means life, Fisher. Eighteen hundred should get you on the path." Tal, both the professor and the student, looked at himself in the mirror as he spoke to Fisher.

◆ TAL'S FATHER: For what?—If he's not in control, he's not happy. What's the sense of always preparing and not simply ask-ing first? In Antwerp, during the sum-mer, Abraham would sit in our apart-ment for hours before coming down to work. I used to ask him, What do you do in the morning? And he would answer, I try to guess what will happen, what I will say, what Pollack will say, what I will say to Pollack. I would reply, If you're so curious, why not simply come down and see what we say to each other in the office? But no, he always had to guess everything in advance. Why couldn't he simply ask this young boy how much money he wanted? Or even if he wanted the money? But everything had to be done for effect. Such a waste. Probably, the boy wouldn't even have imagined Abraham wanted to give him such a sum.

● RACHEL, TAL'S GIRLFRIEND: Money—The money is exactly what will pre-vent them from marrying. Oh, Abraham fretted at the door of my house: How could we make "ends" meet, what if his parents wouldn't support him, my father had no money. Abraham worried that he couldn't earn his own way in his father's business. What if his brother wouldn't help him? What if? What if? And I told Abraham, Let's just go to a rabbi and get married. And then it will simply work out. Instead of this ridiculous $1,800, let Abraham offer $12. That will put the money in its rightful perspective. That is all that is needed: $12 and a willing-ness to risk. Later on Tal can give the $1,800 if he's so keen on helping them.

■ SIMHA BUNAM OF PSHISKHE: Eighteen—We learn, eighteen means life: honor your mother and your father that your days may be lengthened. The only one of the ten commandments that has a reward attached to it is the honoring of parents. For it is not natural and is more difficult.

■ JOAN BAEZ: Blue—I would sing Dylan's song: *"Oh, what'll you do now, my blue-eyed son, Oh, what'll you do now, my darling young one? I'm a-goin' back out 'fore the rain starts a-fallin' . . . Where black is the color, where none is the number."*
And he would sit in the audience in front of me. Between me and the audience. And I would see his face and never theirs.

■ EZRA STILES: Life—*What I shall do in the next life is to speak to our heavenly Father in His native tongue—Hebrew.*

◆ RACHEL, TAL'S MOTHER: Surely not your path—No, that is not it at all. The money is not wasted. Abraham is following exactly the path Suleimani took that June afternoon. Suleimani came to my house with Abraham and sat down ceremoniously in our "tearoom," as he called it, and then asked Abraham to hand him his embroidered Herati money folder and took all the money out of it and, after carefully counting the money, gave the bills to me. "For paint," he said. "Old-mine blue paint. Paint that wall mirror exactly this shade of old-mine blue turquoise," pointing to the ring on his left hand. And then Suleimani told me of his father, who used to travel to Nishtapur for five months at a time. He was the turquoise king. He would come back twice a year before Pesach and before Rosh Hashanah and spread the deep blue turquoise on our table. And the whole room would glow with the color. "Suleimani," I said gently, "My family is not in turquoise, we are in diamonds and colored stones." "Never mind," he replied, "This old-mine blue Nishapur color paint will bring the tearoom peace. And peace will make your fortune." So I used his money and bought the paint. And I liked to sit in the room.

■ KAFKA: A hundred a week—A hundred a week is still possible but already, Herr Joyce, you're speaking of punitive damages. Five thousand two hundred dollars a year with only death to look forward to even the score. Of course, a gift is permissible. We all live on gifts. But to identify the source of manna down below seems unusually filled with pride.

I would urge Mr. Tal not to pay the hundred a week. His brother will get the credit. But a clean gift which is hidden from the bride will help the donor. Abraham is entitled to the ten percent. Fisher is from Broken Bow, Tal from Venice, and the woman from the end of the rainbow. Jews so often are from out of town. That's why the ten-percent rule. The marriages are not made down below. They are made close to us. But the fees are paid down below. It's quite quaint, really.

■ CHIEF CRAZY HORSE: I haven't seen a woman—When I was a baby I was called Light Hair because my hair was the color of the mist at sunrise in winter. Later, when I was a boy, I was called Buys a Bad Woman. These two white men—one afraid to buy a woman and one afraid to pay. They should move closer to the earth and farther from the sky.

■ F. SCOTT FITZGERALD: What path—The whole point, my dear Mrs. Tal, is that Abraham is the path. He is Fisher multiplied twice. So most definitely Tal is a guide to the boy. Of course, Fisher, like myself, only knows what he doesn't want to be: ordinary, predictable, fungible, abraded, and tired. Hence the sprinting up the stairs. And the money is so, so important. He needs the girl as I needed mine. And he has to have the money. Because she has so much; a princess she is. As was mine, a Montgomery princess. If he hadn't the dowry, her father would not have gifted her. Often the money changes hands from the old to the young, from the man to the woman; it simply flows backwards after time. In America, the gold is elderly but the young have the dream.

"And what path is that, Abe? Surely not yours. I haven't seen a woman up here in the seven years I've been here. The only woman I ever saw you talk to is Dosha. Anything going on there?" Fisher asked, with a sardonic grin.

"Don't be disgusting, Fisher. She loves you more than you love yourself."

"I don't need eighteen hundred to marry myself. A hundred a week will do very well, thank you. In any case, keep the money. Maybe she'll marry you instead."

■ MAX BROD, KAFKA'S FRIEND: Maybe she'll marry you instead—Fisher's like Franz. He wants desperately to get married but needs this old man to convince him to go ahead. And at the same time he suspects that the old man's choice will not be suitable for his artistic needs. Dora Dymant vividly explained Franz's predicament to me:

"In the hope that it would enable him to lead the kind of life he wanted, Kafka establishes a concrete but by no means bourgeois relationship to his home, to his family, and to money. I mention this because I remember how quietly and objectively he spoke to me about his former fiancée. She was a splendid girl but completely bourgeois in outlook. Kafka felt that by marrying her he would have been marrying the whole deceitful world in which she moved; and he also feared that he would have had no time to come to terms with middle-class life. That was one of the principal reasons for his engagement; the other was curiosity. He wanted to get to know everything and to get to know it in personal terms."

Fisher wants Tal to make the *shidduch* so he can refuse the arranged marriage on the grounds that it will bleed and drain his art. But the old man is not without his own ruses.

◆ TAL'S FATHER: I haven't seen a woman up here in the seven years I've been here—"Thou shalt not covet thy neighbor's things." What a pair they make, each looking at each other across the hall. After Suleimani moved onto my floor—also due to Abraham's suggestion—every time I'd look out of my office window, I would see Suleimani staring at me, seated at his desk positioned directly opposite the stairwell from mine. When I finally complained, Suleimani simply said that if I didn't look, I wouldn't see him looking at me.

◆ EMIL FISHER, FISHER'S FATHER: Seven years—He read *Parshas Miketz*, the story of Pharaoh's dream, for his bar mitzvah. Raphael was so short that when he gave his speech after reading from the Torah, he had to stand on a chair. My son talked about the seven lean years following the seven fat years. He smiled at his mother and said not to worry, for in just a year more he would start to fatten up. He took those cycles seriously and always was trying to get me to figure out where in the seven-year cycle of plenty or famine I was. But he wouldn't accept my advice when I told him to join my business if he couldn't finish his novel in seven years on the top floor of a Greenwich Village walk-up.

■ JAMES JOYCE: Seven years—While it may be said that Fisher has worked for his Rachel for seven years—alluding to his bright father-in-law's request—Fisher's seven years involved no wedding. Where is Leah? The work was not in the fields but at night. And Fisher wouldn't leap. The old man, Tal, wants to give, so let him give. But what Fisher wants is $100 a week. As well he might: a nice secular sum it would be. Better a "kest" for the Sabbath so that he might study for the week than a lump-sum dowry for a woman he may never wed. "*Bracha levatalah*," a blessing in vain, as we said in school. And of course, if Tal doesn't die (and Lord knows those stairs in rue St. Sulpice almost killed me), he'll be Fisher studying *mishnayos* on his hundred a week. A fine bargain for both. Of course, it doesn't matter now that the seven fat years are over. And a hundred hundreds won't help.

Raphael, *La Velata.*

◆ Tuviah Gutman Gutwirth, Fisher's grandfather: Talks about—When I told my father—my teacher, my blessing—that someone in my yeshiva in Riglitz, while talking about my good friend Jacob, had lied to me, my father said, "One is not permitted to lie but one is not obligated to tell the truth. One can remain silent rather than shame another person."

■ Rabbi Nachman of Breslov: Precious stone—All the special qualities Seguloth possessed by precious stones are found in every Jew and all these qualities together make up a crown, because each Jew is a crown for G-d. All that is necessary is for us to search out these qualities.

■ Bobby Fischer: Family—There wasn't much to say about my father. He just left. Walked. Disappeared. And there wasn't much to say about Mom. But I sure said a lot about my queen. My queen will live forever. Tal's queen never moved, even in his opening against Tartkower in New York in 1924. Capablanca's queen occasionally spoke. But my queen—I reinvented her in the sixties.

■ Max Brod: On a thin rope—Franz would say, "*The true way goes over a rope which is not stretched at any great height but just above the ground. It seems more designed to make people stumble than be walked upon.*"

■ Chief Crazy Horse: If you can find them—These whites are like buffalo cut from the herd. Wandering around in tight circles, howling at the sun.

Where are her parents, this Doe-Sha? When I was courting Black Buffalo woman I could speak at evening for two minutes time. Her mother would immediately pass Black Buffalo to another brave to be spoken to. Black Buffalo's long legs were bound every evening. These parents have dropped their daughter into the void. Is it a wonder that their children's ears have become so closed to their secrets? If they can find them at all.

"Fisher, you're her precious stone, all she talks about. And anyway, I'll get ten percent of the dowry since she's from out of town. It's five percent for arranging a marriage for parties that live in the same city and ten percent if you bring in an out-of-towner, so that's what I can ask her family for."

"If you can find them. She never talks about them. I can't stop talking about mine and she can't start talking about hers. As far as ten percent of her dowry, what do you think that will amount to?"

"Well, Fisher, I've thought a lot about that," said Tal calmly. "And I've decided that I'd like her painting 'White No. 4' that's hanging on the other side of my wall."

"When do you want delivery, Abe? Right now, before she says 'yes,' or at consummation time?" Fisher moved menacingly close to Tal.

"Oh, Fisher, not now and not then. I just want to know I own it. I don't mind at all that it hangs on a thin rope in your apartment. On the contrary, I like it that way.

◆ Rachel, Tal's mother: You're all she talks about—Of course Abraham is right. Dosha loves Fisher. But Fisher won't believe Abraham. If Abraham had been married those seven years and the boy looked at Abraham as an example, that would have been more incentive to get married than all the $1,800 in the world. You don't teach by words, you learn by example, Abraham. My father didn't have to tell me what to do, he just did.

◆ Emil Fisher, Fisher's father: I can't stop talking about mine—That's news to me. He never would call or drop by my office. It was always his mother that was the go-between. The Yiddish proverb my father used, "A father can support ten children but ten children can't support one father," is so true. But it was not money that I wanted from him, just a letter. More than a phone call, I think. I would have put that letter in my wallet rather than the photo of him just before his bar mitzvah. I guess if he talked less about me he could have talked more *to* me.

■ Vincent van Gogh: I just want to know I own it—That's what Théo told me. Sweet of him. Even to the extent of paying me for the painting. He created that love of twilight in me. He was always writing to me that he saw twilight for the first time in my paintings. And it was imprinted on his eyes. Even in the middle of the night he could envision twilight. He didn't have to have the canvas in his house. He thought I was the teacher, but truly I was his pupil. As a dealer he couldn't sell my paintings—there were no buyers. As a connoisseur he wanted to own them. So I kept the paintings, he paid me, and he owned them. And his son inherited them. Tal is right; where the painting hangs is of little importance.

I Ver Meer
MDCLXVIII

◆ EMIL FISHER, FISHER'S FATHER: Too much like my unwritten novel—Nothing can be too much like something that doesn't exist and probably never will. I could have understood it if my son had told me he had finished a novel and handed it to me. Like styles for the coming season. That would have made sense. But then why take Chinese painting courses at Yale? If my silk flower designer told me, "I've got a big secret. It's about my undrawn sketches for next year's silk line," I would have fired him on the spot. It's no secret if it's not on paper. And how can my son claim something undone is his? He is so much like my neighbor Topiol I grew up with in the shtetl. His Jerusalem, just about to be rebuilt. So don't worry about the future.

■ F. SCOTT FITZGERALD: My unwritten novel—All sketched out for the future, I left my notebooks with characters and phrases. Ideas. All alphabetized. This Fisher was born on the French Riviera. Nice touch: to come back as a Jew and a Yalie. A bit of irony. At least I returned as a novelist. I hope Fisher reads my lists. Thank G-d his woman's a painter and not a novelist. Princeton was hell enough.

■ NATHANAEL WEST: Fisher—This Fisher is me. I changed my name to West. Not that Weinstein was a bad name. The other Weinstein got into Brown, and I took his place at college. My unwritten name, which I wrote and called into existence. Fisher looks as I would look if I were reborn when he came in. Instead of trying to be Scott, I should have tried to be myself.

"I like having my assets dispersed—even if they're only on the other side of a dividing wall," continued Tal.

"You're a freak, Tal."

"You're the freak, Fisher. In India, Bombay merchants think like you. Only as far as the eye can see or the hand can reach will they allow their possessions to rest. You're a covert Mahwari merchant, right here on Hudson Street."

"And why are you trying so hard to marry off a nice Jewish girl to a Mahwari like me, Tal?"

"Fisher, why are you always joking when it comes to Dosha? Why can't you ever talk for five minutes about her without drifting into the Borscht Circuit?"

"Well, since you asked, I find the dowry commission on your side too onerous. Ten percent is okay, but 'White No. 4' with an echo of red, her best painting, is out of the question. The process is too much like my unwritten novel.

■ VERMEER: I like having my assets dispersed—They are mad, these people of New York. I kept everything that was important to me in one place—in my home. The paintings I bought and sold I kept in the parlor beside the kitchen. All the masterpieces I painted were upstairs in the bedroom hidden behind the blue curtain facing the river. My daughters and my wife rarely went out. My mother-in-law and her unmarried son were with us most of the day. Coffins are made to disperse us.

■ JAMES JOYCE: Like my unwritten novel—On September 30, 1940, my application to settle in Switzerland was denied. The reason given: because I was a Jew, "C'est le bouquet, vraiment." No one reads my books now. No more books to be written, I thought then. I, shattered. We were admitted into Zurich through a Swiss-cheese hole. It was then, in 1940, that I prayed. Zurich to die. Buried far from the Fascists. Met him Pike Horses. Let me be born again this time a Jew. And let me write a novel about an Irishman. After Mercanton issued an affidavit, "Que je ne suis pas juif de Judée mais aryen d'Erin." Curious fellow, this Fisher of men.

■ NORA JOYCE: Like my unwritten novel—Sure Jim was broken in '40. When in November we got the dreadful news of my mother's passing, he wept like a child. He took my hand and held it to my breast and said so weakly to me, "My dimber wapping dell." I'll return to you again this time as a Jew. This Fisher's novel will be written, not by him but through his red bride.

■ THE RIZHINER REBBE: The highest bidder—"*Look around you. Works of art everywhere are cherished, honored and protected while man—G-d's masterpiece—lies in the dust.*"

■ F. SCOTT FITZGERALD: Precisely forty years after my death—Or at my death. Which is never in the past but simply continues. It's all strained through your religion—but really is your past. "Financing Finnegan," read it 1939. Finnegan. His indeed was a name with ingots in it. My career had started brilliantly, and if it had not kept up to its first exalted level, at least it started brilliantly all over again every few years. I was the "*perennial man of promise in American letters.*" Abraham's not a money-wasting old man. He's starting Fisher off. Fisher is his masterpiece. And I'll tell you something quickly. Fisher was born in 1940. December 22. On the Riviera. In the morning, early Sunday. Get it? I died on December 21 at 5:15 A.M. Get it? He's me. Finnegan. Back again.

■ BOB DYLAN: Great—"*mother say go in That direction & please do the greatest deed of all time & say i say mother but it's already been done & she say well what else is there for you to do & i say i don't know mother but I'm not going in that direction—I'm going in That direction & she say Ok but where will you be & i say i don't know mother but I'm not Tom Joad & she say all right then I am not your mother.*"

■ SIMHA BUNAM: Unwritten book—I would write a book every day. And it would be one page long. And I would rip the page up every night. I saw Fishers in Berlin. And I played chess with Fishers in Vienna. And I sold merchandise to Fishers when I had a short black coat. And the greatest heresy is the belief that a book can be written on paper. Only parchment will last.

"And I quote from my great unwritten book: 'Picture this: a warm June day. Suddenly, a crowd of people in the Guggenheim are startled by an announcement: "Ladies and gentlemen, Solomon R. Guggenheim speaks to us today from his will: 'Precisely forty years after my death, the paintings in my museum should be auctioned off. However, as, I, Solomon, have learned from my father, only cash in your pocket counts—not checks, not bank deposits, just old-fashioned liquidity.'

"So, ladies and gentlemen," says the director of the museum to the astounded museum-goers who just by chance happened to be in Solomon Guggenheim's museum on the day stipulated by the old man's will, "the bidding will commence in twenty minutes. All Mr. Guggenheim's van Goghs, all his Monets, all his Mondrians—indeed, all his masterpieces here today—will be sold to the highest bidder. Anyone wishing to leave now will be allowed to, but no one will be permitted re-entry into this museum once the auction has started." The director intoned these words over the loudspeaker system throughout the entire building.

■ THE KOTZKER REBBE: Book—I could have written a book. But I didn't. And who would read my book? A Jew. And when would a poor Jew read it? On Shabbes. And when would he read? In the afternoon when he is exhausted from the "*vochedike*" work—the work of the past week. And what would happen, he would fall asleep over my words. For him I should write a book?

■ VERMEER: Sold to the highest bidder—Twice in my lifetime, suddenly, all the paintings I dealt with after the crisis of 1643 were sold under the hammer. On the day I died the neighborhood baker purchased all the masterpieces I had painted except for *Allegory of Art*, hidden upstairs in my mother-in-law's linen cabinet with the false back. In both cases the buyers had visited me, coveted my property and the property of my mind. When disaster struck they were ready. It's unnatural, the desire for art. It knows no hour or season. I bet museum-goers entering a gallery dream for a chance someday to buy or to borrow. Just for a lifetime.

■ JAMES JOYCE: My death—Don't Finnegan me, goo goo Googenheim. A renegade heathen you are. "*I pity your old self I was once used to. Now a younger's there. . . . as I was sweet when I came down out of me mother. My great blue bedroom, the air so quiet, scarce a cloud. In peace and silence. I could have stayed up there for always? . . . First we feel. Then we fall. And let her rain now if she likes. Gently or strongly as she likes. Anyway let her rain for my time is come.*"

You only wish the lad was you. It takes a lot longer to return, and you know it. He's himself. And that's the he and the she of it. Like Mrs. McCormick. Offering me thousands if only I lie back and be analyzed. Refuse the money, Fisher. Or you'll spend the rest of your life on your back. Paint your masterpiece novels.

◆ TAL'S FATHER: She leaves in a flash, not believing her luck—Americans can't believe their luck. An open country, greenest in the world. Just run a railroad across it. Kill twenty red-skinned people and call it a skirmish. Kill two hundred and call it a war. That's how they think. Buy cheap for trinkets and "run like a bandit," not believing your luck. G-d forbid she should stay, sell her picture for twice her price, and paint two new paintings instead. No. Make a quick buck—a killing—and get out: the American Dream.

■ SØREN KIERKEGAARD: Not believing—Once one believes, all is possible and what if one cannot believe? Faith: the willing suspension of disbelief. Abraham drawing the knife, losing hope, losing belief, yet having faith. A traveler wandering in a museum seeing beauty beyond any feeling that one has wanting to possess it, no real hope or belief that such a work of art could be a nighttime angel of comfort when one awakes in the terror of one's sleep searching for calmness. It doesn't matter if she believes or if she has luck. All she needs is faith.

■ ALEXIS DE TOCQUEVILLE: She leaves in a flash—"*I know of no country, indeed, where the love of money has taken stronger hold on the affections of men and where a profounder contempt is expressed for the theory of the permanent equality of property.*" An American, even a poor American, will believe that a treasure might at any time be offered to him. A European would think such a scene of a work of art being sold on a democratic basis could never occur. A European would never participate in such a bidding.

"Then, of course, the fun begins. It's basically zero-sum economics, from Yale. The first painting goes for eight hundred dollars to a lady from Scarsdale who had come to New York to pick up a color TV at Macy's. She leaves in a flash, not believing her luck, but lugging her masterpiece with her. By the fifth painting, people are starting to form groups, cartels. People are trading their houses on the outside for a few hundred dollars in ready cash on the inside. Hysteria sweeps. Wartime buying panic. A few accountants and one statistician start to add up the probable amount of money in the house by multiplying numbers of people times average cash balances. They hope to pick up the last paintings for almost nothing. People are swapping pictures they bought. And then, a siren. A long, incredible wail, an end-of-the-world wail. A nighttime, night-rending wail.

◆ EMIL FISHER, FISHER'S FATHER: Zero-sum economics, from Yale—The words don't add up to me. If it's zero, what's the sum? When I would ask my son why he didn't take economics he would quote that Yale professor, Walter Fisher, who said in 1929, "The economy has reached a permanently high plateau." That's what they teach at Yale, Dad. Perfectly reliable economics. If you do the opposite you never make a mistake. So I said, Good, study economics and do the opposite. It was only years later that I found out he would sit in the back of economics classes and listen. But he would never give me the satisfaction of following my advice. My zero-sum son.

■ RABBI NACHMAN OF BRESLOV: Hysteria sweeps—When man understands that money has no meaning, madness can reign. Money is an illusion. Where are the great fortunes of bygone days? Everyone spoke of them. Now they have disappeared. I like this Fisher. *Mayse betoch mayse*—a story within a story. A dream within a dream.

■ DELMORE SCHWARTZ: Hysteria—"*Teach me to stare and not to stare.*" To give. To sympathize. To control. To sit still.

◆ RACHEL, TAL'S MOTHER: You can have—When he was five he would tug at my dress while I was baking, his fingers grabbing at mine so I could barely knead the dough. All the time whimpering for a cookie. I would never let him stick his finger into the cookie batter—he seemed like a cat jumping on the stove. As soon as the cookies came out he screamed and whined until I would tell him, "You can have one now, they're cooled and ready." My Abraham would take the cookie and disappear. After a few minutes I would see him meekly giving his cookie to his brother. It was to be gifted, that's what he wanted. Not to possess.

■ JAMES JOYCE: Such an atmosphere—"To be safe from the rabid and soul-destroying political atmosphere in Ireland, for in such an atmosphere it is very difficult to create good work. At a very early stage I came to the conclusion that to stay in Ireland would be to rot and I never had any intention of rotting or at least I intended to rot in my own way and I think most people will agree I have done that."

■ REMBRANDT: And then I decided never, never to part with any of my pictures—In December 1655 I had to sell everything. I sold the costumes. I sold the props. I sold Saskia's jewels—even the curious Indian miniatures. Those marvels of one-haired brushes done in the land of the Moghul Indian ruler, Shah Jahan. Even those delights I sold. Oh, I kept my copies of the Hindustan pictures. And I kept the paintings that showed the costumes. But it was as though I had spilt paint, which was my blood, on the earth. Those costumes, those miniatures, were my dreams. And now these pictures are my tombstone. Art is creating the future. Pictures are the dead past.

"And then quiet."
"And then?" Tal asked.
"And then I decided never, never to part with any of my pictures—even if Dosha is thrown into the deal."
"But it's not your picture. It's hers."
"That's true, Tal, but it's my novel."
"It's wonderful, Fisher. Such an atmosphere. Did you just now make it up?" asked Tal, wide-eyed.
"No, but I did make it up. Okay. You can have the picture so long as it can stay in my apartment right along with my Dosha."
"Okay, Fisher. Here's the eighteen hundred dollars."
And Fisher folded the money neatly into his blue jeans and gently shepherded Tal to the door, leaving him in the hall, alone.

■ BORIS SPASSKY: Never, never to part—He'll keep his consistent picture but he'll die alone, this Fisher. My wife left in 1961. We were like bishops of opposite color. And this woman, a red bishop, how crude of these Americans to "throw their women into a deal." At least he is not like Bobby. They called me the most handsome champion since Capablanca. Bobby couldn't take that from me. Difficult to balance chess and long hair. Fame springs from skill. Skill flows from desolation.

◆ TAL'S FATHER: Not your picture, it's hers—Here he is, my son, the *dayan*, the all-knowing judge. This is not yours, it's hers. To stay in yeshiva and study Baba Metziah was beyond him. No one asks him to judge but he thinks he must decide for the world.

■ MIKHAIL TAL: And then—All Botvinnik would do is study end games. An *ein fachte* idiot—a complete idiot. In 1960 when I was younger than anyone I beat him and became world champion. Still he continued to study end games. That is what I like about this young Fisher. He knows if he starts the novel, the end will present itself.

■ MIKHAIL BOTVINNIK: Did you just now make it up?—Fisher's like Mikhail Tal, that Riga non-prodigy. No preparation, just walk to the board, mumble, stare, and move. "If Tal would learn to program himself properly then it would be impossible to play him."

■ BOBBY FISCHER: Never, never to part—With my principles, my loneliness, and my vision. I didn't need a second. I can't stand grandmaster draws. Why should Fisher part with his pictures? Any combination Tal is working out for him won't be worth warm spit. He can get it all, the novel, the pictures, and the girl, if he doesn't reveal his planned end game.

■ T. S. ELIOT: And then quiet—
"This is the way the world ends
Not with a bang but a whimper."

■ YITZHAK BUNAM ZUCKER: Like my mother used to—My mother often used to sit in darkness when my father or I came home: alone and staring straight ahead, quietly. I often wondered why and I would ask her why, as evening approached, she didn't turn on the lights, and she wouldn't answer and would respond with a question, What would you like to drink? I suppose my father expected to find my mother sometimes sitting in the dark, but it always unnerved him. He was always uneasy entering the house if she was sitting in the dark. My father would turn on the lights and say softly, "Hello, chérie." Now she is no longer in this world and just now I had a dream of her, more a hint of a dream in daytime. Mother is sitting in darkness and Father, who is named after the Shinyeveh Rebbe, has come home. And Father asks her, Why are you sitting in the dark, my dear bride? She looks at him and says, What do you want to drink? Suddenly my father remembers a story, a story totally forgotten, that his mother told him when he was four years old about the Rebbetzin Feige, the daughter of the *Baruch Tam*, the perfect blessing.

Feige was pregnant with Yehezkel Shraga of Shinyeveh and she traveled to Lubin to receive a blessing from the greatest Tsadik of her time, the Seer of Lublin. The Seer of Lublin rose when she entered and said with deep emotion, "I do not rise in honor of your father the great *gaon*. Nor do I rise in your honor, nor in the honor of your learned husband. I rise in honor of the child you are carrying, for his light will illuminate the world." And then my grandmother asked my father, "And who was that child, Yehezkel Shraga of Shinyeveh?" My father answered brightly, "Oh, I am named after him! He was a great Rebbe." "And why was he a great Rebbe?" my grandmother persisted. And of course my father at four years old was silent. My grandmother promptly quoted a teaching of the *heileger* Yehezkel Shraga of Shinyeveh, who explained a Talmudic teaching:

"'There are fifty gates of wisdom in the world. All were granted to Moses except one.' Since the Talmud tells us all fifty gates were granted to Moses, why does it modify its statement and reduce it by the number of one? A well-known maxim by Ramban will help us understand it. The purpose of all knowledge is to realize that one has no knowledge. The fiftieth gate attained by Moses was the awareness that the wisdom of the Torah is very deep and transcends all understanding. The fiftieth gate is the comprehension of the Oneness of G-d." Now my mother has been able to help my father understand the question he could never pose directly to her, which really was a retelling of a story never forgotten by his mother to him. Of a rabbi he was named after, in whose light the world shines. And are we not all part of that story, because its light is a comprehension of the Oneness of G-d?

CHAPTER 4

THE BLUE of the pitched roof on the sixteenth-century Venetian Jewish wedding ring was remarkable. The light from Tal's window glistened sensuously down the blue cloisons on the shank sides of the ring, like microscopic igloos floating before my eyes, thought Isaac, Tal's oldest nephew, who held the ring in his steady hand for a very long time.

"Open it!" Tal commanded.

"How?" asked Isaac, as if awakening from a most peaceful trance.

"Like my mother used to," Tal replied breathlessly.

Isaac looked down carefully at the ring. The ring's shank was broad and oversized. Placing his right thumb inside the shank, he peered at its wide shoulders. On the shoulder shanks were circular filigree bosses, connected by royal blue enameling, set in delicately crafted cloisons.

◆ RACHEL, TAL'S MOTHER: Like my mother used to—Abraham would stand next to me in the kitchen, pull at my skirt while I was cooking, and ask me, "Mother, how do you know how much spice to put in the soup? How do you know when the bread dough is kneaded enough? How do you know how many eggs to put in an omelet? How do you know how long to cook the meat?" And I would always answer, "I cook like my mother used to." And one day I passed by the open door of the children's room, and Tuviah and Abraham were studying together. At that time, Abraham would ask Tuviah for help before every one of his examinations. Abraham was frozen with fear and weeping, saying to Tuviah, "I'm so frightened I don't know anything. How will I answer tomorrow?" And Tuviah put his arm lightly on Abraham's shoulder and said, "Answer just like Mother used to." And then when Abraham looked bewildered, Tuviah said, "Don't even think; just do it."

◆ TAL'S FATHER: Roof—Abraham always expected a reward when none was due. Manna from heaven was his expectation. He forgot that the manna only fell on our people when we left Egypt and wandered; on the day we reached Israel, my father told me, the manna from heaven stopped. Abraham always lived in a child's wonderland. He expected to live on his back and have manna fall from the ceiling through a tiny hole in his roof—directly connected to heaven, of course. Naturally there would be no leaks through the ceiling, only manna. And if a drop should fall on his face, he would immediately pronounce *Tal Min Hashamayin*—rain from heaven—and utter a Hasidic blessing. Lazy stories. And now to reward not working with money from Tuviah. It is so dreamy. Doesn't he see where it will end?

Jewish wedding ring, Venice, seventeenth century.

◆ RACHEL, TAL'S MOTHER: The ring—I handed the ring to my poor Abraham, and out of the corner of my eye I could see his fingers quiver. "Now it is mine," he said breathlessly. "I can always keep it," he said, shuddering to himself, "even if I never get married." "Even if you never get married, Abraham," I repeated, as though submitting my family prayer book to swear on. I thought I would strike him but I didn't. And I didn't interrupt him. He asked me what those letters meant to my father, and I looked at them and said, "Mazel tov. It's an abbreviation for good luck." And Abraham, after looking around the room and even in back of him, whispered to me, "That is an Ashkenazic expression, mazel tov. Isn't our family Castillano and Sephardic?"

"First of all," I responded, "Why do you look around this room? We're alone. And don't we Castillanos need luck also?" And Abraham said sanctimoniously, "It means Morid Tal, He who brings down the dew of blessings." And I said to him, "In the Shmoneh Esrei, we say each day 'morid Hatal,'" and quicker than I could speak the words learned by rote even before I went to school, Abraham said, "The parallel lines stand for abbreviation marks but are written in the Lurianic fashion as a double *yud*—" "Ah, but Luria was part Ashkenazic," I parried.

He was always clever, my son Abraham. Not only a mother's boast; everyone felt so too. He quickly answered me. "But Mother, that's the whole point. You're always saying we are part Castillano and part Ashkenazic." He wasn't wrong, my son, to look around the room. We were not alone in it. And now is he not right about He who brings down the dew of blessings—"Tal"—from the heavens, blessings that awaken the living from deathlike sleep, blessings that revive the earth in spring, and blessings that will wake the dead?

■ J. P. MORGAN: This must be the side to press on—Before Carnegie entered my study I thought for two days without leaving my treasure library: Should I fight and bid for Carnegie steel or should I offer to buy him out? Which way to press? I didn't know what he wanted and I didn't know how to find out, nor did Judge Gary know how much Carnegie would fight back. I handed Carnegie a check with my signature and told him to fill in the amount. A Scotsman, he wrote in $225,639,000. That was the side to press on, Carnegie doing the pressing himself. Later he asked me if I would have paid $100,000,000 more. If you had asked me, Carnegie, I should have paid it.

The golden pellets surmounting each domed boss burst forth like the sun in Isaac's eyes. Ribbons of green and blue light lifted the sun toward the blue bezel on top of the ring.

On the bezel sat a watchtower, a minute house, more roof than house, a blue-enameled roof with two gold studs at each end. The roof and the ring seemed of a piece, completely fused. As Isaac held the ring he noticed a delicate spiral loop enclosing a small golden peg. This must be the side to press on, he thought. Suddenly, his hand quivered as his eye was mesmerized by the blue-white light reflected on the rooftop of the ring.

Isaac placed the ring on his left hand thumb and, using the slightest pressure, he pressed open the other side of the ring with his right index finger.

The roof opened. And on a small plaque, in a peculiar block script, were the Hebrew letters: Mem Tov.

■ BOB DYLAN: Watchtower—

"All along the watch tower, princes kept the view
While all the women came and went, barefoot servants, too.
Outside in the distance a wildcat did growl.
Two riders were approaching, the wind began to howl."

■ SARAH ABENDANA, TAL'S GRANDMOTHER: The roof and the ring seemed of a piece—The Ashkenazim got married with a simple gold band. And they went round and round in their lives, my husband Benjamin used to say. They never knew where they were. We got married with a ring and a roof. I told my husband that I wanted to live near to my parents. Better still, on the same block or, even better, in adjoining houses. The ring of our love and the roof of my youth seemed of a piece.

■ NUMBERS 15:38: Blue—*Speak unto the children of Israel, and bid them that they make them fringes in the borders of their garments throughout their generations, and that they put upon the fringe of the borders a ribbon of blue.* A thread of tekehelet had to be included in the fringes.

■ DAVID BEZBORODKO: Blue—In Deuteronomy 33:19 we learn: "*Zebulun's treasures are in the sand.*" The tekehelet was extracted from the murex snail, a snail found in the sea near Tyre. The tribe of Zebulun would gather these snails and extract the blue dye that was used in the prayer shawls of the cohanim. And that was the blessing, that Zebulun would be the extractor of the necessary blue dye of blessing.

■ HOFETS HAYYIM: A minute house—Just before the war I was walking in the street in Warsaw with my teacher, Haim Wasserman, who pointed at the huge Shomrei Hadas Yeshiva on Zelninski Street. Do you see all these huge yeshivas? I said. They are all built on contributions by people who worked on Shabbes. They will not last for long. They are "minute" houses.

■ KAFKA: This must be the side to press on—At Zeltnergasse, the house of the three kings, I would peer directly into the Tyn Church. I could see the people walking down the right aisle to receive communion, past Simon Abeles' bone remains, who before his bar mitzvah was supposedly converted only to be killed by his father. Buried in the Tyn, he was so "pleasing to look at," after the six days that the townspeople waited to inspect his holy corpse. I would pace from the view of Abeles' Aisle to the window and stare out at the roofs of Prague. Blue in the early morning. Gold light shimmering off the pitched ends. Then I would pace back again to the Tyn. Then to the distance. It was only later I learned to sit quietly at my desk with my pencil pressed into my right rib, thinking this must be the side to press on.

for my pressing seas in as hereafter must they chirrywill immediately pending on my safe return to ignorance and bliss with my ropes
of pearls for gamey girls the way you'll hardly know me.
After due purification we will and render social service, missus.
Let us all ignite as aposeals and help our Makeline sisters clean
up the hogshole. Burn only what's Irish, accepting their coals.
Write me anyly cursorily for Henrietta' sake on the life of jewvries
and the sludge of King Harrington's at its height running boulevards
over the whole of it. Bear in mind by Michael all the provincial's
bananas peels and elacock eggs making drawadust jubilee along
Henry, Moore, Earl and Talbot streets. Luke at all the memmer
running he's dung for the pray of birds strewing the Castleknock
road and the Marist Fathers eleven out on a rogation stag party.
Compare their caponchin trowbers with the Bridge of Belches
in Fairview, east Dublin's favourite wateringplace and ump as you
jump it. Stand on, say, Aston's. I advise you strongly, along
quaith a copy of the Seeds and Weeds Act when you have procured
one for yourself and take a good longing gaze into any nearby
shopswindow you may select at suppose, let us say, the hoyth of
number eleven, Kane or Keogh's and in the course of about thirty-
two minutes' time proceed to turn aroundabout on your heehills
towards the previous causeway and I shall be very cruelly mista-
ken indeed if you will not be jushed astowshed to see how you will
be meanwhile durn well topcoated with cakes of slush occasioned by
the rush jam of the crosse and blackwalls traffic in transit. When
will the W. D. face of our muckloved city gets its wellbelavered
whitewish? Who'll disasperaguss Pape's Avignue or who'll uproose
the Opian Way? 'Tis an ill wee blows no poppy good. And this
labour's worthy of my higher. Do you know what, little girls? One
of those days I am advised to positively strike off hiking for good
and all until such time as some mood is made to get me an increase
of automoboil and footwear as I sartunly think now, honest to
John, for an income plexus that that's about the sanguine boun-
dary limit.
Sis dearest, Jaun added, melancholic this time whiles his onsa-
turncast eyes in stellar attraction followed swift to an imaginary
swellaw, O, the vanity of Vanissy! All ends vanishing! Personally,
Grog help me, I am in no violent hurry. If time enough lost the
ducks walking easy found them I'd turn back as lief as not if I
could only find the girl of my heart's appointment to guide me
by gastronomy under her safe conduct, I'd ask no kinder of fates
than to stay where I am, leaning on my cubits, at this passing
moment by localoption in the birds' lodging, the pheasants among
full well on into the bosom of the exhaling night, picking sto-

◆ RACHEL, TAL'S MOTHER: It is real. I would like you to keep it—Poor Abraham, I told him when he was a child that he must learn to keep what is real until he can no longer keep it. He is not so old to be giving away his most precious hope. But the burden of hope is too great. Now he will never get married.

■ JAMES JOYCE: Not with your eyes but with your memory—*"Yes, Tid. There's where. First. We pass through grass behush the bush to. Whish! A gull. Gulls. Far calls. Coming, far! End here. Us then. Finn, again! Take. Bussoftlhee, mememoree!"* Isaac's eyes, like mine weak, but his memory will last and last.

■ SON HOUSE TO ALAN LOMAX: Real—This old man Tal is white and the Lomaxes' father and son were white and I asked Mr. Lomax: *"Now if you don't mind, I'd like to ask you one question. Why is it that a white man like you would get into his car and come all the way down here to Mississippi to talk to a fellow like me about the blues? You understand why I'm asking you this? It's not because I want to say something wrong or hurt your feelings. . . . It's a puzzle to me. . . . I'm used to plowing so many acres a week and sayin Yessuh and Nossuh to the boss on the plantation, but for sittin down and talkin about my music with some man from college like you, I just never thought about it happenin to me. So I want to understand it better."*

Lomax answered: *"History wasn't just made by kings and presidents and people like that; real people who plow the corn and pick the cotton have had a lot to do with it. My job is to help you get down the history of your own."*

"That's good," I said. *"That's mighty good-sounding to me. How does it sound to you?"* I asked my wife. She gave them both a smile.

"Mazel tov!" cried Tal, and threw his arm around Isaac. "When we were growing up in Antwerp before the war, that is how mother would hold the ring, by the window. She would show your father and me the ring, one day a year, always before Shavuot."

"I wish I had known her, Uncle," said Isaac, standing as straight as he could, trying to be as tall as Tal.

"Someday you will, Isaac. Someday you will," Tal said, smiling with his hand resting lightly on Isaac's shoulder.

"Uncle, it's really beautiful. All that you said it would be. All that I imagined it would be."

"Isaac, it's real. And that's the whole world. That's what Mother would say. It is real. I would like you to keep it, Isaac. I want you to stand by this window in this room and look at it. Not with your eyes but with your memory. With the eyes of our family's memory. I will be in the next room and I will join you after some time." Tal put his arm once more around his nephew, his only nephew, whom he loved dearly, and squeezed his fingers gently around the lad's shoulder.

◆ TAL'S FATHER: It is real—That's the whole point. It is not real. It is gold. It is glass. It is solder. It is beauty. But it is not real. In the Talmud Shabbat we learn that the world exists only because of the innocent breath of schoolchildren. That is real.

■ MARCEL PROUST: Ring—*"Half an hour later the thought that it was time to go to sleep would awaken me; I would make as if to put away the book which I imagined was still in my hands, and to blow out the light; I had gone on thinking, while I was asleep, about what I had just been reading, but these thoughts had taken a rather peculiar turn; it seemed to me that I myself was the immediate subject of my book."* This ring—Abraham's visual madelaine.

■ HINDA, GRANDDAUGHTER OF THE SEER OF LUBLIN: I will be in the next room and I will join you after some time—At my wedding my grandfather Yakov Yitchak fell asleep. My father waited for a long time and then woke him up. The badkhan called out, "The gifts from the bride's family." My grandfather opened his eyes and said simply, "I give myself. I will be in the next room. After thirteen years the gift will arrive." Thirteen years later I bore a son and called him Yakov Yitchak, and he was as like my *Zayde* as two drops of water resemble each other. His right eye was bigger than his left, just like *Zayde's*.

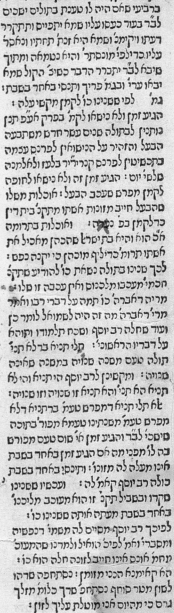

בתולה

נשאת ליום הרביעי ואלמנה ליום החמישי
שפעמים בשבת בתי דינין יושבין בעיירות ביום
השני וביום החמישי שאם היה לו טען בתולי'
היה משכים לב"ד: גמ' אמר רב יוסף אמר
רב יהודה אמר שמואל מפני מה אמרו בתולה
נשאת ליום הרביעי לפי ששנינו הגיע זמן ולא
נשאו אוכלות משלו ואוכלות בתרומה יכול
הגיע זמן בא' בשבת יהא מעלה לה מזונות לכך
שנינו בתולה נשאת ליום ד' אמר רב יוסף מריה
דאברהם תלי תניא בדלא תניא הי תניא ודילא
תניא הא תניא והא תניא אלא תלי תניא דמ'
טעמ' בדתניא דלא מפרש טעמ' אלא אי איתמ'
הכי איתמר אמר רב יהודה אמר שמואל מפני
מה אמרו בתולה נשאת ליום הד' שאם היה לו
טען בתולין היה משכי' לב"ד ותנשא בא' בשב'
שאם היה לו טענת בתולים היה משכים לב"ד
שקדו חכמי' על תקנ' בנות ישראל שיהא טורח
בסעודה ג' ימים א' בשבת וב' בשבת וג' בשבת
וברביעי כונסה ועכשיו ששנינו שקדו אותה
ששנינו הגיע זמן ולא נשאר אוכלברג' משלו
ואוכלות בתרומה הגיע זמן בא' בשבת מתוך
שאינו יכול לבנוס אינו מעלה לה מזונות לפיכך
חלה הוא או שהלתה היא או שפירסה נדה
אינו מעלה לה מזונות ואיבא דבעי לה מיבעא
חלה הוא מהו התם טעמ' מאי משו' דאניס והב'

הוא אניס או דילמ' הת' אניס בתקנתא דתקינו לי' רבנן הבא לא ואת"ל חלה הוא מעלה
לה מזונו' חלתה היא מהו מצי אמ' לה אנא הא קאימנ' או דלמ' מצי' אמר ל' נסתחפה
שדהו ואת"ל אמר ל' נסתחפה פירסה נדה מהו בש"ע ואסת' לא תיבעי לך דלא
מצי'

◆ TAL'S FATHER: Bomberg—A Gentile prints the Talmud and the Bible, and Abraham will seek only that edition. And even when he pointed out to me that a righteous Gentile invested his entire capital of 4,000,000 ducats to open a printing plant, obtained permission for Jewish typesetters to settle in Venice, and convinced Pope Leo X that the entire Talmud should be printed for the first time, I questioned my son, Abraham, perhaps too strongly. And what became of those typesetters; did they not leave our faith within one generation? The words are key, not the quality of the paper it is printed on. Even if the page is of Venetian silk. All else is *Avodat Zaroh*, worship of idols.

■ PSALM 127:1: Watchman—*Except the Lord build the house they labor in vain that build it: except the Lord keep the city the watchmen waketh but in vain.*

■ MISSISSIPPI JOHN HURT: Piece of white paper—In 1963 Tom Hoskins showed up at my door with a map of Avalon and a little crumpled piece of white paper, exclaiming *"We've been looking for you for years."* My first reaction was, *"I thought he must be an FBI man. I said, 'you got the wrong man! I ain't done nothing mean.'"*

And with a determined smile, Tal went into the next room of his cavernous apartment.

Absentmindedly, Tal reached for a dusty volume on his shelf and opened to a page, Isaiah 21. "*The burden of Du'mah. He calleth to me out of Se'ir, Watchman, what of the night? Watchman, what of the night?*" He sat down, took out a piece of white paper, and with a blue felt pen started to write the passage over and over in a neat European hand. And if not now, when? he thought. And is it not all contained here and now? But I can't see it, although I know it is here. And it is always and ever a promise. Once given it is received. Once received it is no longer a promise, but history. And good then until the end of time. But a sweeter time to come, even in exile, Tal intoned to himself.

Tears streamed down his face onto the page of the Venetian Bible. Bomberg. Not foxed but read and read again by twenty generations of his ancestors. And who would regard him as a grandfather?

■ ORSON WELLES: Isaiah—*All those tiny scraps of paper. I used to carry reminders of what to do with me when I went to the studio lot. Gradually I left all the scraps in the desk drawer in my kitchen. I'd put a coffee cup laced with old St. Croix on top of the drawer and rest the mug on the scrap-paper notes. I'd read the papers while drinking the coffee. When I directed The Immortal Story everyone thought I was the fat merchant, but I wasn't. I was the Polish Jew with a scrap of Isaiah hidden in his apartment. My G-d, to have seen the blue light and captured it in black-and-white in Citizen Kane. And I so young. So very young.*

■ WALKER PERCY: Exile—*"There is nothing new in my Jewish vibrations. During the years when I had friends my Aunt Edna, who is a theosophist, noticed that all my friends were Jews. She knew why moreover: I had been a Jew in a previous incarnation. Perhaps that is it. Anyhow, it is true that I am Jewish by instinct. We share the same exile. The fact is, however, I am more Jewish than the Jews I know. They are more at home than I am. I accept my exile.*

"Another evidence of my Jewishness: the other day a sociologist reported that a significantly large percentage of solitary moviegoers are Jews.

"Jews are my first real clue.

"When a man is in despair and does not in his heart of hearts allow that a search is possible, and when such a man passes a Jew in the street, he notices nothing.

"When a man becomes a scientist or an artist, he is open to a different kind of despair. When such a man passes a Jew in the street, he may notice something but it is not a remarkable encounter. To him the Jew can only appear as a scientist or artist like himself or a specimen to be studied.

"But when a man awakens to the possibility of a search and when such a man passes a Jew in the street for the first time, he is like Robinson Crusoe seeing the footprint on the beach."

شبیه شاه شجاع بهادر و اورنگ زیب بهادر و مراد بخش علی بالهند

■ A LUBLINER HASID: Into the room—Once the Seer of Lublin passed a study hall and saw a great light shining within. He thought that Jews must be devotedly studying the Torah inside. He went into the room and saw two students telling stories of great Hasidic rabbis.

■ GRANDFATHER ROJKO MILAN, A GYPSY: Imagine the mistakes in transmission—The only book Gypsies took from India was our language. We are the Rom, descended from Rama. If we had written down a book and carried it with us we would have been weighed down in the sands of Rajasthan and sunk in the mud of Transylvania. Our language became song, and we have glided on its wings across the mountains of the world. Nothing contains more mistakes than the written word. Nothing is more faithful than a mother's lullaby.

■ BILLIE BURKE: Age—Age is something that doesn't matter, unless you are cheese.

And where were his children as numerous as stars in the sky? But one as precious, more precious. An Isaac, his Isaac. Tal, alive, moved into the room again to be close to his Isaac.

"Isaac, where are you?" Tal asked, haltingly.

"Here I am," came the voice of a fourteen-year-old, not quite an adult, no longer a child.

Tal hurried over to Isaac and, with one motion, closed the unhinged and open roof and took the ring off of Isaac's thumb.

"Sit down, Isaac, and I will tell you what I was told and I will tell you what I believe. What I know of the ring's age is that the ring was made in Venice, not in the sixteenth century as the world reckons it, but four hundred years ago as we know it. For that is their counting and not ours, nor can it ever be. Four hundred years ago is only twenty generations. Tell your closest friend, your brother, a secret and let him tell someone else and by the time it passes to the twentieth person, imagine the distortion, imagine the mistakes in transmission.

■ THE APTER REBBE: I will tell you what I was told and I will tell you what I believe—"And I will tell you what I heard." All my life I have tried to remember a haunting tune, a niggun that I heard when I was a sheep in the flock of Jacob. This niggun was carried by Jacob's son, Joseph, to Egypt. Someday, I will hear that niggun again and I will never forget it. When it comes back, redemption will come to the world.

■ LAURENCE STERNE: Here I am—Here I Tristram Shandy am and "I am this month one whole year older than I was this time twelve months ago and having got almost into the middle of my fourth volume—and no farther than to my first day's life—tis demonstrative that I have three hundred and sixty-four days more life to write just now than when I first set out; so that instead of advancing as a common writer, in my work with what I have doing at it, on the contrary, I am just thrown so many volumes back …I shall never overtake myself. And here I am, a hero, hero born in book three, chapter three."

And here am I, Laurence Sterne, writing about Tristram Shandy writing about the birth of Shandy, and I reborn in 1760, dining out, twice a night in London, talked about in the Boodle halls of Major Russell's home, singing my novel for my supper. "To write a book is for all the world like humming a song—be but in tune with yourself." "Nothing odd will do long," said Dr. Johnson to Boswell. But Knights at Yale will sing my song, odd though it be, and here I am, again and again, "all I wish is to let people tell their stories in their own way." And here I am. In love with Elizabeth. Or is it Liza? Or is it in love with Tristram in love with Liza? But here I am.

◆ RACHEL, TAL'S MOTHER: *Pashut mi pashuta*, the simplest of the simple— What did Abraham want. What did he long for? The simplest of warm things. Love. But really a mother's embrace. Which I gave him and his brother. And of course they write books and books about it. Love your mother, Freud. Love your fellow worker, Marx. All those grand complicated schemes to recover the golden flash these children got or didn't get, dreamt of or saw. Why couldn't Abraham have kept it simple, truthful. We receive love. We must treasure it, pass it along. Not write about it. Not philosophize about it. Just pass it along.

■ ALBERT EINSTEIN: Understandable—*"Why is it that nobody understands me and everybody likes me?"*

■ THE VILNA GAON: Message—*"You must chew your food well so that your body can benefit from it. The same holds true for Torah study. You must fully 'grind and digest' all the details of the holy Torah in order to extract the correct Halakah. This is what the message of the sages was when they said: 'If there is no flour, there is no Torah.' Being meticulous in your studies helps to improve your character and behavior."*

■ DAVID WOLFFSOHN: Blue secret—Herzl called me a banker. He called me a yeshiva boy. Either I was too much on earth or too much in heaven. I fixed my gaze on him just like Reb Isaac Ruelf used to stare at me while unraveling a *sugyia* in my Lithuanian yeshiva. Your flag, Theodor, with the seven stars and seven hours and seven this and seven that, you are the banker and you know nothing of our history but you are our leader. We've always had a flag. We have worn it in our palaces, in our homes, and in our synagogues before our heavenly King. Now our nation can—men and women all—proudly display it. Our eternal blue and white, we will wrap it around ourselves, our nation, and our land. Theodor didn't really know of a tallis. He was not aware of our people's secret, but he knew I knew.

"The message at the end would surely degenerate into a garbled-joke version of the original. Except if . . . Except if . . ." Tal stood, weaving in silence. Wearily he summoned all his strength and sat down in his chair, a rocking chair with golden pegs of dark oak. "Except if . . . Except if what, Isaac?" asked Tal looking intently at his nephew.

"Uncle Abraham, except if the original blue secret were as clear as crystal, so simple, so understandable, so stark, as to be immutable. *Pashut mi pashuta*, the simplest of the simple," answered Isaac, with the certainty of a pupil repeating his teacher's message and intonation.

"And that's what this ring is. Four hundred years old. Look at the tiny balls of gold. The warmth of the gold is highlighted by the flat planes on the gold. These are hammering marks on the surface of the gold, tiny tool marks that came from the smallest of hammers used in those days."

■ BOB DYLAN: Clear as crystal—

I went down to the lobby
To make a small call out
A pretty dancing girl was there,
And she began to shout,
"Go on back to see the gypsy
He can move you from the rear
Drive you from your fear,
Bring you through the mirror.
He did it in Las Vegas,
And he can do it here."

■ ABRAHAM ABULAFIA: Clear as crystal—*"The clear crystal (aspaglarya ba'-me'irah). Comprehension of the Name, by the Name, and examination into His name, by means of the twenty-two letters of the Torah. And these letters and the ten sephiroth form the clear crystal, for all the forms that have brightness and strong radiance are included in them. And one who gazes at them in their forms will discover their secrets and speak of them, and they will speak of them and they will speak of him. And they are like an image in which a man sees all his forms standing opposite him, and then he will be able to see all the general and specific things."* A crystal ever translucent to Tal's eye.

■ THEODOR HERZL: Blue secret—The flag I was thinking of is *"a white flag with seven gold stars. The white background stands for our new and pure life; the seven stars are the seven working hours. We shall enter the Promised Land with a sign of work."* But David knew better. One night he leaned toward me with those large yeshiva eyes of his and said, "it's a blue secret—our flag—a simple secret. We've always had as our flag a tallis."

◆ RACHEL, TAL'S MOTHER: Venetian—The wedding ring is Venetian. The enameling is Venetian. The legacy is Venetian. But Abraham is not a historian and not a rabbi and not the teller of my tale.

■ VAN GOGH: Color—"*Vermeer's yellow is a color capable of charming G-d.*"

■ KIERKEGAARD: Handed the ring—And to him who has the ring the spirit of the ring is obedient. In fear and trembling, this Abraham handed the ring to Isaac. You do not need a son to pass the ring to. All you need is an Isaac. And in the handing, the message:

"Isaac saw that his left hand was clenched in despair. Then they returned home and Sarah hastened to meet them, but Isaac had lost his faith."

Abraham thinks Isaac is looking at the object in his hand. It doesn't matter. In one generation a knife, in another a ring. What counts is the handing onward of the ring of transmission. And this Abraham's hand trembled. And this Isaac, having noticed the tremor, will he be able to achieve true faith?

Tal handed the ring to Isaac, who looked at the worked surfaces of the shank.

"What are those lumps in the enameling?" asked Isaac.

"Those are where the enamel was poured again and again into the cloisons, to get an exact color. Characteristic of South German work of the period. Interesting, for the filigree is definitely more Venetian in character. One thing is for sure. To the eye of the craftsman of that period, the lumpiness was acceptable. To our eyes the enameling probably would have been filed down to satisfy our demonic sense of symmetry."

"And why the false catch on the front?" quizzed Isaac.

"Perhaps because there is always a false catch in the front . . . But that I do not know with certainty and I should not be flippant with you. And least of all about this ring."

■ DOV BER OF MEZERITCH: The false catch on the front—"*Every man should possess strong faith that what he does here below stirs great pleasure up above.*" The false catch is in front of us. The true catch that opens all is above.

◆ TAL'S FATHER: Characteristic of South German work of the period—To take our precious heirloom, our family legacy, and calmly call it South German work of the period. Portuguese possibly, Venetian probably, but certainly not German. A fool and a heretic. And to pass his theories on to my grandson. They are a lost pair, my son Abraham and my grandson Isaac.

■ REMBRANDT: Isaac, who looked—And I knew from Titus and by Saskia's dead children, unborn, never to raise their cheeks to me for caressing, that Abraham could not raise the knife and stare into his child's eyes and still be Abraham. A Jew's child or mine, no man with a pinpoint of G-d could do that. So I averted Isaac's eyes with Abraham's etched hand, and in caressing Isaac I diverted Isaac's glance in a different direction, and in teaching Isaac I allowed Isaac to modestly gaze downward. If Isaac's eyes had met Abraham's there could have been no sacrifice. Only madness and suicide.

■ JOSEPH STIEGLITZ: Venetian—There were three communities in Venice which I had Shabbes lamps from. The Italki ones were the smallest. Severe. Brass. Emphasizing light, both in weight and brilliance. Not many curved surfaces. The Venetian Sephardic Jewish Shabbes lamps had another character altogether. Intermeshed sinuous curves. All Arabesques. Looked almost Moroccan. But the Ashenazic lamps were really something. Huge, heavy, precarious, almost chandelier size, gargantuan in proportion to the tiny rooms of the Ashkenazic Jews in the Venice ghetto. Strange how each style interpreted the light of G-d's Sabbath. Could they still be worshiping the same G-d?

◆ RACHEL, TAL'S MOTHER: In the library of your grandfather's house—My husband, when we were engaged, brought me into his father's house and took me straightaway to the library. All four walls were covered with books. It reminded me of my own father's library, except that his books were in Hebrew and Aramaic but also in German and French and some in English. My husband-to-be stared at me as I looked around the room. I guess I hurt his feelings when I said that my own father's library was more impressive. "Why?" he asked. Because all of our books are in the holy tongue, I answered. "How could you possibly know that, as you don't learn?" he asked. Because I dust them before every Rosh Hashanah and every Pesach. He insisted on coming to my house, around the corner on Van Eykelai. He stayed in our library for two hours and finally squealed with delight when he found a two-volume Biblical Concordance in German. "You see! Not all the books are in Hebrew," he gloated. Then and there I knew he would never apologize for anything.

■ JORGE LUIS BORGES: Library—*"I have always imagined paradise will be a kind of library."*

■ THE SANZER REBBE: Free of any sigh—*"Nothing in this world is worth a sigh."*

■ ISAAC LURIA: He was standing in front of the table on which he would learn—"He was" is written but "she was" is read to teach us of the bride of the Sabbath, the holy *Shekinah*.

■ LAURENCE STERNE: I started to cry—On Gerrard Street at Commodore James's house, I had met her—Elizabeth Draper. Mrs. Mrs. Mrs. Mrs. Mrs. She was twenty-two. And I twice her age, and full of ancient wisdom. And around nine volumes of *Tristram Shandy* under my belt. And not much more. And I liked my ninth volume the best, and the monthly reviews calling me a harlequin and my work a PANTOMIME OF LITERATURE. I went home from Gerrard Street and started to cry with tears. Using them as ink, I wrote my sweet Liza:

"I'm half in love with you, Liza. I ought to be wholly so—for a man never valued (or saw more good qualities to value) or thought more of one of yr. sex than of you." All my life I had written with blue ink. Finally, heavenly tears.

"First, let me tell you what I do know. This ring was given to me by your grandmother. She handed it to me in the library of your grandfather's house in Antwerp. He was standing in front of the table on which he would learn. When she handed the ring to me, I started to cry. Father said sharply to me, 'Cry for other things in your life but this ring should be free of any sigh. And if you ever, ever cry again in its presence, Mother will give it to Tuviah.'

"I took the ring and went to the window in Father's study and looked at it for a long, long time. The ring had come to her from her father. And it had been held in his family for at least as long as they had been living in Antwerp, which was over three hundred years, and before that, perhaps when we and our cousins—the Pintos—departed from Venice. For as you know, we were originally Abendanas from Venice and Portugal."

■ YEHUDA IBN TIBBON: Library—*"I have honored you, my son, by multiplying the books in your library. I have not constrained you to borrow yourself from others, while you see that most students wander around looking for a book, failing to find it. Keep your books well. Keep them from the rain above and any other damage. Every Passover and every Feast of Tabernacles bring back home all the books you lent out. Never refuse to lend books to a man who has not the money to buy them for himself, if you are sure he will return them."*

■ VERMEER: Went to the window—When my father left Portuguese Oporto, as a child, because they knew he was a Jew at heart, his mother went to the window. As he walked down the narrow cobblestoned Avenida Salvador, she looked through the glass, tears in her eyes, for she knew my father would never return. He would never, ever, be able to write her a letter or communicate in any way. When he saw the tears—and she knew he saw—she lowered her head and, as my father told it to me, tears that were pure light, diamondlike yet visible, froze in his memory forever.

Once my father came into my second-floor studio facing the river. When he saw the painting of the woman reading a letter by the window, he screamed and threw himself into my arms. "Those are her tears! This is the letter I could never send her!" he shrieked. Even I could see the reflection of my grandmother's tears, on the letter that she never received from my father but that she could see every day.

Johannes Vermeer, *Lady Writing a Letter with Her Maid.*

■ VERMEER: An old man in love with a marriage ring and not with a bride—At first I drew her very close, an inch away from my face. So close I could see beneath her pores, so close my breath could kindle the perspiration on her white skin, rouging the passion she secreted for me. My hand was frozen. Who was I? An old man in love. In an old costume. A disembodied head. At least I didn't think that the true ladder to Heaven lay through that cracked landscape of the Netherlands. Or that a ladder of Black Crosses led to and through her. She would be my trumpet of fame, although she could barely support my weight, much less look in my eyes. But what was I to her and she to me? I: a promise. She: a beginning. I adorned her with a laurel of flowers. She clasped my book to her trembling, delicate oval breasts. Her body glowed sunlike. The leather of my book. The sun of Delft. Her skin kindled. Her child, my work. Her dream became mine. I perched on my chair, pausing before I could touch her. Knowing that touch could not be transmitted to the canvas. Knowing her inner core, bubbling and always burning through her slender body, trailing from the crease of her neck's nape along her shoulders, edging through the flat planes that dissolved in her milk, curving, always a warm center, glowing on the leather outer skin of my book. My hand froze before I could draw her on my canvas. I could not draw her. I could only draw myself drawing my dream of her, the milkiness, the milky warmth of her. The light of Delft instantly illuminated her eyelids. And the map of the Netherlands dissolved. The blackness of the crosses ceased to weigh me down, the broken candelabrum hidden in my attic and hung only when she came to my house ceased swaying. And she knew and I knew that our promises could merge if only for the briefest of times, away from place, away from time, away from art, and away from the future.

■ MEYER AMSCHEL ROTHSCHILD: Why did you receive … and not my father?—He's absolutely right, this Isaac. I gathered them on my deathbed and drew a picture on a piece of ledger paper. Five arrows and a circle. And I told them, Not you and not you. Not you and not you. But "US." If these brothers divided my fortune among themselves, their children won't be cousins, and their offspring won't be nephews and their uncles won't be partners.

Isaac looked at the ring in Abraham's hand and thought to himself, A queer combination: an old man in love with a marriage ring and not with a bride. Embarrassed at the thought, he looked downward.

"I know what you're thinking, Isaac. Why you and not Ephraim? Why should you get the ring and not your older brother?"

"Well, because you mention who possesses the ring, Uncle, why did you receive it and not my father?" Isaac was afraid to look his uncle in the eye, but he glanced at him surreptitiously.

"Your father once told me that he would rather have the woman and not the ring. On another occasion your father told me that he had been offered the ring first but refused it, as he felt that I was the weaker one and needed it more than he did."

"Which is the real reason, Uncle?" asked Isaac, with the curiosity of a young man trying to decipher his parents' past.

"Neither is correct and neither is false," said Tal.

■ CATHARINA BOLNES VERMEER: A queer combination—He was extraordinary, my young Johannes. An old man who dressed up in a queer century-old costume when his model, Morika, came to our house. Locking the door and forbidding me to knock and bring in tea to that poor young stick of a woman who modeled for him month after month. At first the rattling and clanging alarmed me. That is why I knocked. Only through the keyhole was I able to see the odd chandelier he would suspend from the ceiling. Where he got it nobody knew. Nor would he answer when I asked. Oh, he was a magician of secrets. And what was the point of his drawing that little waist of a waif as a pregnant woman? I guess to make me jealous. And when I saw the painting half finished when Johan visited The Hague, I understood how he had tricked that poor young woman. She had to lower her eyes. His old wrinkled eyes could not be drawn. Only the queer ridiculous gentleman's clown costume. And yet after he died, when I sold the painting to pay Mother's debt, I realized the woman had been me. And Johan was unchanged. And the wreath, my favorite laurel flower, would never again bloom. If only he had told me what that room meant to him. If only I had asked.

■ GITTEL ROTHSCHILD: Why you and not—Meyer Amschel, my husband of blessed memory, not only in the next world but far beyond the ghetto in Frankfurt and throughout Europe, was dying. And the boys—Amschel, Salomon, Nathan, Karl Meyer, and Jacob—were terrified. Young Amschel was weeping in the foolish, dusty, padded Leipzig antique chair that my sainted husband bought when he was sixteen at the Leipzig fair. Amschel Meyer would curl up in it and whimper until I came to him and gathered him in my arms. I drew on a piece of paper five arrows with a circle. The paper was torn from an account book near Amschel's bed. I put the paper on Amschel's night table. And I summoned the children to Amschel's bedroom. Amschel Meyer, my oldest and biggest child, had to be practically carried. I said to the boys, "Father has told me he won't hear of who receives what and 'why you and not me.' Father tells us to think of US." The boys stared at their father, who was looking at the piece of paper I placed in his hand. He was so weak, my Amschel. But praise G-d, the most beautiful smile crossed his face when I told the boys, "This paper of your father's is his will to you." We all left the room, and poor Amschel passed away an hour later. If they hadn't seen the paper they would not have been convinced to accept the notary's revised will.

● SIMHA PADAWER, DOSHA'S GRANDFATHER: Hate—Do you hate? Do you love? And I would think of the words of Jeremiah. . . . Poor Rickele, my love, my wife. She would say, I have not brought you even a goosedown blanket for my dowry. And I would quote the Talmud Sanhedrin: "*When our love was strong, we could sleep on the edge of a sword.*" And I would never, G-d forbid, complete the Sanhedrin's sentences: "*Now that our love is not strong, a bed sixty cubits wide is not big enough for us.*" And in Slonim, when I studied—and later in the forests with the partisans, and even later in America—it was always a bed as thin as a sword, but because of love, thank G-d, big enough for us.

■ MONET: Hate—"*I don't approve. Because Sargent makes me into something much grander than I am, and I've always had a horror of theories, and finally the only merit I have is to have painted directly from nature with the aim of conveying my impressions in front of the most fugitive effects, and it still upsets me that I was responsible for the name given to a group the majority of whom had nothing of the impressionist about them.*" And if nature is full of the most fugitive effects and if the path changes each instant, how foolish, how presumptuous to map it ahead and how even more arrogant for one's father to chart it for his child. I should hate this uncle, were he mine.

"Why do you hate Father, Uncle?" whispered Isaac.

"I don't hate your father. I hate his fear of me, his unwillingness to let me be, his certainty that there is only one path and he is square in the middle of it and I must follow after he has cleared the high ground. I guess the certainty is what I find most difficult. But hate? I don't hate anyone. In fact, I think that I regard him exactly as you regard Ephraim. Do you hate your brother?"

Isaac looked at the ring and after a long time said, "I'm sorry I phrased it that way, Uncle. My father has never said you hated him, but he has never, never mentioned your name in the house to me without sighing and looking upward." Isaac bashfully again looked down to avoid his uncle's gaze.

"You and I, Isaac, will show him. Don't worry."

■ SARMAD, TEACHER OF DARA SHIKOH: One path—In my first lesson with Dara Shikoh I told him a teaching his father, Shah Jahan, had heard from Akbar, his grandfather. There is one path. And more than that, there is but one language. And in fact all paths to G-d are but different words comprising different blessings. And hatred and fear both spring from an inability to translate another's language.

■ MARCEL PROUST: Hate Father—Of course this Tal doesn't hate Isaac's father. And doesn't hate his own father. Anymore than I hated mine. But the certainty that there is one path—that I could not accept. My life would have been twisted into hatred. In 1895 my father had wanted me to develop a career. I wanted to take another path. My job at the Mazarin Library was not a job. Five years of absenteeism. Finally my own path to Venice, to Venice with Mother. To Venice with Mother to translate Ruskin. And away from Mother on a gondola in the mornings, only to return and see her books and shawl, all framed in a window. Did the path lead away from Father? Toward or away from Mother? The certainty of Father about my path and yet . . . even he ultimately was afraid to be firm. To Mother he said, telling her not to worry, our son is no longer a child, "'*He's quite capable of knowing what will make him happy in life.' Such unexpected kindness from him had always given me an urge to kiss his red cheeks above his beard, and if I did not give in to it, it was only from fear of displeasing him.*"

■ AKBAR, MOGUL RULER OF INDIA: Hate his fear of me—Babur, my grandfather, took a stick one day and drew a circle by the river. Humayum, my father, was ten years old. Babur, The Tiger, had just conquered India. "This stick is you, Humayum. Put it in the ground of India, and the Hindu people will fear you. Drag your armies around this immense land in a circle, and you will come around to the same place. They will fear you, and this fear of you will cause them to hate you. And this hatred will cause you to fear them. And this fear of them will cause you eventually to hate them. And the more you move in that circle, the deeper the rut and the less likely you will be able to escape from the cycle of fear and hate."

My father, my poor, weak father, Humayum, asked Babur, "Then what is to be done?"

"Float above India," Babur said. "Make no marks. Build on no Hindu temples. Do not hate the Hindu, nor his fear of you."

But Humayum was weak and relied on the stick and eventually lost India. I vowed on my return to engrave my grandfather's sayings on my heart. But these are lessons more easily learned by grandsons than sons.

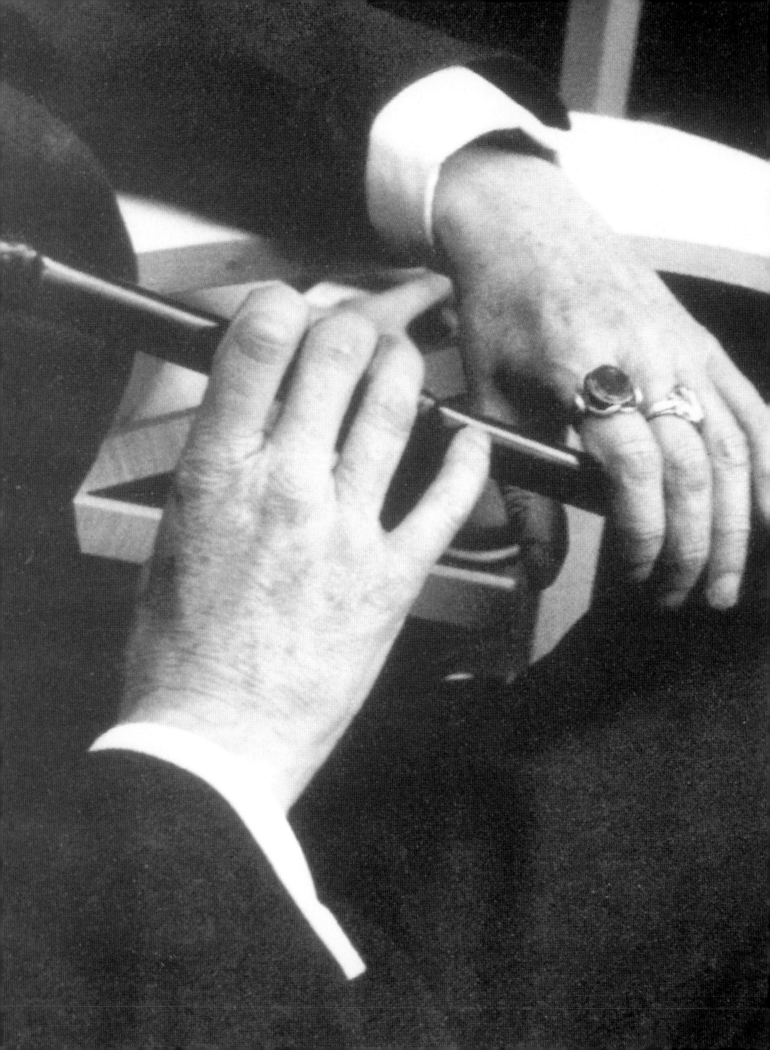

◆ RACHEL, TAL'S MOTHER: Father said we were jewelers—I told Abraham a stone dealer and a jeweler were like the braided rope candles used in the Habdalah service at the end of the Sabbath. Either my husband was in his office with my father showing gemstones to a jeweler or he was visiting the jeweler's office with stones. The gems were either pried out of an old setting and recut or they were recut to fit a jewel or a ring. But poor Abraham, he would only accept his version: that we were aristocrats, not working with our hands soldering metal, mixing enamel. And what of my dear father, with all that diamond dust on his priestly hands? Sitting at the wheel, hour after hour, until I would visit his office, after my school let out and Father would leave his office with me, walking by the river when the weather was nice. It was one vision—the stone and the jewel, one partnership. And just as Abraham couldn't see that partnership, he will never be a partner.

■ JOSEPH STIEGLITZ: A Torah crown set with precious stones—I remember purchasing on Haruskah Street in Cracow after the war a Torah crown. With all blue and red stones glistening. The antiques store owner wanted a fabulous price, but I assured him the stones were false, glass. We went to the university to the Department of Mineralogy. The professor put the Torah crown under a microscope and pronounced the stones to be glass. Only when the professor swore he was a Catholic did the antiques dealer realize I wasn't a swindler. He was so depressed that he quoted me only 1,200 zlotys. I paid 2,000 zlotys, telling him at least the stones were original, pointing out that the jewelers' prongs had not been altered. It bothered me always that glass would be used and not precious stones. But then I visited the Morgan Library and saw the Lindau Gospel book cover with its occasional glass stones and bent, misshapen prongs. If the jeweler had used only precious stones, they would have been switched long ago. Not for a moment do I believe this Tal that a Torah crown with precious stones was donated.

One day he will come to realize that we and souls like us have kept this ring alive for four hundred years since Venice."

"What did our family do in Venice? Father said we were jewelers." Isaac waited for Tal's answer, which was long in coming.

"No, not jewelers, Isaac," Tal answered, enunciating each word, "stone dealers. Dealers in precious stones. One of our ancestors, Yitshak Askenazi, was the *parnas* in the synagogue close to the Palazzo del Vecchio. He donated a Torah crown set with precious stones that later was exhibited in the Vienna Jewish Museum before the war."

"Why did Father say we were jewelers and not stone dealers?" Isaac was surprised to hear that his always precise father had made a mistake.

"Probably for the same reason that he may have refused the ring. He doesn't regard it with as much importance as I do. He even tried to convince me it was not genuine."

■ ISAAC LURIA: Souls like us—*The souls of the righteous, they alone affect the true devotion of the community of Israel to G-d. Her souls longing for Him make possible the flow of the lower waters toward the upper, and this brings about perfect friendship and the yearning for mutual embrace in order to bring forth fruit.*

■ JAMES JOYCE: No, not jewelers, Isaac, stone dealers—Before *Ulysses* was published, precisely on my fortieth birthday, I wore a ring with a pale white gold band, Gypsy-set with a deep blue sapphire in it. I had promised myself to buy it for years. Nora commented, Jim, what a lovely ring you've on. And I replied, I'm not wearing a ring but rather a sapphire jewel.

The shade of blue of the sapphire matched the blue of my dreams: the blue of the Greek sea, the blue I chose for the cover of *Ulysses*. The printer, Darantière, botched the job and printed a cover more green than blue and I insisted on having the cover reprinted. Nora argued with me. What's a difference in blue, Jim? Finally the right shade arrived, and I inscribed the thousandth copy to Nora. She even tried to sell her copy to Arthur Power.

It all hinged on a blue stone, the essence of a jewel. Of course they would be fools to exchange their profession of trading gems for that of jewelers.

■ KAFKA: Souls like us have kept this ring alive—Odd character, this Tal. Instead of thinking of a woman he could give a ring to, to wed, he weds himself to a ring. Not that I don't sympathize with him. My father would tell me over and over again, Marry! Marry! You're not a man until you do. You can't hide yourself up in your attic and study Kabbala until you wed. Even Tal knew that. If I had had a ring to give, it might have made a difference.

■ HENRY WALTERS: Fake—Father could never understand my collection of fakes. If you want to develop a taste for quality, stick to quality. Did he tell that to Morgan or did Morgan tell him that? Father was certain just having a fake in the collection tainted the other pieces. And even if you keep a fake in a separate box, in a separate room, in your museum hall of fakes, it could get confused with your good things. And what do you collect, Father? Napoleonana, he would bark. And I would think, The greatest little fake of all time but of course would say nothing, and in any case Father had already left the room.

■ WILLIAM WALTERS: Fake—First-class business in a first-class way, Morgan would say. And his son kept up his collection. And young Henry will keep up mine. These Tals have no tradition, pass nothing along, keep no records, don't know what they have, show their treasures to strangers. Of course they'll part with these icons come the next Depression.

■ MELVIN GUTMAN: The Walters Art Gallery— Oh, I would pace around the Henry Walters house when I visited my aunt in the 1930s. Lots of apple sellers on the southeast corner. The lanterns always on in the vestibule in the Great Man's house, even though he and I both lived in New York. I could imagine box after box of treasure inside, probably unopened. If my father had been his father, imagine all those Morgan treasures I would have had. But then again, if his father had been my father either he would have been a businessman or a collector but not both. I couldn't stay in Baltimore and not be in the family business. When they opened the gallery to the public in 1931, I was the third person in. Not surprisingly, they pronounced poor Tal's piece a fake. Oh, if Henry had bought it, it would be on display in the *Wunderkammer*; and if William had bought it, it would have been on a pedestal by the entrance. Too bad it wasn't offered to me.

"When we came to America and were dreadfully short of capital, your father went to the Walters Art Gallery in Baltimore and tried to sell it. They examined it and pronounced it a nineteenth-century Neo-Renaissance piece. The lettering in Hebrew was too simple, out of character with the rest of the piece, the filigree work too eastern, and the enameling was suspect. Since that time your father has always called it 'my ring.' Our mother always called it 'the ring of blue!' Tal's voice rose with excitement.

"Why, Uncle?" asked Isaac.

"I am not sure, but I am certain that Mother's name is the key to understanding its importance. As to its being a fake or a nineteenth-century ring, the enameling is corroded at the edges, and you can see the underpaste, exactly in the style of South German workmanship."

■ ISAAC LURIA: The name is the key to understanding—The name of G-d cannot be pronounced, cannot be whispered. It is distinctive: Hashem Hameforash ("the unique name"). And that name contains both G-d's essence and character. But one path to understanding is through understanding the names of G-d's creations. And that is why my synagogue was blue. The word for blue sapphire is *sapphir* and the root essence of the word for a story, *sippur*. The colored stone *sappir* is a variant of the word for counting, *mispar*, and the name of the sapphire stone throne described by Ezekiel. No wonder Tal's mother calls it the ring of blue. She, one generation closer than Tal to Sinai, understands. Imagine forgetting the meaning of one's name.

■ LAURENCE STERNE: My ring—This Tal. His hobby-horse is his ring. "*A man and his hobby-horse tho I cannot say that they act and react exactly after the same manner in which the soul and the body do upon each other: Yet doubtless there is a communication between them of some kind, and my opinion rather is, that there is something in it more of the manner of electrified bodies, and that by means of the heated parts of the rider which come immediately into contact with the back of the hobby-horse—by long journies and much friction—it so happens that the body of the rider is at length filled as full of hobby-horsical matter as it can hold; so that if you are able to give but a clear description of the nature of the one, you may form a pretty exact notion of the genius and the character of the other.*"

Now this hobby-horse is Tal's ring and his father's hobby-horse may have been this ring. But his brother's is most certainly not this ring. And never have I ever imagined one could will a hobby-horse to a nephew.

"*He had of books a chosen few.*" So perhaps this lot of chosen few might choose instead to be a people of the ring. Quite a turn.

◆ TAL'S FATHER: We originally came from Germany—When Abraham came home one day he had a book by a Professor Agus which stated that from the sixth century until the tenth century, the Jewish population in Europe numbered but 10,000 people. The Jews who remained survived unbelievable pressures: Jews who chose Judaism even over life, Jews whose whole life was centered on the faith in one indivisible G-d. "Heroes of spirit," Agus called them. Didn't we originally come from Germany, Father? Abraham wrote history forward and backward. No, we came from Hamburg and lived with Jews. Those German Jews were Ashkenazim. We were Sephardic goldsmiths who left Portugal in the early 1600s. Then we went to Hamburg and then to Venice as agents for the Bank of Portugal. But those Jews who spoke only Yiddish who perished in Cologne and died at York—their martyrdom is not part of you.

Abraham did not reply. Two weeks later he showed me a long letter he had sent to the professor with each name of our family—Tal, Del Vecchio, Abulafia, da Costa Nuñez Pinto, and Uriel—with questions whether the professor had done any research on our family's history in Hamburg. But I never heard another word from Abraham about it. A Sephardic heritage was not enough for him. He had to be Askhenazi, too.

■ HARRY BOBER: Weightness—I remember Tal well. A crumpled man with a beautiful ring. Not my field, I told Tal. Mine's medieval. Your ring's high renaissance. Tal fenced with me: "But you've got a Jewish heart, Professor," he said. Perhaps I've a Jewish eye, I parried. And in any case, Tal, your ring is good.

I taught him how important it was to hold the piece in one's hand and feel its weight. *Fingerspitzen*, the German scholars called it. I even told him how to convince anyone you're an expert. First you hold the object in your right hand. Then you pretend you're weighing it. Then you turn it around and look at its reverse side. You nod vigorously to yourself and reach into your left pocket, swiftly picking out an imaginary jeweler's loupe. Then you mumble yes, yes, or, better still, Yah, yah, and everyone assumes you're an expert. Tal thanked me elegantly with a courtly bow I had never seen outside Vienna and on his way out mumbled, "Thanks for making me an expert, Professor Bober."

Jewish marriage ring brooch, seventeenth century.

"I thought you said the ring came from Venice?"

"Yes, but Nuremberg and Augsburg are not far from Venice. Also, we originally came, in fact, from Germany. In any case, this ring differs from the fake Jewish wedding rings I have had in my hand. It has a different weightiness, and there is no green in the blue. It's well named, indeed. Also, four years after the museum refused to buy the ring, we got a call from the curator, asking to see it again. I'm not so sure he understood what he was looking at." Tal's eyes were half shut as he remembered the day the curator called. Tuviah was out of the office and Tal took the call. But Tuviah seemed hardly interested in Tal's tale of the Walters Art Gallery curator.

"Why are you choosing me to get the ring?" asked Isaac suddenly.

"Do you want it, Isaac?"

"Yes, very much," answered Isaac, with great clarity in his voice.

"That's why I am giving it to you. And I want to give it to you very much. More than you can ever imagine.

■ JOAN BAEZ: Ring—

I got you a ring
And you got me diamonds and rust.

■ SIMHA BUNAM: Ring—"*Just as one who has made all the preparations for his wedding but has forgotten to buy a wedding ring, so is one who has worked his whole life—but forgotten to make himself holy—in the end he wrings his hands and is overcome by overwhelming sadness.*"

■ DYLAN: Blue. It's well named indeed—

Oh baby, baby, baby blue
You'll change your last name too.

When I was Zimmerman in college, I read everything. I could remember every line of Eliot. That first year I must have read *Ash Wednesday* over and over one hundred times. But that acned, scrawny, corduroy-suited graduate student who led my creative-writing discussion group simply ignored me until the end of the semester. Until he wrote on my last poem, "Mr. Zimmerman, if you stop copying others, perhaps—just perhaps—you might be intelligible." I'll never forget when three years later he saw me at a performance at Gerde's Folk City and said, "Bob, remember how I encouraged you in university? I'd recognize you anywhere, even though you've lost weight and changed your last name, too."

● Rachel, Tal's girlfriend: Utterly alone—He would take me to the park in Antwerp and draw a big circle in the sand in front of a park bench. Here will be our house. And in front will be a square hedge park and in the back we'll have an enclosed courtyard in which the children will play. On the top floor facing the east will be our apartment. The house on the far side of the courtyard will be your father's. And then he would describe the furnishings and his library. And how the books would be ordered. And where we would allow the children to play. And where the housekeeper and her husband the gardener would live. Two seventeen-year-olds playing house with the gusto of four-year-olds. And now he's sixty, utterly and completely alone.

■ Kafka: He returned to his apartment—At least Tal could return to his apartment and be alone. When I was in the apartment beyond Stupartgasse I would lie down on my bed in a swoon, only to hear a low roar of petitioners—always women, always sixty, always weeping at the side altar, imploring the blessed Virgin to clasp them as the crowned Christ Child, protect them, restore them. Over and over I heard the words *hell, save, above, never again, always*. After two in the morning the roar would suddenly cease and the church door would be closed with a deafening clang. Then I would rise from the bed, bolt awake, and write until dawn. When the door of the church would open again the petitioners would stream in, once more hypnotizing me in half a slumber. But I was never on my bed and alone. Either I was writing at my desk or I was prostrate on my bed with the sounds of an infinite variety of drowning souls.

"But now that I have promised it to you, I beg you to keep it a secret. I will hold it for you. And when the time is right, it will be yours."

And with these words, Tal reached into his pocket and pulled out a very frayed leather cushion-shaped jewel box and placed the ring inside. Then, ushering his nephew to the door, he returned to his apartment and lay down on his bed, utterly alone.

■ Mikhail Botvinnik: Time is right—Asked in 1947 why I spent so much time studying end games that rarely occurred, I replied that if I were to be champion I had to be master of every kind of end-game solution for when the time is right.

■ Elie Wiesel: Secret—*"And yet the secret of the secret cannot be divulged."*

■ Elihu Yale: Utterly alone—My G-d she was a beauty, Hieronyma de Paiva. Jacques had died three months before, and she had come to my office to beg for transit papers to transfer her husband's merchandise back to England. I examined each of the inventory records, taking an eternity over each sentence, and each time I looked up from the documents her gaze was fixed intensely on mine. How do I know that your furnishings match these descriptions? I asked her. "You must see for yourself," she replied. I asked her shyly if I could come and verify the furnishings and seal and stamp them for the long voyage home, and she said, "Does not my lord trust me?" And I said of course I do, but England trusts no one.

I went up the narrow stairs on King Street, not two doors down from Salvador, where the other Jewish diamond merchant, Abendana, later lived. I mounted the stairs and knocked, but the door was ajar and I didn't wait for an invitation for I could hardly breathe. And I looked about the room, seeing her there, her black hair glistening by the Madras sunlight. My G-d, you're completely alone, I said. "No, my lord, it is you who are completely alone." And then I knew what could not be avoided.

■ James Joyce: Secret—*"Her secret: old feather fans, tasseled dance cards powdered with musk, a gaud of feather beads in her locked drawer."*

Those secrets Mother kept. All through the descent from the Bray house ten miles from Dublin nestled by Bray Head, down to Blackrock Halway toward Dublin, and finally into Fitzgibbon Street, spiraling not merrily ever downward to Millbourne Lane, the feathered fans gathering dust, never leaving a drawer. No weeping in pubs, wandering through parks accosting strangers with secrets. Pity Tal's mother didn't keep the ring—then the secret would always be kept.

עין משפט נר מצוה

מאימתי קורין את שמע בערבין וכו'. פי' רש"י ואם היו קרין מבעוד יום אין אנו מומחין ללאת הכוכבים כדמפרש בגמרא. על כן פי' רש"י דקריאת שמע שעל המטה עיקר והיא לאחר לאת הכוכבים. ול"כ לומר שזו קריאה בצ ירושלמי. והכי איתא בירושלמי הכנסת כדי לעמוד בתפלה מתוך דברי תורה. תימא לפירושו והלא אין העולם רגילין לקרות סמוך לשכיבה אלא פרשה ראשונה (לקמן דף ס') ואם כן שלש פרשיות לא יקרות. ועוד קשה דלריך לברך בקריאת שמע שתים לפניה ושתים לאחריה בערבית. ועוד דאותה קריאה סמוך למטה אינה אלא בשביל המזיקין כדאמר בסמוך (דף ה.) ואם תלמיד חכם הוא אינו לריך. ועוד קשה דא"כ פסקינן כר' יהושע בן לוי דאמר תפלות באמלע תקנום. בין שני קריאת שמע של שחרית ובין קריאת שמע של ערבית. ואם קיימא לן כוותיה לכן לריך לקרות מיד קריאת שמע של ערבית. ואנן קיימא לן דאותה קריאה סמוך למטה אינה אלא בשביל המזיקין. לכן פירש ר"ת דאדרבה קריאת שמע של בית הכנסת עיקר. ואם תאמר היאך אנו קורין כל כך מבעוד יום. וי"ל דקריאת שמע שבבית הכנסת עיקר...

גמ' תנא היכא קאי דקתני מאימתי ותו מאי שנא דתני בערבית ברישא לתני דשחרית ברישא. תנא אקרא קאי דכתיב בשכבך ובקומך והכי קתני זמן קריאת שמע דשכיבה אימת משעה שהכהנים נכנסים לאכול בתרומתן. ואי בעית אימא יליף מברייתו של עולם. דכתיב ויהי ערב ויהי בקר יום אחד. אי הכי סיפא דקתני בשחר מברך שתים לפניה ואחת לאחריה בערב מברך שתים לפניה ושתים לאחריה לתני דערבית ברישא. תנא פתח בערבית והדר תני בשחרית עד דקאי בשחרית פריש מילי דשחרית והדר פריש מילי דערבית: **אמר מר** משעה שהכהנים נכנסים לאכול בתרומתן מכדי כהנים אימת קא אכלי תרומה משעת לאת הכוכבים לתני משעת לאת הכוכבים. **כהנים** אימת קא אכלי בתרומה משעת לאת הכוכבים והא קמ"ל דכפרה לא מעכבא כדתניא **ובא השמש** וטהר ביאת שמשו מעכבתו מלאכול בתרומה ואין כפרתו מעכבתו מלאכול בתרומה ו**ממאי** דהאי ובא השמש ביאת השמש והאי וטהר טהר יומא

מסורת הש"ס

מאימתי קורין את שמע בערבין. משנה שהכהנים נכנסים לאכול בתרומתן. כהנים שנטמאו וטבלו והעריב שמשן והגיע עתם לאכול בתרומה: עד סוף האשמורה הראשונה. שליש הלילה כדמפרש בגמרא (דף ג.) ומשם ואילך עבר זמן דלא מקרי תו זמן שכיבה ולא קרינן ביה בשכבך. ומקמי הכי נמי לאו זמן שכיבה לפיכך הקורא קודם לכן לא ילא ידי חובתו. אם כן למה קורין אותה בבית הכנסת כדי לעמוד בתפלה מתוך דברי תורה. והכי תניא בברייתא בברכות ירושלמי. ולפיכך חובה עלינו לקרותה משתחשך. ובקריאת פרשה ראשונה שאדם קורא על מטתו ילא: עד שיעלה עמוד השחר. שכל הלילה קרוי זמן שכיבה: הקטר חלבים ואברים. של קרבנות שנקרב דמן ביום: מצותן. להעלות כל הלילה ואינן נפסלים בלינה עד שיעלה עמוד השחר והן נאמר בהן מן הבקר לעולם ולא תבא עליו השמש:

Berachoth Tom. I.

◆ Tuviah Gutman Gutwirth, Fisher's Grandfather: Blue—My blessed father-in-law Abish Rheinhold would quote from the Medrash Rabbah, and when he would come to the word *blue*, he would stare heavenward and pause. *"Ten things will G-d bring to pass in the future: He will give light; He will cause fresh, curative waters to come forth from Jerusalem; the trees will bear fruit each month; all cities that have been destroyed, including even Sodom, will be rebuilt; Jerusalem will be rebuilt with blue . . . sapphires; a cow and a bear will graze together; all animals will be domesticated; there will no longer be weeping or death; and everyone will rejoice at all times."*

■ Dylan Thomas: Who I'm living with—

Not for the proud man apart
From the raging moon I write
On these spindrift pages
Not for the towering dead
With their nightingales and psalms
But for the lovers, their arms
Round the griefs of the ages,
Who pay no praise or wages
Nor heed my craft or art.

Dylan's taken my name and now Fisher has taken his. But that's the whole idea of writing. Backdrop music for entangled lovers on a cool autumnal night.

■ Kafka: Who I'm living with—Corngold was right when he understood that *"someone must have traduced Joseph K. for without having done anything wrong he was arrested one fine morning"* is commentary. Not action, not plot, and not life. Fisher wants Dylan to be commentary on himself, and Dosha wants Fisher to be plot. Perhaps each should accept that each is commentary on the other. That is life. For if our nighttime dreams are commentary on our day, cannot Dosha, Fisher's daytime dream, be a commentary on his night? And how do we separate night from day?

CHAPTER 5

Blue-eyed *young son."*

Dylan, Dylan: that's all Fisher plays, every minute of every day. If he keeps this up he won't be able to string together one simple sentence of his own, thought Tal. Tal got up and pulled on a string attached to a hammer which pounded into the steam pipe. Smiling, he adjusted an earphone with a sensor plug against the wall adjoining Fisher's room.

"Dammit, Dreamboat, turn off Dylan! I tell you I've got something to talk about, and you turn up Dylan. Sometimes I wonder who I'm living with, you or Bob," shouted Dosha, barely hearing herself above Dylan's wailing voice.

"Who do you prefer?" shot back Fisher, as he abruptly turned off the record player and faced Dosha, as though asking her to dance in the echoes of the music.

"That's it. Now I can hear," said Tal softly.

■ Bob Dylan: Every minute of every day—It's sweet. It's nice. Playing my records day after day. Every minute of every day. Foolish this Fisherman—holding flowers—and asking her, Who do you prefer? Should be whom, I think.

And anyway, don't my gal look fine when she's coming after me?

She's living with Fisher and with me. In the same way that I lived with Sarah and with my angel.

I got this graveyard woman, you know she
keeps my kid
But my soulful mama, you know she keeps
me hid
She's a junkyard angel and she always gives
me bread
Well, if I go down dyin', you know she bound
to put a blanket on my bed
—from "A Buick 6"

The same angel. The same thirst for bread in every village apartment and in every Parisian garret. And probably in every Argentine walk-up, in every dream being dreamt. Fisher and Dosha look to be 56 together. 28 each or 30 and 26, whatever. Nice to be included. That's why I wrote. That's why I sang.

■ Isaac Luria to a disciple: If he keeps this up he won't be able to string together—*"It is impossible because all things are connected with one another. I can hardly open my mouth to speak without feeling as though the sea burst its dams and overflowed. How then shall I express what my soul has received and how can I put it down in a book?"*

Dosha is right. He knows she is. And that is why he plays this music every minute of every day. So as not to allow one minute for her to enter his soul. Once she enters, she will never leave.

◆ RACHEL, TAL'S MOTHER: Your father? Are you nuts?—It is Fisher who is mad. Never asking about her family. Never mentioning her mother. As though Chicago were a different star. Extraordinary how in America no one visits relatives in another city. They might as well be dead. Even in Europe we would visit the graves of our dead relatives. How much more so the living. To think that Fisher never offered to visit her father's grave with her. And to use the name of the dead to revive the living. If Abraham's stratagem were not so ridiculous it would be tragic.

■ TALMUD BERACHOT 32: Crying—*Even if the gates of prayer are shut the gates of tears are not.*

■ PAUL GAUGUIN: To finish—*Van Gogh would never let me finish anything: a painting, a thought, a sentence, a joke, a story, a seduction, a scream, a walk, a sleep, a nap, a meal. He hovered, he shrieked, he pawed. He bragged. He wept. I wrote his brother Vincent, "We simply cannot live together in peace because of incompatibilities of temper, and we both need quiet for our work."* This Fisher needs music. And if Dosha keeps interrupting him, not letting him finish, all that will be left of him is a painting of hers.

■ SOMERSET MAUGHAM: Story—*"I could not spend an hour in anyone's company without getting the material to write at least a readable story about him."* What a pleasure it is for Tal to have this ingenue act in his play. Breathtakingly clever.

"Whom do you prefer, me or Bob?" asked Dosha, suddenly taking Fisher in her arms and spinning him around in a waltz step.

"What did you want to tell me that couldn't wait for Bob to finish?" asked Fisher, feigning exhaustion and dropping onto the floor, dragging Dosha down with him.

"I met my father today, my mad father who came to New York to take me home to Chicago," Dosha whispered.

"Your father? Are you nuts? Your father died five years ago! Dosha, what are you talking about?" Dosha freed herself from Fisher's embrace and leaped off the Herati prayer rug with its torn tassels.

Impulsively, Dosha burst onto the bed, crying, and then just as suddenly sprinted into the next room.

"Dosha!" shouted Fisher, as he followed her into the living room.

Tal removed his ear sensor from the wall and hurried into the kitchen, which abutted Fisher and Dosha's living room.

". . . not five years," said Dosha. Tal had missed the first part of her story's sentence.

■ REB NOSON OF BRESLOV: Whom do you prefer?—After the death of the Rebbe Nachman everyone would ask me whom do I prefer to be the next Rebbe. But the Breslover told us, *"I want to remain among you."* And that is why I now say what the Rebbe says: I prefer a dead Rebbe who is alive to a live Rebbe who is dead.

■ REMBRANDT: I met my father—*In my painting of Abraham and Isaac, I have Isaac's eyes covered. If Isaac had met his father's gaze it would have been impossible either for Abraham to take Isaac up to Mount Moriah or for Isaac to go. But to listen and to do without eyes meeting—that was possible in the fury of the moment.*

■ BOB DYLAN: Wait for Bob to finish—I'll bless Fisher if he'll bless me. And as he plays me he blesses me.

May G-d bless you and keep you always,
May your wishes all come true,
May you always do for others
And let others do for you.
May you build a ladder to the stars
And climb on every rung
May you stay forever young,
Forever young, forever young,
May you stay forever young.

■ BOB DYLAN: Dylan hasn't been pop for years now—In July 1965 I strode on the stage with an amplified electric—628-volt—guitar. I could see Seeger off to the left, pulling at the mike plugs in the circulator box behind. Screaming, flailing, not allowing me an inch. As long as I had my harmonica and visited Woody and sang about unions and no louder than the birds, that was just fine with Seeger, but a new instrument, electric, truly popular? Old Seeger would have brought down the temple if he could have. I may have been no David, but he was no Samson.

■ JOAN BAEZ: Don't put on that G-d damned record—Extraordinary that Tal would call Dylan's record—his unsung voice—*G-d damned*. My record "Hey Blue You Good Dog You"—my highest note would have melted Fisher's resolve. Tears won't touch Tal, he's dewy enough. Better my early Elizabethan ballads, and kiss the back of Fisher's neck by candlelight. An unpublished novelist will always respond to a candle-lit ballad.

"Can I put Dylan back on? That way, at least we can listen, not fight," Fisher pleaded.

"Don't put on that G-d damned record, Fisher, or I'll come in and take my money back," Tal snarled under his breath.

"Don't you have anything to say for yourself, Fisher? My G-d, I tell you I just saw my father, and all you can think of doing is to play pop music." Dosha was whispering, but Tal could almost sense what she was saying before she spoke.

"Dylan hasn't been pop for years now. On the other hand, your pop hasn't been pop for years either," sneered Fisher. "And your mums been mum too."

"Fisher, I'm telling you I saw my father. He didn't die. He . . . he . . ." Suddenly, Dosha threw herself on the floor, thrashed around, and grabbed a nearby chair, throwing it against the wall.

The earphone suctioned against Tal's wall fell off. Tal scrambled around to pull it up and replace it against the wall only to realize Dosha had darted into the bedroom.

◆ TAL'S FATHER: Threw herself on the floor—Suleimani, in fact, was born in Zakho in Kurdistan and he would tell me how the women stood on the roof at the start of a wedding raising their *klilili*—cries of joy—at first quietly, then more firmly, and finally with such joy the roofs themselves would shake. Little girls walked by with colored candles in mountainous Amadiya where his mother was raised. In Sinne, horses pranced through narrow streets whinnying their way to the bejeweled silvery bride. But here, in golden America, a woman must throw herself at her would-be groom's feet. Suleimani said that a beggar in Kurdistan lived better than a prince here.

■ FRANK WALKER: Record—In 1926, Chris Bouchillon and his brothers from Greenville, South Carolina, came to me with their version of singing—more like steam escaping from the foundry. *"I said to them, Don't sing it. Just talk it. Tell them about the blues but don't sing it. . . . and that's how Chris and his brother Uris, the guitar player, created Talking Blues. 'If you want to get to Heaven, let them tell you how to do it.'"*

The record was issued in 1927 and sold 90,000 copies. Robert Lunn performed Talking Blues and then added his own verses; only later did white musicians perform Talking Blues. Woody Guthrie used the Talking Blues. And now Fisher's listening to Dylan who listened to Woody use his Talking Blues to this darling dream of his. We all use our own words on songs of others.

◆ EMIL FISHER, FISHER'S FATHER: You're Jewish—I always wanted to be Jewish; I was young, hungry for new things. To be modern. The whole world had come to Paris to see the Exposition des Arts Décoratifs et Industriels Modernes. For six months, every hour I could spare from work, I would spend wandering through the Pavillon de l'Elégance. Architecture. Clothing. Furniture. Endless necklaces fashioned with diamonds, natural pearls from the gulf, strings of pearls, ropes of pearls, pearl brooches. Sapphires. Gems beyond one's dreams. But I always ended at the very same address, the Worth fashion house just beyond the Cartier display—not in the Grand Palais but precisely in the center of the Pavillon de l'Elégance. I would rush past the enormous emerald epaulette of Cartier breathless to see our feathers!

Ostrich feathers from South Africa. Bird-of-Paradise feathers. Peacock sticks. Goose satinettes. And one day I had my chance. There was the Mâitre Couturier, Mr. Worth, talking about the white egret feather in a lady's hat. "This, madame," he was saying, "originally comes from Egypt." And on and on Monsieur Worth went, for more than an hour. I waited until the customer left and walked over smartly to the booth and said, "Mr. Worth, those feathers actually come from the rue Daunou, Maison Judith Barbier." "And how do you know that, young man?" Monsieur Worth asked calmly. "Because we sold them to her." And with a flourish, I handed him my card: Fisher et Fils, Emil Victor Fisher.

Mr. Worth smiled and said, "Are you Jewish?" I stiffened. This wasn't Poland but this *was* France. I blurted out, "Yes, I am Jewish and I've always wanted to be Jewish." "Let's take a walk," Worth said, and we walked over to the Cartier booth. He pointed out a glorious diamond aigrette lit by diamonds with an extraordinary egret feather resting in its central shaft. "Why don't you go over to Monsieur Louis Cartier and tell him you know where he gets his egret feathers from? He will confirm your belief he purchased the feathers from me, and I from Madame Barbier and she from you and you from Egypt." Then, with a smile, he gently turned my body on an axis completely around and facing a mannequin wearing the emerald epaulette. "Now if you knew where Monsieur Cartier purchased that glorious bouquet of flowers, that would shock him," he said, pointing to a 114-carat gem, the most paradisaically green emerald imaginable. What could I say? I was so humiliated.

But suddenly Worth said, "I apologize. I should not have spoken of religion. The truth is I was just like you when I was your age. *Plus ça change.* It was a great pleasure to meet you, Monsieur Fisher." He touched my shoulder with a gesture that I believe wished me luck. Then he vanished.

Tal grabbed the suction piece and sprinted back to his bedroom, thinking, She's going to kill me. Heart attack, for sure. Breathing heavily, he again adjusted the listening device.

Through the dividing wall, Tal could hear Fisher. "My G-d, you're no Gypsy, Dosha. This is crazy. You're Jewish. Your father came from that town in Russia. You told me that. I once met your mother's cousin from Chicago—or was it Omaha—Pinky or whatever his name was."

"That was no cousin, jerk. He was my high school boyfriend. I always wanted to be Jewish. You would also if your father was a Gypsy." Dosha arched her head backward at an almost impossible angle, as though she were looking at Fisher from a high peak.

A long silence. Not just long but totally quiet.

After a few minutes: "If I had told you what it was like I don't think you would have wanted me. The nights I would come home after school. And my father alone in the house, not having worked for months." Dosha was whimpering more than speaking.

◆ RACHEL, TAL'S MOTHER: You're Jewish—Of course Fisher talks about his girlfriend's parents. As though one should be proud—or ashamed—of being Jewish because one's mother or father was Jewish. To take joy in, to observe, to honor the Torah. To be proud that his girlfriend might have lighted candles, candles at sundown on Friday. Proud that his girlfriend smuggled a tattered prayer book into Russia. Proud that she taught herself Hebrew, gave charity, wrote a poem, read scriptures, dreamed of Jerusalem, visited a Venice ghetto synagogue, sat in the back of an Argentine Hebrew school, walked an elderly Jewish blind woman—or any blind woman—to a bakery. *Thou shalt not put a stumbling block before the blind.* Any Jewish—any human—deed that would be "Jewish" and not some genealogical record. "*What doth the Lord require of you but to do justly and to love mercy and walk humbly with thy G-d?*" (Micah 6:8). Not simply: be born Jewish. Far more subtle is what the good Lord wants.

◆ TAL'S FATHER: Pinky—No one has a name that anyone else has. Abraham in the first generation will be Abe, in the second generation Big A, then Pinky, then A. Preston. But never Abraham and his grandson Abraham and his great-great-grandson Abraham. We even named our ancestors by the books they wrote. Sfas Emes, Pardes Rimonim. Of course, no one now will be able to remember where they came from. Only nicknames, no place of birth. They're killing their memory.

■ DANA NISWENDER: Was a Gypsy—This young man should use the subjunctive, *were* a Gypsy, as this is contrary to the fact.

■ ISAAC LURIA: Your father came from that town in Russia—In this country of Tal's, not only can a Jew not remember where his bride's family came from, he cannot even remember where his own father or grandfather came from. I would walk down the steep hills off to the right of the ravine to the east of Safed and think and think as I walked with Vital, *Sha'ar ha Gilgulim*, the gates of transmigrating souls. Suddenly it would come to me in a kind of bluish haze surrounding my head, dense, almost opaque. I could hardly walk.

Vital would help me hobble up the hill to my house. Hours later I would awake, generally after almost a day of sleep, and I would know—beyond knowledge, beyond smell or taste—where a person's soul had come from. I would rush to their house and beg forgiveness of them and tell them where their soul had been before. And which prayers and whose forgiveness they should seek to free their past souls of all sins. To know where a Jew came from. In Safed it could be done. You could hear the murmur of the hints of souls in the air. How different, America.

■ GAUGUIN: A pretty picture—Oh, they were a pretty picture, the French in Tahiti when I arrived in June 1891. Come immediately to the Circle Militaire and we can watch the Tahitians from a balcony in a banyan tree." What a pretty picture they make," they eagerly told me. Not that I was such a pretty picture myself, with my hair down to my shoulders. A *mahu* they called me. I asked whether I was handsome, and my woman—or my mademoiselle, as my fellow Parisians would call her, though she was more woman and more mademoiselle than they dared dream—giggled and whispered to me, "You are not handsome, you are a pretty *taata-wahine* [man-woman]." Being forty-three, I cut my hair the next day.

■ KAFKA: Strange—Each evening after work in the insurance company, three men who sat in the office next to mine would go to the King's Bar to drink and smoke until eight or nine o'clock, when they would catch the last bus to their homes just outside the city. I don't drink, I told them, or else I would most certainly join you, when they pressed me week after week to come drinking with them.

Once I had a sensation, after I left at precisely 4 P.M. as I always did, that the ringleader was about to pull some mischievous prank on me. I thought, when I was sitting in the café with Brod, that I saw the ringleader that evening. The next morning Axel came over to me with that extraordinary smirk of his and said, "I thought you didn't drink. I saw you with another cadaver at the café." I wasn't drinking, I answered summarily; I was reading a short story about a man who became a bug. As I left the room I saw Axel turn to Klapper and whisper, "G-d, the fellow's strange."

"Pestering me about where I went after school. Following me. Desperately jealous, especially after Mother left. It wasn't a very pretty picture."

Fisher put his arm around Dosha's shoulder and licked the short hairs on the back of her neck.

"It's strange," Fisher mumbled. "Tal's always talked about your red and white canvases as 'Gypsy red.' No Jew would use your palette, he once said."

"He's no stranger than you, Dreamboat. And a lot kinder than my father, though just about as sad and confused." Dosha lowered her head, as though resigned to an inescapable destiny.

Tal winced. He never thought of himself as confused. "I'll show them," he shouted. "I ought to record this conversation! Then they'll see who's confused."

Dosha turned to Fisher and, holding his hand in hers, rubbed her hand against the side of his chin. "Why don't you stop shaving, Dreamboat, and grow a beard? You'd look really great."

■ AMEDEO MODIGLIANI: Gypsy red—The Gypsy wore a red dress to my studio three times. First for the sketch in charcoal, which took barely an hour. I told her I would give it to her when I had finished her portrait. The second time I sent her home after painting her for half an hour. She had changed her dress from red to black. I told her straight out that I couldn't sketch her wearing one dress and have her posing next in another. "What difference could it possibly make," she asked, "since your first drawing was in black-and-white? And what will you pay me?" I told her, I'll feed you with a meal that will fill you for a week. She said she would return to me for one last sitting, but I warned her, No Gypsy red dress, no meal.

A month later at eight o'clock in the morning, she returned. I laughed when I saw that she had brought her child and painted them both until the late afternoon. When I finally showed her the canvas she exclaimed, "But my dress is Gypsy red! And your painting is orange." Your skin is what I see it as, your hands are what I see them as, the curve of your chin, the bridge of your nose, the slope of your ear, your extraordinary neck is in my hand, guided by my eyes, I replied, and added, But your heart is Gypsy red. And she and her baby and I ate together for seven days.

■ BOB DYLAN: Always talked—It's not who I always talk about and not who I always sing about but who I always think about. Robert Johnson was my man.

"Corrina, Corrina. Stone's in my passway."

One whole Johnson verse simply appeared in the song. Got inside me and never left. But why should I 'fess up to that? And critics telling me who I am and from where I got this. And that's none of their business. More precisely, why should critics build their business on my business and bootleg off of me, always talking about where my takes and songs and picking come from? He was right, young Robert Johnson. Never let 'em see your finger pickin' too closely.

Amedeo Modigliani, Gypsy with Baby.

◆ RACHEL, TAL'S MOTHER: Your first girlfriend . . . your mother—Abraham came home breathless. Sixteen. Looking down at his feet. Stammering. Hanging around the kitchen although I asked him to change his shoes, which had mud on them. He didn't hear me. I asked where he had gotten so muddy. He pointed out the window toward the park. Which was odd as he never went playing with his classmates after school but came straight home supposedly to work but never finished his homework by the time he was due for his eight o'clock class in the morning. "Playing?" I asked him. "No, talking—Rachel," he said. I thought it odd that he called me by my first name. The first and last time he did so. "You mean Mother, don't you?" "No, Rachel. Rachel Beller, the daughter of Shloimi." "I don't know her," I told him. "Where does she go to school? What does she look like? How did you meet her? Does Tuviah know her?" Abraham just stared mutely down at his shoes. "Well, tell me something, anything, about Rachel," I said to him. "I've told you all." "You've only told me her name." "That's enough," he replied. "Don't you understand, Mother? Her name is the same as yours so I can't marry her." He wept and held my hand against his face by the window. I looked down at him and asked gently, "What do you mean?" "The Talmud," he sobbed, "It's all in the Talmud." "My, my," I said. "So many books and you don't think there is an answer to this problem about a girl you've just met this afternoon." "I met her before." He sighed. "Well, I will ask your father, Abraham. He will have a solution." At night I told my husband. He said it was ridiculous but that he would pose the question on Thursday night when he was studying with Rav Gamliel. He came back late Thursday and knocked on Abraham's door, but Abraham wouldn't open it.

"And why don't you stop cutting your hair?" Fisher's hands formed a delicate comb plowing its way through the furrows of her dark glistening diamondiferous hair in the afternoon sunlight.

Dosha sat up in bed, ripping her locket off her neck. "I can't stand it," she screamed. "You keep at me. I'm not your first girlfriend, your sister, your mother, all rolled into one. They all had long hair. I don't want long hair. I'm me!" Dosha jumped to her feet on the bed again, surveying Fisher from the heights. Suddenly Tal heard the rustle of metal shades against glass.

"Why did you do that?" shouted Fisher, genuinely alarmed.

Before Tal could move, he heard Fisher exclaim, "You must have hit the top of the window shade. It just goes to show why so few major league ball players are Gypsies." Tal could picture Fisher's sardonic smile.

Dosha suddenly hit Fisher on the hand with all her might. "Cut it out, Dosha!" Fisher shouted, more from surprise than pain.

◆ TAL'S FATHER: Your first girlfriend . . . your mother—I went to Rav Gamliel's house and posed the question. "It is true," said the rabbi. "Your son is correct. It is not allowed to marry a woman who bears the name of his mother. However, Torah is a way of life, not death. It is permissible to add a name to the woman. She could be Leah Rachel or Sarah Rachel. And then it is allowed. If G-d forbid she got sick, another name could be added to her. She could become Deborah Sarah Rachel. Again, the Torah is life. Now as to whether their daughter could be named Rachel after Sarah Rachel's living grandmother, for example, is another question. You Sephardim have no problem with this. We Ashkenazim rarely do it. But why add more things for your son to ponder about alone? Bring him to me. We could study together before our Thursday evening *shiur*."

■ BOBBY FISCHER: I'm not your first girlfriend, your sister, your mother, all rolled into one— She's good, this Dosha. She's got a great opening, a good middle, and she's moving into her end game. Fisher doesn't understand that the queen is the mother and the sister and the girlfriend all rolled into one. That's why he'll never hold his own with Dosha. As soon as my sister taught me the rules of chess, I grasped the connection. That's why I never lost to her afterward. Dosha's smart to claim mother and girlfriend, queen and sister, are not one. Of course, she's just feigning, keeping Fisher off balance. She's more Fisher than he. I don't think her boyfriend Fisher has a move left.

■ ROBERT JOHNSON: More from surprise than pain—*"Johnny Shines and me rode buses and trains. We walked every which road, in and out, from Helena to Vicksburg. Now Johnny would look like a mouse that done got caught by a dead cat, but I'd be clean. And it rattled Johnny. And he'd say, R.J., with those old ladies you're looking to hook up to, t'aint no difference what you look like. All you're gonna do is fasten on the oldest, sorriest, biggest friend girl we see."* And I'd smile and say, All you see is how much Annie from BoBo (right down near Clarksdale) weighed, but as I see her, Johnny, the pain I sees in her reminds me of my momma. It's that simple. But when I walked over to BoBo Annie last Thursday night at the Duncan Juke Joint, she accepted me more from surprise than pain.

◆ TAL'S FATHER: Honey and . . . milk—A land flowing with milk and honey. Milk, the finest of foods, a term of abundance, and honey, the epitome of sweetness. Imagine a land with the body of a woman. No wonder the land of Israel was longed for, yearned for, for two thousand years. No wonder they sang of her, praised her on the Russian steppes, in cold Polish winters. First the milky dream was a land, then a woman, then a mother. Now just American packaged goods, dated, spoiling, and disposable.

■ MONET: Kisses on your eyelids—Dr. Coutela lifted my eyelids gently, almost a kiss, and peered at me an inch from my face, just as I peered at my canvas and brushes on my oak table. I wondered if he could see my pupils from afar. The next thing I knew I felt an intense pain in my right eye, as though he had grasped my right eyelid and stretched his foot flat against my head. I shrieked. Blanche held my hand with a firmness I didn't know she possessed.

Hours later Coutela told me the news. I thought he said I was nearly blind. Blanche explained to me. "Papa, he said you're nearly *blue*-blind. You see too much yellow and too little blue." I wept for days. Everything I was painting was not the way I saw it. An old xanthopsic clown pretending he was painting nature when all he was doing was painting himself.

"You cut it out. You'll never know. With your warm baths and your honey and your milk at night and your mother and her kisses on your eyelids. And all I have is this locket Father gave me. I hate him. Him and his cunning ways. And I hate him following me. I can't draw a human portrait because I would have to draw his eyes. And those eyes follow me. Now he's found me and he wants to take me home, as he puts it. I hate him. I hate him. My G-d, those eyes suddenly here on the street, in New York. How the hell did he find me, Fisher?" And like a spent top, Dosha collapsed on their bed.

Fisher put her head in his hands and stroked her tearful face. He brought her lips to his, and the salt from her tears touched his mouth. Fisher removed her red scarf, tied Vermeer-like around her head, her dress, sticking to her like a wrapping, her sheer white stockings, then gently slid her frilly underwear off the edge of the bed.

■ BLANCHE HOSCHEDÉ-MONET, MONET'S DAUGHTER: My eyelids—Papa raged and screamed, "I'm blind, I'm blind! I will never paint. My eyelids are shrouds. That scoundrel Rebière, that crook, the so-called Dr. Coutela!" I said, "Papa, what do you care if your canvases are too yellow? You always insisted nature followed you, not you nature. That is why you planted and painted, painted and planted." "Don't tell anyone I'm blind," he screamed. "It is our *petit secret*." By now, Papa, it is our *grand secret*. You shouted it down to Madame Jallou in the churchyard. Later I told "the tiger" Clemenceau everything. Perhaps he could explain the sickness to Papa.

■ CAMILLE PISSARO: Eyes follow me—I painted myself at ninety with eyes that follow the viewer wherever he goes in the room. My father's eyes, Mother would say. And indeed my four boys' eyes, remarkable, three generations of pairs of eyes that never varied. But not G-d's eyes. And certainly not the eyes of the synagogue elders, which would not deign to rest on Papa after he married Mother—she seven years older than Papa and his aunt to boot! I never wrote of G-d to Father and I never spoke of the judgment of the synagogue or him; nor could they judge me, for I would not stand before them. But I judge myself and probably more severely than they could ever have judged me.

■ KAFKA: How little he knew of her—"*It is almost as though the girls in my great love Felice's school were my children and I had acquired a mother.*" To marry Felice Bauer. To have children. To take them to dinner at my parents' house. To walk my children to school. To marry Felice Bauer. To remain in my house. Not to visit my parents. Not to have children. Not to take them to school. To think. To write in one's room. To make the pen dance. How little it all had to do with Felice. How little I knew of her.

■ BEAVER CLAWS: Long hair—When I saw Elk River's daughter's long hair I knew that, should I die in battle searching for horses to give to her father, I would be the happiest Arapaho. I found forty-six horses in one moonlight raid but did not rest. Only after I drove twenty-four more horses to Elk River's lodge did I speak. Elk River's daughter often asked me if I could see in the dark to be able capture seventy horses. Yes, I would tell her. If I were buried in your long black hair I could see the moonbeams high in the sky. And we would roll and roll and roll and roll down the night slide of love. And those seventy horses gave me seventy years of joy.

■ JONAH: Bed—*Now the word of the Lord came unto Jonah the son of Amitai, saying, Arise and go to Nineveh, that great city, and cry against it; for their wickedness is come up before me.*

But Jonah rose up to flee to Tarshish from the presence of the Lord, and went down to Joppa; and he found a ship going to Tarshish: so he paid the fare thereof, and went down into it, to go with them unto Tarshish from the presence of the Lord.

But the Lord sent out a great wind into the sea, and there was a mighty tempest in the sea, so that the ship was like to be broken.

Then the mariners were afraid and cried every man unto his G-d, and cast forth the wares that were in the ship into the sea, to lighten it of them.

But Jonah was gone down into the sides of the ship, and he lay on his bed, and was fast asleep.

They met in the center of the bed, not so much lovers as mountaineers, climbers, exhausted and sweetly dozing under an alpine tree. A tree whose leaves slowly fell on Dosha's fragrant face. Fisher gently brushed Dosha's face, her long hair shining even in the darkness.

"I love you, Dosha." A shudder swept through her body. She dug her fingers into his back and clung to him with all her might, shouting, "Never, never! Don't let him take me!"

"I won't! I won't! I won't. I won't," moaned Fisher. And when he looked again, she was fast asleep in his arms.

My G-d. How little he knew of her. She had approached him years ago on a Village street. He hadn't even seen her coming. And she had flipped her head sideways and her hair parted; it was silken-fine and glorious.

■ VERMEER: A village street—Just across from my window, I would gaze for hours to try to capture Henrika sitting in the doorway, or Annika sweeping the path between Six's house and Ten Eyck's door. Henrika would look out and shout at me, "Johannes! Tend to your daughters. It's ridiculous. You're gaping at me as though I were twenty years old again." It was impossible to catch her still and quiet. And then Leeuwenhoek told me of the hidden camera, *camera obscura*, he called it. Simply a reflection.

I sat in my room in the dark and the image appeared on my wall upside down. I painted for hours. When I finished three months later, I invited Henrika to my home, fed her biscuits and tea, and unveiled the painting. Her jaw dropped wide. "Johannes. I thought you had gone away to The Hague. Why waste time on an old woman and an even older building? You'll never sell this painting." "I painted it for you," I said. "You can keep it in your house if you'd like." "And what should I do, throw away my mirror and stare at my painting? Thank you kindly but I'll come here every now and then to look at it." "You'll come for the biscuits and tea." I laughed. And so she did, every Wednesday.

■ JOHNNY SHINES: Never, never—Robert Johnson always looked neat, never, never looked like me. "*Robert could ride highways and things like that all day long, and you'd look down at yourself and you'd be as filthy as a pig and Robert'd be clean. How, I don't know. In those days we had nowhere to go. People would just pick you up on the streets. They'd see you with your instrument, say: 'Man, you play that? Yeah, play me a piece.' You say, Well I do this for my living, man, and by that they knew automatically that you're not going to play for free. Maybe you stand there and play two or three pieces. Well, by that time, hell you got twenty-five people around you.*"

◆ TAL'S FATHER: My G-d—The G-d of Abraham, the G-d of Isaac, the G-d of Jacob. And why do we say *the G-d* three times? Did not Abraham, Isaac, and Jacob worship the same G-d? They each actually found their own method of worshiping in their own way. And that is why they were able to maintain their faith. Simply copying the faith of their father would have meant that eventually they would have lost their faith. Even I understood that. Teach the child when he's young and let him choose his own path when he is older.

■ MARI BOLNES, VERMEER'S MOTHER-IN-LAW: My G-d—Still more secretive than his father, Johannes was. But Catharina would have followed him to the Zuider Zee, across the waters to Cadiz, and beyond to the East Indies if he had just gestured with his holy painter's hands. "What do you know of him," I asked her. "He's Protestant from Delft. You are a Catholic from Gouda." I told her. "And what does he do?" "His father, Reynier Vermeer, is an art dealer." "Catharina, his father's name is not Vermeer but Vos and he owns a tavern and sells Caffa silk and I don't trust the father and I don't trust the son. They have a whiff of the East about them." But of course Catharina wouldn't listen and I figured better a Catholic baby than an illegitimate one on our doorstep.

But strange: the night before the vows— Johannes dead drunk and whispering in my ear, "Oh, I will sign anything you want. Children, Catholic mass, I'll sign it all"—and then that odd statement: "I'm more Catholic than you, more Spanish than the Spaniards, more Jewish than our Lord." I told him to shut up and accept 2,000 guilders and leave, but to his credit and to my horror he said, "I am not Judas but a Jew." He never got drunk again, nor did I ever mention this to Catharina. I wonder where those odd Mechlin vases of his came from anyway?

But what he remembered most of all was that he couldn't turn away from her gaze as she asked where he was going. My G-d, she never let up, not that he ever knew where he was going or wanted to.

Soon she stirred. He'd better decide. He really knew nothing about her—Gypsy, that's the end. And pretending she was Jewish. Tal will have a fit when he finds out. Serves him right, that demented matchmaker.

She stirred and opened her eyes only to have Fisher kiss them shut. "I love you and your milk and honey," she said.

"I want to marry you, my darling," said Fisher. "I'm serious this time. I want to offer you my hand. I've saved sixteen hundred dollars. We can take a trip anywhere. I love you."

■ KAFKA: I want to marry you. . . . I want to offer you my hand—"*Milena, for me you are not a woman. You are a girl, as real as I ever saw. I don't think I'll dare offer you my hand, girl, this dirty twitching clawlike unsteady uncertain hot-cold hand.*" This Fisher is like me at thirty-seven with Milena. If I had met Milena at his age, maybe marriage would have been possible. Quaint the way in America they still call it "offering one's hand." But Fisher and Dosha are both like my Milena. All three have a future because none of them has a past.

All I had was a past. The clock tower in Prague running backward. And I clutching for dear life to its hour hand either being borne ceaselessly backward or tumbling to an instant death on the pavement stones of the old Jewish quarter. And Milena shouting, pleading, whispering, cajoling, begging, entreating, asking, almost convincing me, "Jump, slide, wiggle, descend, Franz, into my arms, I will save you, bear you into my present, into the future," and I unable to offer my hand.

■ VERMEER: My G-d—My mother-in-law flatly told me, Enough of the new religion. "Johannes, if you take my daughter, you will have to take my G-d. And you will take my daughter to the church on Hoogenstraat and pray at mass." What could I do, tell her I too had enough of the new religion? I said casually, "My painting is my G-d." She jumped. I clarified slowly to appease her. "Look at the cross in the painting *The Allegory of the New Testament*.

"What cross?" she protested, then added, "It's barely visible in the painting. And our blessed Jesus looking like a slab of Leyden sausage."

"Not that cross but the clear cross on the tiled floor," I said, which quieted her. And the red blood of Christ and the killed serpent, all these quieted her too. But of course I didn't point out for her the drops of blue blood— *Sangre azul*—also running on the floor, nor the reflection of the Sabbath lamp in the glass ball reflecting the one true G-d's light in the window. These I did not point out to her, nor paint out for her.

■ IRVING A. AGUS: This is where I'm going— "*The forefathers of Franco-German Jews, the five to ten thousand persons who survived the repeated invasions, the wholesale destruction, as well as the religious persecutions and forceful conversions of the fourth through eighth centuries, in Italy, Germany, and France, were very unusual and very remarkable individuals. At the end of this horrendous period, these five to ten thousand Jewish survivors constituted but one half of one percent of world Jewry; while by the first quarter of the twentieth century, the descendants of this small group numbered about twelve million and constituted more than eighty percent of the Jewish people. In the past twelve centuries, the descendants of the Jews of Catholic Europe from the dawn of the eighth century thus multiplied in number more than a thousand times, while the descendants of all the other branches of the Jewish people multiplied but three to four times. . . . The Ashkenazic Jews of the twentieth century are overwhelmingly the descendants of the above-mentioned five to ten thousand persons.*

"*The ancestors of German Jewry alive in the eighth century possessed to a very marked degree two main characteristics: unusual commercial skill and tremendous dedication to study and the observance of Judaism. . . . Beginning with the second half of the eighth century, therefore, Jews of Europe possessed all the important characteristics of a nation, except for geographic contiguity. Its members were of common origin; they married only among themselves generation after generation; they clung together with great brotherly devotion; they possessed a strong feeling of mutual responsibility; and very few of them ever deserted the group. And moreover, for the following thousand years, the group possessed a high degree of political and legal autonomy.*"

And she took him into her, doubling his arms around her, and after rolling down the river-washed grass, they arose with the dawn light and Dosha said, "Dreamboat, I have two hundred of my own. We're taking a cab to Centre Street so we can be first on line."

And he thought, This is where I'm going, and, overcoming a twinge of hesitation, carried her down the stairs and out of the building, leaving Tal upstairs to roll over on his bed, finally to fall asleep into his past, alone.

■ LAURENCE STERNE: Alone—26 March 1759. Tristram Shandy and I. Or perhaps, Tristram Shandy and Uncle Toby Shandy and Walter Shandy. Or perhaps Trim and the Widow Wadman. But not I. I dined at Stillington— three hours and twelve minutes—oporto from Stephen Croft caves, so could I refuse to read? And the Parson Grimadge and Croft himself first smiling, then both snoring. What was I to do but heave my manuscript into Croft's fireplace? Alas, Croft bestirred himself and pulled my family—all the Shandys and even Widow Wadman—from the flames. I am ever alone, Croft. I laughed with a plethora of tears. The Shandys have each other, but I do not even have my readers. Or listeners. It's all laugh-at-able in its own way.

■ ST. FRANCIS OF ASSISI: The dawn light—It was the dawn light, and the dusk that taught me all I know. The dawn light, which lit the world with the voices of the cuckoo and the dove, the oriole and the warbler. As a child in our garden I could imitate a cuckoo so well that I could awaken a mother from her nest and have her fly and rest on my hand for hours. By the time I was sixteen I spoke to the birds just as they spoke to me. But I always wondered why they did not sing at dusk, until one day I saw the blue night settling over the hills of Perugia and I understood that the birds had gone back to G-d and their morning wisdom was received from angels. I did not only preach to them, they preached to me. And I told Elias, Spread my word after my death. Teach great things in my name, from small things. Just as I have learned great things from the small in the dawn light. And Elias nodded and said, "Through your small pupils will I spread your great teachings." And I tried to correct him saying, "Small is great," but Elias did not understand.

■ BROTHER ELIAS, VICAR GENERAL OF THE FRANCISCAN ORDER: The dawn light—Brother Francis would awaken one hour before the dawn light and we would say matins together. It was impossible to hear myself pray because Francis would chant and murmur in a language that was more bird word that the word of our blessed Lord. There must have been at least two hundred cuckoos echoing Francis's prayers each morning. It is true that he spoke their language and they spoke his, but those pine nuts that I left outside before I went to sleep could not have harmed Francis's songs.

The day after his death, I set out to make his small teachings great. Giotto's angelic brush and my design inspired by the great cathedrals of France spread my Lord and his shepherd Francis's words to every pilgrim from as far away as Greece who came to worship in Assisi on their way to Rome. What did I care that the other brothers claimed I had made the "great" small. But no matter how many pine nuts I or my assistants left out at night, we never had a choir of two hundred birds after Francis's death. And till I died I wept at night and at dusk both for Francis and for my Lord.

Claude Monet, *Poplars on the Epte.*

■ Eduard Guilhou: Blue-blood—The rings filled the vitrines in my study. They spilled out of the cases in my library, into the salon on the first floor of my house. They marched up the stairs and filled the attic. They multiplied. They danced all day before my eyes and filled my dreams. When I would show my collection to my guests, one was sure to ask me which was my favorite. My favorite child. And I would remove the most marvelous blue sapphire mounted in a renaissance enameled ring and put it on the finger of the asker of the question. They would then always comment, How delicate, how blue. I could feel the blue running in my blood.

■ James Joyce: Jew—"*What, reduced to their simplest reciprocal form, were Bloom's thoughts about Stephen's thoughts about Bloom, and Bloom's thoughts about Stephen's thoughts about Bloom's thoughts about Stephen? He thought that he thought that he was a Jew whereas he knew that he knew that he knew that he was not.*"

■ Bob Dylan: Blue—

The highway is for gamblers, better use your sense.
Take what you have gathered from coincidence.
The empty-handed painter from your streets
Is drawing crazy patterns on your sheets.
The sky, too, is folding under you
And it's all over now, Baby Blue.

BLUE-BLOODED. Of course you're blue-blooded. And in the best sense of the word. You and your ancestors and your relatives in the East, and your mother, a Jew who hints at Sephardic relatives in Venice. What do I have to compare?" said Rachel Beller, a tall wisp of a girl who, at only twenty-two, looked far less than that.

"Rachel, Rachel," cried Tal, clutching his pillow. Tal opened his eyes and stared up at the ceiling, a completely blue-painted surface. The twinkling lights of the Empire State building twenty-five blocks away cascaded into Tal's Hudson Street windows, casting a whitish glow on the photo Tal had taped on the ceiling directly above his head.

■ Isaac Cardozo: Blue-blooded—Amazing to hear these words a thousand years after we heard them in beloved España from Visigothic rulers. And then in the Sentencia Estatuto of Toledo (1449). And almost two hundred years later in the academy in Valladolid. It was not enough that I said their prayers, ate their Host, signed their contracts. I was not one of the pure-blooded ones—*limpienza de sangre*—and therefore could not be trusted to truly utter prayer, truly taste the Host, truly write my assents. My mouth, my throat, my limbs did not posses the *sangre d'azul*, the blue blood of a true Christian, free from a spot of Moorish and Jewish "ancestral blood." Rather I was said to have a tail because of the sins of my ancestors in denying the body and blood of Jesus. And the color of blood was all important. I wrote on the excellence of green. And Brandam on blue and Villareal wrote on green again. Blue blood was the color of a passport to sleep at night, to go to university, to travel abroad, to return in peace. I hated and loved the color blue. Only when I came to Verona did I appreciate the blueness of the sky, G-d's sapphire given to Noah lighting the world. But for a Jew from Antwerp to use the phrase blue-blooded for a Jew in Antwerp is extraordinary. When we escaped there in the sixteenth century, not even as a pleasantry did we ever utter the words blue-blooded again.

■ Rabbi Shimon ben Eleazar: I—In the Talmud it is written: "*In all my days I have never seen a deer as a farmer, a lion as a porter, or a fox as a storekeeper. They make their living without suffering. But they were created only to serve me while I was created to serve my Maker. If they, who were created only to serve me, are supported without suffering, then surely I should be, for I was created to serve my Maker. Except that, I have corrupted my deeds and thus denied myself an easy livelihood.*"

◆ Rachel bat Elijah, Rabbi of Chelm (d. 1583), wife of Ephraim ben Jacob Katz, Fisher's ancestor: A rolled-up parchment—What is on the rolled-up parchment in her hand? For in her hand it is different than in anyone else's hand. If her hand is holy, the message on the rolled-up parchment she holds can be holy or can become holy.

I saw it in my blessed father Elijah's time. He was known far beyond Chelm as the Baal Shem Tov, the master of the good name, and I could feel his hand when he took mine on the way to the synagogue. A warm hand. And with his fingers, he wrote the words, Emet—Truth, on a yellowing piece of parchment. And from the dust in out attic, a golem paced back and forth. When I asked him, "Father, is it your hand that has molded a golem? Can I, your daughter, create one too?" Father took my tiny hand, for I was less than ten years old when I asked him and a ten-year-old speaks of everything, questions everything, and lifted my hand up and said quietly, "Just as I lift your hand now, so too the Holy One lifted mine. If the Blessed One chooses your hand to create, you too will bring a golem into this world."

And when our child Hezekiah had died and our second, Aryeh Judah Leib, was dying and my saintly husband asked me to lift my hand and pray to G-d that Aryeh Leib be spared and my husband's life be taken, I said in our child's stead to Ephraim, "If the Holy One wishes to lift your hand to create life, surely He can do it. If the Holy One chooses to take you to the other side of the curtain, surely He can do so. But I cannot pray for it. It is beyond me. Can I be both Abraham and Sarah? Can I bind both my child and my blessed husband? But by my father's power given to me, I give you leave to pray as you wish." Was there ever a more difficult choice for a wife or a mother?

The yellowing photograph is a portrait of a woman standing in the rain in front of an Antwerp brownstone. Two stone lions flank a staircase that leads directly up to the brownstone's dark oaken entranceway. The girl's vision is slightly strained as she stares directly into what must have been a 1922 box-camera lens. In her left hand is a curled-up newspaper, like a rolled-up parchment. She looks eager to go inside out of the rain. What is most noticeable is her unusually long neck and intensely black eyes. Her hair is braided into two concentric knots, and her tubular black dress (or some dark color) looks rather Parisian Art Deco, 1925. Light raindrops glisten on her dress, and her feet are so tiny that she appears to float upward into the Antwerp mist—although that effect might be the result of the photograph's position on the ceiling above Tal's head.

■ Henri Cartier-Bresson: Photograph—Photographers deal in things that vanish instantly. Nothing on earth can bring those things back again. Now this Tal has a photograph of his lady friend. When he took it I'm sure he didn't write anything on the back. Because, of course, he knew her so well. And he knew the building, and the two lions, and her mother, and her father. But soon he, too, will vanish. And the girl has already vanished. And the building perhaps has vanished. A recipe for madness, these family photographs. Better a photograph of someone you don't know, whose parents you don't know. With only the country and perhaps the year known.

■ Modigliani: Unusually long neck—When I showed Jeanne my painting of her, she said, "I have a long neck but not that long. Paint me again." "Let me stroke your neck each night for twenty years until it lengthens," I said. And she said, "Stroke me tonight but paint me tomorrow."

And when two weeks later I showed her the new portrait, she teased, "Now my neck is too short. I need more stroking." And we lay in bed for two days, not eating but feeding on each other's eyelids, and never have I dined more delicately. The first words she uttered after her bath were, "Now my neck is the proper length," and threw on a black dress which darkened her hair, then said, "Paint me, Amedeo, as you dream of me." And I did, but I wept as I painted her eyes as two tears. And she wept when she saw it. "Is this your dream of me?" she asked. I told her that it was her dream of my dream of her, and that it had no future. All I could see was her mourning my death. She looked at me and said, "When we will have no future, I will have no dreams."

dit is naer mijn huijsvrou geconterfijt
do sij 21 jaer oudt was den derde
dach als wij getrout waren
de 8 gunijus
1633

■ GENESIS: Rachel—*So Jacob served seven years for Rachel. And they seemed unto him but a few days, for the love he had for her.*

■ RABBI NACHMAN OF BRESLOV: Rosh Hashanah—*To me the main holiday is Rosh Hashanah and as soon as Rosh Hashanah is over, I listen to hear if there's a knocking at doors and Jews are arousing themselves to penitential prayers for the next year. For the year is over in the twinkling of an eye.*

■ BARUCH SPINOZA: A merchant's son—We were both merchant's sons, my beloved brother and myself. And we followed my blessed father into the trade together, Bento et Gabriel d'Espinoza, fruit merchants. One day my brother returned from the docks where he had inspected the crop of fruits from the East, El Kahir, I believe. I was reading a text in Latin. "How can you read at a time like this?" he asked. "We have just lost a quarter of our remaining capital." I replied, "Let me study for two years and then let me go down to the docks for the next two years. And you can stay in peace for two years." He answered me, "I know, Issachar and Zebulun. One studies and one works and both share in Paradise. But I am a merchant's son. And I know we will lose our capital if you don't work full time." "And I know I will lose my eternal capital," I said, "if I do work full time." And he shouted in anger, "Your way will lead to bankruptcy and excommunication." And I left that day saying, "Keep the fruit and I will keep the faith." In truth, he was right. He became bankrupt and I was excommunicated. But we would have survived had we remained together as Issachar and Zebulun.

"Rachel! Rachel! We're going to get married today," sobbed Tal.

"You're never going to marry me," said the photograph peering down at him. "You're never going to marry me. And your mother is not going to marry me. And your father is not going to bless me. And your venerable brother, G-d forbid, is not going to marry me. Avram, look at yourself. For all your camera equipment and your fancy shoes and your Champs-Élysées raincoat and your hat, you're still a merchant's son."

"Rachel, Rachel, I'm a Rabbi's grandson. Your father is a holy man. Of course our families will let us marry by Rosh Hashanah, for sure."

■ PA TA SHAN JEN: Look at yourself—This man must look at himself first. And he must look at others with the same eyes. But he looks with the "white eye"—the eye of disdain and indifference. This disdain of himself will mean that he will never be able to join himself to this woman's family. Any more than I could have joined the deceitful Manchu court. I kept a distance of half of China between myself and them. And I suspect this man will double that distance soon.

■ SIMHA BUNAM: Bless—In Genesis 48:20 we read that Joseph took his two sons, Manasseh and Ephraim, to visit their grandfather Jacob. And Jacob blessed them that day, saying, Israel will use you as a blessing. They will say, "*May G-d make you like Ephraim and Manasseh.*"

And Joseph blessed them that day. "*This phrase teaches us an important lesson. His blessing was contained in the words 'that day.' That day means today, the only day that counts. Concern yourself with the present. Don't worry about tomorrow. That was Jacob's blessing.*"

And Tal sobs because he knows his today is weighted down by his possessions. I, Simha Bunam, was a merchant's son. I was even a merchant myself. And my father read to me at the seder table:

"*Matzoh, why do we eat this unleavened bread? Because the dough of our fathers did not have the time to become leavened before the king of kings, the Holy One, Blessed is He, revealed Himself to them and redeemed them. Israel was driven out of Egypt and could not delay, nor had they prepared any provisions for the way. To be redeemed from Egypt, Israelites must leave their homes, abandon all their possessions, and make their way into the desert. Such is not the practice that is in fashion today.*" My father, a merchant, brought me to this understanding.

A man must realize that this is the way of redemption. Tal's father doesn't show him the path into the desert. Tal cannot not accept the blessings of the day and thus may not be able to share either in redemption or in Rachel's tomorrows.

◆ RACHEL, TAL'S MOTHER: Your father will never ask my father—She is right, that young girl, Rachel. My husband would never ask. He would tell me or he would say, Why should I ask a simple *shohet*? Let Abraham do the asking if he's so sure. But I would have told my husband, and it wouldn't have taken more than a day and a night for me to get him to agree. Of course, It would always have to be known as his idea.

■ JAMES JOYCE: Ask Father—Ask Father. Ask Father. Which father? Our father. Her father. His father. My father and my father's father lived on Clambrassil Street just north of the Grand Canal. The center of the Dublin Jewish community. And Father would tell me how the Jews would not have an entrance on the street. The entrance to their houses would be off an interior courtyard, so that the mezuzah wouldn't show and no one would know their comings and goings. And probably a protection for their daughters, so that no stranger would easily find the way to father's door to ask for a daughter's hand. But Nora agreed to live with me as man and wife, though she never gave up from asking me to ask Our Father for her hand. I held her off till 4 July 1931, when we wed by His leave. But Tal should cross an ocean or at least a sea with Rachel. Iseult the Fair. That will put her hand in his forever.

■ SASKIA: Ask Father—I told Rembrandt that before he could marry me he must ask my father for my hand. His eyes froze with horror and he said, "Saskia, your father is dead and buried with your mother, in Leeuwarden. The cold Friesland wind howls over their grave, though they are buried beside the churchyard's thick stone wall. Uylenburg your cousin told me the gravestone has started to crack from last winter's freeze though it is less than ten years old." I answered him, "Rembrandt, that is where you must go, to the churchyard in Friesland, and I cannot go with you for you must go alone." He left immediately, my young prince, the talk of all Holland as a painter. He took his theatrical fake sword and his plumed hat and gloves and he didn't return until the next week, staying eight days away. White he was, and rather than answer me he spent another week in his studio. He handed me an etching of himself with the very same saber and, weeping, said, "I have spoken to him. I have seen him and he has given his permission."

"Then go in, Avram, and ask Father. He's leaving in a few minutes to go to the Rebbe's house. Tomorrow is Shabbes Hagadol. There's not much time. If you're so sure, go in and ask for my hand. He'll give it to you and then you'll be committed. I'll kill myself if you break your promise to my father. Ask him." The face in the photograph moved seductively toward him, and he could feel Rachel's skin touch his forehead.

"Rachel, Rachel, my father must ask him. That's how it should be. You don't want to spend your life fighting with my family. My father will ask, and then before next Rosh Hashanah we can get married. If it doesn't work here in Antwerp, we can go to the Holy Land. It's quiet there now. Yes, that's what we should do."

"Avram," said Rachel, suddenly moving away, inching back toward the ceiling. "Your father will never ask my father. Your father won't speak to my father."

◆ TAL'S FATHER: Your father will never ask my father—Why do they always ask me? They supposedly know their parents. And what will we say? What will we do? And then children say we don't understand them. Or listen to what they tell us or ask us. Of course I would have gone to Rachel's father. Of course I would have asked her father for permission for my son to marry his daughter. A small family, two sons. All the princely dreams of Abraham would not have meant anything, if our children remained unwed.

■ KAFKA: Ask Father—Of course he should ask her father. But he should not ask his father for help, nor should he ask his mother. "*My mother lived only for my father. I wrote my father, saying, Mother loved you too much, she was too loyally devoted to you to act for any length of time as an independent spiritual force in a child's struggle.*"

No, my mother brought her dowry to the marriage, and that's what started Father off in his business. She played cards with him each night—and, I suspect, lost on purpose as often as she could without his knowing it. She bore him six children and never took their side in their arguments with him. He was king, although his kingdom was exceedingly small. And no prince or princess was prepared for the future. Now this Tal can't ask his mother or his father to ask this young girl's parents for her hand. Instead, Tal will go back and forth from his parents' house to her house like a messenger who has lost the message and is uncertain which destination to travel to.

■ KAFKA: Absolutely white—"*Even the last tip of the blue and white prayer shawl of Judaism was denied me.*" When Jiri Langer returned from that small town in eastern Poland, Belz, he invited me over to his room to pray. "Bring your tallis," he said. "I don't have a tallis." "Then bring your grandfather's tallis," he said. I asked my mother for her father's tallis, and my father burst into the room laughing and said, "Ask her father yourself or perhaps ask Jiri to ask him. If you want a tallis, you can find one in the hall closet. It's in the black box on the top shelf"—tossing the bronze closet key to me.

I mounted a short oak ladder. I felt dizzy but finally found a tattered, battered, very dark blue box. Curiously my bar mitzvah tallis and Father's tallis were hopelessly intertwined, moth-eaten, and completely unusable. I never accepted Jiri's invitation and sheepishly returned the key to my father. He smirked and said, "If Jiri needs a tenth man he should ask me and not you."

■ A KOTZKER HASID: Pure—Once a Hasid came into the Kotzker's synagogue just before the Sabbath. He didn't have time to go to the *mikvah* but started to meditate on the "redemption of the sparks" of G-d, from the teachings of the pure one, Isaac Luria of Safed. My master, the Kotzker Rebbe, burst into the room and shouted:

"*Who dares to meddle around with meditations and mysteries here? What impudence! Let him never do it again!*"

"My father is a nothing, a *shohet*. There's blood on his hands. He has one daughter, no sons. He stutters. His only blessing is me. His only language, Polish-Yiddish. His only happiness, Mother's memory. He's nothing. Your father wouldn't walk into my house. Never."

"Rachel, there's no blood on your father. He is absolutely white, more pure than any stone Father has ever cut. How can you say such a thing? Father will do what I ask him to do."

"Your father, Abraham Tal," said Rachel evenly, climbing up the stairs toward the door, "will do what your mother tells him to do, and your mother told you never to mention my name in your house."

Tal clutched his pillow to his chest, stroking Rachel's long unwound black hair. "How can you say these things? You're driving me mad, Rachel. Your name is spoken every hour in my house. It's her name too."

■ MONET: Black—"*I am completely discouraged. After several days of beautiful weather, the rain has started again and once more I have to put aside the things I have begun. I am going crazy, and unfortunately it is my poor canvases I take it out on. A large still life of flowers that I have just finished, I have destroyed, along with three or four canvases that I have not only scraped out but slashed. I see the future as too black. Doubt has taken possession of me. I feel lost, I'll no longer be able to do anything.*"

■ ST. COLUM, ABBOT OF IONA: Pure—A man must be pure and his gospel must be pure. And the parchment that his gospel is written on must be purer than himself. I told my cousin Braithéne to take a calfskin and remove the hairs with lime. And when after a week all the hairs are removed, set it aside for a month. And then examine it in the light of day and not by candlelight. And keep removing hairs for another week. And set it aside for another month and return to it. And after six months if you have done this diligently this parchment will be pure enough to write the immaculate gospel on. And reflect, Braithéne, G-d examines our souls in such a fashion. Picking us up and putting us down at His will. But we can become pure.

■ Rabbi Nachman of Breslov: Share—The question is, do they share the essence of the name they share? When my soul yearned for something, when I knew part of myself was floating, reaching, grasping, clawing through a darkness I could barely breathe in, when I was drowning and diving at the same time, I met Rabbi Nathan, on the 22nd day of Elul 5562 (September 18, 1802). I was twenty-two; he was eight years older. He said to me in a whisper, very evenly and very slowly:

"We've known each other a long time, but it's been very long since we've seen each other face-to-face."

They do not see each other, this Tal and this Rachel, face-to-face. And she does not see Tal's mother face-to-face. And Tal does not see Rachel's father face to face. How can even a hundred Rebbes join them together? But one prayer could.

■ Tung Ch'i-ch'ang: Your ancestor—I was born in Shanghai to no ancestors. For four generations we were poor. We had no office holders. No land that was free of taxes. I fled at sixteen. It was only at Ku Ching's house that I saw paintings and began to write. I began to paint my own ancestors. Could I not be the heir of Wang Meng? Could not Ni Tsan have been one of my mother's ancestors? A true artist creates his children and creates his past.

When my pupil became Emperor in 1620, Emperor Kuang Tsung, and asked, "Where is my teacher Tung now?" I had perfected even myself. But like so many of the great rivers, quakes can change their course. A month on the throne and Kuang Tsung died. Then I moved to the capital and tried to create the past, writing the veritable records of Wan Li's reign, 1573–1620. And that failed. At least I was able to create my children, those painters who by moonlight look through my eyes and paint the rivers, mountains and streams, scholars and fishermen, as long as China shall breathe.

"Yes, we share a name." Rachel nodded pensively. "We share a name—and your all-too-holy-brother, merchant-cum-yeshiva *illuyi*, quotes the Hatam Sopher that a Jew cannot marry a woman with the same name as one's mother—and you a Cohen, even a double Cohen! A Cohen on your father's side and a Cohen on your mother's side. Can twice a Cohen marry such a woman?"

"Rachel, this is horrible, crazy. Stop crying. Your father asked the Rebbe at Marienbad last year. The Belzer said that Rashi—"

"Yes, Rashi your ancestor, precious Avram, your ancestor." Suddenly, even the lions on the staircase flared their nostrils and awoke to the disputation.

"—Rashi said that in such a case there is a custom, a *minhag*, that one may take a woman to a shul and she may take a new name and be called before a minyan and be known forever, in this world and in the next.

■ Van Gogh: Share a name—A woman shares a name with another woman alive. Well. Healthy. There might have been a thousand Vincents crossing my path each day in Holland. Or a woman is named after a grandmother. The grandmother's memory becomes alive through her grandchild. Well. Healthy. But I was named after a brother. Stillborn, he was. And not to rise from the grave. But I, was I dead? Was I he? And if I were he, who am I? Am I anyone?

When I shared a room with Görlitz I smoked my pipe until the whole room filled up with blue curling clouds of Chinese wispiness. Görlitz would ask, while he studied for his high school certificate, "Is that you, Vincent, behind the cloud and the fire?" "It is Vincent, but I do not know if it is me," I would answer, and I read the Bible night after night. I dreamt of G-d and not of color. I dreamt of understanding how a name that is supposed to be a blessing could be detached from a curse. Certainly G-d loomed larger than art, and there was no question that the countless ordinary joys of life would have to wait until I could unlock the essence of myself locked within me.

■ Echo Star Helstrom: Share a name—One afternoon in 1958, Bobby came running up the walk to my house, hauling a book and half chanting, *"I've finally found a name. I'm gonna call myself Bob Dylan."* But he pronounced it Dial-in. Of course, he would never admit later that he shared his name with the Welsh poet. Or that he made it up so he and I could share together, I the Viking woman of his dreams and the nightmare of his mother. Perhaps I would have had a ghost of a chance had he remained Zimmerman, the man in my room. But not once he embarked on his Welsh saga.

בסימנא טבא ❧ ✦ ❧ ובמזלא מעליא

בששי בשבת עשרה ימים לחדש מנחם שנת חמשת אלפים וארבע מאות חמשים וחמשה
לבריאת ׳עלם ׳למנין שאנו מנין בו פה וירונה מתא דיתבא על נהר אדיג׳ נא נאההשוב והנכבר
כבר שלמה ה׳ יצו במלהלהיר וענה מסק׳נד׳ אנו יומ׳ ואמר לה לבתורה הצנועה והחשזוכה מרת
לאה בתולתא מבת בת הרמנוח כמלהר׳ רפאל ׳משה חיב הולל הורהטירה זלהה הוי לי לאנתו כדרית
משה וישראל ואנא בכי ׳עמא רשמויא ׳אפלה ׳ואוקיר ׳ואזון ׳ואפרנס יתיכ מהלכת גנבין הודאין
רפלחין ומוקרין וזנין ומפרנסין לנשיהון בקושטא והיבנא ליכ מהר בתוליכי כסף זוז מאן דחזו
ליכי ׳מזוניכי ׳וכסותכי וספקוזכ ׳זמיעל לותיכ כארח כל אינ׳שא ׳וצבאת מרת לאה בתולתא רב׳א
תמא והות ליה לאנתו לכמר׳ שלמה חי ׳יצו חתן רנ ׳ורא נדוניא דהנעלת ליה מבי אוז ׳אבוה
ארבע מאות וחמשים דוקאט׳ בזלכ מ׳עת דחושבים לערך שישה זהוב וארבעה מירקטי לא מזבע
קרינטוני בירוטו ׳ויער שלש מאות דוקאטי בכל כך כרים ׳עפים ותכשיטים רהיבוי מובילי השייכם
לגזה הכלה מבת תהל ׳וצב כבר שלמה חי יצו חתן רנ ׳ואסיך לה מדידיה עשרים מאה לכל הסכר
הלכ כפי המוסכב כגויה רהיזא מאה וחמשש דוקאאתי לערך הנזכר סך הכל כתובתא ונדוניא ותוספתא
תשיע מאות דוקאטי ליערך הנזכר ׳וכן אמר כבר שלמה חי יצו חתן רנ אחריות כתובתא דא קבלית
עלו ׳ועל ירתי בתראי להתפרע׳א מן כל שפר ׳ארג נכסין ׳וקנין ראית לי תחות כל שמיא דקנאו וראקנה
נכסין ראיתלהון אחריות׳ ואנבגן דלית להון אחריות כלהון יהון אחראין ׳וערבאין למפר׳ע מנהון כתובתא
דא יצו גמירא ׳ואפילו מן גלומא׳ על כתפאי בחיי ובמותא מן יומא רנ ׳ולעלם ׳וקבל עלו כבר שלמה
חי יצו חתן רנ חמר ׳כבר שלמ׳ חי יצו חתן רנ כחמר כל שטרי כתובות רהוגין כבנות ישראל הבתולות
הצנועות והמשויות דלא כאסמכתא ׳ודלא כטופסי דשטרי וקנינא אנן סהרי רחתמי׳ לתתא מן
כבר שלמה חי יצו חתן רנ לזכות מרת לאה בתולתא מרת תמא ׳על כל מאי דכתיב
ומפרש לעיל בכנא בדבר למקנא ביה ׳והכל ׳שריר ׳וקים ׳וקם

■ HIERONYMA DE PAIVA: Gravestone—When Jacob died I went to Elihu Yale's house and asked him for the right to buy a gravesite so I could bury my husband in a marsh field just outside of Fort St. George. "My dear lady," he told me, "Jews are allowed by my company to live here, but I must wait for permission to grant your request." "And how long will that take, Mr. Yale?" I inquired. "I shall dispatch a note immediately. Perhaps three months." When I entered Elihu's house he would often taunt me. "What will you do with your own bones?" I told Elihu that never for all eternity would I consent to be buried next to him, and he laughed. "If you die before me I will lie with you forever." And I said, "Your name will be on my gravestone but I shall rest far, far away."

■ MIANTONOMO, A NARRAGANSETT SACHEM, 1638: Get married first ... be rich first—"*When I was a boy my father owned a quarter of all the whelks and quahogs along the shore of the Blue Mountain edge to double-heeled woman's feet on the eastern shore of the Long Island of New York. All maidens in our village were married and all braves became rich. Now the white man has come. He has told us that first one should become rich and then and only then can one marry. We harvest quahogs and whelks and drill their shells all evening. And though we have tenfold the number of wampum and less than half the number of women to marry we are poorer now than ever before. I speak because I am not afraid. When I tell the white man that he will never be rich no matter how much wampum he takes from my brothers, his smile tells me I will not have long to wait to join my four brothers and sisters who have passed beyond the sunset.*"

"In her *ketubbah* and on her gravestone, in her own right and in her granddaughters' names with names and—"

"And, and, and!" screamed Rachel. "So, if it's accepted and the world agrees, why don't you go in and ask my father?"

"Rachel, there's an order to these things. A time. An order. First, my brother must agree."

"Your brother won't acknowledge that I exist! And the thing you don't want to see is that he hates you, hates what you could become. And he's half mad over what we can become. He must get married first. He must be rich first. He must pick your wife for you, his children must be your children's bosses. I curse the day you told them about us.

■ RABBI NACHMAN OF BRESLOV: What we can become—When a person discusses spiritual matters with a friend, he can become an observer of the "encircling light." He can see what he couldn't before. He can rise higher and higher until he reaches the transcendent level—which is the joy and delight of the world to come. Thus without you I am nothing, and without me you are nothing.

■ JACOB (JACQUES) DE PAIVA (d. 1687): *Ketubbah*—Hieronyma did not want anything in her *ketubbah*. No land. No money. Not that I had it. Neither ducats of Venice nor sovereign gold of London. She only wanted to be sure that if I traveled across the seas I would have to take her. "But Hieronyma, no Jewish merchant travels with his wife," I would tell her. But she begged and would not have her brother agree to the *ketubbah* unless I stated that on any trip outside of London she would accompany me. And her brother also. She told me her father had come to her in a dream and made her swear she would live her life each night always at my side, and only death and a gravestone would separate us. I laughed and said only G-d can decide when we shall separate. And she said meekly, "At least I can write my own *ketubbah*."

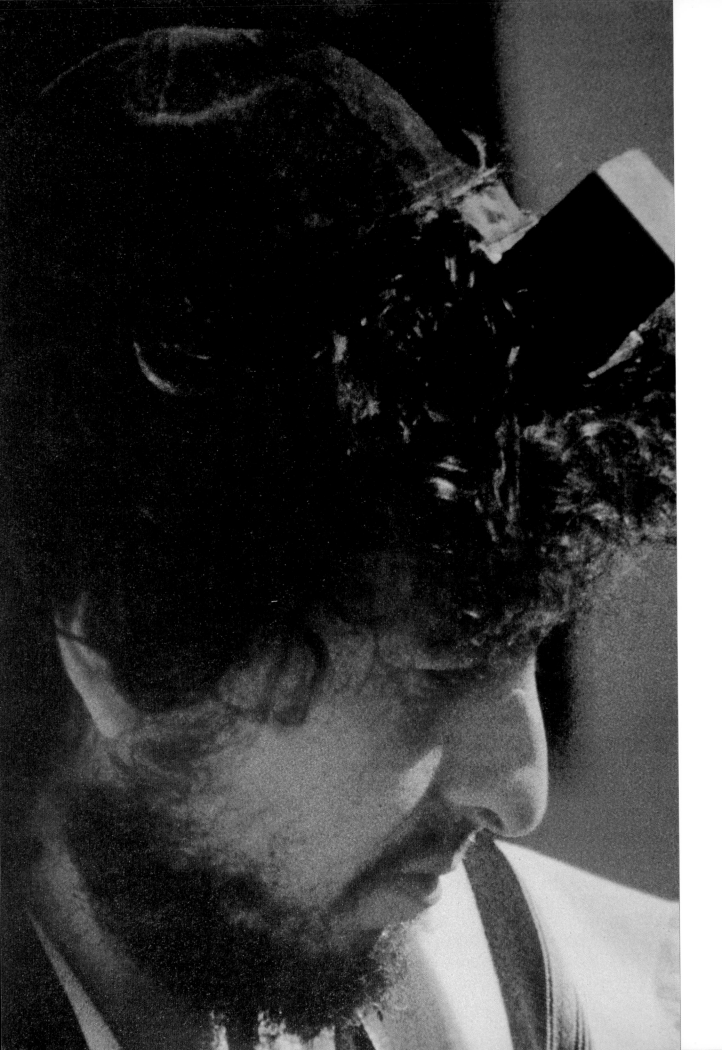

● EPHRAIM BEN JACOB HAKOHEN (GUT-WIRTH FAMILY), FISHER'S ANCESTOR (1616–1678): I'm going with you—I'm going with you, Aryeh Leib kept whispering to me. Father, I'm going with you. But Aryeh could barely mouth the words, so ravished by the plague he was.

Rachel, my wife, his mother, did not leave his bedside for weeks. Over and over Aryeh chanted, Father, Father, I'm going with you. I could see in Rachel's eyes that Aryeh was sinking. The same look he had as when the Lord took Hezekiah from us just four months before.

I asked Aryeh softly, "Where are you going, my son?" And Aryeh said, so softly that only his mother could hear (for she and her father could see and hear everything), "I am going with you, Father. I am going to Jerusalem." I pleaded with Rachel, "Let me pray that the Lord take me and not Aryeh."

Rachel looked from me to Aryeh and from Aryeh to me. And understood and said nothing. I gently took Aryeh's hand and said, "My son, I am going to Jerusalem but not with you, G-d forbid. Bring my words into the light. Copy them. Explain them. Print them."

"And where am I going, Father?" Aryeh feebly responded. And with Rachel holding my hand in her right hand and Aryeh's hand in her left I said simply, "Aryeh, you are going to Safed." And as with her blessed father, Rebbe Elijah, so said, so done.

"I'm going inside, Avram. Or I'm going with you. Either way." All at once there was no picture on the ceiling. Rachel was lying next to him on the bed.

"Rachel, we can't go away," Tal murmured. "What will we do in the Holy Land? Go to Safed? Study? What will we live on, your father's income? What will I do? That's not a life. Step by step is the only way." And Tal moved yet closer toward Rachel.

"Don't come near me, Abraham Tal," shouted Rachel. "Not in front of my father's house, or I'll throw this at you." Rachel held up her arm with the rolled up newspaper clenched in her fist and brandished it at Tal.

Tal retreated two steps. "All right, I'll ask your father. I'll speak to him alone. Don't worry. It will work. It has to work. We will be married. We have to be."

■ ISAAC LURIA: Rachel, we can't go away— They could go away on a boat together like Jonah. They could go toward the Holy Land. Or away from the Holy Land. Either way it would be the same direction. For a storm would overtake their ship; they would be cast out and swallowed by a fish. And grieve unto death. And how they would repent out of terror.

Not to voyage, but to eternally plan. To pay for the passage but not to board the ship. That is no life because it's not a choice. All the nervousness of planning and none of the joy of arrival. Step by step, even if never reaching the end. One must leap from the shore onto a boat of one's dreams and not inquire its destination first.

■ BOB DYLAN: What will I do—*If I lived in a different age, I might have been a Talmudic scholar.*

Tal wants to be here and his heart wants to be there. Ages ago. First go, then do. If he goes to Safed he will be one thing. If he goes to the Holy Land but not to Safed, he will choose another. But to choose the place and to sketch his life before he gets there is like writing poetry without a pen. He won't remember it and who will read it?

■ GAUGUIN: What will we live on?—We will live on love. Or we will die on money, I told Mette. All Tahitian women have so much love in their veins that it is always love even when it is bought, I told her. Come here to Tahiti with me and we will live on love.

Of course, it would have been more complicated. She would have come and for weeks I would have done nothing but peer at her for days under the sheets, nibble on her ears, tickle her by moonlight. But love would have guided my hand. And the heat of my brush strokes would have melted the glacial heart of Durand-Ruel Junior. Alphonse Mucha would have sent us money. From across the seas in coconuts would float franc notes saying, "You are doing what I dream of. Here is a franc for Mette and you. Bless me." Mette dismissed all of this, called me either insanely sober or crazily drunk. Tal and Rachel could never support themselves, but they could live on love.

■ AKBAR: Closed his eyes—When Khurram was nine years old I brought him to my palace and asked him to stand on a rug that I was sitting on. I asked him a question. "Khurram, you will someday be greater than I. Whose rug is this that I am sitting on and you are standing on?" "I cannot tell you, Grandfather. Let us step off the rug and I will study the treasury inscription and then I will tell you." I moved off the rug onto another rug nearby and watched Khurram as he studied the marks on the back of the rug, and he came over to me and said, "It is your rug. The inscription says it was removed from the treasury by you on the twentieth of the month of Shawwal." "And how about the one I am now reclining on?" Again Khurram asked me to move and again he examined the inscription. And again he said simply to me, "It's yours." "You were right now but wrong before."

I showed him the design on the second rug—the many glorious red orbs finishing in one fiery orange red flamelike center—and I traced the elephants and tigers and leaping gazelles. I explained to Khurram how I had seen this rug in a dream on a hunting trip and had ordered it to be made. That is why it is mine. The other treasured rug I had received from blessed Babur. "A human's possessions are only what he creates or causes to be created," I told him. The boy said nothing for a long time and then whispered, "Someday I will create a vast rug miles long and it will be all colors, even white, filled with jewels, and it will glisten by night and day." And I took him into my arms and said, "That is why, dear Khurram, you will be greater than I."

● MAX MEYER, BROTHER OF JULIUS MEYER (d. 1909), GRANDFATHER OF DOSHA (FATHER OF SUSANNA JULIA MEYER): His right hand clenched in a fist—I brought Julius from Blomberg, Germany. I taught him English. I offered him a one-third interest in our Farnum Street store in Omaha. "Call it Max Moritz and Company," my brother Julius said crisply, and then he would deign to agree, "Its always been Max Meyer and Bro. Co." I said, "We'd lose our customers." And Julius, cheeky he was, said, "I'll round 'em back up." I offered Julius a stake in the twelfth and Douglas Street place, and he said with no smile but just plain deadpan, "Call it Julius Meyer and Bro. Co. and then I'll join." I imagined what Adolph would have said to that.

Julius never cared what we thought or what Omaha thought or even what Paris thought. All he cared about was Chief Standing Bear. And Red Cloud. And Swift Bear. And Spotted Tail. Julius sat in front of his shop, the Indian Wigwam, and would shake hands with anyone and introduce himself as Box-Ka-Re-Sha-Harh-Ta-Ka, white chief who speaks with one tongue.

Julius never married. He spoke six Indian languages. I didn't understand one bit of any of it. When he died, his right hand was clenched in a fist and his left hand was holding a revolver—right there in Hanscom Park. A suicide, the Omaha police called it. But my brother Julius was right-handed. I didn't understand one bit of any of it. But how I miss him. How I miss him.

Tal closed his eyes. With his right hand clenched in a fist and his left hand open, he wept hysterically for his Rachel, above him—and for himself, alone.

■ GEORGE SWORD, AN OGLALA HOLY MAN: Left hand open—As I stood with my mother night after night in the last six months of her life, her left hand was open and her right hand closed in a fist. She told me she was signing for the-word-of-G-d and the clenched fist meant that if she received it she would never let it go. Two days before her death I sat next to her by the Missouri River and both her hands were clenched around mine. And her dream of G-d's word became mine and I spoke the dream to a white man—Walker—who promised to write them down in a book whose fist would never be opened.

■ RASHI: His right hand clenched . . . and his left hand open—His left hand is open to receive from the angel Raphael a ring to give to Rachel. With his right hand under his head, using his fist as a pillow, he waits patiently for Raphael. And did not Raphael bring a magic ring to Solomon, who had prayed for help to build the Temple, a ring enameled with a five-pointed solomonic star? A ring that gave Solomon power to guide the imps to complete the superhuman effort to construct the Holy Temple? If Tal can keep his left hand open, surely Raphael will answer his prayers.

■ ISAAC LURIA: Left hand—His left hand is open as Gabriel sits on the left side of G-d. And is not man an angel descended from heaven? And is not man an angel ascending after death? And is not Tal wrestling with his brother as Gabriel wrestled with Jacob? But Tal is not in balance. Not in balance with above and below, not in balance with his mother and his bride. His right hand is in a fist and his left hand open—and thus he is alone.

■ ROSE WEASEL, NAKOTA: Left hand open—Tal is holding his left hand open because he is talking in his sleep. And his left hand symbolizes a tree which his young bride represents to him. My people, the Nakota, the Lakota, and even the Dakota from the edge of the plains, would understand; the Great White Father who gathers all dreams will accept his left-handed open-handed sign. But what does this white man mean with his closed right fist? For that means farther away. And how can a tree move farther away each night?

■ LAURENCE STERNE: His right hand clenched—"Books, painting, fiddling, and shooting were my amusements." And what books and what fiddling shall young Tal do if his right hand is clenched?

125

Old Horn Weasel signing at Fort Belknap.

■ SARA LOWNDES: Piled with photographs, books, and frayed magazine photos—Share a name, share a bed, share a life, share. Of course, IN THE BEGINNING, G-d created. We were in Albert Grossman's place on Gramercy Park. And it had to be hush, hush. Hush from Joanie, of course. She was Bobby's meal ticket to fame. Or who knows, or maybe he always had to share me with another, another with me. Probably he didn't think the way we all did. First you go here and then you get there.

I enter the apartment walk-up, hearing him sing—not surprising, he sang all day—"*Hey Mr. Tambourine Man, play a song for me.*" And we wouldn't make love because he hadn't eaten all day but we would roll around in the kitchen.*"I'm not sleepy and there is no place I'm going to,*" Bob would sing, tapping on my shoulders or my neck or the kitchen table, "*laughin', spinnin', swingin' madly.*"

And all the wine bottles half drunken and every night pasta, only half eaten. And then into the living room with the Bukhara rug we called bed—never in the bedroom because he always worried about the neighbors. The Bukhara piled with photographs, books, and frayed magazine photos. In the beginning— "*I'm not sleepy and there is no place I'm going to.*" It was so sweet. Although with Dylan, you knew you had to share. But he didn't share anything. He gave me a song. And when I left exhausted for work at 8:30 each morning, I would hear his voice on the staircase as I descended into the hell of Manhattan:

"*In the jingle jangle morning I'll come following you.*"

■ WILLIAM MOORE: Absolutely no hair—A man that got no hair is bound to be blue. When I was in Rappahannock, Virginia, I had a customer that would pay me a quarter a month to cut his hair. But he didn't have more than ten little itty bitty hairs. And I asked why are you coming here, so bald and all, just to get these little itty bitty hairs cut? And he said, "William, I listen to you every weekend at Mama Jean's but I miss you and I like the way you hum while you cut." It was doin' his hair that I got the first bars of Ragtime Millionaire: *Any man that pays to have his hair cut if he ain't got hair must be a millionaire.* And I'd hum it for him every time he came into my shop.

CHAPTER 7

BLUE. You're always blue," said Tal to Amnon Eliyahu.

Tal looked at Eliyahu before him: a short man with absolutely no hair on his head and dark eyes set impossibly far back in their sockets. Eliyahu was seated at a jeweler's bench, long and narrow, piled with photographs, books, and frayed magazine photos cracked with age, photos now more gray than black. On the corner of the bench was a silver cup with a repoussé representation of a bear, a lion, a deer, and an animal that appeared to be a crude combination of an eagle and a dove.

"You'd be blue, too, on what you pay me." Eliyahu winced.

"I pay you three quarters of what my brother pays me. Complain to him, Amnon, not to me," said Tal jovially.

■ JEAN BAPTISTE TAVERNIER: Photos cracked with age—No fool, this jeweler. All his good sketches in his drawer, away from his customers' eyes, tucked away like Mumtaz in the tomb of the Taj—white and then black. Or they would say, Could I just show this drawing to my partner? My wife? My friend? Just for a week, a day, an hour? And then return with the sketch copied. Tal is drinking the pictures in with his eyes. I wouldn't loan him even a tiny scrap of paper. But strange all that effort of repoussé only to work in silver. Gold would have been more like it, especially for a wine cup. I never commissioned a single piece of silver.

■ RABBI ISRAEL OF STOLIN'S SON: Before him— My father was at a wedding, and they were waiting for him to come out of a room. They were waiting for a long time. Finally, someone peeked in and saw him standing before a mirror, saying, "*Hello Rebbe. How are you? Sit down.*" He was praising himself to the Heavens with words of respect and greeting. Later they asked him, "What does this mean?" He said:

"*I'm going out into the public and I'm going to get all this honor. I'm practicing to myself. What does all this honor mean? It means the same as if I were saying them to myself—nothing.*"

שמריים אותו חזקיהו אל הינה פקיצות
לילה פתח מיצרים פריצא גבותך
על אדום יהוצצי פתחנה דוד
מישריב שרב ובזמירנו בנפש הרך
הלינה בריך אפריעל המעריב
ערבים

The Body of

B. Franklin

Printer

(Like the cover of an old book,

its contents turned out

and stripped of its lettering and gilding),

lies here, food for worms,

But the work shall not be wholly lost;

For it will, as he believed, appear once more,

In a new and more elegant edition,

revised and corrected

by the Author

■ VERMEER: Let's drink and eat—In my painting *Girl Being Offered Wine*, one rogue peers at a woman while the other looks off, dreaming. Strange, these two bachelors, Tal and Eliyahu, drinking and eating with each other. And not talking of women but of rings—not speaking of art but of copies of art. But even if they had a woman in the room, it would not make a difference. For she would not notice them—much as Katrinka had no eyes for her suitor, Willem Herik, but lived only for me. A painter's meager wages are paid in the coins of love.

"Okay. When can I go?" Eliyahu rose from his workbench.

"Later, after you've shown me the pieces," answered Tal, resting a patriarchal hand on Eliyahu's shoulder.

"Here they are, Tal, right on the tray." On a pewter tray lay a dozen house rings, each like a fallen Jerusalem, once proud, now the object of pity, with only old men gazing at them.

"First, let's drink," said Tal, walking toward Eliyahu's cupboard, where Tal himself always kept two bottles of Kedem.

"What do you think of this, Eliyahu?" Tal asked, picking up a ring with half-filled enameling in the roof and the underbezel still containing pitch that had oozed from the false gold bottom.

"Amnon, *habibi*," exclaimed Tal, rushing back from his personal wine cellar. "Let's drink and eat. A forger should never, G-d forbid, be in a hurry."

Tal got up again, walked into the kitchen, and, unwrapping a newly bought glass cup from the side of the sink, poured water on both his hands.

■ RABBI NACHMAN OF BRESLOV: A fallen Jerusalem—"*It is impossible to come to the land of Israel without difficulties and suffering. The root of all the difficulties and suffering lies in the slanderous image of the land which is put about by the wicked. They are the source of all the obstacles.*"

And of all the obstacles, all the difficulties, none are greater than those surrounding Jerusalem. Once-proud Jerusalem is an object of pity now, fit only for old men. But the day will come when Jerusalem will no longer be fallen. And what will the reaction of the world be then? She will still be portrayed by the wicked as difficult to live in. And Jew more than Gentile will fear to travel there. But when the Messiah will come, even the faint-hearted will follow into her gates. And she will be seen as she is, no longer fallen but forever raised.

■ ISRAEL FRIEDMAN OF RUZHIN: False gold bottom—Gold is always false because behind it are people's false hopes and distorted dreams. Abraham Dov of Ovrueh sent me from Safed a siddur that I would put on my study table and show to my children. What do you see? I would ask. "Golden pictures worthy of the word of G-d," my children would answer. Only the words have reality. "The gold is false, but the letters will remain." I told them, and I knew in my heart that just as the manuscript came from the Holy Land to me it would return there to those who would understand its true meaning and not be blinded by its golden illusion.

◆ RACHEL, TAL'S MOTHER: Suddenly grew silent—At home every Friday night, Abraham's father would ask Abraham if he wanted to say *kiddush*. "Ask my brother Tuviah if he wants to," Abraham would immediately answer, and if Tuviah said *kiddush*, Abraham would barely touch his meal. But if Tuviah would say, "Oh, let Abraham say it," then Abraham would start in the most miraculous, melodious way, but midway through, as though his mind were elsewhere, he would simply stop. And it would be left to Tuviah to finish. Abraham had to be first but he couldn't finish.

■ JAMES JOYCE: Eliyahu, who drained the cup—*"Ireland sober is Ireland stiff."*

■ KAFKA: This is how I learned to work—*"What do I have in common with Jews. I have hardly anything in common with myself."*

I did not learn to work at home. I could not work at home. I could only work at night in quiet in an apartment that would never be a home because I could never share it with another. And I could not work in an office because that was not work because I could never create something, I could only follow directions. My insurance work was more of the nature of an army barracks after the war was over but before the peace was signed—full of frenetic activity and confusion. I like this Eliyahu's home and craftsman's atelier combination. I guess I should have mixed my ink with wine—rather than with my blood.

"Blessed art Thou, Lord our G-d, King of the Universe, who sanctified us with his commandments and has commanded us regarding the immersion of—" He suddenly grew silent and peered down at his trembling hand.

"—vessels . . . Blessed are thou our Lord, our G-d, King of the universe, who has commanded us regarding washing of the hands," finished Eliyahu, standing next to him, after he, too, had poured water on his hands.

This is how I learned to work in my homeland, thought Eliyahu.

Returning to the bench, Tal picked up the goblet of dark red wine and, barely balancing it in his right hand, cried out, "Blessed art Thou. . . . And is he not blessed, our Lord, our G-d? One, one, always one, who makes the wine holy." And Tal drank two sips and passed it to Eliyahu, who drained the cup.

● RACHEL, TAL'S GIRLFRIEND: He suddenly grew silent—Abraham would talk and talk about everything he had read in a newspaper or a book, gossip overheard at a school lunch table, a story he remembered his mother telling him when she was growing up in Holland. The stories were remarkable because each time a character was introduced, the character's parents' stories would also be told, and even the character's grandparents', and often the descriptions of a physical peculiarity of a child would be an echo of a grandparent's, and in the end each story, like a wheel revolving within a wheel, seemed related. But Abraham never finished an entire cycle; instead, at a certain moment he would grow silent. At first I thought he had lost the thread so I said nothing. Sometimes I touched his hand and softly encouraged him to continue, but he was immovable. Sometimes I finished the story for him. And he wouldn't correct me but simply listened, childlike. I once asked him why he stopped before the end and he said with trepidation in his voice, "Certain things will be resolved—*teku*—when the Messiah comes. Eliyahu the Tishbite will solve all difficulties and finish all philosophical debates." And I said, "Such as our marriage date?" but he did not laugh or even smile.

ICI REPOSE

VINCENT van GOGH

1853 – 1890

ICI REPOSE

THÉODORE van GOGH

1857 – 1891

■ MOSHEH FUTERMAN: Start the day—In Dachau we would start our day in the darkness of the night. We would put on tefillin even before the light shone. We relied on the Rabbi of Kovno, who had ruled that although Maimonides had forbidden tefillin to be worn at night lest a person fall asleep and not be in a state of purity and mental and physical cleanliness, there was no chance that a prisoner in Dachau would willingly fall asleep. Reb Oshry also allowed the Bracha on the Shmoneh Esrei to be pronounced in darkness. He quoted the Rambam, who allowed the Shmoneh Esrei to be prayed in the dark when setting out on a journey. And the Rabbi from Kovno added, "Would that my portion in the hereafter be with them on their coming journey."

■ FAN CH'I, NANKING PAINTER, c. 1645: Copier—Eliyahu reminds me of myself reminding myself of Wu Pin. It was not that I copied Wu Pin or that he copied foreign artists from the West. Rather I thought about Wu Pin, who had been born in Fukien province and moved to Nanking, where he was the court painter for the Ming emperor, Wan Li. Wu Pin's mountains danced in my mind, and I saw the silk scroll spread before me through the clouds that rose straight from his scrolls. The Nanking artists of my day would say, "Aha, you are copying Wu Pin who was copying from the West." And I would say, "I am Wu Pin who has come again to Nanking—work undone—brush strokes to be completed." This Eliyahu is wise to deny his birthplace, and he is doubly wise to work with the hands of his uncle.

Sinking into a deep chair, Amnon Eliyahu brushed the beads of sweat off his forehead and looked at Tal.

"This is how we would start the day in Isfahan." Amnon was sunk in the deep recesses of his Kabuli armchair upholstered with rug fabric.

"Amnon, you grew up in Herat!" Tal corrected him sternly.

"Tal, for a watered-down Sephardi, you think you're my twin. Were you there?" queried Eliyahu, floating a bit, although he had drunk only one glass of wine.

"What do you think?" asked Tal, abruptly picking up the tray of rings for Eliyahu to study. "You've held the ring in your hand. You're the copier, not I."

"I am a worker, a worker with my uncle's hands, Tal. It would have made things much simpler if you had left your ring with me to study." Eliyahu did not return Tal's gaze but continued to look at the scattered rings on his workbench.

"What do you think, Amnon? Which one's most acceptable?" Tal passed the tray back to him.

Ici Repose

VINCENT VAN GOGH
1853–1890

Ici Repose

THÉODORE VAN GOGH
1857–1891

■ VAN GOGH: You think you're my twin—My mother would tell me that I was my dead brother Vincent's twin. And my brother would tell me, Vincent, you're my twin. And Cézanne would tell me, Leave me alone, Vincent, you think you're my twin. I wrote Théo in 1888 (24 March):

"Thank you very much for all the steps you have taken toward the exhibition of the Independents. On the whole I'm very glad that my pictures have been put with the other Impressionists. But though it doesn't matter in the least this time, in the future my name ought to be put in the catalogue as I sign it on the canvas, namely Vincent and not van Gogh." But Théo of course had his way in the end—and twinned his tombstone to mine. At least our birth and death dates were discrete.

■ YIDDISH PROVERB: A worker—If I made candles the sun wouldn't set. *Ikh zol handlen mit likht, volt di zun nit untergegangen.*

■ MILENA JESNSKA: It would have made things much simpler—Kafka told me when he was in a room full of Jewish emigrants passing through Prague in 1922 waiting for visas to America that, had he been given the choice to be whatever he wanted, he would have chosen to be a little Eastern Jewish boy in the corner of that room without a worry in the world. It would have made things a lot simpler, he said. No choices; that's what he would have chosen. One model to copy, not a choice of an infinite number of models to follow. I like this Tal not leaving the ring to be copied. Better Eliyahu should have to choose which "original" to duplicate.

■ EAGLE CHIEF (LETAKOTS-TESA), NINETEENTH-CENTURY PAWNEE: Put the best on the right—Tal would have Eliyahu put the best on the left. He is incorrect. Eliyahu should only use pairs. "*All things in the world are two. In our minds we are two, good and evil; with our eyes we see two things, things that are fair and things that are ugly. We have the right hand that strikes and makes for evil and the left hand full of kindness near the heart. One foot may lead us to an evil way, the other to a good. So are all things two, all two.*"

● JULIUS MEYER (CURLY-HEADED WHITE CHIEF WHO SPEAKS WITH ONE TONGUE), Dosha's grandfather's brother: The customer is always right—These are my people, Tal and Eliyahu, and they are in a Jewish home. But they are not in America. When I traveled with the Pawnee they were first my customers and then my students, but they did not know of the white world beyond the Mississippi. I taught them about that world and even took them to Paris. And I became a "one-tongued" Pawnee Chief. In my tepee they were in a Jewish home, and in their tepee we were in a Pawnee dwelling. But the land of America doesn't reveal any truth, anymore than the Great Plains or the stone streets of Paris. Only people speaking from their hearts can tell the truth.

Eliyahu arranged the rings in a long row, one next to the other, almost touching.

"Why don't you put them in a descending order of acceptability?" commented Tal languidly. "You know. The best on the left, then the second best next to it and so forth, until the one on the extreme right is the least good," Tal swept his hand from left to right.

"Why not put the best on the right?" questioned Eliyahu belligerently.

"Fine, put the best on the right," replied Tal immediately.

"Look, Tal, the whole idea doesn't appeal to me. You are the Ashkenazi, you put them in order."

"You," insisted Tal.

"Well, the customer is always right!" Eliyahu interjected brightly.

"We're not in America. We're in your apartment," Tal said, sweeping his eyes across the floor of Eliyahu's living room, each square foot of which was piled high with three or four carpets: bundled, spread, fraying at the edges, swimming with color.

■ KAFKA: We're not in America—Tal and Eliyahu are not in America any more than Jiri Langer and I were in Prague. Or than the Belzer Rebbe and Max Brod and I were in Marienbad. We were floating somewhere above the ground, and Langer would tell me that since Jews were in so many countries wandering about, how could we be assembled quickly when the Messiah came? So, therefore, the good Lord raised us above the ground and our discussions floated in the air, enabling us always to be ready to be gathered for the coming journey.

■ AKBAR: Why not put the best on the right?—I showed Prince Khurram a miniature painted with a single-hair brush by Hashim and I showed the Prince a page of calligraphy and I asked him, Which page would you put on the right side of the album and which would you put on the left? He was no fool, my grandson. He said, Grandfather, which would you put on the right? I said, Khurram, I would put the best on the right, for our holy script is written from right to left. And Khurram said, Which is the best, this picture of you and Timur and me or this divine script, the throne verse? I smiled and said, I ask you, my grandson, which is the best? He had to answer, The likeness of you, Grandfather, for in it is contained the teachings of the Koran.

I thought for a long time and answered him gently, I would put the script on the right, for we are all contained in its letters. And Khurram shot back, You always say we started from Timur; would you not put his picture on the right? Then I knew that afterward all his albums would have our pictures on the right and the suras on the left. But Jews are people of the book. Surely they should agree on the proper order.

■ JACKSON POLLOCK: Gently—Lee would take me out just before Montauk Point and we would walk all afternoon and half the night. And by moonlight I would roll her on the beach with the sand filling her ears and I licking them clean. And she saying, Gently, gently, and when I could no longer move she would take my hands in hers and coo, Guide me to drop clumps of sand on her body gently, gently. I scooped up the moist moonlit sand and squeezed it all over her in a thin jet stream of lust. I pelted her with sand balls. I rolled huge piles of sand all over her and the waves echoed her lover's instructions of gently, gently. During the week on Sullivan Street I squeezed the tubes of paint on my own canvases. I could still hear her voice calling, Gently, gently.

■ HENRY WALTERS: To the past—He's good, this Tal. I would carry two classes of objects with me when I would go "hunting" in Europe. In my right coat pocket a fake icon, a fake Etruscan ring, a nineteenth-century cameo imitating Teresa Talani's elegant gem carving. Any object as long as it was spurious. In my left coat pocket a wonderful renaissance pyramid diamond ring. I'd look at them in my quarters at night. It would train my eye in the daytime. An object has to be believable to the past. Morgan never understood that. He bought stories. If the people were believable, he believed the object.

"This is the best, Tal. This is a masterpiece," said Eliyahu, holding up a completely finished ring and placing it before Tal.

Tal went to the window and examined the work. The filigree was right, that much was certain. All of the bosses joined differently at the junctures. The pitch of the roof was correct, matching precisely the photograph of rings in the 1905 *Jewish Encyclopedia* that lay on the corner of Eliyahu's bench. Tal examined the catch and opened and closed the roof several times.

"Gently, Tal. It took me two months to make that peg closing. Gently."

"Just trying to give it a patina of use, Amnon," Tal replied professionally, and then added as an afterthought, "There's green in the blue enameling, Amnon. The shade is wrong. The blue isn't believable."

"Believable to whom?" Eliyahu was starting to lose interest in Tal's games. He wondered if Tal would reject the whole lot.

"To the past," said Tal, sweeping his hand lazily across Eliyahu's desk.

■ VERMEER: To the window—Of course Tal would go to the window, but not to see more clearly, rather to receive the light by which he could think more clearly. My grandmother told me how she had received a letter from Oporto when she was a girl and she took it over to the window to read and knew instantly that her brother had perished in the auto-da-fé of 17 June 1612. I asked her on her deathbed if she had kept the letter and she pointed to her dresser drawer. This was the letter I used for the blue Catharina painting. When I held her hands in mine and showed her the gesture I wanted for my painting, she laughed and said, How can I stay still, pretending to read this letter, when it is blank? I sighed and said, It is blank but it has the deepest of messages. And she quivered and moved her lips as though reading a love note from me.

■ SARMAD, DARA SHIKOH'S SUFI MASTER: Green in the blue—When Shah Jahan summoned me to the Diwan-i-khas he was alone with his preferred son, Dara Shikoh, a boy of fourteen. You will be his teacher and I will be *darvish* (master), said his father. I am a Jew, I said, surely you know that. Shah Jahan looked out at the sun, which was starting to set, and put his hand on my shoulder and said, Put a touch of green in the blue. And I did. And I did.

◆ Isaac Tal, Tal's father: Working from a photograph—Abraham would always bring my photograph to the office. And before he would ask Tuviah for money he would ceremoniously put my photograph on the table, shine its matted silver edge, and intone his request with an almost cantorial air. Tuviah would gently remind Abraham that he kept my photograph on my desk and thank you very much it was enough because of the small surface area that Tuviah sorted diamonds and sapphires on. Abraham would ceremoniously exclaim, You're working for a photograph and I'm working from a photograph. Our father was a great scholar and he should be present when we are together. Once Tuviah gave Abraham $3,000 and told him he would give ten times the amount if Abraham would leave my photograph on his desk, but he remarked, "Tuviah, I would, but you still wouldn't be working from a photograph."

■ Bob Dylan: Working from a photograph— A different blue. That's what the king said to me as I walked onto the stage. Oh, it was a simple twist of fate that put me up there, not in the audience of those—what did the king call them?—seaside resort man of wars. Or menopause. Why was I working from a photograph of Dylan Thomas and the king with a photograph of Blake? And why was Joan carrying my photograph in her locket and calling me Bobby? And all of us singing "This Land is Your Land" at the end of it all?

"How should I know? I'm working from a photograph. I've already told you." Eliyahu shrugged and lifted another ring off the tray. "How about this one? This has a different blue."

"This one? This one is good," Tal said, as he put the ring on his thumb. "But the gold is wrong. This must be eighteen karat. Why do you have to be so cheap? I told you time and again, twenty-two karat pure, almost."

"I gave it out. I can't make these models overnight."

"You've had months, Amnon. You said you could do it. Also, the drawn wire here: the pattern's wrong. Look at the squared edges on the filigree." Tal handed the ring, the bezel upside down, to Eliyahu.

"You know, Tal, you could make a good jeweler," said Eliyahu. If only your hands didn't shake, he thought.

■ Allen Ginsberg: This has a different blue— In the beginning Dylan told me, You haven't found your kingdom but you've always been the king. In the Seacrest Hotel before 236 mahjong players (182 of whom had blue hair), he gently led me onto the stage and said, "Here's your kingdom." I could see my mother in every face before me. How is my son doing? she would write. Had I eaten? What books had I read? Do I remember a walk we took and all the time she improved in Greystone, only later to lie in the Beth Moses Cemetery in Farmington. This my kingdom all present with Moses at Sinai. And I reading my kaddish for the 236 faces of my mother. And how my son Dylan mounted the stage and I whispered to them, And now a different blue. And he sang "A Simple Twist of Fate."

■ Edward S. Curtis: Working from a photograph—I knew I had no money. I had three children. I had barely a silver coin for each. The Blackfoot tribe I hoped to photograph would not accept such meager wages. I knew that only Morgan could bankroll me. The letter from T.R. got me an interview with Morgan himself in his renaissance velvet, leathered library. I spoke for twelve minutes of the sunsets in Durango, the Sioux tepees, of Custer's Crow scouts. I spoke of Apsaroke children, of the Hopi weaver's marriage robes, of all the Indian civilizations that were vanishing and only Morgan could keep them alive forever in photographs.

Morgan stood and said abruptly, "There are many demands on me for financial assistance. I will be unable to help you work." "I do not need your help, Mr. Morgan. I will be working from a photograph," and I showed him my photograph of Slow Bull, the Oglala Sioux. Morgan studied, peered at, and almost swallowed the photograph. Slow Bull had fought in fifty-five battles. Slow Bull stared at Morgan. After half an hour Morgan said, "Mr. Curtis, I want to see these photographs in books. They must be the most beautiful set of books ever published."

◆ TAL'S FATHER: The tool I gave you—I gave Abraham eighteen years in our home. Never did he have to lift a finger to support me or his mother. I gave him the tools of education. After school at night and on Sundays I asked Van der Heyden to teach him cleaving. I gave him my father's diamond cutting tools. In short, I gave him everything. And he used nothing. The school he didn't go to. Our home he would leave every chance he had. Van der Heyden told me he would never sit still although he did tell me that Abraham had a remarkable visual ability. He could envision a diamond at any angle, unlike Tuviah, who saw everything from one angle only. The one thing Abraham would concentrate on was any story I knew of his grandparents. He would ask Rachel and me to tell each tale over and over and over again.

■ VERMEER: The tool I gave you—Anton van Leeuwenhoek once came to my painting room without knocking, simply put down this enormous package. Amazing that with his bulk he could climb my winding stairs. "Breathless," he said. "Don't thank me, just give me a commission on your painting," and laughed with that hollow smoker's laugh of his. It was a magic camera (camera obscura) and it was amazing. I worked with it for months on end and kept it in my studio all my life. But it had no life. One day he casually asked me in a tavern if I used the tool he gave me. I said not the tool you gave me but the tool you showed me. He looked puzzled and said, "Always clever by half you are, Johannes. Always trying to avoid a commission." But I didn't explain that his magnifying machine could enlarge a canvas so miraculously that I was always careful to place my guide points well below the surface of the paint so even he could never know how I created.

Tal picked up another ring, slightly smaller, and opened the roof to reveal the letters. The edge of the *mem* continued in a straight graver's line.

"Did you use the tool I gave you?" he asked.

"Yes. Can't you see the line it makes at the end of the stroke?" Eliyahu knew that without a jeweler's loupe Tal could not see the flourishing of the engraving line. And he had purposely hidden all the loupes before Tal arrived.

"Yes. That's good," Tal agreed. "Wonderful. And how about this one? What does it weigh?" Tal picked up a ring dented at the edge.

"Slightly more than the others. It corresponds to the weight given in the Pforzheim catalog you gave me of that show after those madmen lost the war," exclaimed Eliyahu with a schoolboy's pride.

"I *loaned* you the catalog, Amnon. Did you drop the ring three times, as I told you?"

"Yes," replied Eliyahu, staring down at his multicarpeted floor.

"On the floor or on your rug, Amnon?"

■ JIRI LANGER: Lost—In Marienbad I met two Hasidim, one from Jikov, the other from Belz, who argued which one of their Rebbes was the greater miracle worker. The first told me of the great miracles the Jikov had done for him—when as a yeshiva *bocher*, he had been told by the Jikov Rebbe to go to Cracow into the tailor trade and always charge half of what the tailor across the way charged and within five years he would be blessed five-fold.

One day a wealthy man from Tarnov came into his shop and after hearing his prices asked him, How can it be so cheap? "You will never be able to make a living and certainly not become rich like me." The tailor replied, "Oh, I will be blessed five-fold; this I know from my Rebbe, who knows it from G-d." The rich man became his customer, and the Hasid never varied his prices.

After a year the rich man came to the Hasid exasperated and said, "I have been coming here a year and you are getting poorer and I am getting richer and you never vary from charging me too little, unlike every other tradesman I deal with here does after he discovers how wealthy I am." "I will be wealthy too, wealthy like you. And my wealth will come from G-d just like yours does. I am not worried. In fact, I will be blessed five-fold," said the tailor. The rich man became white and suddenly said, "My Rochele, I would like you to meet her. A bridegroom such as yourself is G-d sent." The Hasid met Rochele and both agreed.

Now, five years later the Hasid had come to Marienbad to ask the blessing of the Jikov to celebrate the birth of their child, named after his wealthy father-in-law. Just before the rich Tarnov Jew, his father-in-law, had died he told the Hasid that he had had a recurring dream that his daughter Rochele would be wed to a tailor, a poor Hasid, a bridegroom who eventually would be blessed five-fold with children, but to find such a son-in-law he would have to search in Cracow.

"That is nothing," said the Belzer Hasid to the Jikover Hasid. "I was told by Yischar Dov to go to Meletz and leave my partnership of feathers that I exported to Paris from Jeshev and go into the goosedown business. I sold every feather I had and went to Meletz into the goosedown trade. I lost every groschen I had." "Lost!" the Jikover Hasid said. "Lost? Where's the miracle?" "The miracle is that I remained faithful to the Creator of the World, and to my dear Rebbe."

◆ RACHEL, TAL'S MOTHER: Drop your children—It is strange how the curse one utters in one's life at a parent comes back, as an echo. Even if one has no children the curse comes back, either spoken by a lover or a friend. But never by an enemy. Abraham would try to talk to his father at night, just for a few moments. He would hurl himself at the door, sobbing, "You've dropped your children!" His brother, Tuviah, would try to wrestle him down the stairs but always to no avail. And here Eliyahu is saying to him the same question, which must sound like a curse to Abraham.

■ SIR ERNEST OPPENHEIMER: Do you drop your children?—Harry asked me in 1934 what we were going to do. Of course I asked him back, What are we going to do? The banks had been advising us to shore up the Diamond Trading Company's dwindling cash reserves by selling the interests in the Witwatersrand field. On the other hand, Lamont at Morgan felt the price of gold had risen, so that perhaps it might make sense to sell either a portion or all of AngloAmerican's holding in DeBeers. "Well, Harry, what do you feel?" Of course, Harry was too smart to answer before me, and I gently asked him, "Do you drop your children?"

"I dropped it. Do you drop your children on the floor, Tal?" Rachel's photograph on Tal's ceiling suddenly appeared before Tal's eyes.

"You dropped it on the rug," said Tal, moving menacingly close to Eliyahu.

Eliyahu answered. "Tal, my uncle once told me something that may help you a lot: You are not permitted to lie, but so as not to shame a person, you don't have to tell the truth either."

Eliyahu and Tal sat facing each other, neither saying a word. At length, Tal whispered, "I want this blue, Amnon. I want you to make the filigree like the work on this ring. I want the peg from the same piece. I want the pitch of this ring. Actually, all the angles are good. The letters on this one are good." Tal picked up the second ring. "Very good. If you can't copy this lettering, forget it. And I want nine of these."

■ SAMUEL SANDERS: Do you drop your children?—I asked Daniel Boone, "Do you drop your children?" in anger one day because he wanted me to paddle down through the Cumberland basin of the Tennessee River with only two scouts when the Shawnee had been east of there just a month before. He embraced me and said, "I dropped one child before, but now you're my last. I won't drop you anymore than you would drop your own and only child." It was a hundred twenty miles downriver and in moonlight you knew it was like honey to the bears. When the Shawnee captured me I thought I, too, had been dropped. But then I remembered what Daniel said about my dropping a child. I knew then that first moonlight night that if I had a chance to live and be given a chance to have a child I would never drop her. And by moonlight I saw Ears of Corn looking at me and by moonlight not two years later our daughter Star Bright was born. And the Shawnee never dropped me, nor I, them.

■ BLACK ELK (OGLALA SIOUX HOLY MAN), 1863–1930: All the angles are good—To these whites all the angles are good. And you don't have to tell the truth. But to the Sioux it is not so and never will be.

"You have noted that everything an Indian does is a circle and that is because the power of the world is always in circles, and everything tries to be round. The sky is round, and I have heard that the earth is round like a ball and so are the stars. The wind in its greatest power whirls. Birds make their nests in circles, for theirs is the same religion as ours. Even the seasons form a great circle in their changing and always come back again to where they were. The life of man is a circle from childhood to childhood, and so it is in everything where power moves."

■ Jeanne Hébuterne, Modigliani's mistress: Time—Any simple question would agitate my Momo, throw him off. But the simplest question which I would always ask him in English would send him sailing. Momo dearest, what time is it? His eyes would focus on mine, almost jumping out of their sockets, rolling about, and then he would jabber in French or in an Italian slang I could never make out. Always running on about "I need a live model to paint." But this is too much. Do I have a watch? Ask my grandmother, raving about his mother. I'll tell you when I'm through, *cara mia*. Not long, not long, he would plead. My G-d, I wanted just to walk about a bit, just for a minute. One night he jumped up in his sleep and screamed, "What time is it?! How much time do we have left? Nothing." Then I understood.

■ Bobby Fischer: Time—Spassky had his hair cut and was looking especially greasy. I'm sure he had spent all the afternoon time break in a hotel room with that woman who interviewed us for French radio. But I wouldn't talk and he wouldn't stop talking. I was shaking my right foot once every three moments of the second hand on the chess clock on the table. His eyes were riveted on mine. But his ears were counting my leg movements against the movement of the clock. Suddenly in the middle of the fourth game, I knew he had left chess time for the time of the so called real world. The world of female interviewers, the world of chess clocks, the world of getting older, flabbier, weaker; and he left me alone in the timeless world of castles and bishops. I walked all over him. P.Q.2.

6th match game

27 . . . Nh7

28 Rcf1 . . . Qd8

According to Tal, "*A textbook example of an attack on a King.*"

"Fine. It will take time."

"How much time?" asked Tal.

"Three months . . ."

"No. I must leave within a month."

"Where are you going?" asked Eliyahu, more shocked than curious.

"Where I should have gone years ago," Tal said with resignation. Visions of Rachel in the photograph. "Which would you say is the poorest ring, Amnon?"

"This one," answered Eliyahu, immediately holding up a dully finished ring with gold beads too bright and too dramatic for the roof.

"I'll take this with me," said Tal, placing it in a box and putting it in his pocket.

"Now leave me alone to examine your work for some moments."

Eliyahu rose and went into another room, closing the door.

■ Rashi: Time—Time would be satisfying to them if they could rest. But Eliyahu and Tal both have forsaken the Sabbath. Sabbath comes, rest comes. And so without the Sabbath their minutes, their hours, their days, their years, their lives, pile one upon another like manuscripts one on another until they tumble over onto the earth.

■ R. C. Zucker, poet: Photograph—"*The impossibility of photographing the past.*"

■ Modigliani: Time—"What time is it?" Jeanne Hébuterne would ask me. And not only she. Everyone I painted. And twice as often if they were nude and seated. And three times as often if they were lying on my divan. And I would not ignore them so much as not hear them. And what could I answer? My time? Paris time? Livorno time? My mother Eugenia Garsin's time as a young girl in a Catholic school just before matins? Five minutes after vespers? My grandmother Regina Spinoza's time? Oh, she would not have told me the time but rather answered that my ancestor Baruch Spinoza would argue that time in reality did not exist.

In any case, they didn't want an answer, they wanted to move, to stretch, to break from the mold into which I had poured them. And they didn't realize that as fast as I could paint I could not overtake time to slow it down and then freeze it—to burn it onto a canvas. So that they could have a sliver of their time unchanged forever.

■ CHARLES ZUCKER: Catch—Some people called me lucky. To be in the right place at the right time. So many have the same chance. I caught luck as it passed by me. To be born in Mielec on June 17, 1905, was not in and of itself terribly lucky. I suppose one has to go in a kind of middle way. I wonder what would have happened to me if I had started a year and a day earlier, June 16, 1904, or a year and a day later, June 18, 1906.

■ J. P. MORGAN: Jeweled city—I was cabled that the Weingarten Gospels would be mine. The most important medieval manuscript to come on the market in thirty years. And I told the dealer I would pay more than his princely price provided that the book cover was studded with genuine jewels. "It is my lord a sapphire and ruby encrusted vision of the heavenly jeweled city of Jerusalem," he cabled me. When the book arrived it was breathtaking, the gold leaf on each parchment page glistening even in the darkness of my study, the repoussé design of the Virgin and child haunting like my mother. But most of the gems were glass and there was but one true blue sapphire and a smattering of tiny rubies.

I wrote to the selling agent hoping to reduce my price. "I am not your lord and there is only one sapphire. Is this the vision of the jeweled city?" He calmly cabled me back: "Perhaps, Mr. Morgan, you are right and you are not my lord. But kindly check my original offering cable and note 'sapphire' and 'ruby' to be in the singular. As to the vision of the heavenly jeweled city, we both will judge soon enough." I paid him.

Tal reached into his left pocket, pulled out the cushion-shaped box, and placed his ring in the midst of the jeweled city. Moving the ring from one neighbor to another, he compared his and Eliyahu's rings from all angles.

"Visions of Venice, visions of Jerusalem, visions of Safed," Tal whispered reverentially.

"Amnon, come in again," he cried, as he placed his own ring back in his own ring box. "I want you to complete these rings and give them all to me. And I want you to be very careful with the pegs and the closing catch. Use this one instead," he said, picking up the damaged ring. "But keep the blue faithful to this one."

And Tal walked slowly to the door and let himself out.

■ KAFKA: Closing catch—*In the Carolinum, the old college where I studied law, the Rigorosum I, II, III had to be passed before one could receive a doctoral degree. I was intellectually fed on sawdust, which moreover had already been pre-chewed by other mouths.*

Brod and I would laugh till tears rolled down our faces about the closing catch. One would think that Rigorosum I would begin our hell and Rigorosum III would end our nightmare or perhaps III would begin our studies and I would close our academic year. But no. First we had Rigorosum II. And I managed to get three of four votes to continue. Then came Rigorosum III and I got three votes, just barely passing. And the closing catch, Rigorosum I, I passed. But really it was Brod's notes and my doodling that got the degree on June 18, 1906. And the close again was a deception, for it was not an end and not a beginning. I couldn't start to become a lawyer and I couldn't stop being a writer.

■ SAMSON RAPHAEL HIRSCH: Visions of Venice, visions of Jerusalem, visions of Safed—At first it would seem it should be Jerusalem first in Tal's thoughts, and then Safed, and later and only last, Venice. Did Tal study in Venice? Did he prostrate himself on his ancestors' graves in the Lido cemetery before going to synagogue on the high holy days? Did he give to the poor outside the courtyard of the Spanish Synagogue in the Venice ghetto?

But he is describing the righteousness of his family. As Rashi teaches us, "These are the generations of Noah. Noah was the righteous man of his generation." And the true descendants of the righteous are good deeds. And because Tal's ancestors lived and prayed, gave to charity, and were buried in Venice, he invokes that city first. And then of course his heart utters the name Jerusalem. But Tal has no children, and these rings to be given to his brother's family will ensure he will be buried in Safed. His good deeds will accompany him upon the coming of the Messiah. Amen.

■ JAMES JOYCE: Catch—"*I have given only catchwords in the scheme but I think you will understand Ulysses all the same. It is an epic of two races (Israelite–Irish) and at the same time the cycle of the human body as well as a little story of a day.*" And the day had to be June 16, 1904, Bloomsday. My day. My catching Nora Barnacle. She who my father said would stick to me forever.

■ KAFKA: Spiral staircase—This Eliyahu, he's terrorized Tal. He is no different from any of the high-level authorities on the fourth floor of the Assicurazioni Generali. I had been told clearly: "*no lateness ever tolerated, overtime without compensation, no private property in the office desk, no resignation without three months' notice.*" What if I died? What if I went mad? And for any change, any relaxation of these rules, I would have to climb the spiral staircase to ask permission only to find I had spent an hour going up and down, down and up, totally losing my bearings until I forgot why I originally wished to climb in the first place. Brod told me the architecture had been commissioned by the devil himself, who, once he had received one Prague commission, succeeded in cornering the whole market. But my father scowled at me when I told him of my difficulties in mounting the staircase to ask for vacation time. "Some lawyer you are, Franz. Can't get from point A to B."

■ SIMHA BUNAM: Wonderful—"*One day I felt like telling a story, or rather, I felt a story in me that wanted to be told. Except that I was afraid; it was what you would call a daring story. I felt that if I told it, my most ardent followers would stop calling me Rebbe. As for my enemies, they would know why they hated me, yet I could not repress the story. It wanted to be told, so I told it. And to my great surprise, even my enemies thought it wonderful and began to admire me.*"

He walked down the spiral staircase. Halfway down, peering up at Eliyahu, whose head was framed in the sunlit skylight, he exclaimed: "They are wonderful, but watch out for the blue!"

■ LAURENCE STERNE: Eliyahu—Liza told me of Eliyahu. Her horsical tale, over and over. Lord Elihu Yale this. And I that. And I wrote her simply, with all truth of my Christian soul: "*My wife cannot live long. . . . And I know not the woman I should like so well for her substitute as yourself. It's true I am ninety-five in constitution and you but twenty-five—rather too great a disparity, this! But what I want in youth, I will make up in good humor.*"

Elizabeth barred me from her door.

■ DARA SHIKOH: Head was framed in the sunlit skylight—In my dreams I would always see Father and myself as a boy of nine, his head framed in a sunlit sky in the Jaroka portal just at sunrise. We would be awakened an hour before sunrise Timuridly ascending. My brothers Daniel and Shashujah and I would wear our white robes, each with our *padkas* neatly tasseled. We would stand on the marble parapet at attention and loud kettle drums would echo and the sweetest silence would follow and Father would float out into the Jaroka Darshan window, his head framed in the sunlit sky. It would only be for a moment. But a moment that engraved itself on my memory so that no night, moonlit or dark, could ever erase that image from my sleep.

■ LIZA DRAPER: Eliyahu—I heard of Elihu Yale and his young woman, Jewess she was. Hieronyma de Paiva. Young like me before aging suddenly. The old men imbibe our girlish blood.

"*It is in the case of all girls destined for India—no beings in the world are less indebted to education—none living require greater assistance from it. For the regulation of time in Eastern countries is such that every woman must naturally have a large portion of it; leisure—this is either a blessing or a curse as our minds are disposed. The majority of us are extremely frivolous; this I grant. How should it be otherwise? We were never instructed in the importance of anything but one world point, that of getting the establishment of the luxurious kind, as soon as possible. A tolerable complexion, an easy manner, some degree of taste in the adjustment of our pursuits, a little skill in dancing a minuet and singing an air are the summum bonum of perfection here. These are all that matters. Aunts and governesses inculcate these with some merit—into our accomplishments. The very best of us leave Europe and commence as wives in the East at fourteen. Climate, custom, and immediate examples induce to indolence. This betrays us into the practice of gallantry that imprisons all that's amiable and good.*"

Elihu and Laurence, Yale and Sterne, Paiva and I, simply descending down down down in a minuet of death. Not very pretty.

■ HIERONYMA DE PAIVA: Eliyahu—My Elihu, my Eliyahu, but not my Lord. And on my son's tombstone, far from India, on the Cape of Good Hope:

Here lies: Charles Almonzo
the son of Hieronyma de Paiva and the
*   son of Lord Yale,*
once Governor of Madras, but not of
*   Hieronyma.*

My Elihu but not my lord.

■ VERMEER: As though resting—These gems, these sapphires, and even these diamonds: They will always rest, never leap, never live. Had I sold a thousand pictures I still would not have painted Morika with sapphire or diamond earrings. The pearls I placed on her ears and took off after each sitting would glow on my canvas long after she had left the room. At night I would look by candlelight at the canvas and I could feel her skin pulsating off the white silken surface of the pearl. My heart stopped in an ecstasy of longing for her so that I could not rest until she returned to my studio.

● SHABBETAI SULEIMANI, SULEIMANI'S FATHER: Buying or selling—"What's the price, buying or selling?" Tal's brother would say to my son in their office when he came from Bombay. My son would answer, "I'm not buying, I'm not selling." Even an Ashkenazi could understand. "Give me the diamonds. Moshe Baruch Suleimani will sell them and come back to you and give you the money and your family can keep whatever you want." And Tuviah would look at his father and say, "Father, he wants the selling price." And my son would interject and say, "I don't want the selling and I don't want the buying price. I want to make you happy." And Tuviah's father would say, "Give Suleimani the goods and let's see what happens."

And my son would sell the diamonds or colored stones, come back with our check, and hand it to Tuviah, and he would hand it to his father, and his father would hand it to Abraham. Tuviah would say, "Hakofos, what is your share, Suleimani?" And my son would say, "Whatever makes you happy." And Abraham would write with a flourish a check to my son and sign it and leave the amount blank. But Tuviah would grab the check and say, "We'll post this in the mail to you, Suleimani, after we've discussed this." Abraham was wiser but Tuviah was shrewder.

CHAPTER 8

BLUE OR PURPLE depends on whether you're buying or selling," said Tuviah Tal to his brother Abraham. Tuviah spread the fourteen sapphires on the table. Thirteen stones oval in shape and one pear-shaped sapphire, lying on its side as though resting, glistened in the direct sunlight in Tuviah's office.

Tuviah picked up the twenty-four-carat pear-shaped stone. "This would be for the necklace, with these four oval sapphires interspersed with pear-shaped diamonds, forming the balance of the necklace." Tuviah arranged the five sapphires on a wax board.

"These six oval stones, between twelve and twenty carats, are for the bracelet, especially this twenty-carater. This could be the center of the bracelet. Now these two matching twelve-caraters are left for the earrings. And, finally, this specimen twenty-eight-carat oval sapphire is perfect for a ring."

■ LEE KRASNER, JACKSON POLLOCK'S WIFE: Buying or selling—I would tell Jackson, Let's talk "shop talk," not "small stuff." What's shop talk? he would ask me. Who's buying and what's selling, prices in a shoestore mean nothing, small stuff. The stretching of the last to the undersole, that's shop talk. I'll never ask you why you paint the way you do, but how Picasso painted, that's shop talk, and that's the heart of art.

■ DANIEL GUGGENHEIM: Buying or selling— That's what Benjamin and Will would always say. "The price of Guggenheim Exploration depends on whether we're buying or whether we're selling." And I would answer, We will do both! And Benjamin would scream, "John D. Rockefeller and J. P. Morgan will never sell to us." And why not? I'd ask, whispering so that Father couldn't hear. And Benjamin would roar, "For one hundred thousand reasons. One, we're Swiss, and—" And Benjamin screamed, "John D. Rockefeller will never sell American Smelting to us!" "Let him finish," shouted Bill.

"—and the other 99,999 reasons are we're Jewish." And I told Benjamin and Will, Either you let me run this or you're both out. Benjamin simply said, "Well, then, I'm out because Morganization simply means not selling to a Benjamin even if his name is Guggenheim."

After they left the firm I explained to Father that we would buy shares of American Smelting from under the Rockefellers and force the company to buy us. This way they could save face as it would be a merger and not a buy or sell. Father chuckled and said, " If only Simon could be here." But then he grew pensive and said, "And what about Benjamin and Will, do you prefer Morgan and Rockefeller as partners to your own brothers?" And I said calmly, After they see we neither bought nor sold they'll come back. And Father mumbled very quietly, "In Lengnau we had a saying: 'Just as I can't see my right ear, I won't see that day.'"

■ MIKHAIL BOTVINNIK: Blue—Tal was a revolting mass of blue noxious smoke. Once when he was having a kidney operation he talked chess until the oxygen mask was placed on his face. Mikhail Tal had no program. No real preparation. He could only play his own way—frantic, obsessive, wild, free, and barreling toward a blue grave.

■ HIERONYMA DE PAIVA: Specimen—My lord Yale snarled at me, "Is this specimen?" following me around my chambers, even placing the stone on my neck as we lay in bed. He hounded me until I answered. "What do you mean by specimen?" I asked him. "What the English Jewel House of Chardin says is specimen," he answered. "For example?" I pressed him. "The stone I sent London five months ago that doubled our money in Amsterdam, a high-domed sharp-edge pure diamond, 32 and 1/4 carats." "I thought you told me the stone was of the second water and not pure." And Lord Yale smiled at me like a mischievous prince and said, "Anyway, like that 32-carater."

I asked him further and he always mentioned the profits made first and only later the quality. "For you, my lord, the margin of money earned would seem to dictate the rating," I would say. "Blast the profits, Hieronyma. I owe Sir John Chardin a fortune if I don't send him remnants of Shah Jahan's treasury. He will be your lord and not I." "He will never be my lord. And don't fear his opinion so much. Listen to your heart," I told him. "Only when you give it back to me." With immense charm, he removed the stone from my person and whispered, "You're the only specimen in all of Madras."

"Why not use the pear shape for a ring and the specimen as the centerpiece of the necklace?" asked Abraham Tal.

"Because of the silk in the pear shape. It will be less noticeable if mounted in a necklace. And the ring should stand by itself." Tuviah looked at his brother with a self-congratulatory smile.

"But the color of the pear shape is an absolutely perfect blue, Tuviah," protested Tal. "Although it's from Ceylon and not a Kashmir, it's a blue without any hint of purple, gray, green, or black in it. The twelve-carat ring, on the other hand, is purple."

"Abraham, not purple. We're sellers. It's blue." Again, Tuviah smiled.

"Tuviah, what is it with you?" Tal said. "Why can't you ever see things as they are. It's purple and you know it."

"Fine, Avram. Call it purple. Call it off-color. Call it unsellable.

■ JAHANGIR: Kashmir—"*Kashmir is a paradise of eternal spring, or an iron fort to a palace of kings—a delightful flower bed, and a heart-expanding heritage for dervishes. There are running streams and fountains beyond count. Wherever the eye reaches, there is verdure and running water. . . . The flowers that are seen in Kashmir are beyond all calculation.*"

■ ELIHU YALE: Specimen—All Daniel Chardin wanted was specimen this and specimen that. My dear brother Sir John Chardin could only sell a specimen diamond if the stone was above four carats. I was told: I will ship this fine colored but dull-luster green emerald to England but doubt if there will be much of a profit for the Madras side. We will have to wait for my brother John's report. And Sir John would send his meaty letters so salted with the word "specimen" that I found them indigestible. What was I to do but ship and pray?

■ MIKHAIL NEKHEMYEVICH TAL: Less noticeable—I was shaking. Simply shaking. And Botvinnik to his credit asked if I wished to go to Moscow Narodni Hospital for a checkup. But I simply continued smoking. Botvinnik laughed and said through the tobacco haze, "The pieces are less visible, dear Mikhail, but your strategy is crystal clear." What did he know of hospitals? For all his preparation strategy analysis, I learned chess in my father's waiting room. All the patients smoked one last cigarette while they waited for their doctor, my father, to see them. They smoked, they played chess with me, and they went in pawn-like for the news. I beat Botvinnik—a non-smoker—but I also defeated myself.

■ MONET: Purple—Venice at sunset. Impossible to be so purple. Not pleasant to be whispered to that I am an old man who can not distinguish shades of blue in an old city. And I, responding with a flourish of Socrates:

"I wish I had been born blind and that my eyesight had been suddenly given to me so that I could see nature as it really is."

Still, hemlock ended those doubts. And I weakening and my eyes going, especially the left one. But standing at sunset and the mixture of the fading red of sunset with the Venetian night's blue is a purple vision. It goes so quickly one must remember it more than see it, like life.

"You're the one who can never see things as they are. Here is the most extraordinary layout we've ever assembled. One stone has a very slight hint of purple—and that only by comparison with the purity of color of the pear shape—and you are already knocking it. This isn't an intellectual exercise. This is for real. I can't afford to knock my best piece. If I follow your advice, the ring will be unsellable because it has silk and the necklace will be weaker because the twelve-carater will be dwarfed by the remaining stone. Net result: no ring sale, no necklace sale." Tuviah stood up from his side of the jeweler's desk as though he were resting his case.

"Look, Tuviah, the color of the pear shape is perfect. It must stand alone. The color of the twelve-carater is purple. It should be grouped with the stones in the necklace." Abraham Tal met his brother's eyes with his own as would a wrestler, exhausted, still hoping to overcome a rival through sheer will.

■ SUBRAHMANDAN CHANDRASEKHAR: Dwarf—Tal understands and his brother does not understand. Oppenheimer understood and the others did not. A sun will collapse into a compact and immensely dense state, a white dwarf. And if it is more than fourteen times the density of the sun it collapses so totally without end that it will be a black hole—a neutron star—that nothing, no light or other object will escape it. As in the sky, so on earth: Certain things can, must, stand alone. Chandrasekhar's Limit, Tal's law.

■ EXODUS 19:5: Alone—
Now if you will hearken unto my voice alone
And keep my covenant
Then you shall be my own treasure
from among all peoples
for all the Earth is mine.
And you shall be unto me
A kingdom of priests and a nation alone and
*   apart (a holy nation).*

■ VERMEER: Silk—Curious that Tal sees silk in a gem. Morika always told me I saw silk everywhere. And so it is. The silken thread held in your left hand and spun tight and white around the taut spool and the liquid silk pouring out across my canvas and the silken lace hugging your neckline. My tongue quivered as I painted her embroidering by the hour before my eyes. But I'm nothing in your eyes, Johannes, she sighed, nothing more than a daytime of working and an evening of pleasure. Soon to be forgotten after your next model.

How could I tell her that my scarlet sins had been transmuted into snow-white light on eternity's canvas? Because you're nothing, you're everything, and there will never be another. "Hand me the neesk cushion," I teased her, "and like magicians we'll change nothing into everything," and she blushed in the dark at the playfulness of *neesk cushion*.

■ Peggy Guggenheim: Too pure—In '45 I heard the same drivel from Lee about Jackson. How he couldn't stand alone. How Pollock (like this Tal) was too pure for New York, too perfect for a city. They just had to live out on Long Island. The house was only $5,000. All Lee and Jackson could borrow was $3,000. They needed an extra $2,000. And they had all of $40 between them. Of course they blackmailed me with Kootz—they thought, Take the painting they owed me to sell to him and sell me out. I agreed to give them the $1,960 ransom.

They were too pure to live together unwed and they needed me to witness their sham wedding. It didn't matter, a cathedral, a synagogue, or a Dutch Reformed church. It was all the same to Jackson and Lee, if only I'd be witness to their purely fictional rites. That seemed delightfully Venetian and I would have gone but Jackson had mistakenly mumbled October 26 as the wedding date instead of the previous day and I was busy on the October 25. So they got the church janitor as their stand-in witness for a Guggenheim. Too perfect. Too pure.

■ Thomas Hart Benton: Special—Pollock was special. "*The only thing I taught him was how to drink a fifth a day.*"

"Abraham," said Tuviah, without a trace of modulation, "That's you to perfection. 'It's perfect; it must stand alone. . . .'" You don't have an obsession just about rings, Avram, you have an obsession about standing alone to show how perfect you are. You're too pure to stand with the rest of us. You're too special to mix with us. G-d forbid, we might contaminate you!"

"Listen, Tuviah, and hear me well. You made me stand alone. You destroyed my chances of marrying Rachel in Antwerp. You blocked me from her. You poisoned Father's heart. If I am alone, it is because you have tried to separate me from everyone in the family!"

"Avram. I pleaded with you to marry. That girl wasn't for you and you knew it. She had tuberculosis. She was dying. She would have died in childbirth.

■ The Jerusalem Talmud Sukkah 5A: Holy—
The Holy Spirit rests only in a heart that rejoices.

■ Jackson Pollock: You have an obsession about standing alone to show how perfect you are—Why can't you have two people who care about each other who don't mimic Tal and Tuviah? One wants to be alone, and one wants to get into the other's skin. I could sit in my studio for hours rolling the tubes of paint unopened on my floor. I could visualize the contents comingling, running together, coagulating, and suddenly in the middle of an afternoon's dream Lee would come in talking, squirming, jostling, giggling, anything to get into my skull, under my skin. "I miss you, honey. Too pure for company, are you? Let's go out. Let's go to bed. Let's talk shop." Always let's, let's, let's. She drove me to the Cedar Bar. At least there I could drown alone in a sea of drunken women's eyelashes.

■ Lee Krasner: Standing alone—Oh, this Tal is my Jackson. Wanting to be alone and his definition of alone so simple. Stare at a row of unopened paint tubes, read the contents over and over again, cobalt blue, for hours, until early evening, and then walk slowly to University Place and throw yourself at the first woman who knows you and how great you are and is willing to wait until you've had four Jack Daniel's and a good cry.

Thank G-d I never let you snow me with that aloneness routine and told you simply we had to get married or you would drown in alcohol or freeze in a desolate ditch just outside the Village. But of course how could we raise the $2,000 for the lovely house in Springs? We wanted to get out of the city. And when we got the money from Peggy Guggenheim, Jackson said how could we live together in Springs without getting married and how could we get married without witnesses, without a church or a synagogue. He always had an excuse to try to stand alone.

■ VAN GOGH: Half mad—*"Color expresses something by itself. Let's say that I have to paint an autumn landscape with yellow leaves on the trees. If I see it as a symphony in yellow, does it matter whether the yellow that I use is the same as the yellow of the leaves? No, it doesn't."*

My G-d, if I had a sou for each man who called me half mad. And they half mad also. What is their vision of the world? This Tuviah is the one who is totally mad, with all his half measures, his "half the business" talk. The Tals of the world will always be considered half mad by the truly totally mad.

■ SONNY BOY WILLIAMSON II: Alone—I was older than Robert. Lots older. Wiser. Lots wiser. Robert kept on with that "Sonny Boy, you watch out for the devil stuff, he don't blink." But I told him, "Robert, forget the devil. You watch out for the houseman because you lookin' at his wife and it ain't gonna end well." And then somebody brought Robert a drink with that broken seal on the top of the bottle. I shouted to Robert, "Man, don't never take a drink from an open bottle. You don't know what could be in it." Robert answered me with sass. "Man don't never knock a bottle of whiskey outa my hand." Simple as that.

But Robert, he couldn't play much guitar after that. He just crumpled up like a little child, sweating and crying. I took him to Grandma Hopkins's place, just outside of Three Forks, and left him alone to fetch the doctor. But it was the devil's brew. And by the time I got back, Robert was nothing but a heaven-sent memory of every Jack man and mama who ever heard him jingle those hot Delta nights.

"She would have died on the way to the *huppah*. Her mother died in her twenties, and her father was half mad. I have tried to arrange six marriages for you since we came here, every one from a good family. I offered half of this business to Pollack if his daughter would marry you. The girl should bring the dowry, but for you to wed I would have done the reverse. So, that's what I think about your 'alone' theory. No, you have to chase every straggly-haired hippie in the Village and G-d knows where else. Not a single one of my choices—all of whom wanted you—were good enough. Alone you are and alone you'll die. And no one will say kaddish over you."

"Tuviah Tal."

Abraham went to the shelf behind his brother and pulled down a tractate of the Talmud.

■ DR. PAUL-FERDINAND GACHET: Half mad—Van Gogh would tremble in my presence, quiver, shake. He paced much like Tal from room to room, from object to object, from subject to subject. *"Why are my objets d'art all black, black?"* he asked. And I would answer, "And which of the Impressionist paintings in my office is black to you, Vincent?" And he would ask me, whispering, "Dr. Gachet, are you half mad, now that your wife has died?" I didn't answer him. I put my hand on his, calmed him, but broached the inevitable question, "Am I half mad, Dr. Gachet, as all people say I am?" I cradled him in my arms and whispered to him like his dream mother, *"You must work boldly on and not think of what is wrong with you."*

■ MAIMONIDES: Half mad—*"Were it not for the half mad the world would still be a ruin."*

■ THÉODORE VAN GOGH: Mad—*"My brother's work does not express a mad mind but all the ardor and all the humanity of a great man."*

What a revolting sight, these two brothers: Cain and Abel. Instead of looking about themselves at the miracle of the world, each thinks the other mad. No sense at all.

Vincent would often ask me in his letters to make one painting sing by placing it next to another. To place a color scale of yellow next to a scale of blue, a scale of green next to a scale of red. There is no such thing as half mad or half normal or half business or half a lover. Any more than only one single color could exist in a universe in my time or now or in the everlasting future. They could sing together, Tal and Tuviah, eternally. If they wished.

◆ TAL'S FATHER: *By the books Father spent his life learning*—One day Abraham came to me and asked whether my Shas was given to me by my father. I could see where he was going: to find out in his own terms if the copy of the Shas was holier than any other book in my library. That idea is simple idolatry. Without raising my voice, I said, "These books are yours now. Furthermore, here is enough money to buy your own books. But the only way you will learn is together with your brother." Abraham took the books and the money but while he can swear using my books as witness, he still hasn't accepted my lesson.

■ THE VILNA GAON: Learning—The sanctity of a place where one learns the Torah or Talmud exceeds that of a place where one prays, a synagogue. And yet we learn that one can eat and sleep in a *Bet Midrash*, a house of study. This is done for the convenience of the students so they will not be forced to leave the house. Abraham would seem to regard the very books his father studied as sacred, rather than regard the place where they were studied in as an echo of holiness.

As to swearing on them, from this oath he would be easily released even by three ordinary men if three scholars were not available. The Maim Raybav states: A person will say I swore an oath concerning such and such a matter and I now regret it. Had I known I would be in such distress through it I would not have sworn. You are released—*sharui lekha*. You are absolved—*mutar lekha*. You are pardoned—*machol lekha*. Tuviah, is not a loving brother worth three judges? He can release and absolve and pardon Tal from his past.

"By the books Father spent his life learning from and by Mother's memory, I swear to you that you destroyed my life. Now you must pay."

"And just what must I pay, Abraham?" said Tuviah Tal evenly.

"You built your family on my ashes. You married and had two sons. I want Isaac. I want him to say kaddish for me when I die. I want him to visit me. I want him to close my eyes when I pass away. I want him—" Suddenly Tal broke down crying. He fell to the floor and crumpled like a small animal. "But I'll give him this. I'll give him this."

Reaching into his pocket, he pulled out the ring box and collapsed onto the carpeted floor.

"Get up, Abraham. Get up."

Tuviah pulled his brother up and threw him into a chair.

■ RACHEL, RASHI'S DAUGHTER: By the books Father spent his life learning—The sun goes down but the sun also rises. When the light of the exile Rabbenu Gershon ben Judah passed in 4800, my father Rashi was born and given to all Israel. When on the 29th day of Tammuz 4865 at sixty-five years of age my father was called to Heaven, it was simply too great a loss for our family. A people mourn the loss of their king. But imagine the grief of those who are extraordinarily close to the king, those who eat and drink, who study with him, those whose every day is spent with him. My brother-in-law Yehuda ben Nathan lost the power of speech when my father died. For three months he would not talk. I told him what Father told me, that Father's teachings were only the starting words, we were the continuation. But Yehuda could not accept the teaching. I fought with him when the tractate of Ta'annit came out because they used my father's blessed name. One of us should have gone behind the curtain to ask if it was permitted to write in Father's name. We were the books Father spent his life learning with.

■ RASHI: By the books Father spent his life learning—The word or phrase I always began my commentary with—"*Dibbur ha mathil*"—why did I call them "starting words?" Because I knew my daughter would one day ask the question no one else would ask. The answer to which she and I did not know. Would I finish my commentary on the Talmud? Tal's children have the books their father learned with, but they do not speak of learning with their father. When my daughter Rachel finally asked, "Father, will you finish all the tractates?", I simply looked at her and said, "Each writing we finish together is stitched into its own booklet—*perush hakuntres*. We are the *dibbur ha mathil*. Others will be the "*dibbur haaharon*," the closing word. Starting is even more blessed than finishing.

■ YISCHAR DOV OF BELZ: Tractate—The print is holy. The press is holy. The paper is sanctified. Even the Mitnagdim are angels. They themselves do not understand the sentence:

"*Said one to her companion, my dear, come let us wander about the world and let us hear from behind the curtain.*"

These Mitnagdim, they planned where to divide the text of the Talmud, but their hands were guided from above, and of course this page has to appear on page eighteen of the Berachot Talmud. Torah is life: *Chaim*. And Page Eighteen because this world is divided from the next by a curtain as thin as a page of the Romm Talmud.

HERE LŸES THE
BODY OF Isaac
Abendanasardo
OF MADRAS HEBREW
MERCHANT TO HO
DŸED THE 10th OF
maÿ ANNO 1709 iN
THE 47th Year OF HIS
AGE

■ JACOB (JACQUES) DE PAIVA: Let me find someone for you—I was dying. And I knew it. I knew where I was going. To Peddenaipetam. And even in what corner of the Memorial Hall Cemetery. I knew it in Golconda, as soon as I fell next to the river sluice, examined diamond rough to send to Madras onward to London. I knew it by the intense pain in the back of my neck that could not be quieted even by Hieronyma's heavenly hands, ever warm when we met.

And because I was dying I looked at my bride and said simply, "Let me find someone for you." And she lowered her head and wept and said, "You are for me, Jacob. Do not go." And I whispered to her, "The road to Peddenaipetam is but two hours long. Let me find someone for you. I can in Cochin. I can in London. I can in Amsterdam." But she was a child in love and she kept sighing, "Do not go." A husband can not pick a groom for his wife. An unmarried brother cannot choose for a brother. A mother and a father can choose. Or a person can choose for himself. But more often it is the place that chooses, not the person. Would I had died in London or in Amsterdam and not in Madras. With my heavenly Hieronyma.

■ JACOB BEN JOSEPH ABENDANA, 1630–1685: The hell with worrying about a hereafter—Antonius Hulsius wrote me quoting Haggai's verse (Haggai 2:9), "*The latter splendor of this house shall be greater than the former. Indisputable proof,*" Antonius said, that I and my brother Isaac Abendana, as dear to me as David Maimonides was to Moses Maimonides, should join, needed to join, must join, in the great glory of the new house. I wrote Isaac in the language of the old house, Hebrew, and asked simply, "Should we become Christians as we were when we were Marranos in Spain? Or should we bless G-d for having found our way back?" My brother Isaac sent me his reply—his Latin translation of the Mishnah he had just completed in Cambridge with the inscription on the flyleaf: "*Jacob, Blessed art thou our Lord, our G-d, King of the universe, who has kept us alive, sustained us and brought us to this time.*" Who is Tuviah to speak of Hell? Or of the hereafter? Breaking the Maimonidean chain, he is. No wonder the brother does not heed his words.

"Get up and stay up. Let me tell you, this ring has brought your life to absolute madness. Stop it. Forget it. Let's destroy it. What you need is a wife. The hell with children. The hell with worrying about a here-after. Comfort. Why shouldn't you have someone in your old age, my G-d, someone to be with? Forget Greenwich Village. Forget those nothings. Let me find someone for you if you're afraid to find someone yourself." Tuviah Tal wrapped his arms around his brother, cradling and rocking him at the same time.

Abraham Tal straightened up in his chair and, wiping his wet cheeks, slowly intoned, "That is why Mother gave me the ring. That is why. Because you talk of destroying it. I'll give you rings to destroy. I'll give you rings to destroy. I'm leaving. That's right! I'm leaving!" he screamed. "And listen to me, brother!

■ CONFUCIUS: Stop—*It does not matter how slow you go as long as you do not stop.*

■ BOB DYLAN: What you need is a wife—

*She knows what you need
But I know what you want.*

Of course, Tuviah knows what his brother needs. Of course Tal's mother knew what he needed. Of course his father knew what his son needed. But did any of them ask Tal what he wanted? Naturally not, because the answer would have struck such a wild chord that their whole family would have been singing off tune—if they chose to sing together—for the next two generations. And that's why I never answered my mother when she would ask me, "Bobby, what do you want? Bobby, what is it that you want?" Or when Joan, knowing my mother called me, would whisper through that impossibly long hair of hers even while we were making love off Abingdon Square, "Bobby, what do you want? Bobby, what do you want?"

Even when I thought I knew what I wanted, I knew well enough that I probably didn't know for sure and why should I lie and why should I speak for the unsaid spoke so much more finely? And Joan and my mother really speaking to my need in any case. He's got some nerve, Tuviah, telling Tal what to forget and what to need. Tal should simply run off with Dosha. That's probably what he wants. Even if just around the block with her. Even for an afternoon. Better a brief gallop by moonlight than a lifetime under an unforgiving, scorching sun.

■ ISAAC SARDO ABENDANA, 1632–1709: What you need is—As surely as I could see a flaw in a diamond rough that I would show to Pitt in Fort St. George, Madras, as surely as I could show Pitt how the stone needed to be severed and cut, Tuviah can look into his brother Tal's heart and tell him what he needs.

But it means nothing.

It goes nowhere.

It ends differently.

Even should Tuviah write on the walls of Tal's home, "You, my brother, need this. If you do not follow this path this or that will happen." It would mean nothing. Did I not tell my wife, who was more to me than a brother and dearer than a mother by far, that if she "needed" to remarry she needed to do so only "in a city where there is a synagogue"? And did she not assent and swear on my testamentary in front of two witnesses, a Sephardi and a Lutheran? And did she not marry the Lutheran in Fort St. George when my body was not yet three years cold?

■ ISAAC LURIA: Where are you going? . . . Safed—Abraham Tal understands what Tuviah does not. Tuviah is asking two questions: Where are you? and Are you going toward something or are you stationary? And Abraham doesn't have to wait for his brother to finish the sentence. He answers simply, Safed. Now there are two journeys in the world, one toward Safed and one toward every other place. Those who travel toward Safed are given a special blessing. Once they truly set out toward Safed, they immediately arrive. It all depends on the sincerity of the voyager. Tal is already in Safed.

■ CLOVIS GAUGUIN: Where are you going?— They all asked me in 1849 in Paris. I, a radical republican journalist, and they? They could be anyone; certainly the concierge must have been surêté. And my neighbor probably not police but rather gloating that I had to flee, and watching my family scattered was for him like watching startled mice disperse in the light of a candle carried by a farmer surprising them suddenly in a barn we called home. And the police themselves asking me, Where are you going? That was equally dangerous, so I answered, Lima or Louisiana, it's all the same to me as long as I have relations there to watch out for my family.

"I am giving you nine rings just like this one. Almost but not quite. You can give them to Ephraim, to your grandchildren and your great-grandchildren, but I want Isaac. Swear to me you will send him to me. And I will give him my ring. And don't stand between us. And let him close my eyes when I die. And let him bury me. And let him say kaddish over me."

"Where are you going, Abraham?" asked Tuviah, with a sudden coolness.

Abraham Tal paused and then whispered fiercely, "I am going to Safed."

"Then everything is signed, clear and accepted. Isaac will do this and you will be what you have always wanted to be, completely free of me and completely alone."

■ ALINE GAUGUIN: Where are you going?— Clovis would scream at me, "Where should I go? Where can I go?" And I would say, "Clovis, we can go anywhere. We can go to Italy. We can go to England. We can start anew in Germany." Then he would shout again at me. "We can't go to Italy! We can't go anywhere in Europe! You and the children can go anywhere in Europe." "Don't be such a journalist and quibble over words."

"I am not quibbling, Aline. I don't have family in Europe. We are trapped, although I could travel anywhere myself." "Then we can go to South America to Lima to our family there," I pleaded with him. "We can, we must go to Lima." He persisted. "I thought you said we could," I answered mystified to Clovis.

"You can. We can't because I can't. Leaving Europe will kill me." I held him in my arms awake all night in Paris and lullabyed him to sleep, and he boarded the ship in the morning . . . and died en route.

■ PAUL GAUGUIN: Where are you going?— They all asked me. My wife, Mette, her parents. Shrewd, they were. I shouldn't have been flippant, so offhand with them, by introducing myself as a "savage from Peru." They knew I had sailed for six years in the French merchant navy, so they were placated when I said simply, "Anywhere I have relatives, famille Gauguin," not knowing that's what killed my father.

And Mette with the same question over and over again. Where are you going after Paris? she asked. After Rouen, after Copenhagen, after glorious Brittany. "What I want most is to get out of Paris . . . which is a wilderness for a poor man. I'm off to Panama to live like a savage." After Martinique. After van Gogh's razor in Arles.

I answered Mette simply. Where am I going? I am going into my canvas. There is a mysterious affinity between my brain and my lines and colors. I am going into my own art." She said sadly, "I thought you would only go where you had relatives?" But she could not ever, would not ever, understand that I had come finally and forever in my house of pleasure on the edge of the Marquesas in Hiva-Oa, to my ancestral home.

■ VERMEER: I've watched you come here for a month. . . . and you've watched me—She came to my studio and stood hour after hour with the stillness of a startled deer or women who have never been wronged. She did not speak for what seemed like an entire cycle of the moon. Only when I finally broke the silence at the end of a four-hour sitting with the words, "I've watched you come here for a month and you've watched me," did she reword my entreaty with, "And I've watched you watch me."

She, like the moon, never blinked, and the more I painted her moonlike eyes the more heartsick I became that she would leave me. Over and over I painted the pearl on her ear, the yellow river of silk flowing downward on the small of her back, until in the fourth month I held her in my arms and whispered, "Never leave. I want to watch you forever." And she looked at me and said simply, "Johannes, you are painting yourself, not me. My canvas will be with you but I must go."

■ TALMUD, HULLIN, 84b: Indifferent black suit—*A man should always eat and drink less than his means allow, clothe himself in accordance within his means, and honor his wife and children more than his means allow.*

■ JACQUES DERRIDA: And one thing you know is that I know—It is not simple. My Talmudic-studying rabbinic grandfather would say, "It is not so simple." The Torah given orally to Moses and he writing part of it down and transmitting part of it orally. Generation after generation dancing around the text. I remember the excitement in my Algerian synagogue when the Torah seemed twice my size on Simchat Torah.

What are we to make of the Kabbalists still dancing about the Torah but whispering its secrets one to another on camel voyages across the deserts of North Africa, ships across the Mediterranean? And what to make of an old man's mirror, a young man's esoteric knowledge? Is this text? Is this speech? Logo centrality. If there is one single thing that Tal knows then my grandfather was right. It is not so simple because it is so simple. We search for texts that "*make the limits of our language tremble.*"

"*What interests me is not strictly called either philosophy or literature. I dream of a writing that would be neither, while still keeping—I've no desire to abandon this—the memory of literature and philosophy.*"

CHAPTER 9

BLUE, this shade of blue for a *bimah*? thought Tal, dazzled by the shimmering painted blue *bimah* in the center of the Ari Synagogue in Safed. Here in this very synagogue, Isaac Luria had prayed four hundred years ago, and it was called the Ari Synagogue after the Lion of Safed ever since.

A thin man in his early twenties approached Tal. He had a disheveled beard, an indifferent black suit, flecks of dandruff on his shoulders, and blue eyes that only Russian Jews have.

"I've watched you come here for a month, American. And you've watched me. I wonder who you are and you wonder who I am. But one thing I know; you are a seeker. And one thing you know is that I was a seeker and now I am sure you know.

■ JOSEPH KARO (1488–1575): This shade of blue for a *bimah*?—Be careful to avoid thinking about anything at the hour of prayer except the words of the prayers themselves. This even includes avoiding thoughts of Torah and the Commandments. At first it seems that Tal should not be thinking of shades of blue while praying. He is standing in the center of the synagogue, and is not Safed at the center of the heart of the world? But blue is his melody and blue is his color and blue is his vision. My angel, my *Maggid*, instructed me never to become angry about anything at all having to do with material things. This blue is not material but a section of Heaven itself. Tal is closer than he has ever been.

■ HAYYIM VITAL (1543–1620): An indifferent black suit—I can remember my master, Isaac Luria, the lion of our exile, indifferent to his own clothing, but when it came to his wife's apparel he was exceedingly careful to honor and clothe her well. He used to satisfy her every desire, even if it were not within his means. When my master died we wondered how to decorate the ark in our synagogue, and in a dream the Holy Ari came to me, saying, "Was not the Sabbath my bride; and is not Israel the bride of G-d?" And his words were written in the deepest blue script on a background of the purest white.

I remembered that shade of blue on the dresses he gave his wife before each Simchat Torah, and thus we came to cover the ark in our synagogue in the deepest blue cloth woven in our holy city.

■ MODIGLIANI: Hot, cramped hotel room—Jeanne would rail at me that it was stifling in the hotel room we lived in on rue de la Grande Chaumière, an appropriate name, she noted. By the time she mounted the stairs to the apartment, 2 Bis, she was steaming. She would never stay during the day in the summer of 1919 but instead wandered about, zigzagging cunningly across Paris. Once I followed her when she left at daybreak but lost her somewhere in the Jardin du Luxembourg. She could smell my presence. She would tease me lavishly.

I would prepare my canvases and clean my brushes and sketch my colors on the wall by the window—huge swatches of yellow and orange for her neck—and she would enter and say wearily, "*La chaleur*" or "*Le diable*," and disrobe immediately and lie on our bed inches from my canvas. "What is it to be now, my dear, art or life?" Then I would sketch and paint all at once trembling, knowing of her silky rewards after I finished. Generally, I painted until the moon was above the brown mansard roof of the house across the park on rue Emmanuel Joseph. And she would look at the canvas and smile and glisten.

"I do not look like that. My neck is not as long. No woman looks like that. You do not know me, Momo. You must be painting your last woman. Perhaps you have confused us." And only when I stroked her hair, following the follicles of her neck down slowly across the ridge of her back, crisscrossing each inch of her arms and voyaging through her and across her, was my sense of distance confirmed and I knew as I had always known that space was an illusion and a canvas was not flat and that Jeanne Hébuterne was light that never melted in heat or moonlight.

"And I will tell you what you need to learn, but only on one condition."

The young man stopped speaking abruptly, gazing into Tal's eyes with an intensity that recalled something to Tal from his past he could not place. Tal thought of his hot, cramped hotel room five blocks away, and of the summer heat, uncommon for Safed, nestled in the mountains and always supposed to be cool. And yet here he felt stifled, almost faint from the heat. For the past week, his left arm could hardly move and the small of his back felt as though someone had punched him. Yes, he had noticed this half-mad tourist guide, this rabbi manqué, a few days ago. But he hadn't thought to speak to him.

From out of the hot mist, the young man spoke again.

■ VAN GOGH TO HIS BROTHER, THÉO: Stopped speaking—"*Really we can speak only through our paintings.*"

■ RASHI: Rabbi manqúe—In the language of our neighbors, a half rabbi or a missing rabbi. Here the *peshat*, the simple meaning, is a half. For Tal is half a rabbi in the sense that he studies by himself. He lives, but by himself. And without students how can he be a whole rabbi? But the *remez*, the hint, is one of missing. Tal when he was in exile, *galut*, was a rabbi manqué. His heart was in the Holy Land and his head in a land far away. He was not a rabbi in exile and he was missing from the Holy Land. Now that he is in the land of Israel he is no longer a rabbi manqué. If only his lot were to have lived his youth wandering in search of wisdom, and then returned to be a rabbi, I myself would have given him *smicha*.

■ MICHAELANGELO BESSO: Stopped speaking—Once the coffee cups arrived in our café just off Bahnhofstrasse in Zurich, Einstein would pour the coffee into my cup and stare at the liquid as it left the spout with an intensity that would suspend the liquid for an additional second in midair. "And is it not like a light particle . . . a beam? If we could travel, Besso, on a beam of light would we see it faster and faster? What would we see? And the space? Contracted, until at the speed of light the space we see outside our raft of light would be so thin, so elongated that all sides of our 'outside' would be visible all at once. Space is an illusion. Only light exists." Sometimes we would simply sit and think together. The fewer words we spoke, the more clearly we saw and thought. And one month we stopped speaking and Einstein changed the way the world was understood.

■ SAMUEL BEN MEIR, RASHI'S GRANDSON: Rabbi manqué—My grandfather of blessed memory once called me a rabbi manqué. I had just shown him a commentary I had written on a page of Talmud, and he poured over the twelve pages I wrote, a month of work, and looked up at me and simply said, "You're a rabbi manqué." And I asked, "What have I left out from my text?" My grandfather smiled and said, "*If you were to explain the whole of the Talmud in this fashion you would find your commentary so heavy you would need a carriage to carry it.*" He took my work and a week later returned it to me on a single page. Clear and simple, every word a diamond drop. And then I understood the phrase in French, manqué one can be greater than two.

■ TALMUD TRACTATE SANHEDRIN 21B: Song—
Said Rabbah, *"Even though our ancestors have
left us a scroll of the Torah, it is our religious duty
to write one for ourselves, as it is said, 'Now then,
write down this song and teach it to the people
of Israel, put it in their mouths, in order that this
song may be my witness within the people of
Israel.'"* Deuteronomy 31:19

■ AKBAR: Me forty years ago—When I saw
my grandson, Prince Khurram, wrestling with
his brothers, I smiled. They, so much bigger
than he, and always defeating him. And he,
weeping, because they would so rarely deign
to wrestle with him. And then one hot summer afternoon, hot even in the paradise that
is Kashmir, I saw Khurram run wildly in a circle, tumble and turn, spin about on his feet,
and land full force on his side. Laughing, I
shouted, "Khurram! Whatever are you doing?
Won't your brothers wrestle with you?"
He smiled gently and said, "No, Grandfather,
even when I wrestle with them, what I truly
am doing is wrestling with myself." Then I
understood all my conversations with the
Jesuit fathers, all the discussions with Jews—
people of the book—all the talks with my Sufi
Murshid. We all must wrestle with ourselves.
Khurram is me forty years ago.

"Good, I think you know instinc-
tively what the condition is." The
man's blue eyes rested on Tal, and
suddenly Tal understood: This man
is me forty years ago. Not his eyes,
for mine are greenish-brown. Not
his beard, for I have never had one.
Not his freckles or his thin, ethereal
physique, or his impossibly white
rabbinic hands, but his wild spirit,
like mine, his mystical song, that
doesn't wait for an answer but is
answered in a silent echo.

"The condition is," said the
young man, "that I do all the talking
and you do the listening."

Tal felt as though he would doze
off if he could lie down on the
narrow wooden bench in the back
row of the Ari Synagogue. He could
barely stand, let alone open his
mouth to talk. He tried to lift his
arm but suddenly found himself
crumpled on the back bench of the
synagogue.

■ VAN GOGH: Wild spirit—*Everywhere and all
over the vault of heaven is a marvelous blue,
and the sun sheds a radiance of pale sulfur and
it is soft and as lovely as the combination of
heavenly blues and yellows in a Vermeer of Delft.
I cannot paint it as beautifully as that but it
absorbs me so much that I let my wild spirit go,
breaking rules as I go.*

■ BOB DYLAN: This man is me forty years
ago—

*May your voice always be sung . . .
May you stay forever young.*

Tal never needed a beard because he
looked like an old man when he was young.
And this young man looks like Tal never
looked because Tal is listening to his song and
realizes he has heard that song a long time
ago. And not just a lifetime ago. Longer. People
wouldn't believe it if I told them I heard my
songs before they were born and before I
was born. It wasn't simply the angel Gabriel's
harmonica humming in my birthday band,
teaching me music. Songs are more than
music and words. Separate them and you die.
Listen and sing them together and you're forever young. Tal and this young man are singing
together, just as they did forty years before.

■ ISAAC LURIA: Song—In my synagogue, on the
street where I lived, in my world, Tal is not
being spoken to. He is being sung to. The song
he is learning is the song he has spent a lifetime learning. Although he knew the words
and the melody forty years before. Is not the
Torah G-d's song? Does not G-d hear Tal
singing this song to himself, but really to G-d?
What is our life but a preparation for these
final moments? The song at the moment of
death that we sing. The notes are the wheels
of the chariot that lifts us heavenward.

Juhanghir with portrait of his father, Akbar.

■ KAFKA: A story—Milena wrote to me that I regarded the whole world as a secret, something I could not cope with. That I regarded with awe my director because he was such an extraordinary typist. That I regarded her philandering husband, unfaithful to her a hundred times a year, as an extraordinary phenomenon. In short, she knew my fear that I could not exist with her and live with her and share with her in a mystical way the ordinary. The daily. The simple. That man and woman have had together in all times and in all places. I expected miracles. I could not deal with the ordinary, said Milena.

But I had sent her my stories. Not simply to be translated but as an offering. She pressed me and would brook no excuses. I must come to Vienna. I told her she had the whole of me: my stories. I had to go. We walked and we fed on air for one hundred hours. I wrote her, "*Since I love you, Milena, I love the whole world.*" Lovers are simply storytellers who sit and walk together, listening to and repeating the same story to each other.

"May we continue?" said the man to Tal. "Why did you come here to this synagogue? To find me. Why did I come here? To find you. And who am I? I am you. And who are you? Not whom you seem to be, but finally who you wish to be.

"A story, your story: one day Simha Bunam of Pshiskhe was chosen to become the Rebbe. The night before he was to assume his position, his Gabbai said to himself, 'I was the Gabbai when the previous Rebbe was alive. It was always such a mess, everyone with his *kvittel*, no order, pushing, shoving. The important thing is to make order, especially the first night. As it will be the first night, so will it be the next one hundred and twenty years for the Rebbe.'

"So the Gabbai arranged all the seats in absolutely straight rows.

■ REMBRANDT: A story—Not *the* story. Not what happens. Not whether it ever happened. Not whether it happened in long-ago Israel. But rather the time spent in the telling. And in the listening: I a boy in Leyden in my grandmother's room, and she reading the great leather-bound Bible she received from her grandfather. By candlelight. I, afraid of the dark, unable to sleep. Walking quietly into her room. Her aged hand on her Bible. She smiling at me and holding my hands in hers and telling me a story. Isaac and Abraham. The great fish. The hair of Samson. The fall of Adam. A snake. An apple. It was all one long tale. All I remember is the warm glow of the light of the story.

■ MILENA JESENSKA: Story—"*I knew Franz's fear before I ever knew him. And I armed myself against it by accepting it. My Franz will never get well. Franz will die soon. Life for him is entirely different than it is for the rest of us. . . . His stories are amazing. He himself is much more amazing.*"

He gave me his story and I read it and reread it and after the fifth rereading I could almost recite it by heart. And after the tenth rereading I could chant it. I sat in my cold room on the fourth floor while Polak my husband caroused in Vienna until morning. I took out the lined notebook Franz had given me in our four-day marriage and chanted and translated and wrote until I had finished my Czech version of Franz's German. When I posted the version to Franz he answered, "It is your story, not mine, Milena, just as I am yours, not mine anymore." Whosoever tells his story totally to another loses himself forever. Tal has handed his *kvittel* to the man who has given it to the Gabbai who is giving it to the Rebbe. And he has also given the young man his soul. Just as Franz gave me his in Vienna.

■ VERMEER: A story—A story. My story. What is my story? What is my history? What is his story? That is what I was asked from the moment I entered my studio on the second floor. Not only by my wife, Catharina. And by her mother. And by the people on the street across the way who would pause and wonder why I stayed indoors peering at the light hour after hour. What is my story?

And Ameka, who glowed in yellow, curtained from my touch by an ever-youthful green under my brush, kept asking me, "Johannes, tell me your story." I responded gently, "It is all written on the letter you are reading." Only she didn't have the eyes to see what I wanted and simply furrowed her brow in confusion.

But I was ready for Morika. I saw her when she crossed the street in front of the alley by the Handles market. I left her a note of white paper inviting her to my house to be painted. I let her set the modeling fee. And when she inevitably asked the question "What is your story?" I told her I would tell her through my art, and day after day in my studio she read my story. Slowly. While we merged in a river of white and blue.

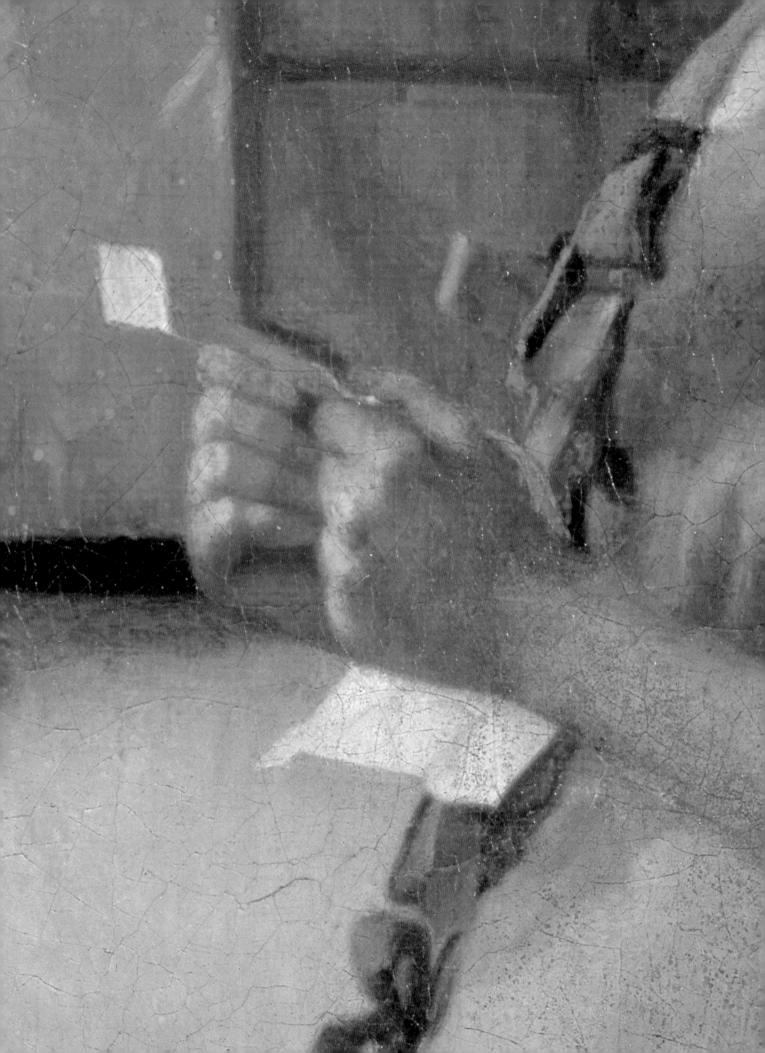

■ KAFKA: A well-dressed German Jew—That was me. Or Brod. Or Brod and me. Or every Western Jew. With our long amber cigarette holders. Our homburgs. Our curiosity to see all and to travel and to taste and to experience. And butterfly-like to suck honey from each charming mouth we see in cafés and railroad dining cars from Warsaw to Paris. But never to dwell, to sit, to pour over, to commit, to be certain, to say, This is the place where I will be born, where I will live. Where my children will bury me. That is me. That is Brod waiting with me or, should I say, waiting for an audience with Yischar Dov of Belz in Marienbad, 1922. And of course the Belz Hasidim are looking at me. At us. Brod and me. I will be part of their stories. The Gabbai will tell his tale of us and it will be passed down to the next generation of Hasidim and I will tell my version of the story but G-d forbid that Brod pass down mine.

■ HUDDIE LEDBETTER (LEADBELLY): Masses of poor—We would sit and stare, my Mamma and my three brothers, simply sit in the Mooringsport Baptist Church until suddenly from a side door in would burst Reverend George C. Johnson. The poor people would start to clap their hands and the roof would jump up and down as we shouted and prayed and spoke to the Lord. And as suddenly as he, Johnson, had entered, he would leave. He was the man who could lead us to the Lord.

And wasn't it just the same with Mr. Lomax, who took my song to the Governor and sprung me? Whenever you see a mass of poor people, you can just bet they're waiting and hoping for the man to come to lead them to salvation.

"The first Hasid to come in was seated in the front row and each subsequent person was seated carefully row by row. At length, when all the seats were filled, the Gabbai heard the *heileger* Simha Bunam stir within his room. As the Rebbe opened the door slowly from the back of the room to face the masses of poor Hasidic women and men each clutching their small letters of requests, suddenly a well-dressed German Jew, with a long amber cigarette holder and a homburg tilted rakishly on the side of his head, bounded in. The Gabbai gave this *daitcher* a look of absolute disbelief, until Simha Bunam, stepping directly into the crowd, said, 'Shmuel, I'll see him first,' pointing to the dandy.

"'Rebbe,' exclaimed the Gabbai, 'he just came! These other people have been here for hours. I told you that from now on I want order, Rebbe.'

■ MORIKA ABENDANA, VERMEER'S MODEL: Letters—Week after week I went to his room. My cousins and I had just come from Spain and not yet gone to our Uncle Jacob's home in Amsterdam. I had shown Vermeer's note to my cousins, and both of them came with me to his house. They sat with me for weeks on end as Vermeer painted me. He changed my outfits innumerable times and charmed young Daniel with questions of our life in Spain. The colors of every garment our family wore. How our table looked, how our rugs, and even how our shoelaces were made interested him. Daniel's brother Jeremiah (known before as José Pedro) never uttered a word. How do we know he is not a spy from the Inquisition? he would mutter, as soon as we were in our apartment across the canal. Jeremiah yawned and ate biscuits and fell asleep.

After several months the boys trusted Vermeer to be alone with me and no longer accompanied me to visit Abraham, as they wittily called Johannes. And the day they stopped coming, the letter I would read as he painted suddenly contained script in Dutch, difficult to read and even harder to understand, changing each day. Each letter written from his heart. To me. How strange. A courtship of letters. Without a word spoken between us. He was cunning, dear Johannes. Charming and cunning.

■ VAN GOGH: Letter—Vermeer's letter. After all it is not the girl's letter. And it is not a letter sent from a simple suitor. I would go to the Rijksmuseum each morning at nine and try to read it. To digest it. To swallow it *"This strange painter's palette consists of blue, lemon yellow, pearl gray, black, and white."* The white letter's light itself was the key. It warmed the woman's face, burnt the soil of the Holland map glowing behind her, and breathed life into the baby growing within her. I vowed then and there in the halls of the Rijksmuseum to be able to post my own letter back to dear Vermeer, letters of grateful thanks written with my tears of white.

◆ RACHEL, TAL'S MOTHER: Almost indecipherable writing—As a boy, he would come weeping into the kitchen after school with his homework assignment, returned from the teacher without a grade or with a comment: "I can't read this." "Copy again." "Maybe you're brilliant but how would I know? I can't decipher this." Or, simply, "Failure but recopy carefully if you wish another grade." I would sit Abraham on my lap and ask him to read his own assignment and he would, slowly, with the charming pomposity of an eight-year-old. But often even he couldn't read his own almost indecipherable writing. Laughing, I would interrupt him and say, "I think, Abraham, this is what you wrote," and he would storm out, his pride shattered, crumpling the school assignment on the stairs, stumbling up to his room before he slammed the door shut. How strange. We all offer our notes to others. Love is the greatest decipherer.

■ SIR ARTHUR EVANS: Almost indecipherable writing—In the middle of my life I started to dig. Half a lifetime earning and half a lifetime learning, I would tell my daughter, Joan, the indecipherable writing on the walls in the wide dark palace, on the clay tablets, in stones strewn around Crete and by G-d even on the mainland at Pylos! Oh, I could work out the numbers, for what were all writers initially but overworked accountants keeping track of goods and treasure—just as I, retired businessman working even in my dreams, almost deciphering, nearly deciphering, but not deciphering.

Once, I dreamed that my daughter picked up a tablet and read its meaning to me: "In four months O King of Heaven my four-wheeled chariot will bring you 1,000 jars and 10,000 cups of—" And then I awoke only to realize I had been staring at my own pictographs half scrawled at my desk when I had fallen asleep. No, I knew in the depths of my bones it would not be my family but some other young person who would carry on. And that is why I "advertised." Had exhibitions, spoke, wrote. To attract that unknown youth to carry on. Forty years is a long time to nearly decipher and not to fully decipher.

"But Simha Bunam turned his back on the Gabbai and retreated to his room to sit behind a long oak table. Resigned, the Gabbai ushered the young man, dressed in a shimmering gray suit, into the Rebbe's study. The Gabbai left the door slightly ajar and stood beside it so that he could hear. Through the slit in the door he could see the tip of the youth's cigarette holder and the back of his head, as well as the eyes of the Rebbe, who was watching the youth patiently. The young man said nothing for a long time. He inhaled and exhaled bluish smoke rings.

"'Why did you come?' asked the Rebbe gently.

"'Well, as the almost indecipherable writing in my *kvittel* says, I have a deep conflict. I am in love with two women.' The youth ended each of his sentences with circles of cigarette smoke."

■ MICHAEL VENTRIS TO SIR ARTHUR EVANS: Writing—"Did you say that Minoan writing is almost indecipherable, or did you say that it has not been deciphered, Sir Evans?" I asked Evans. He, eighty-five. I, fourteen. My classics master Patrick Hunter repeated the question louder for Evans to hear. But Evans moved closer to me, waved Hunter aside, and, smiling, handed me a small tablet with Cretan writing which danced before my eyes.

"It has not been deciphered yet is what I said." He stared down at me a centimeter from my forehead, whispered, "It is you," and walked abruptly out of the hall.

Master Hunter immediately strode toward me and queried, "Ventris, what did Sir Arthur whisper to you?" I shrugged as though to say I didn't hear Evans, but the blessing never left me day or night.

■ THE SEER OF LUBLIN: Almost indecipherable writing—They would come to me and write their *kvittlach* in indecipherable script and hand it to my Gabbai, Hersh Leib Sassov. He would hand me their *kvittlach*, stealing a glance downward, not being able to understand a single written word. I guess they felt that as I was the Rebbe and all-seeing I should be able to read their script. They were often ashamed of their requests, ashamed at the smallness of their desires. Often, I could not make out even one line but the answer to their request came out of my mouth. In Lublin, my Hasidim said I could tell from their foreheads where they had come from and where they were going. So many came with their hats resting on their noses, as though I could not see through their hats. The *kvittel* is writing indecipherable to the writer, unreadable to the Gabbai, illegible to the Rebbe, but intelligible and perfectly visible to the All-Seeing One.

■ F. SCOTT FITZGERALD: Beautiful—"*You took what you wanted from life if you could get it and you did without the rest.*" Those words and dreams mingling inside my skull. As long as I could remember, sitting on the red stairs in front of my house in St. Paul. Waiting for the vision of my mother at the end of the long avenue of chestnut trees, walking slowly down the street, fixing her eyes on mine, and smiling always. Words about school or the weather or something floating just a foot above in the walkway reaching me before I could taste her perfume in the air. At Princeton, Anne Watson enters the room: all eyes on her. Even Richard Truslow knows she's finer than anything he's seen in Greenwich. And she, simply speaking my lines. My words. My undergraduate play. My directions. Speaking to no one in the audience but me, looking only at me. "*I don't know whether I'm real or I'm a character in one of my own novels.*" And Zelda knew what I dreamed of before I dreamed of it. Beautiful. The first girl. In the first southern moon of my life. I, a novelist, in a play written by myself, starring us two, a play touring on the road, even after the show closes.

■ PAULINE PFEIFFER HEMINGWAY, HEMINGWAY'S SECOND WIFE: The second girl . . . comes from a fine family—I moved into Hadley and Hem's flat. As simple as that. Just brought in my hatboxes, my old copies of *Vogue*, and my red heels, which turned Hem's eyes from Hadley's hair to my legs whenever I walked down the stairs and knocked on their door. I was the second girl but my family was finer and I knew I could convert Hem to the Catholic beliefs of my parents and after his conversion I would be the first and only. The red of Hadley's hair would disappear from his mind and his memory forever under my red heels. The greenness of his eyes would merge with my emerald-jeweled ears forever.

And we did. And our prayed-for sons were given to us. But our rainbow of red and green vanished with Martha, who became the second girl. How incredibly stupid to set the trap for Hadley, only to leave it in our house waiting to be used by Martha on me.

"Already on the balls of his feet, the Gabbai was on the verge of barging into the room but could hardly move for fear of losing the next sentence.

"'The first girl,' continued the youth languidly, 'is very beautiful. Her skin is completely pure and her eyes reflect the moonlight each evening of the year. She is slender and fine and when she speaks, her voice is like a song I heard as a child long ago.

"'The second girl is not as beautiful. Her eyes stare back at me opaquely, and I do not see any reflection in them in winter or fall, in summer or even in spring. She is not slender but substantial. Although her voice is a whisper, she has great strength. When I see her, I do not fear. Most important, she comes from a fine family.'

■ ZELDA SAYRE FITZGERALD: The first girl . . . is very beautiful—"*I used to think until you're eighteen nothing matters. That's right. And afterward it's the same way.*" I don't want to be famous and fêted. All I want is to be very young and very irresponsible. I stared deep into his eye sockets. Deep into the mirror of his irises. I could see my reflection off the shiny buttons on his uniform. He was an officer, the highest ranking one present, seated with me, the most beautiful woman present, at the officers' ball. It was torrid in Montgomery. Still I see my eyes on his buttons as I spoke slowly, more slowly than Mama would speak when Jimmy Driscoll's father came to visit us. I was hardly speaking, just jumbles of words, sentences running, red with blushing. And I asking Scott, What did you think of the play, and he didn't hear me or couldn't hear me or would not speak, and I, volunteering, "The first girl is very beautiful," even though I hated the first lead, Martha Jackson, far more than she disdained me and then his honor Scott said, "You are the first girl." And when I looked down at my feet, protesting that I wasn't, he proclaimed, "You are and you always will be."

■ ERNEST HEMINGWAY: The first girl—"*They said I needed a new woman for each big book. There was one, Hadley Richardson, for the stories and* The Sun Also Rises. *Pauline Pfeiffer for* A Farewell to Arms. *If there's another big book I think I'll have another wife.*"

And what did they ever know—who the first girl was. Or the second girl. Or the third girl. Dos Passos put it simply when he told me, "*Hem, you are the only man I ever knew who really hated his mother.*" You simply could not make my dear mother my first girl. As for memories of warmth and love, of the first heart needing kindness from dear old mom, try the gift to me of the gun Dad killed himself with sent by my first "mom" after Dad's funeral.

Hadley thought she was the first girl, too. Especially after Pauline moved in. G-d she was lovely. Droplets of shimmering emerald crystals she wore as earrings dazzling her body and smile. But Hadley was not the first girl. Not anymore than Pauline was even after my conversion. And even Agnes von Kurowsky caring over me and I, dying, before living, her face before my shattered body in Milan in 1918. Blond hair over my body at night washing my wounds with her eyelashes. She wasn't the first girl either. And the pain of her leaving. And the letter Agnes wrote me. Perhaps Father never had a first girl. Perhaps neither did I.

Amedeo Modigliani, *Head of a Woman*.

● GUTMAN GUTWIRTH (FISHER'S GRAND-FATHER): Simhah Bunam did not speak—Reb Bunam said we should learn to be careful of every move we make in life just as a chess player takes great precaution before he makes a move. Before making a decision, we should think in advance whether we will have cause to regret it.

■ KAFKA: I find her irresistible—Dora was the second girl. She was irresistible. On the other hand, Brod told me that if the "first" girl Milena or Felice had been irresistible, there would have been no second girl. To which I replied, "The second is always irresistible because the first girl is not compared to any other and therefore one finds all kinds of excuses to fault her, find objections, delays in committing, and so forth."

Brod and I would banter endlessly about courtship and love and first and second girls, but the truth was the Gerer Rebbe had said no to my letter asking for Dora's hand that I gave to Dora who gave it to her father who passed it as a kvittel to the Gerer Rebbe who said no to Dora's father who said no to Dora. How could I resist Dora? I was dying.

"'Her father and mother are so wealthy that I find her irresistible.'

"Had he not been horrified, the Gabbai would have burst out laughing. This serves the Rebbe right. A Rebbe who thinks he is a good Gabbai will soon become a Gabbai, but will no longer be a Rebbe.

"The Rebbe's head moved back and forth, back and forth, looking at each woman as though they were seated at either side of the young man. The Rebbe barely paused to look at the young man himself. Simha Bunam did not speak. Finally, hesitating, he said softly, 'Young man, you should marry the wealthy girl.' And the man arose, and without pausing to thank the Rebbe, turned on his heels and left.

"The Gabbai rushed in, shouting, 'For this, for an apikores I make order. I set up the chairs. I keep your yidden waiting. It's sacrilege.'

"'Sit,'" said the Rebbe. But the Gabbai stood, glaring.

"'Didn't you understand his question?'" thundered the Rebbe.

"'What question?'" bolted back the Gabbai.

■ MAX BROD: Irresistible—Franz and Dora were like children. They would dip their hands together in the same washbasin and call it the family bath. Franz would ask me to take a long drink of water before him because he didn't have the strength to do it himself. On the day Dora's father's rejection of Franz's marriage proposal came, it was only one word. Franz fell into the deepest of sleep. Dora confided to me that Franz awakening in the middle of the night saw an owl outside his window. The bird of death. And then Franz understood what made Dora so irresistible. Her love for him, her thousand gestures to bathe him, warm him, feed him. Who knows Dora, only he can know what love means.

■ REBBE MENDEL OF RYMANOV: Didn't you understand his question?—When I was in the yeshiva of Daniel Yafe in Berlin, I would pour over Maschet Berachot in the Talmud day after day, night after night. Gradually through repetition, through singing the pages of the shas to myself in my sleep, I came to the level where I could recite the entire maschetah—the entire section of the Talmud—by heart.

After two years I went to Daniel Yafe and asked him how to continue my studies. He said to me, "A favorite saying of Rav was: 'The future world is not like this world' (Berachot 17A). What does this mean?" I answered from memory, "Rav says in the future world there is no eating or drinking or propagation or business or jealousy or hatred or competition but the righteous sitting with their crowns on their heads feasting on the brightness of the divine presence. Rif says, "They beheld G-d and did eat and drink." Reb Yafe said simply, "Thus written but you can see the Rif?" and abruptly left the room.

In the middle of the night I awoke, and before me stood the Rif. He quoted the Jerusalem Talmud: "He who quotes a tradition in the name of a sage should at the same time be able to sense his presence." I wept because I knew that what Reb Yafe meant was that I had concentrated on the question and not on the person. And then I fell asleep again and slept through the entire day and night and suddenly awoke and there was the Rif before my eyes again, and he said, "Did you not understand the codifier of Jewish law? Go to Elimelech." That is how I went to Elimelech of Lizensk. And that is how I became the Rebbe of Rymanov.

◆ RACHEL, TAL'S MOTHER: An old man hearing a tale from a young man—I told Abraham of my father's house in Antwerp. Of my mother's ancestor who had come from Portugal, become rich in India, died in Amsterdam. Of Jacob. Of Daniel. Of all the Abendanas. A tale of diamonds and prayer. I spoke of Madrasi spices while Abraham stood by my side. I can remember him at six when I said, "I have told you everything I know of my family, Abraham," and he burst out crying. I said to him, "Your father will be coming home soon, and now it is your turn to tell my stories." I told my husband at the door, "Listen to your son now if you would wish him to listen to you later." From that day over and over again, from the time Abraham was six until he was ten, his father would patiently sit and hear the Abendana saga, an old man hearing a tale from a young man. But who ultimately has such patience? It broke Abraham when his father once reprimanded him: "Cease these family tales for now and do your homework, Abraham." And no amount of entreaty could ever get Abraham to ask for or to recount another of my tales.

■ VERMEER: He had heard that story long ago—Did not any story I ever heard in any town in Holland, in any tavern, from any woman I ever painted, bring me back to my mother, who took me in her arms and placed me in a little wooden box bed by the rocking chair in my grandfather's house and began the self-same tale?

"Once there was a great prince who was a little child. He was discovered in the bullrushes and destined to be a savior of his people. In Hebrew his name was Moses but in Dutch we must call him Johannes, so that no one will ever discover his princely secret."

Always at the end of the tale she would intone, "Johannes, go now for forty years and then tell this tale to another. But not to more than one, or else the secret will no longer be ours." And why the forty years? I would ask. And she talked of a wilderness that had to be crossed before the tale could be told. I knew that although I was forbidden to tell the tale I could paint it, but only in the shadows of a corner of my paintings.

"'The young man stayed up every night for the entire year seeking. He wished to know if he should begin his studies of those on high beginning with the teachings of Rabbi Moses Cordovero—whose elegant lines of thought have never been equaled—or with the teachings of the holy Ari, Isaac Luria, the Ashkenazi, who built his works on the treasures of our past. Looking at him and his gaze, I advised him to begin with the riches of Luria.'"

Tal studied the young man. Not bad. Not bad at all. He had heard that story long ago, forty years before. But still, it was remarkable to hear it here. An old man hearing a tale from a young man. But Tal was exhausted and longed to go back to his hotel room.

■ SIMHA BUNAM: An old man hearing a tale— The young man can hold the old man's attention just as David could calm Saul, half mad because David could see the future. David would close his eyes and then he could see within himself. That is how he composed the Psalms. When David sang, Saul could accept his words. The old will never listen to the young unless they are sung to. I can barely hear this young man's voice. I would wager he's merely humming a melody. Probably without even a word.

■ CAITLIN THOMAS, DYLAN THOMAS'S WIFE: An old man hearing a tale from a young man— Young Dylan, he would be in Brown's Hotel near the boathouse. Watching me talk in the morning to whomever entered the bar. I'd roll a cigarette on my thigh with one hand in front of my audience, which would stop young Dylan in the middle of whatever he was saying in another corner of the bar. I could feel his hot breath as others looked at me and he wouldn't stop panting until we left before lunch. He walked to his father's house and helped his dying father with the crossword puzzle and rhyming words for a warm-up.

And then in the room above the boathouse I would hear him mumbling words, rhymes tumbling out of him, but he an old man then, hardly moving except his hands and his eyes, looking across out at the water. Simply transcribing what the barroom lad thought up as he watched my thigh across the room. After writing all afternoon until sunset, Dylan would fall asleep at his desk, only to be awakened at six by Colm and me.

An old man he was, hearing a tale from a young man. I would take my two babes Colm and Dylan into my arms and rock them back and forth. And one I would hush to sleep and the other I would take to my bed. And awaken again and back to Brown's for a late-night drink and up again for breakfast in the bar. Aging and being reborn each day and he and I giving birth to poems forever green.

■ BOB DYLAN: An old man hearing a tale from a young man—I was young with a very old name, Zimmerman. A name heard in Hibbing. In Duluth. Zimmerman's son. Zimmerman's grandson. How could I be forever young? Only with a double first name and no history. And why should I even explain any change? Each of my explanations would only lead to other people telling me why I had done this or that. Or why I said what I didn't say to someone who misheard a joke I didn't mean in the first place, but all those rhymes in my head bulleting and ricocheting off my skull. I knew I was like that poet in Wales and I could hear the ocean echo in the name. I knew that in taking the name I would be blessed, that the old and young would listen to my tale.

■ RABBI NACHMAN OF BRESLOV: The prayers were sung like those in Safed—In Safed, the holy Ari prayed the same prayers as in every other synagogue in the world. And in Safed the synagogue looked in its essence the same as any other synagogue in the world. Weren't the seats wooden? Did not the ark point to Jerusalem? Were there not windows that opened to the mountains? Did not the door need to be fixed each year before Pesach? But in Safed the prayers before the prayers were special. People prayed so that they might be able to pray. The holy Ari would walk by the wall on the road leading down to the synagogue, slowly, silently but with joy. Hayyim Vital would walk with him, beside but not in step with him, a young man, and each was floating in their own prayer.

When I go in Uman toward my synagogue, by the time I get there I know whether my prayer to pray has been answered and whether I can start to pray. Always think you are walking to the Ari's synagogue in Safed even when you voyage to my Uman grave, and you will have your prayers to pray answered.

■ VAN GOGH: The intention—I would take each brush to my sink on the second floor of my house in Arles and wash it with turpentine. Every brush had its own color, and while washing I would think of Théo, my mother, the part of the field I would go to that day to paint.

Gauguin once asked me how much time I needed to clean those brushes. I looked startled and said, "How much time have I taken so far?" He answered, "You've been here for two and a half hours and you've washed each brush four times." I told him I was thinking about the painting, and when I returned to the house from the tree-filled field in mid-afternoon, Cézanne, laughing, stated, "You spend more time cleaning brushes and talking about painting than actually painting."

But I knew that once my intention was set I could not stop for even a minute. It was all so automatic: the vision of the countryside, the overwhelming light, the colors, the brushes, the palette mixed helter-skelter with a finished canvas lying on my bed, dreaming of the next day.

He started to get up but a weight pressed on his shoulder and he couldn't rise.

"So you, too, are here for the riches of Luria, as am I, as are we all." His clear blue eyes met those of Tal as he continued in a whisper, "Indeed, the world asks, 'If all the synagogues in the world were like those in Safed, and all the prayers were sung like those in Safed, would not the Messiah have come?'

"But then why are there different prayer rites in Safed: the Aboab Synagogue, the Ashkenazi Synagogue, and the Sephardi synagogues? Which order should we follow? There is no uniform Safed rite," continued the young man.

"And the answer is, 'It is not the order or the song of prayers that counts, but how one prays—the intention, the *kavanah*.'"

■ HAYYIM VITAL: If all the synagogues in the world were like those in Safed—"All the synagogues in the world are like Safed," said my master, Isaac Luria. "Enter my synagogue alone," he would say. "Enter before sunrise, and the cool light streaming in is full of waiting angels flying in through the windows, buzzing across the synagogue seats, and escaping through the other side of the hall. Back and forth you can hear the wings of the angels as they prepare for the day's transport. Three trips back and forth they make: in the morning, midday, and at night. That silence which is not silence, emptiness which is fullness, is present in all synagogues. If you cannot feel the presence of angels, then you may be sure your prayers are not carried above."

■ JACKSON POLLOCK: Intention—It was the death of everything. All that calculation. Shine your shoes. Get your lunch box. Brush your teeth. Leave ten minutes before the school bus. Get the homework assignment. Get your library card. Speak to the teacher. See the principal. What are you going to say? All for nothing. All the shrieking and endless whining and Mom yelling: "When your Dad comes home, if you haven't . . . !" And I hadn't.

And preparing for New York. Bring this. Bring that. Write your cousin, Peter Knowles—as though he answered any of my letters. And what was the point, living in his garage and paying him rent anyway? And in art school: If you don't prepare your canvas it will, in hundreds of years . . . Let it. And what makes Botticelli so great anyway? I'd rather eat the egg yolks. You can take all your intention, all your preparation. I simply dripped the paint exactly where I wanted it to be. Nothing accidental in my universe. If Lee wanted to make love to Botticelli, she knew where to find him.

● SHABBETAI SULEIMANI'S FATHER: Was Luria a Sephardi? Was Luria an Ashkenazi? —All his life Tal has been puzzled. Is he Ashkenazi, is he Sephardi? . . . . And it meant so much to him to be a Sephardi. A prince, one who looks at the underpinning of the argument, the essence of the law, rather than the minutiae. One who sees the heart of it all. And I would always discuss with him only patterns, directions, market tendencies. And then his brother would come in, and each stone would be examined, each nuance of cuttings, could a piece be recut, what would be gained or lost. And Tal would say, "We're the only Jewish family that has one Sephardi son and one Ashkenazi." But here he is, aging. And suddenly he sees, as we all do eventually, his own brother in himself.

■ SIR ERNEST OPPENHEIMER: A businessman . . . a trader—"*I owed everything to my older brother, Louis.*" But he was not a businessman. He was a trader. The rough diamonds came to our Kimberley office in sacks, and we would sort the rough into series. Louis could look at a series of stones and without weighing them could tell instantly how much they would yield after cutting.

In the 1930s, when month after month our stockpile grew, he hit upon the idea to break up the parcel series and sell them as individual stones. I was in England with young Alfred Beit, Otto's son, to see the Rothchilds when I got Louis's cable: "Sold October production 42 stones mined at 12% increase in profits by breaking the series." I said to Beit, "The only thing that counts in business is a series of repeatable transactions. If not, one is just a trader." And I knew it would take me years to clear up the trouble Louis had caused by breaking up the series.

"For all the rites are separate gateways, and Jerusalem's emanates from Safed.

"Was Luria a Sephardi? Was Luria an Ashkenazi? Both. You're right and you're right. His father was an Ashkenazi, but his mother was a Sephardi Tahor, a Frances from Cordoba, then to Cairo. And it was his mother's brother who taught him."

Isaac should be coming soon, thought Tal. Perhaps I shouldn't have alarmed him, but still, I feel so weighted down since I came here. Maybe it's the altitude.

"Are you a Sephardi?" asked the young man, rhetorically. "No, but you will become one, for you are standing here in the center, and we are all one.

"Are you," the young man continued, "a businessman? Was the holy Luria a trader? He sold pepper. He bought salt in Cairo."

■ SIR ALFRED BEIT: Businessman—I was in London with "Uncle" Ernest (my father always told me I had two uncles, Alfred Beit and Sir Ernest), and Father said one uncle would leave me a fortune and the other would teach me how to make an even greater fortune.

I remember the cable arriving from Kimberley from Sir Ernest's brother, Louis, and Sir Ernest saying, "Series, series, everything is a series. How could Louis be such a fool!" And I thought I was being charming when I said, "Oh, yes, Uncle, your brother married a Pollak and you married the next in the series, Mary Lina Pollak." But Sir Ernest didn't find it funny, he was so distraught.

I took him to Hunt's to get his mind off business, after telling him I would show him the greatest, most remarkable, most breathtaking series in the world. We came into Hunt's Gallery Room at midday but, as bright as the interior was, the picture was even brighter. Sir Ernest looked for a long time at the passage in the picture that had a swatch of Vermeer's heavenly white light on a billowing window curtain. "My G-d," he said. "That light is pure blue-white, just like our finest gem diamonds." And I told him how there were only three dozen known Vermeers in the world and that this was the only and last one in the series available and that he should buy it.

Sir Ernest paused for what seemed to me at least an hour and said, "Alfred, you buy it. If I could buy the entire series I would. That would be good business." Right then and there I bought the Vermeer and resolved never to be a good businessman.

■ NATHAN OPPENHEIM, FELIX WARBURG'S GRANDFATHER: Businessman—*To sell a man pearls you have got and that he wants, that is not business. To sell a man pearls that you have not got and that he does not want, that is business.*

■ JAMES JOYCE: Pray while doing business—Probably. Possible. But improbable if business is good. As the Talmud says at one point, *"We Jews are like the olive. We give our best when we are being crushed, when we are collapsing under the burden of our foliage."*

My career reminds me of an opera with a magnificent overture. While the audience is applauding just before the curtain goes up, in comes a group of bailiffs that arrests the fiddlers for debt. And how am I to write if not during business hours? And what are my words but dunning letters, requests for a shilling, for Parisian wine from Mother, Father, from her lordship Mrs. McCormick, shoes from Pound, moralizing from Monier and Beach? Were I an angel I could write while doing business, but not until then.

■ MODIGLIANI: Can he not pray while doing business?—She would smile and hold her pose. Languid. Always languid. Stretched across my bed. The bed sheets already fiery red on my canvas. She smiling and whispering, "Momo, Momo. What are you doing?"

I would gaze down at the canvas and speak to her, alive at the edge of my brush, and answer, "Painting, painting." And she would whimper, "Love me, love me, Momo." I couldn't form the words in my throat because that was what I was doing, loving while painting, painting while loving. There is no difference.

"If a man can think of business while praying, can he not pray while doing business?

"So you are both, or were for the moments when you were whole. You were never one, never another.

"And where are you going? Up? Down? What is your future? Exactly like your past.

"You are moving in both directions at once. Look at the top of this synagogue." A small shaft of light fell directly on Tal's face. "Now look at the floor next to the *bimah*. Exactly the same. White light. The same white light. From the Academy on High we have a mirror of our Academy here below.

"And you say the light is not white? It is blue?" the young man asked.

Tal's eyes widened. How did he know what I was thinking, he asked himself.

■ ISAAC LURIA: While doing business—"I can pray while selling pepper but I can't write while doing anything else.

"In fact, it is impossible for me to write a book because all things are interrelated. I can hardly open my mouth to speak without feeling as though the sea has burst its dam and overflowed. How then shall I express what my soul has received? How can I set it down in a book?"

■ VAN GOGH: Pray while doing business—We are all pushing, grasping, crawling. Businessmen. Adults. Sober citizens. At the same time we are children, hopeful, yearning. We pray while doing business. We are doubles. We are mirror images. We seek our angelic opposite. I am a painter in a field of Arles and I am Wil, my sister, two self-portraits. She, too, is me. Two pillows on my bed. Two candles on a table. Two brushes and two yellow chairs filled with sun warmth. My prayer, Gauguin, coming soon while I live in my own daily prayer of painting, longing, and yearning for my reflected image.

■ BLACK ELK: Blue is not an accident—The Holy Spirit did not choose the rainbow colors by accident. Nor do blue or green or yellow or red appear by accident. I was thirteen when I saw Sitting Bull and White Bull paint their tobacco blue. No accident, White Bull intoned to all under the moonlight. Now this tobacco is united with the sky and we are one, and tomorrow Long Hair Custer will go to the distant valley never to return. The tobacco, which is the secret of the earth, and blue, which is the sky, bore witness. Long Hair was no more. But as I saw that battle, so too I saw a lifetime later, at the age of ninety, another battle at Pine Ridge—the end:

"I did not know then how much was ended. When I look back now from the high hill of my old age I can still see the butchered women and children lying heaped and scattered all along the crooked gulch as plain as when I saw them with eyes still young. And I can see that something else died there in the bloody mud and was buried in the blizzard. A people's dream died there. It was a beautiful dream. The nation's hoop is broken and scattered. There is no cemetery any longer, and the sacred tree there is dead."

■ TAO CHI: Painted again and again—The old masters were the old masters. Mei Ching would sit in Huang Shang and study from his collection, sit in his study and look. Look from his study out at the mountains. He would paint, and paint again, and yet again. I could see him in his painting, alone, a single brush stroke. I could see his eyes dotting the landscape. Again and again. Painting and writing, writing and painting. He was my friend. But if I had never left Huang Shang I would not have been able to paint. It was an ancestral tomb. Beautiful, quiet.

Mei Ching would implore me: "Stay a while longer. We will paint together, walk the narrow paths south of Huang Shang." I could not answer him. The paintings I brought to him every few years—the paintings I did again and again, far from Huang Shang—were my conversations with him. This, Mei Ching told me when I would leave him. He said he would gaze at my landscape scrolls and without words talk to me.

"It is blue by reference to the *bimah*, by reflection. The *bimah* is so blue that it intensifies the blue in everything. It is painting, albeit slowly, the canvas of the world. This blue was chosen by the Ari, may his memory of a Tzaddik be a blessing, and painted again and again in exactly the same hue for four centuries.

"Know then one thing, that nothing is accidental. You and I were meant to meet. We were talking before. This blue, at this instant in time, is for your eyes only.

"The shade of blue is not an accident either. Where did the sefirot come from? The holy sefirot that brought the world into existence? They came from the blue of the sapphire. They were named 'sappir' by the Holy Name. And where did this sapphire come from? It came from the tablets of the Ten Commandments.

■ MEI CHING (1625–1697): Painted again and again—Again and again. The snow fell. Lightly on the pines. I painted again and again. The weight of the snow brushed the pines, and suddenly, with an elegant swaying sound, the branches of the trees were bare and the snow was on the ground. Again I started to paint, and yet again the snow fell, and the pine trees became full yet again. And Tao Chi visited, not often but yet again. From far away. He told me simply, "The village of Huang Shang is your mistress. Why can you not leave her even for a season?" And I replied, "I shall leave Huang Shang soon enough. Just as the master whom I copy. Who painted these pines? Again and again I have left. Why must you leave me, Tao Chi, no place is as beautiful as Huang Shang." And Tao Chi looked over his teacup, shaking, but could not answer.

■ JAMES JOYCE: Blue is not an accident—"*A genius does not err. His mistakes are the portals of discovery.*" And blue. Did I ever see it? As it is. As it was. And what do we make of color? Like love. Tommy loves Rosy. And Rosy loves Jeff and Jeff loves Mummy. And is their love the same? And when I told the conductor of the Dijon-Paris Express to tell. Darantière that the cover of my treasure—*Ulysses*—was not blue but "an accident," the train conductor smiled at me as though to say, You are an old man at forty. You do not know of accidents. I am a train conductor.

There is no accident, he protested. I brought this book to you from my friend, Monsieur Darantière. But what did I care what the conductor thought. Or Darantière or Beach. Or whoever or Nora or G-d Almighty. Or Nutting, who mixed the colors so that the blue of my book cover would be the blue of the sky covering Greece. It was my blue. And my cover. And my birthday. But in the end it was all an accident.

■ MAX BROD: Blue—His accursed blue note-books. Over and over Franz would tell me, "My days are numbered. My manuscripts are counted. My message is outlined. I am nearing the end." It was maddening.

Once I said to him, "Franz, you will recover. You will marry Milena. You will outlive me. You have not written your last words yet." Franz answered simply, "Go and look. Look and read." And one day when he was not in his room, I glanced at Blue Octavo #8 and on the last page I saw:

"There is no need for you to leave the house. Stay at your table and listen. Don't even listen, just wait. Don't even wait, be completely quiet and alone. The world will offer itself to you to be unmasked; it can't do otherwise. Enraptured, it will write before you."

■ KAFKA: Blue—My reality was my little pile of blue notebooks. I purchased eight on Haruska Street just by the St. Michael's bridge. I took them to my room and left them on my desk.

"Everyone carries a room about inside him. This fact can even be proved by means of the sense of hearing. If someone walks fast and one pricks up one's ears and listens, say in the night when everything round about is quiet, one hears for instance the rattling of a mirror not quite firmly fastened to the wall."

Max would come to my room every few months, month after month, and remark after absentmindedly fingering through my fraying and dog-eared notebooks, "Franz, let me get you new workbooks." But I brushed him aside with my words: Max, these books are all I need.

"Moses found this sapphire buried in the sand by the burning bush. Where did it come from before? It illuminated Noah's ark for forty days and nights. And who brought it there? The angel Raphael. And where had it come from before? From Adam, who received it directly from The Blessed One, G-d.

"And why are we standing here? Because of Israel, and her flag, and all the *tallitot* with blue threads over these past centuries.

"The light is unbroken. And we are the ladders going up and down. This blue teaches us that there is a reality. And it is one. And there is only the One, and our eyes are the mirror."

Tal looked at the intense blue eyes of the young man. All gray vanished from them, and they seemed to float toward him.

■ LOUIS GINSBERG: Raphael—*"When G-d resolved to bring a flood upon the Earth, He sent the archangel Raphael to Noah bearing the message, 'I give you a holy book with all the mysteries of the universe.' Noah took the book and studied it. The book was made of sapphire. All the time Noah spent in the ark, it served him as a timepiece to distinguish night from day. Before his death, he entrusted it to Shem, and he in turn to Abraham. From Abraham the sapphire descended through Jacob to Levi and then to Moses, Joshua, and Solomon. Solomon learned all his wisdom from it, his skill in the healing art, and his mastery over the demons."*

■ HIERONYMA DE PAIVA: Raphael—Elihu spoke in his sleep and was barely awake for two days running. He kept murmuring, "What will I say to him? He is a fanatic. A heathen. His advisors are worse. They will not suffer a Christian in their presence for more than a minute. And only if an extraordinary gift is proffered to his Majesty." I asked, "Why must you say you are a Christian?" And Elihu said, "To Aurangzeb, all Europeans are Christians." And I told Elihu simply, "Tell him your full name is Elihu Raphael Yale. And indeed you are named after Rafil, the angel who instructed Noah, and is there not one angel over us all?" Elihu laughed and said, "Shah Jahan, his father, might have listened, but Aurangzeb is a great heathen." And I said simply, "Even a great heathen loves a great tale." Elihu implored me to come with him but I refused, saying, "You go with a man's body—but with a woman's tale."

■ ELIHU YALE: Raphael—It was preposterous: sent to an audience with the Great Moghul himself, and the Company refusing to allow me even the smallest of gifts. What was I to do but follow Hieronyma's tale—she more Muslim than I—probably half a heathen herself. Like Open Sesame. I said my name *Elihu* softly and fairly shouted *Raphael*, pronouncing it in the Muslim-Jewish way, Rah-fil, and mumbled *Yale*, and then I was asked immediately how did I get such a treasure for a name?

I talked of Wales, and my mother, and how the mountains were green with emeralds, how the color of Rafil/Raphael was green. I told him everything I had rehearsed with Hieronyma and he was entranced. I was brought closer to the great Moghul and fed from his Treasurer's hand. The next day we dined alone with an interpreter and a guide and then he showed me his father's emerald, modeled on the Taj Mahal. It was engraved with three flowers: a lotus, a poppy, and an amaranth. "Here, Raphael, this is your color, and this is my father's gem." When I returned, I told Hieronyma about everything but the flower garden gem.

■ SIMHA BUNAM: Backward—Once Pessah, the wife of Menahem Mendel from Barenov, came to me three days before Rosh Hashanah and said, "Rebbe, can you do me a great favor? Can you move the clock backward for my husband just forty-eight hours? Two days ago his store was burnt down. His fortune is gone. He can't give charity and he feels too weak even to come to you." I suddenly felt almost overcome by laughter inside. Although I realized that Menahem Mendel was not present, I said to Pessah, his wife, "Let me tell you both a story.

"Once I was a manager for a timber producer outside of Voidslav. Hundreds of acres, thousands of trees. The job was good: simple planting of the seedlings, counting the trees, and making sure the timber was sold in Leipzig or before the fair at Leipzig so that the price was fixed. Once the selling price was set, I had time for myself to study in daylight hours, eight hours a day—paradise itself.

"The first seven years the profits always increased and Count Poliakov stopped even coming to collect the money but simply sent his servant to me for my accounts. But then one year, two days after the fair, out of nowhere the Count pounded at my door, screaming, 'Jew! Come out! I'll make you wish you could turn the clock backward. You sold my lumber in Leipzig before the fair, you fool, you crook! If you had only waited until the fair the price would have been double.' And then and there he threw me out and where could I go? Who would hire me? Only in Pshiskhe was I able to find a home to stay in. What could I do but become a simple grinder of medicine, a pharmacist. And barely enough time to learn, just one hour a day.

"Then one day the following year to my tiny shop came the wealthiest Jew in town, Abraham Lustig. 'Bunam,' he said, 'You were wise to leave Voidslav. Have you not heard that all of Count Poliakov's forests burned before he could sell the lumber at Leipzig? And of course his manager has fled in fear for his life.' Backward or forward. What does a clock mean? Take my watch and give it to Menahem Mendel, your husband, and may G-d grant joy to be the portion of his time from here onward and backward."

From behind them came the voice of Isaac, and he felt Isaac's hands move toward his eyelids, and suddenly he felt a softness of touch he hadn't felt for many years, and then, waves of blue. He felt himself floating backward, and he heard his nephew intoning, "Blessed are you, Hashem, our G-d, King of the universe, the true judge."

Tal could feel Rachel's hand lightly on his. Together, one again.

■ YEHEZKEL SHRAGA ZUCKER: Floating backward—My father, Yitzhak Bunam, used to tell me in the name of the Rebbe I was named after, explaining the sentence:

"Moses and Aaron said to Pharaoh: The G-d of the Hebrews has revealed Himself to us. Please allow us a three-day journey into the desert and let us sacrifice to the Lord our G-d lest He strike us down with the plague or with the sword" (Exodus 5:3).

This referred to the Hebrews as a people whose name derived from the word avar, "to pass." All of us should know that this world is but a passage way to the world to come. We are just a people passing through. The main thing is the world to come. Floating backward to the great name.

■ PESSAH OF BARENOV: Floating backward—I don't remember what Simha Bunam, our holy Rebbe, said. It was a long, long story. I felt as though I could not breathe. Menahem Mendel forbade me to go to see him. I will surely die, he said. It is hopeless. Yet I went to see our holy Rebbe. At the end I remember almost fainting, floating backward through the doorway walking all the way to Barenov. And coming into the house, Menahem Mendel looked at me. He hadn't eaten since I had left. "What did the Rebbe tell you?" he asked. I had to confess, "I can't remember a thing. I left empty-handed." Then I felt the cold metal in my pocket and I took out the watch and we could see the heavenly blue minute and hour hands moving gracefully. The chime each hour was the greatest medicine for Menahem Mendel. He never failed to smile when it chimed. Two years later a son was born and we called him Yitzhak Bunam, after Simha Bunam, because the Rebbe brought laughter into our house even after he had gone to the world to come.

■ YITZHAK BUNAM ZUCKER: Isaac—Children. Grandchildren. No children. It is all the same. Glasses full of wine and glasses with the wine emptied. Long serious stories or short tales told by others because their lives were too short to complete even a sentence. But all with one breath. And that is the laughter that is the meaning of my name, Isaac. My wife, Rachel, told me on the morning I proposed to her. We met, we walked, and she said simply, "Of course, I will marry you. Isaac, you're named after your grandfather Isaac Bunam, who was named after Rebbe Simha Bunam. But his joy was not enough so Isaac was added, and your laughing name will make me smile through a dozen births." I shuddered and bashfully said, "What if G-d forbid there are no dozen births?" and she said simply, "Then you will be laughter itself for me. That is enough."

Rabbi Leibel Eisenberg and his gabbai.

CHAPTER 10

THE BLUE stain in the igneous
mineral that Benjamin Tal held
firmly in his hand was evident in one
direction as he turned the crystal
matrix on its axis toward the setting
Beersheba sun. He took off his
glasses and mopped his forehead,
then went back to the tent and lay
down on the cot. Holding the matrix
in his fist, he closed his eyes.

I shouldn't be afraid, but I am, he
thought. The area has been safe for
years. He could visualize the electric
lights from Beersheba slowly being
turned on in the twilight. Benjamin
Tal's father Isaac would take him
there years ago when Benjamin and
his twin brother Akiva were kids.
Akiva would hide and Benjamin
would seek. The problem was that
Akiva would disappear for hours,
leaving Benjamin to look for him
until Benjamin became exhausted.

When Benjamin returns to his tent, his
dream will come to him.

◆ RACHEL, TAL'S MOTHER: Akiva wanted us to search—Akiva, my great grandchild. And Benjamin, my great grandchild. And my father saying, quoting Rabbi Baruch, "The apple doesn't fall far from the tree." Abraham, my child, and my other apple, Tuviah. They did not fall far from the tree, and yet they rolled far from each other, hiding. Seeking. Not wanting to hide. Not wanting to find each other. Endless games played out in successive generations. Always being played out. Touching. Love or lack of love at the bottom of it all.

■ MONET: How to die and then come back—Simply by looking, Cézanne spoke of me: *"Monet is only an eye but my G-d what an eye."* Simply by looking. Looking in the morning before you can see anything. By watching the light on the pond as it comes up through the brush toward Vétheuil. By sitting in the heat of the day, not moving even for lunch, by sleeping in the afternoon by the pond and dream-looking at the water, by awakening before nightfall, and by remembering the image of the trees in the reflected water, by painting after dark from one's memory, by painting each day, by painting canvases so that the reflection on the canvas is a mirror of creation, by bridging and piercing a vision of reflection. But understand that the canvas is us and that the reflection fades not and that we return with spring for we have left with water.

■ RABBI BARUKH OF MEZBOZH: He wanted to hide more than I wanted to find him—My grandson Yehiel was playing hide-and-seek with another boy. He had hidden himself in a clever place and after a long time he emerged from his hiding place, only to realize his friend was not even trying to find him. Yehiel ran to me and wept. What could I do but tell him that G-d says the same thing: "I hide but not one wants to seek me." But in fact I also saw Yehiel's future grandchild and he was playing hide-and-seek alone. It can be a hard, hard thing to see the grandchildren of one's grandchildren. Even for a tzaddik.

Akiva disappeared for the entire day, and it was only late at night that Benjamin and his father found him. Akiva was singing Alkabetz's song.

"Why does Akiva always stand apart from us?" I asked Father. "Almost as though Akiva knew how to die and then come back to us reborn?" Father always answered that Akiva wanted us to search for and find him, but it didn't make sense to me. I would look as hard as I could: all the boundaries of our games were always destroyed by him, especially on that last trip before our bar mitzvah. Benjamin could remember the scene like today. If the army hadn't found him, there would have been one fewer glass factory today in Acre.

The matrix in Benjamin's hand bit deeply into his palm. He jumped with a start. "Who's coming?" Benjamin asked warily.

■ NATHANAEL WEST: Knew how to die and then come back—On Friday the thirteenth, Scott came to my house, walked over to me while I was mixing a drink for myself, and said, "Do you know how to die, Nathanael?" As he always called me Nat, I knew he was serious, but I parried nonetheless. "Friday the thirteenth? Scott, nervous? Want this martini? Do you know how to die?" He looked at me with the vacant look of a character of his entering a room and seeing an extraordinary woman at the far side of the dance floor—Daisy Fay, twenty-two, spring-in-the-world look—and said, "Know how to die," and, appropriating my martini, added, "What's more, how to come back."

And I said to Fitzgerald, "And how will you come back?" He answered simply, "*As a Yale man with a knowledge of the interior of Skull and Bones*, pots of money, and late success rather than early." I laughed and said, "Well, then, it's all settled. But it sounds like a cliché. At least make it through Brown as I did." Fitzgerald said, "Nathanael, it's got to be Yale." And I said, "Well, you'll come back a Jew." "All right," Fitzgerald agreed, "But I insist on coming back on the French Riviera." A nice reentry.

■ F. SCOTT FITZGERALD: How to die—He was sweet, Nat. And gifted. And in a way I thought that he might have a second act in his life. *Although in American lives there are almost no second acts.* He was in love. And he was married. He was haunted but not by a past, for he had invented himself amazingly. First he was Wallerstein-Weinstein and then he was Weinstein and entered Brown with the other Weinstein's grades and credits. Then he became West. Then he moved west. He simply invented and reinvented himself.

I asked him once, when he was too drunk to hide behind those endless series of masks, "Nathanael, do you know how to die?" Without hesitation he recounted his accident on the road in '37 with Leonard Fields. Of his color blindness, of his indifference to death in the past. Then I asked, "Do you know how to come back?" He answered so sweetly, "I know I'll die in a car, but I want to come right back here with her," pointing to Eileen in the next room. And then, of course, he turned his gaze on me, and I told him, "I know how to come back." I had been practicing that, as much as he had been practicing how to die.

■ ESTELLE FAULKNER: Hear—I told her right there in the Peabody Hotel—she or Joan or whatever her name was—that Bill, aged fifty-two, was going through menopause and he had all the whiskey and paper and tobacco he needed and that to throw in a twenty-year-old woman to heat up King David was too Old Testament for me. And, of course, she or Joan or whatever her name was squirmed about and wanted to know what I knew and how I knew it and what I would do, and I said nothing except that I could hear the echo of their breath.

And praise G-d she vanished with the spring.

■ VERMEER: No one appeared on the horizon—I painted over and over again. And DeJongen came to my house and said, "I will pay, pay, Johannes. Whatever you want. I will marry my son Hendrick to your eldest daughter." But I could not part with the painting. It was not simply a view of Delft. It was much, much more. Each year I would paint the figures in on the horizon. And each following year I would paint them out. "The Lord giveth and the Lord taketh away," DeJongen would say. I miss them, Johannes. Who are they? Are they your grandparents arriving from some distant shore to Delft? Why do you never speak of your mother's family? A thousand questions. As though the painting could only speak to him if there were figures on the horizon.

When I was sick, more than sick, I called my eldest daughter into my studio and showed her the painting hanging on a nail by the casement window facing toward the river and said to her in a whisper, "Never sell this but rather give it as bread to your children lest it leave our family." And she was astonished, telling me, "Father, you are mad with fever. The painting is upside down. The figures on the horizon are floating." And I quietly told her I have never been mad. We are all angels.

One could barely hear a sound. Benjamin took out his army search-light and shone it into the dusty air. Slowly, he swung the searchlight from right to left in an arch. But no one appeared on the horizon.

Why am I so jumpy? he thought. It must be my two scouts, Hayyim and Levi. But they're not due back for another hour. Only after night-fall. No sense wasting batteries.

He took off his skullcap, rested it on his pillow in the army bivouac tent, gently placed the crystal matrix specimen alongside the skullcap. He trained the searchlight directly onto the crystal matrix. A tiny bit of soil still adhered to the crystal face. Strange how the color of the crystal was intensified in the artificial light. The matrix was of white quartz, similar to the sands of Acre that his brother mined by the ton to make glass.

■ BOBBY FISCHER: Why am I so jumpy?— Spassky would ask me over and over, Why am I so jumpy? Noise. Squirming opponents. Glaring lighting. Pieces that were overpolished with shiny surfaces to blind me. Spassky would keep hammering at me. I already had a mother. One more queen was unnecessary. That's why I didn't play in the International Chess Federation for three years. I like this Benjamin. Stays up all night, preparing himself. He's not jumpy. He's waiting for their next move. His advantage is that he's one against two, so he knows he can only count on himself in the end game.

■ WILLIAM FAULKNER: Soil—"*I discovered that my own little postage stamp of native soil was worth writing about and that I would never live long enough to exhaust it and by sublimating the actual into the apocryphal I would have complete liberty to use whatever talent I might have to its maximum. I can move these people around like G-d not only in space but in time, too.*"

All I needed was paper, tobacco, food, and a little whiskey.

■ RABBI NACHMAN OF BRESLOV: Hear—Before the coming of the Messiah, the summers will be cold and the winters will be hot. Men will dress as women and women will dress as men. Rabbis will be crooks and crooks will be rabbis. That which was written in a holy language will be unreadable. That which was spoken won't be heard. But an echo of the breath of the speaker will serve as an opening.

◆ TAL'S FATHER: Father would be so happy to see—It happened just before Abraham's bar mitzvah. He chanted the Chapter Tetzeh: Exodus 28:3. He came directly to the office, after his bar mitzvah lesson with David Kimhi, Parnas of our synagogue, and asked, "Are we ordinary Cohanim or high Cohanim?" I answered, "I am an ordinary Cohen," but added jokingly that the Abendana family probably were high Cohanim. It was foolish to joke with Abraham. Everything was so literal with him. "Well, then, Father, all I need is a *migha'at* head covering and not a *mitznefet* mitre." But it didn't end there. He proudly took his skullcap off when he walked home after the Sabbath services, quoting Shabbat 118b that he was no Babylonian scholar.

I went to Kimhi and told him flatly in front of Abraham that before he was taking these classes he was normal and Kimhi was filling his head with nonsense. Kimhi took down Shabbat 156b and said, "Speaking of Shabbes, it says that we believe covering a child's head will ensure his piety and prevent him from becoming a thief." Cheeky Abraham said, "All right." He would wear it until his bar mitzvah but not afterward. An obsession of his: Ashkenazic rabbis allowed praying without a head covering, but David Halevy of Ostrog said, "As others pray bareheaded, Jews should act differently." Maimonides felt bareheadedness was lightheadedness, lightmindedness, and on and on. Finally his mother simply told him, "Father would be happy to see you wearing a skullcap." And he did, but only with a great flourish of putting it on when he saw me.

● SHABBETAI SULEIMANI, SULEIMANI'S FATHER: Long leather roller—My wife had a long leather roller on her night table in India when Suleimani was a child. My sons, Ezekiel and Suleimani, would play in our bedroom, rolling the leather cylinder between them on the floor and flipping silver rupees to get it to roll toward the other. Whoever had the roller farther from him won all the coins. Ezekiel was so awkward he always overshot the mark. But one day Suleimani hit the roller so hard that it rolled away from Ezekiel all the way under the wooden bed, bolted down to the floor, and disappeared between the cracks. They were so frightened that they picked up their rupees and fled.

Weeks later my wife asked me where her *ketubbah* and its leather roller case could have gone. And of course when we brought in our sons, Ezekiel immediately pointed at Suleimani and screamed, "He hid it under your bed, Mama!"

But a thin, intense blue line lay embedded in the matrix. In the artificial light, the blue seemed to flow directly into and from his yarmulke.

Father would be so happy to see me here this evening, wearing his Uncle Abraham's yarmulke and waiting. The news will be good—it must be good, he thought to himself.

He went to the rear of the tent and opened a long leather roller and took out a map of the nearby wadi and rivulet. The high ground stood out in the gray shading, and the tiny Aramaic words that Benjamin had inscribed seemed to dance on the page. Benjamin had seen them so often that he could feel them in the gloaming, much as his mother could do after she had become blind in Safed.

◆ RACHEL, TAL'S MOTHER: His Uncle Abraham's yarmulke—Abraham would take off his yarmulke as soon as he entered the house and look around to see if his father was home. Childish, it was. Sometimes when he knew his father was on a trip he would wear his yarmulke even when he lay down to sleep. Sometimes he wore it until dinner and sometimes only during dinner. I once told him it was like the mysterious Shabbes guest appearing without warning and leaving without anyone noticing. But it made my husband very angry.

■ HIERONYMA DE PAIVA: Leather roller—I did not have anything. Not a single Madrasi silver rupee. Not a *dhiram* of gold. Not a hectare of land. Not a carat of diamond rough. It happened so suddenly. Jacob was out in Golconda. I heard he was feverish. I heard he couldn't walk. I went to him and I could see him churning in the heat, the flies everywhere. His face had gone greenish white. His skin was caked with scales. And his eyes. Just staring at me with incomprehension.

"What shall I do?!" I shrieked at him. "You are everything to me!" I was a child again, and ten thousand miles from my family home. As he lay dying I pressed my head to his lips and heard him whisper, "Take your leather roller with your *ketubbah* in it and …" I couldn't hear the rest. He never said another word. All those flowers gaily painted in London with trumpets proclaiming a lifetime of future joy. The parchment year by year fading before me. So much promise. And I was left with nothing.

● Aryeh Judah Leib ben Jacob HaKohen, (Gutwirth family), Fisher's ancestor: Leave Safed—I could not leave Ofen, even to finish father's work, Sha'ar Ephraim, his commentary on the Mishnah. Not after my brother Hezekiah perished during the plague. Then father prayed that he be taken in my sick stead.

I could not leave Ofen until mother departed this world. Only then could I go to Jerusalem, and the air of Jerusalem, the light of Jerusalem, filled my heart and sustained my hand. So I brought Father's manuscript and sunlight and candlelight teachings to me into everlasting light. The printing of Father's words.

Then and only then could I leave Jerusalem for the Prague yeshiva. Then and only then could I return to the Holy Land to fulfill the words of my mother—her hand is ever in mine. I shall go to Safed. I can never leave Safed. Until the Messiah comes.

■ Isaac Luria: Leave Safed—"Why did my father leave Jerusalem?" asked Vital. And I could not answer him but simply pointed to Cordovero.

Cordovero could not answer but simply pointed to his desk. On top of the desk was the Or Ne'erav (the Sweet Light) and on top of the Tomer Devorah (the Palm Tree of Deborah) was the Pardes Rimmonim (the Pomegranate Orchard).

Vital and I left Cordovero, who was very weak, and walked beyond Vital's house past the garden of Abendana out into the fields on the side of the hill. We walked and walked. Vital could not talk and I could not speak. Suddenly a voice came from within me, a soft voice, the voice of my father, which asked him simply: "Hayyim Vital, have you left Safed?" Vital was so startled that he whispered, "Heaven forbid." The voice followed with, "Did Cordovero leave the Heaven of Pardes Rimmonim when he leaned over to our earth to write the Or Ne'erav?" "Heaven forbid," whispered Vital. And then we all understood that one does not leave Jerusalem. Or Safed. Or heaven.

We never should have left Safed, Benjamin thought. Of course, the schools were terrible, but there we had each other. Why did Father leave Safed? Why did we come to Jerusalem? Mother could walk by herself anywhere. Everyone knew her. And it was a Jewish city full of her friends. Change didn't bring back her eyesight. Nor did her joy at seeing me receive my degree in topological mathematics. Nor did her doctors in Shaare Zedek. At least she had those last seven years of her life in Jerusalem. Miracle? Akiva said she had visited the wrong department in the hospital. He was always so sure of everything. Afterward.

"Where are my scouts? They said seven-thirty at the very latest. My watch must have . . ." Benjamin rubbed his wrist against his clothing to remove tiny grains of sand from the watch face.

■ Monet: Eyesight—Her eyes. When I went to Le Havre as a boy of seventeen people would smile indulgently at Papa and look at me and say quietly, "But Claude, you have your mother's eyes. Claude, you must be the eyes for your father. Claude will look after you." Mother had just passed away, leaving Father and me to play chess with my life.

Boudin had opened my eyes on the beach of Le Havre. I could see his colors wherever I walked. I knew I had my mother's eyes that had looked longingly at the gloaming outside our house before she rushed in to cook Father's supper. He raved at me. "You will go into my wholesale business or into the army. You will see which is more difficult. But you will not use your mother's death to soften my decision." Either, or. I simply said, "Mother wanted the sunsets, you wanted the supper." And I walked to Casimir de la Vigne Street and signed up for seven years of military service.

■ Kafka: After—"The Messiah will come only when he is no longer necessary; he will come only on the day after his arrival."

Because time is not discreet and place is not discreet. One day one can be alive, the next dying. Brod knew I was dying and a day later knew I had not been alive, but not so Dora. Even after my death she knew I was alive. That is love. It is before you meet and after you are not together.

● Shabbetai Suleimani, Suleimani's Father: His father's eyes—Many people have perfect eyes. Some women have eyes of extraordinary beauty, eyes that glisten in one's memory after one has seen them. My eyes had a memory and could tell a story.

My son and I would sit in Jaipur, examining sapphires. I would pick up a four-carater after it had been cut and I would say to him, "This color, hold it to the light, turn it between your fingers, lift the stone up to the light. Look at the color at the edge of the stone. The color just at the star facet is the color of the fourteen-carat cushion-shaped sapphire I sold twelve years ago."

My son would listen. When he saw another stone with that shade of blue he would ask, to give me pleasure, "Is it the color of the fourteen-carat cushion-shaped sapphire you sold years ago?" And I would say, "It had less green in the blue," or, "Very close but not exactly." Gradually he learned from the diary of my eyes the secret of stones. My son could have passed this on to young Abraham Tal, for Abraham was a willing pupil, but his father wouldn't let him and neither would his brother.

■ Abraham Mordechai Leib of Ger: He had never examined such a pair of eyes—My great-grandfather, the Hidushei Harim, Isaac Meir, would say, in the name of the Kotzker Rebbe, "Man has two pockets. In one he must keep the belief that for him the world was created and without him it could not exist. And in the other pocket he should keep the opinion that he is dust and totally in need of redemption and forgiveness."

Everyone would nod their heads at this teaching except his teacher, Simha Bunam of Pshiskhe. Simha Bunam would whisper but so softly that only the Kotzker could hear: "And he who has examined such a pair of eyes as Isaac. Why would He call for . . ." The Kotzker could not answer him. And would not answer.

My great-grandfather Isaac had never examined such a pair of eyes as those of his thirteen children, and yet those thirteen children were taken from him in his lifetime.

And I, in Ger, escaping to Warsaw, the Nazis—may their memory be blotted out forever and ever—everywhere. Examining our papers, our bodies. How are we to understand the faith in pain if G-d has not examined such pairs of eyes as ours? How could we be called upon to suffer so? And yet the yeshiva wall of Sefat Emet was still standing. And the siege of Jerusalem raging. And I, dying. And I can hear the Kotzker's answer in silence. I can see and taste that G-d is good.

"When I was tested in Jerusalem at the Hillel Street Infirmary, the ophthalmologist told Mother that he had never examined such a pair of eyes. On the Kesselstein test I scored 1,408, clearer near and far vision, more discrimination of color than anyone else in the city. 'A jet pilot is what we have here,' Dr. Vital said. 'He just needs a bit more of the outdoors.' Mother lowered her voice and said, 'His father's eyes.'

"And that's when Father gave me his *kippah*. He said, 'Benjamin, this is a gift from my late Uncle Abraham Tal, who brought it here to Israel from America. Blue runs through our family like the River Sambatyon.'

"'Does it stop flowing on Shabbes?' I asked, and Mother laughed.

■ Rembrandt: Examined such a pair of eyes—I, looking into Saskia's eyes at night. By candlelight. Examining her eyelashes. Looking at the bags under her eyes. Hour after hour. She staring vacantly at me murmuring, "Rembrandt, Rembrandt," over and over. But it sounds like Rombartus, over and over. I whisper to her, "Our son is dead," and she looks at me as though I have killed him. Why isn't he here? And paint on my hands as I have painted Isaac over and over. And overpainted Isaac again and again.

"Rombartus is not here, my love, but you are, and as you gave life to him so there will be another one of us," I tell her. But I know she doesn't believe anymore. Can my Abraham's eyes look at my son's eyes again? Never. I can only examine my angel Saskia's eyes.

■ Rabbi Yitzhak Meir of Ger: Examined such a pair of eyes—The Heilige Simha of Pshiskhe would tell me:

"When a newborn child is brought to a mother, she examines the child. She holds the child close to her heart. She hugs the child. She looks again. Over and over. Day after day. Every part of the body is examined. But none more than the child's eyes. A mother's eyes and a child's eyes meet in song. 'Taste and see G-d is good, they sing' (Psalms).

"And G-d, putting Abraham to the test, said to him, 'Take your son, your favored son whom you love, and go to the land of Moriah and offer him there as a burnt offering at one of the heights that I will point out to you' (Genesis 22:2).

"Don't relinquish the love for your son in favor of your love for G-d. Don't fulfill G-d's commandment to offer him in a spirit of ruthlessness and harshness towards your favored son. Offer him as a burnt offering with all the fatherly love you can muster."

■ MARGUERITE KORNITZER: The crystal—Father called Mother and me into the library. He always held court there. Books on four walls. Two desks: "One for writing and one for dreaming," he would say. On the table were nine gem-paper envelopes, each open and containing a sapphire. One an enormous shimmering cabochon. And seven stones all faceted like soldiers standing in file at parade rest, dwarfed by the giant sapphire. In addition there was one gem paper mysteriously closed, marked *The Patiala Gem Star Sapphire*. Through the window the light shone on the stones and one could see a star shimmer on the giant sapphire's surface.

Father was quivering with excitement, as he stared at Mother and me, but strangely he was not saying anything. "Well," said Mother. Father said nothing. "Well," said Mother again, and Father clasped his hands and said, "I've cut the crystal." He took out from his wallet the drawing he had shown us five years before. Instead of eight stones I've got nine," he said. "A 126-carat extraordinary star I've sold to Erdheim along with eight cut stones. And I've recovered all my costs." "I thought you were in this trade to make a profit, not just to show how much you know," said Mother, laughing. "Oh, I've made a fortune here," and he opened the last stone paper.

There was the most beautiful blue I had ever seen. A virtual match to the slightly smaller star but just a nuance more perfect. More pure, more heavenly, more blue. And Father handed the stone to me and said, "Here's our 204-carat fortune, purchased and paid for. It comes from the Maharaja of Patiala. He wore it in a fabulous belt buckle. I've had it recut to a perfect—if I dare use the phrase—204-carat star sapphire. Now that I own this fabulous Burma gem and have recut it, I can part with the rest. It always pays to settle your bills on time. I just had to have the Patiala Blue."

■ MRS. ROSE KORNITZER: The crystal—At first it was the crystal. For years during the Depression, Louis would come home, set down his hat on the stand by the door, make his way to the kitchen, smile at me and slump into his library chair, and sip absentmindedly the cinnamon tea I brewed for him and had poured when I saw him cross the park into our house. Marguerite and I would wait patiently as he unfolded the latest news flash about the crystal. It was from Burma. It was 656 carats in the rough. Morgan would see Louis. Morgan was thinking about the purchase. Morgan wouldn't see Louis. Feldheimer didn't have the money to buy him out but wanted to and couldn't. But would as soon as the Depression ended.

By 1936, Father had owned the rough for more than five years. And suddenly one day (I remember it as now) he turned to us and said, "I've got it. Bring me paper." And he sketched hurriedly on a piece of thin rice paper the shape of the crystal. From three angles: side, top, and bottom. And put his finger in his tea and moved his index finger across the top, moistening the side view. And then on the bottom. And then with his finger drew six other little circles. And he literally ran out the library, out of the house, shouting, "I'll be back! I solved it! I'll show Feldheimer who's cracked!" And when he returned, I asked him: "And when will you sell it, dear Louis?" "Only when," Louis answered coquettishly. "Only when?" I retorted. "Only when I find another as—or more—beautiful."

"Coincidence how these blues compare—they virtually match." Benjamin picked up the crystal, took out a pocket knife, and gently tapped the crystal on one of the obverse angles. A thin sliver of blue, almost a snowflake, rested in his hand.

Holding the sliver between his index finger and thumb, Benjamin took it outside into the twilight. He held the sliver close to his retina and peered through. The entire world became a darkened blue vault. The distant hills looked like a sleeping woman turned away from him—Hagar at night, with her child, Ishmael, silhouetted against the opening of the tent.

"I should have brought Ariel or 'little miracle' Rachel to visit me here. Then I could have stayed another few days." Suddenly, unmistakably, Benjamin heard the faint sound of footsteps cracking dry earth and pebbles in the distance.

■ LOUIS KORNITZER, 1930: The crystal—It was a huge sapphire rough perched on the table in Feldheimer's office. The old man was up to his boyhood tricks and politely excused himself to go to the men's room. "I'll be right back, Prince Louis," he chortled. I could see tiny pencil marks on the white pad just underneath the sapphire crystal's edge. I hovered over the specimen, trying to look at it, resisting with every fiber the desire to pick it up. What was I supposed to do, Feldheimer being indirect .to the end? The blue was extraordinary. But there was a flaw running directly through the base two-thirds of the way along the crystal's edge. After about two minutes, Feldheimer suddenly appeared directly in back of me but I had already retreated and was slouched in my chair looking for all the world as though asleep by the angel's pond in the park across the street.

"Sapphires don't interest the prince any longer?" asked Feldheimer dryly, noticing the gemstone hadn't been moved. "Listen, Jacob, I can see the flaw running through the sapphire crystal from here." "Don't be a fool, Kornitzer. I can see your perspiration all over the crystal as you studied it when I left the room." "And I can see your pencil guide marks to check if I moved the uncut crystal," I responded.

"Let's cut to the chase, Louis," said Feldheimer, lifting and handing the sapphire crystal to me. "This is the greatest blue Burma uncut sapphire crystal in the world. I want to buy it with you and cut it into the most miraculous sapphire ever known." Then he lifted the crystal out of my hand and said, "It will cost twenty-five thousand." "Twenty-five thousand dollars!" I gasped. And Feldheimer said, "No. Twenty-five thousand English pounds." I got up and walked toward the door and at the transom turned and said, "The crystal is cracked and you're cracked." Feldheimer laughed and said, "I guess it's a deal."

■ FELIX ERDHEIM: The crystal—He was no fool, Kornitzer. But he was lazy. Or more precisely, he was given to intrigue. Or even more precisely, he was a bit too European for my taste. Indirect to a fault. They were a pair, Kornitzer and Feldheimer. Whose goods were whose, I could never figure out. When Kornitzer would bring stones to me they would be in Feldheimer's white ratty diamond papers. Feldheimer would show me the light blue immaculately starched Kornitzer gem papers with his code still on the outside flap.

Then one day in 1936, it was Louis who entered my house and simply, with the humility and delicacy of a flower seller in a Montmartre café, placed the most glorious blue 330-carat star sapphire before me, saying, "Here it is. Now you are a king." I examined the splash of blue from place to place in my office. From window to window. I was faint. I couldn't see in front of me. I had never seen such purity of blue in any star. After an hour I said, "So you've finally cut your crystal." And Louis said nothing. How was I to imagine he had found a star sapphire even more beautiful?

■ THE SANZER REBBE: Coming—*I told my son, Yehezkel, that a Rebbe who doesn't know when a disciple is leaving home to see him, and the purpose of his coming and his needs, should not accept kvitlach.* Yehezkel was in front of me, silent. I waited and waited. Finally I asked, "Do you know this?" I knew he did. But I, as a father, could not treat my son as a disciple. So I could not let him believe I knew beyond all certainty what he was thinking. But it was odd how long Yehezkel was silent. He was always so quick to answer.

■ YITZHAK BUNAM ZUCKER: Coming—What could I tell my father, Yehezkel Shraga? It was not easy for me to tell him a Hasidic story. For I was no Rebbe and he was no Hasid. But he was one who was proud of knowing the future, of who was coming to see him and of what they would say. It was uncanny how often the phone would ring and he would say, "It's Joe Hostyk," and it would be. Father explained effortlessly. "Joe came home late. It's the height of his business season. He ate quickly. It's his custom. And now he's calling to ask me and your mother to go for a walk."

But Father was silent for a reason. And that is because he couldn't understand how the Sanzer Rebbe asked his son, "Do you know this?" How could he know what his disciples knew and not be sure of what his son knew? And my father was silent because he knew that I knew that he wondered also.

"Hayyim," shouted Benjamin. "Is that you?"

"Yes, we're coming," two lieutenants' voices returned simultaneously.

They must still be ten minutes away, he guessed.

Benjamin carefully placed the crystal sliver in a white folded gem paper that he had gotten in Tel Aviv and nestled the gem packet in his army jacket pocket. "All they dream of is stones," Benjamin mused.

"Come to me, first," Levi had told him. "We can market these stones together. I'll do the selling. We'll make a fortune, not just a professor's fortune. You come from a jewelry family. You shouldn't be an academic. We'll work something out. I'm not telling you to do something illegal. The other officers will botch it up. It will take years for the army to decide what to do with this treasure. In the meantime you can have more children. Go to America. Just come with me first.

■ YEHEZKEL SHRAGA, THE SHINYEVER REBBE: Coming—My father, may his memory be always a blessing, told me that any Rebbe who doesn't know the purpose of a disciple's coming, and when he is leaving home to go see him, should not accept *kvitlach*. My father looked at me for a long time and asked me, "Do you know this?" This was not his custom, for he was quick to speak and quick to answer.

I waited for a long time—no bonds are as deep as silence—and then I answered, "Father, I know this." For my father wanted to show that he was different to me than to his Hasidim. I was his son. He wanted to show me he was not certain he knew my thoughts but loved me and was close to me as a father. But what father does not fear that a child does not feel the love deeply enough? That is why he paused. I paused, too, for what son does not fear that he has not been able to return love to his father.

■ YEHEZKEL SHRAGA ZUCKER (1905–1982): We're coming—I heard from my son, Yitzhak Bunam, a story: The grandfather of the Klausenburger Rebbe, the Sanzer Rebbe, said, "A Rebbe that doesn't know the time a disciple is leaving his home to go to see him, and doesn't know the purpose of his coming and his needs, should not accept a *kvittel*." He said this in front of his son, the Shinyever Rebbe, and he asked his son this question: "Do you know this?" And his son the Shinyever Rebbe said, "Father, I know this."

When my son told me this story, I said nothing. After a long time my son said, "Father, the Shinyever was the Rebbe you are named after." And I said, "This I know. As for the story, I have not heard it before but this I do know. If you have someone close to you, you know how they think, when they go to sleep, and when they wake up. You know when they go to work and when they leave. This doesn't surprise me. I'm sure the Shinyever's father could do it. But I was silent for a different reason."

■ MENACHEM MENDEL SCHNEERSON: Every flower—My father would walk with me when I was a young boy in the fields outside of Lubavitch: long walks through the mountains, all day. Often he didn't speak for hours. But he sang softly while we walked. Before a new flower he would stop and say the Psalm: *See*—and then he would walk farther and continue—*and taste*—and then walk farther and recite that *G-d is good*. I must have been five years old. Every flower was my study partner. After he passed away and I was in Lithuania, and still later in Paris, and then at 770 Eastern Parkway, I could hear his *niggunim*. I could smell the flowers. I could taste the blessing through his songs of prayer. I was in flowering mountains my whole life.

■ MORIKA ABENDANA, VERMEER'S MODEL: Mad—I told Johannes, "You are mad." And, laughing, he answered, "Mad for you, Morika." And I said, "No. Mad, period. You never go out. You paint in one room upstairs. Your children call. You paint and then paint and then over-paint and overpaint again. And you have painted my portrait over and over again and yet, yet again, month after month, for almost a year."

He just looked at me and asked, "And what would I see if I left this room?" I told him of the dew on the pale pink poppies I had seen that morning in the town square. He answered with shock: "I should cross into the town square? And then think of other town squares where my grandfather and grandmother were carried, wailing, with their cousins burning before crowds of curious blue-blooded aristocrats of España. I should go out and show my face? Who knows what rumors fly and where? No, thank you. As for dew, here is a droplet on your lip. Come and see it. Come and touch it on the canvas."

I walked over to Johannes and fixed my eyes on his and whispered, "There is dew all over me." He reached his hand into my cloak of silk and ran it down my back, licking the moisture on the side of my neck and I, moaning, as he ran his tongue all over me. Mad, mad, it is I who is mad for you, Johannes.

"But above all, don't talk to anyone in the Bourse about your find," Levi said.

My father once told me that gems made his Uncle Abraham mad, Benjamin thought. His last days were spent in that stiflingly hot synagogue in Safed. He died in my father's arms. I don't think Great-Uncle Abraham weighed more than one hundred twenty pounds. But how could Father have carried his uncle all the way down the hill to Rosh Pinah Hospital? Father was weak even then. And my father's uncle raving about the family and the color of the *bimah* and the holy Ari. They both should have been rabbis, my great uncle and my father; they were spiritual brothers—even more, mystical twins. Father would have been a remarkable teacher. All those walks together. He and I making our voyage books— with every flower pressed and labeled—and our bird sighting diaries and star maps.

■ MANSUR, COURT PAINTER TO JAHANGHIR, c. 1605: Every flower pressed and labeled— At first we would walk in Kashmir together, the shadow of G-d on earth: the emperor Jahanghir and I. We started in the morning at sunrise; sometimes her highness, Nur Jahan, would accompany us as far as the lake, and then we two would continue on. Jahanghir would point at a flower. I would scamper and get it for him and he, sitting on the ground, would look at it for a long time. Then he would hold it up in his hand for what seemed only an instant and I would hurriedly sketch the flower as it wilted. Just as the shadow of G-d fleetingly passed across the Paradise on earth that is Kashmir, Jahanghir would press the flower between two pages of a book I had brought with me, write his name on the page, and hand me the book. What was so beautiful and alive had been chosen, labeled by him, and now had passed into the next world. And then Jahanghir would grow weary, and we would go back to the encampment and he would eat and sleep. All night I would stay up in a fever of painting with my one-haired brush so that when he awoke the next morning and immediately summoned me, the drawing was ready. Sometimes it displeased him and he would scream like a child, "This is not my flower at all!" and rip up my work and stomp on it. Sometimes he would call Nur Jahan in and squeal, "Look what I have chosen and created! Is not Mansur the Nadir-al-Dor, the wonder of the age?"

■ REMBRANDT: Gems made . . . mad—Of course they made him mad. Did not painting make me mad? And not just painting itself. Not just searching for a patron and waiting for the portrait sitter. And haggling over the payment before I started. And stretching the canvas. And hoping for payment. Now on a far deeper level—getting older. When Hendryx brought me those curious Indian miniatures and asked me if I wanted them, I was a fool to blurt out, "They make me mad. I'll give you anything!" And then to look at them, how they were made. I would have walked to the Indies if I had been younger. But Saskia wouldn't let me. Mad I was, not only about my painting but made mad by others' painting, gems in other places and in other times.

■ Rabbi Leib, son of Sarah the Wandering Tzaddik: Singing—My great friend Rabbi Pinchas of Korets would always say: "When a man is singing and cannot lift his voice and another comes and sings with him, another who can lift his voice, then the first voice will be able to lift his voice too. That is the secret of the bond between spirit and spirit, friend and friend."

I worked and taught all over the world, in secret. And Pinchas would not leave his town, for he felt that only there was he destined to teach. And when my voice began to falter each year, when I felt I could not sing anymore, I would go to Korets and suddenly my voice would soar on the wings of Pinchas's singing.

■ Shlomo Carlebach: Singing—It was always singing. And dreams of singing. And thoughts of songs. The holy Lubavitcher said simply, "Your song will be my *shaliach*," and I went forth. There was not a country I did not visit. No *yidden* who didn't clap. But what voice needs no rest? And whose voice does not grow hoarse? And how many times can one go to Rhodes to rest? Suddenly no new songs came to me, and I went to the holy Amshinover and, through my tears, I told him the singing continues but the heart of my singing, my composing, has stopped. And the Amshinover sadly put his face in front of mine and said, "It is time to put everything in order."

All the time Father was holding my hand. Father would have loved my maps of the wadi. I still use his code to mark the probable site. Funny, neither Hayyim nor Levi has ever deciphered it. They can dig but their eyes are closed, Benjamin mused.

"Benjamin!" shouted Hayyim. "Here I am! Levi found it!"

The two men appeared at the tent door, exhausted, their faces caked with camouflage makeup. Levi, the stockier of the two, held out his closed fist to Benjamin. "Right where you told us to look, Rabenu," he exclaimed, more singing than speaking.

■ Pinchas Ehrenberg: Levi found it—Seven years after the Holocaust I returned to Poland, wandering, searching, and what did I find? Nothing. No relatives, not a trace of them. And then one day in Breslov, a Polish Jew brought a package of papers and a letter saying:

"To him into whose hands this manuscript may fall: These papers contain one volume of commentaries by the illustrious Rabbi Pinchas of Koretz, one of the disciples of the Baal Shem Tov. They are the only originals left. They contain a vast treasure of priceless holy thoughts and insights. Since I left my home three years ago, a deportee driven from place to place, I have carried these papers in my valise, never abandoning them until now. Now that the 'rage of the oppressor' has overtaken me, and my dear wife and son and daughter have been stolen from me, may it be the will of our Father in Heaven that I will see them again. And we the ones who remain know the life we face is precarious and we do not know what the day will bring. Therefore I decided to give these manuscripts which are so dear to me to one of my non-Jewish acquaintances who will hide them until G-d will return the captives from among His people. I ask him into whose hands this letter will fall to be aware that Heaven bestowed on you this holy treasure in order that you bring to light the teachings of the saintly Rabbi Pinchas of Koretz. My request is that you include also my own commentaries, so that they can be an everlasting memorial for me. I praise and thank G-d for enabling me to be a commentary on a commentary of His holy name."

■ Rabbi Pinchas Shapiro of Korets, Sefer Imrei Pinchas: Singing—"Ribbono Shel Olam [Master of the Universe], if only I could sing I would not allow you to remain in the Heaven above. I would sing and sing and keep singing until you have no choice but to come and dwell with us."

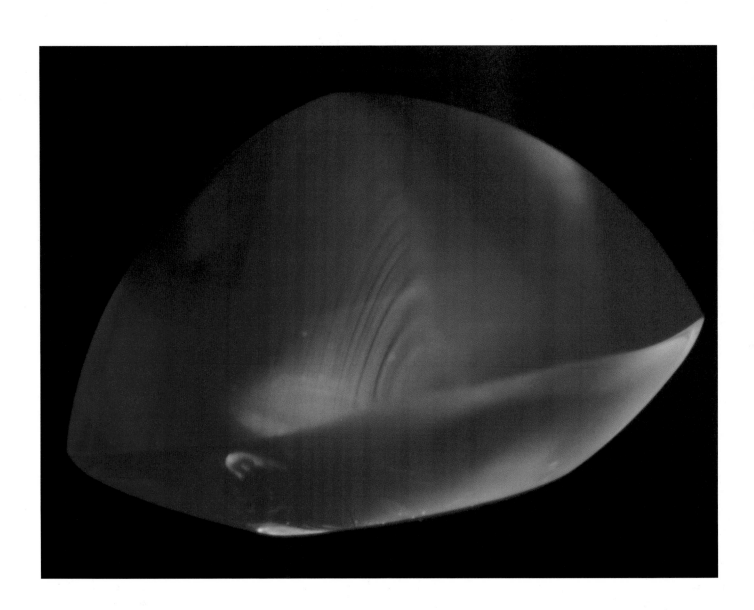

■ GEORGE C. WILLIAMSON: Comparison—Mr. Morgan wanted eight sumptuous catalogs as he put it—"World-class studies of my collections of art objects." I asked what the purpose of the catalogs was and he answered simply, "If anything happens to the originals, if they should ever be dispersed, students can work from the exact replicas, faithful comparisons, as though they had the originals in front of them."

"And how many copies would be printed, Mr. Morgan?" I asked. He answered, "Oh, not more than twenty each of the deluxe version, I should say, Williamson." "And who would you give them to, sir?" I asked. "Oh, the King of England. The President. A few friends." Morgan paused. "And myself. I should like one by my bedside as nighttime reading."

And so it was that Mr. Morgan on his deathbed had as his last nighttime tale, the extraordinary gilt-and-silver-catalog of Mr. Morgan's watches.

■ MAX BROD: An extraordinary strength— *"An extraordinary strength emanated from Franz, the likes of which I have not found even in encounters with very important, famous men."*

Franz would look, peer, and follow my every move. He knew we all have our secrets, some small ones, some big ones. And we all hold our secrets in tightly clenched fists so that others will not see. But of course, we flaunt them, secretly hoping they will be revealed. Franz would look at my secret and quickly, all in one motion, pry it from my hand. How gently he would examine it, how delicately he would treat it.

With an extraordinary strength Benjamin quickly pried open Levi's hand to reveal a small, perfectly formed, double pyramid crystal. It was a much darker midnight blue than the crystal in matrix, which appeared almost grayish by comparison.

"Look at this color! I can't believe my eyes." Benjamin marveled to himself. He rushed inside the tent and flashed his light on both the new crystal and the matrix. "Look how the color of the matrix bleeds slightly, whereas this crystal holds its color."

Levi, the younger of the two men, said, "Isn't the termination perfect? The crystal planes are in absolutely flawless symmetry!"

Benjamin examined the crystal under a jeweler's loupe and nodded his head vigorously. "There is not one single imperfect or water-worn plane. We've found a crystal directly from the source—not an alluvial stone!"

■ BAAL SHEM TOV: Eyes—*"Man was given two eyes. One eye to see his own faults and vices, and the other eye to see the virtues in others."*

◆ RACHEL, TAL'S MOTHER: Benjamin quickly pried open Levi's hand—How like my dear Abraham at six. He would return home, simply fly through the door, barely opening it. In an instant he was in my arms and I already had his surprise. In one hand a *hopje*, in another equally tightly closed fist, nothing. He never failed to guess which fist held the gift. He pried open my fingers and in one motion opened the thin wrapping, put it into his mouth, and told me, "Mother dearest, you'll never believe what happened." He talked without stopping for a breath until he had covered every detail, every slight, every triumph, every failure of his school day.

Once, years later, I asked how in all those years did he never pry open the empty fist. He simply said, "It was not a *hopje* you had in your closed fist, Mother, it was love."

■ MODIGLIANI: Eyes—Poor Momo, poor Momo, each night Jeanne Hébuterne would whimper. I would awake at any hour, hearing the same words over and over: my name an incantation. I would hold her head in my palms and wrap the folds of her ears in my mouth. I would encircle her and spin her around and around and even when awake she would repeat my name like a dream. Her dream was always the same: Her poor dead Momo stretched out on a canvas, my hands pressed against my legs, frozen. My eyes closed, my mouth, in astonishment. And quiet beyond sound. Quiet beyond movement. Quiet still frozen, lifeless, and suddenly Jeanne leaps on my body screaming through the body of Modigliani, through the canvas, through the catafalque, falling endlessly into blue space.

How could I reassure her? I tried, but she would not be comforted. I caressed her, but she would not be stilled. I painted her with eyes closed, but she continued to see.

■ Marcel Proust: Let me be alone for a while—"*Soon after, our housekeeper came to tell me Mama and Papa were only on the salad course and that the butler had not been able to deliver the letter but that as soon as the finger bowls were passed around, he would slip it to Mama.*"

■ Hayyim Vital: Section seven, section seven—My master, Isaac Luria, walked slowly an hour before the Sabbath in Safed and revealed to me that on the seventh day the Holy One rested and the seventh of the lower Sephiroth then descended on that day to Safed. And the seventh Sephirah comes as the Shekinah—the Sabbath queen—to us. "Look, Hayyim, you can see her garment sway in the trees as she makes her way toward the synagogue," the Ari would marvel.

I could feel a breeze on my face as the Shekinah passed us, ascending the sharp rise of the hill just between the row of olive trees by the walls of Cordovero's house. My master, Isaac Luria, was the first one into the synagogue, his eyes strangely brilliant as though something not of this world were reflected in them. I would lower my eyes because in those days I could not face the pure light. Seven times purified are the pure words of the holy name, purified as silver (Psalm 12). Seven times blessed was I to hear my master's teachings.

"We didn't find it. They're your maps, Benjamin. You found it," replied Levi generously.

Levi and Hayyim sat down on the cot inside Benjamin's tent.

"Hayyim," said Benjamin, "Wire Jerusalem. This is an order."

Hayyim looked reluctantly at Benjamin, took out an army scrambler set, and dialed an eight-digit number. "Section seven, section seven," said Hayyim. "Do you read me? Do you read? Benjamin found one tallis. Repeat. Found one tallis. Exactly where he told us it would be. Over and out."

"Let me be alone for a while," said Benjamin. As soon as the men left, Benjamin reached into his pocket and pulled out an old leather cushion box. Opening it up, he slowly pulled out a Venetian Jewish wedding ring. His hand began to tremble. The blue of the roof matched the blue of the crystal precisely. The color jumped electrically from the hinged roof of the ring to the crystal, forming a solid rainbow of color.

■ Talmud: Jerusalem—"*Ten measures of beauty were given the world. Nine were taken by Jerusalem. And one by all the rest.*"

■ Rabbi Nachman of Breslov: Repeat—*G-d never repeats Himself.*

Each human is a new creation. Each flower is different from every other flower in the universe.

■ Van Gogh to his mother, July 1890, Anvers-sur-Oise: Let me be alone for a while—"*I myself am quite absorbed in the immense plain with wheatfields against the hills, boundless as a sea, delicate yellow, delicate soft green, the delicate violet of a dug-up and weeded piece of soil chequered at regular intervals with the green of flowering potato plants, everything under a sky of delicate blue, white, pink, violet tones. I am in a mood of almost too much calmness.*"

I must be alone for a while, I think. I'd like to reflect on my end. I'd like my canvas to reflect all the colors that drip through my head while I sleep. The blues and the yellows that course through my body. The pinks and the violets that wash down through my insides and clot my feet while I walk. I must be alone, Mother, and not just for a while.

Jewish wedding ring, Venice, c. 1600.

◆ TAL'S FATHER: And then he understood—Abraham asked me when he was three the simplest of questions: Did I see G-d? Did I feel G-d? Did I sense G-d? Did I hear G-d? He looked at me and fixed his gaze on me, holding my hand tightly in his and not looking away. Not for an instant could I avoid his gaze. At first I was so shocked I could not even tell my dearest Rachel. What can one say to such a small boy with such large questions? I wouldn't answer. I told him simply, "*In the beginning . . . I am the Lord thy G-d.*" I quoted and quoted, and read and read from the Bible, and each story he would listen to and then return to me: Father, did you ever touch G-d? And I would speak of Moses. Of David. Of Jeremiah.

Slowly, over the years, the questions stopped. In synagogue, in school, and on the street when we walked he would talk of everything but G-d. For he understood that I could not explain what I understood. But my dear Rachel told me on my last Rosh Hashanah eve, "Abraham has asked me to tell you that he now knows the answer to his boyhood questions and you should not worry even about a blade of grass perishing for so soon would you understand."

Blessed is the father who is taught by a child the wisdom he cannot teach his child. According to our holy Talmud, "Every blade of grass has its angel that bends over it and whispers, 'Grow, grow.'"

■ BOB DYLAN: Angel—
Sara, Sara
Sweet Virgin Angel, sweet love of my life
Sara, Sara
Radiant jewel, mystical wife.

You see it twice, if you're lucky, in a lifetime. And when you see it the first time it is so ordinary that you simply put it aside and go back to what you were doing: Drinking coffee. Talking. Walking. Sometimes you see it in a dream and forget it by midmorning. And then you sense something is missing but glide by it. And you search but you can't ask anybody because only you saw it, only you felt it. Then after many years it comes back to you. It's not, at least for me, an overwhelmingly loud sound. And it's not a whisper that you have to strain to hear. It's a very simple, totally peaceful, unforgettably sweet understanding. When you catch it the second time, your first vision comes back, and not only is your life forever changed, every love, every sight, every song is forever altered.

He closed his eyes and felt transported, soaring as an angel above Beersheba, beyond the Mount of Olives, beyond Tiberius to Safed. Here was the *bimah* of the Ari's synagogue and the exact shade of blue matching his father's tallis. The tallis his father had received years before from his great-uncle, Abraham Tal.

Then the thunderclap came. There was no sound, only a wide beam of lightning. And not a white beam but a long, intense blue flash crossing the sky. A pure blue shaft of color surrounded his head with light, a dense blue that weighed upon each centimeter of his flesh, a blue light that permeated his entire frame. Benjamin suddenly felt no demarcation from the outside atmosphere and his interior self. Benjamin and the blue world were one. And then he understood that, indeed, there was, through all the centuries, above and below, One and only One.

Benjamin couldn't speak. He could not move. Finally, removing the shoes from his feet, he called out, "Hayyim, Levi. It's time to pray."

"Is it night already?" Levi asked. And Benjamin softly intoned:

■ RABBI NATHAN, DISCIPLE OF RABBI NACHMAN OF BRESLOV: One and only One—The disciples entered the room and found Rabbi Nachman holding a sheet of paper. On the sheet was his writing. He turned to them.

"'*Numerous are the teachings of this page and numerous are the worlds that are nourished by its smoke.*' He held the sheet of paper against the flame of the candle."

And not only this page was burnt but also my master, Rabbi Nachman's, entire book of mysteries that he ordered burnt in Lemberg in 1805. This was the book, Rabbi Nachman explained to Rabbi Simeon, that had caused the death of his wife and of his son and would kill Rabbi Nachman unless it was burnt. And Rabbi Simeon burnt that book of mysteries. It is not on this earth any longer.

And what is left? Another of Rabbi Nachman's books—a secret of secrets, *nistar denistar*. A secret that no one on earth can read. There is one and only one book and when the Messiah will come he will write a commentary. And then we shall finally and truly understand.

■ ELIHU YALE: Closed his eyes and felt transported—When I came to Hieronyma's room that afternoon in July 1682, two vessels, the *Abigail* and the good ship *Discovery*, both loaded with calico cloth and 1,234 *ratis* of Star Diamonds, were believed lost west of the Cape of Good Hope. Hieronyma wanted a loan from me to enable her to return to her family in England.

I had mounted the narrow staircase to the top floor of 8 King's Street, across from the trader Abendana's apartments, and she opened the door herself to her rooms. Not a servant in the house. Madrasi daylight streamed into the house's windows, and she said, My lord, please sit in this chair. The climb must be wearying to you. But I had already sunk into the peculiar lion-headed chair of blue velvet that she later told me came from Portugal.

She prattled on and on. She didn't want to go to England, she wanted to go to her family. I said, "But your family is in England." She countered, "Their house is in England but not them." I was thinking about my lost fortune on the *Abigail* and the *Discovery* both and could barely see and certainly could not breathe. I asked her politely, "I thought a Jewish wife was not allowed to be in a room alone with another man." (Salvador had told me that.) And she answered, "I am now alone, my lord."

I could barely hear her voice and suddenly I felt her hand on my eyes, closing them. I was transported beyond myself, beyond my one wife, my three children, beyond diamond Golconda, India, beyond my years of work balancing the books of the East Indies Company, beyond my past in Wales, and beyond even the future. I was totally joined to her for that moment and was never alone apart from her for an instant, even after she left me.

◆ RACHEL, TAL'S MOTHER: Evening Shema—My child's child's child. My children's children's children. My blessed Father, holding my hand. *Do not be afraid of the dark. Say your prayers and I will stand by your bedside.* He did. And I slept. As well then as ever. And when he left us I felt him still. But sleepless for years. And now Benjamin. And the evening Shema. Will he sleep? Will he love and laugh through it all? Worrying how he will continue. And sons like big men. And women's eyes green, blue, sparkling even more when old at the music of it all.

■ VERMEER: Blue—Blue is a color I can remember from when I was three years old. We had visited my grandmother's house in The Hague. The kitchen faced the green garden by the river. I was thirsty. I came into the kitchen in the middle of the night. But it was not the middle of the night. It was morning. Grandmother was very old and the milk she had lovingly ladled out for me in the gold beaker was on the floor. It was blue. "It is blue, your blue," she said and gathered me into her apron and told me, "In the light of The Hague everything looks blue in the morning, my little darling."

And yet it is still night for me and the garden outside the window is green, very green inside my mind. I am quivering and there is a diamond of liquid on the edge of her lip and my brush reaches across the years to touch her and her greenness envelops me and flows onto the canvas of my soul in a river of blue.

■ RABBI AKIVA EIGER: From when—From when, from where do we know? my students would ask me. All my life a question would no sooner be asked than I would open the relevant tractate of the Talmud and point to the page and let my pupils see the answer themselves. For far better than quoting by heart was the showing of the passage itself. We are all here for so few turnings of the pages.

As I got older I always wondered, What if I cannot remember the exact page of the Talmud? What if, G-d forbid, my mind weakens? But thank the Holy Name that did not happen, even though my strength weakened and weakened. Still I could always open the tractate to the right page. I could open to just the right citation. Praise be to the Hand that has guided me.

"'From when do we recite the evening Shema?' And the Riziner Rebbe said, 'Read not from when but from the Awe of the Name. But the rabbis teach, from that time when we cannot tell green from blue.'"

■ CHIEF SEATTLE: We cannot tell green from blue—"Day and night cannot dwell together. The red man has fled the approach of the white man as the night must flee before the morning sun. It matters little where we pass the remainder of our days. Every part of this soil is sacred in the estimation of my people. Every hillside, every green valley, every blue sky, hallowed by some sad or happy event in days long vanished.

"And when the last red man shall have perished and the memory of my tribe shall become a myth among the white man, these shores will swarm with the invisible dead of my tribe.

"In all the earth there is no place dedicated to solitude. At night when the streets of your cities and villages are silent and you think them deserted, they will throng with the returning hosts that once filled them and still love this beautiful land. The white man will never be alone. Let him be just and deal kindly with my people. For the dead are not powerless. Dead, did I say? There is no death. Only a change of worlds."

■ KAFKA: Read not from when but from the Awe of the Name. But the rabbis teach—All my life, before and since, I read and read. And I wrote and wrote. And Brod swore that he would take my blue books and burn them on my gravesite. For who would be my pupil? Who would be my student? And as I was lowered into my grave, feather light, the Belzer's words of awe were quoted by Brod and I received yet one more teaching. And now my words are read and my name is invoked and I am a teacher. One writes but others edit and yet others rewrite.

● RACHEL, TAL'S GIRLFRIEND: When— When. When. When, I would ask Abraham. When will we wed? When will we start? When will we build? When will we have? And he spoke of the Awe of the Name. And now. I know that *when* is not a simple droplet of light or an instant of time but a fusion of a river flowing so swiftly that we cannot see its movement, yet we feel it, we see it, we can touch it, and *when* is recurring again as it didn't before and my Tal is not my Tal and yet I am again and there is no waiting this time.

NOTES

Guide to the Reader
First quote: James Joyce, *Finnegan's Wake* (New York: Viking Press, 1976), p. 3. Copyright © 1939 by James Joyce; © renewed 1967 by Giorgio Joyce and Lucia Joyce. Used by permission of Viking Penguin, a division of Penguin Putnam, Inc.

Second quote: F. Scott Fitzgerald, *The Great Gatsby* (New York: Scribner, 1992), p. 152.

CHAPTER 1

Page 1
Franz Kafka: For eleven years (1896–1907), Kafka's room in his family apartment on Zeltnergasse fronted directly onto the interior of Tyn Cathedral. He was able to see Prague parishioners pray and receive the Host. See Max Brod, *Franz Kafka: A Biography* (New York: Schocken Books, 1975), p. 8; Frederick Karl, *Franz Kafka: Representative Man* (New York: Ticknor & Fields, 1991), p. 205.

Shema (Yisroel): Literally, "Hear (O Israel)." The central prayer in the Jewish liturgy, it is to be recited daily, in the morning and the evening ("Teach them thoroughly to your children and speak of them while you sit in your home, while you walk on the way, when you retire and when you arise"). The prayer proclaims the absolute oneness of G-d as well as Israel's love of G-d.

Bloom's Day: The evening of June 16, 1904, when James Joyce and Nora Barnacle went for a walk, the day that Nora made Joyce "a man." Joyce set the entire action of *Ulysses* on that date, and it has been known ever after in the Joycean calendar as "Bloomsday," after the central characters in the novel, Leopold and Molly Bloom.

James Joyce: Dimber wapping dell. *Ulysses* (New York: Random House, 1961), p. 47. Copyright © James Joyce Estate.

Page 3
Rashi (1040–1105): An acronym for Rabbi Solomon (Shelomoh) ben Isaac, a great commentator on the Bible and the Talmud. His commentaries combine a search for the plain meaning of the text with an often allegorical oral tradition of the Torah. In the modern printed version of the Talmud, Rashi's commentary appears on the upper right-hand corner of the text. His three learned daughters, Jochebed, Miriam, and Rachel, all married Torah scholars. His grandchildren and descendants included Jacob Tam (1096–1171). Esra Shereshevsky, *Rashi: The Man and His World* (New York: Sepher-Hermon Press, 1982), p. 22.

Troyes: Rashi's birthplace, the capital city of the Champagne district of France. Rashi received his early education there but later moved to *yeshivot* in Mainz and Worms, Germany.

Maimonides (1135–1204): Rabbi Moses ben Maimon, known by the acronym Rambam, was one of the greatest rabbinic authorities. He was a codifier of the Torah and a philosopher. For eight years he was supported by his brother David, a precious stones dealer. After David's drowning in the Indian Ocean, Maimonides started to practice as a doctor, rather than being solely a scholar. "Better to earn a drachma as a weaver or tailor or carpenter than to be dependent on the license of the exilarch to accept a position as rabbi," he wrote. Maimonides became the personal physician to the Sultan in Al-Qahirah (Cairo). His *Guide to the Perplexed* serves as a philosophical guide to Judaism and his Mishnah Torah as an explanation of the laws of Judaism. Both have been studied for the past eight centuries. *Encyclopedia Judaica*, vol. 11. (New York: Macmillan Publishing Company, 1971), p. 762.

Page 5
Dora Dymant: Dora Dymant was Franz Kafka's last great love. A woman of twenty-one, she shared Kafka's last year of life, inspiring him, living with him in Berlin, planning to emigrate to Palestine with him, and, finally, nursing him lovingly in his final months. At his funeral, distraught, she attempted to leap into his grave. Frederick Karl, *Franz Kafka, Representative Man*, pp. 722–727.

Kadosh: To be holy, in Judaism. That which is holy is that which should be set apart (*kadesh* = to set apart, distinguish). "You shall be holy, for I the Lord your G-d am holy" (Leviticus 19:2). The Sabbath should be kept holy, set apart from the rest of the week. After marriage, the act of *kiddushin*—making holy—sets aside husband and wife from all others.

Kvittel: Literally, a "piece of paper" or a "note," on which a follower of a Hasidic rabbi would write his question or problem for the Rabbi. Accompanying the *kvittel* would be a monetary contribution for the rabbi's court called *pidyon nefesh*, or "redemption of the soul." The Gabbai, assistant to the Rabbi, would often hand the *kvittel* to the Rabbi. *Kvitlach* dealt with questions of health, religion, marriage, business—every area of human concern.

Facing east: When Jews pray in the Diaspora (outside the holy land of Israel), they are enjoined in the Talmud to pray in the direction of Israel. In Europe this means facing east; when in Israel, Jews pray toward Jerusalem; when in Jerusalem, Jews pray in the direction of the Temple Mount. In the early centuries of Islam, Muslims too prayed in the direction of Jerusalem. A prayer niche, called Qibla, guided the worshiper. Subsequently, the Qiblated direction was changed toward Mecca.

Page 7
Milena: A young writer named Milena Jesenska, born in 1896, non-Jewish, wrote Kafka asking to translate his German writings into Czech. A descendant of an aristocratic Czech family, she had married a Jew, Ernst Polak. More than any of his other "lovers" and "would-be love sharers," Milena was able to communicate with and confront Kafka on spiritual, intellectual, and physical levels. Also a consumptive and daughter of a tyrannical father, she was a "secret sharer" with Kafka. Frederick Karl, *Franz Kafka: Representative Man*, p. 602.

Ceneda: A town just north of Venice in the Veneto. Jews had been compelled to live in the ghetto, *gheto nuovo*, literally "new foundry," in 1516 and also in Venice in the adjoining *gheto vecchio*, or "old foundry," in 1541 and in the *gheto nuovissimo*, or "newest foundry," in 1633. The word *gheto* came to mean a closed Jewish quarter. Conditions for Jews in Ceneda were often somewhat freer.

In 1597, Israel di Conegliano was given permission to open a loan bank in Ceneda which remained open throughout the seventeenth century. Members of the Abendana, Gentilli, Luzzato, Pincherle (Alberto Moravia's ancestors), and Conegliano families (Lorenzo da Ponte) lived in Ceneda. Part of Ceneda's beautiful wooden synagogue may be seen today in the Israel Museum in Jerusalem. *Encyclopedia Judaica*, vol. 16, pp. 95, 96.

Talmud: Compiled circa 3rd century B.C.E.–2nd century C.E. An elaboration and discussion of the Mishnah, which itself is an elaboration and discussion of the five books of Moses (Torah) and the Oral Torah. The discussions in the land of Israel are written in the Talmud Yerushalmi (the Jerusalem Talmud). There is another version with less legal discussion and more legends (Haggadah) called the Babylonian Talmud. The printed Talmud studied today is thus a multilevel commentary—eighteenth century commentators, Renaissance commentators, early medieval commentators, all commenting on themselves and on the Talmud and the Mishnah, which in turn comment on the Torah.

Page 9
Ketubbah: The agreement between husband and wife that is signed and read aloud before a wedding. Its text derives from the Talmud. It ensures the wife a sum of money, generally enough to live on for a period of years should her husband decide to ask for a divorce. This amount is the wife's in preference to any demands of children or third parties. This early example of "women's rights" is credited with preserving strong and lasting marriages. These ketubbot were often illuminated in the style of the country in which they were drawn up.

James Joyce: From *Finnegan's Wake* (New York: Viking Press, 1976), pp. 627, 628.

Breslover: Rabbi Nachman of Breslov, 1772–1811, was the great-grandson of Israel Ba'al Shem Tov, founder of the Hasidim. A charismatic personality, Rabbi Nachman voyaged from his home in Podolia, Poland, to Palestine in 1798. He visited Jerusalem and Safed and left when Napoleon invaded the Holy Land. Rabbi Nachman is said to have responded to questions from his Hasidim by instantly fashioning a most wonderful tale. These tales of Rabbi Nachman are a unique treasure of Hasidic mystical lore. On his deathbed, Rabbi Nachman, in response to who should be rabbi to his congregation after his death, replied, "Better a dead rabbi who is alive than a live rabbi who is dead." To this day, Breslover Hasidim tell Rabbi Nachman's tales and study his teachings in Jerusalem, Safed, and other Jewish centers. No rabbi has ever been chosen in his place. Aryeh Kaplan, *Rabbi Nachman's Stories* (New York: Breslov Research Institute, 1983), pp. viii, 437.

Page 11
Bob Dylan: "When the Ship Comes In," copyright © 1963, 1964 Warner Bros.; © 1963 by M. Witmak and Sons. Copyright reissued by Special Rider Music.

Joan Baez: Anthony Scaduto, *Bob Dylan: An Intimate Biography* (New York: Grosset & Dunlap, 1971), pp. 191–192.

Isaac Luria (1534–1572): A Kabbalist known as the sacred lion "Ha Ari" from the initials ARI (Adonanu Rav Itshaki, our master Rabbi Isaac). Luria's father was an Ashkenazi from Poland or Germany and emigrated to Jerusalem. His father married into the Sephardic Frances family. When he was a child, Luria was taken by his mother to her family in Cairo after his father's death. Initiated in kabbalistic mystical teaching, Luria retired for seven years to a life of solitary study on an island in the Nile, Jazirat al-Rawda. In 1570, Luria, a businessman trading in pepper and grain, moved with his family to Safed. Gathering around him a devout mystical circle of people, for several years he taught an intricate mystical system that has become the code of Hassidic and esoteric Jewish belief. His doctrines of creation, the shrinking of G-d to make room for the world, the divine sparks emanating from the presence of G-d, the doctrine of *tikkun*, the restoration of the world, the connection of the inner and outer cosmos, have all inspired and altered Jewish prayer and philosophy. *Encyclopedia Judaica*, vol. 11, p. 578.

Judeo-Persian: A combination of Hebrew and Farsi, the language of Persian Jews.

Ladino: A combination of Hebrew and Spanish, the language of Sephardic Jews in Spain that they took with them to northern Africa and, later, throughout the world.

Page 15
Tuviah Gutman Gutwirth: Noted Rabbinic scholar born in Riglitz, Poland (Galicia). Emigrated to Antwerp, where he led a weekly Talmud *shiur* (lesson) and became a leading diamantaire (diamond dealer) and perhaps the most knowledgeable diamond expert in Antwerp in the 1920s and 1930s. A Belz Hasid and a noted Kabbalist, his library of writings on Lurianic mysticism was open to all interested in mysticism in prewar Antwerp. He was a descendant of Ephraim Katz (the Sha'ar Ephraim [1616–1678]), Elijah of Chelm, who is said to have created a golem, and many other Torah luminaries. Tuviah Gutman Gutwirth fled to Cuba during the war and passed away in New York City. Among the eight children born to him and his wife, Chaya Rheinhold Gutwirth, was Lotty (Sheindel) Zucker, the author's mother. May their memory be a blessing.

Page 19
Rachel, Tal's girlfriend: Zohar Ha Kaddosh (III, p. 115b).

Moses Hayyim Luzzato (1707–1746): Mystical Rabbi in Padua, Italy. When he was twenty years old, Luzzato heard the voice of a *maggid* who revealed to him heavenly secrets. This message from a *maggid* (normally only vouchsafed to a married man) caused great debate in Italian rabbinical circles. Luzzato's Kabbalist teachings aimed to achieve *tikkun*, or repairing the ills of the world, and to join the holy Shekinah (the feminine principle of divine) and all of Israel. Luzzato interpreted the Lurianic doctrine of G-d's withdrawing into Himself (Zimzum) as an act of divine justice to establish contact with the world. Luzzato's *The Path of the Upright* (Mesillat Yesharim) is considered to be one of the great ethical guides in Jewish literature. It is a concrete and simple guide on how to avoid sin and attain holiness. His work was one of the few accepted by Hasidim, Mitnagdim (opponents of Hasidim), as well as by members of the Enlightenment movements. *Encyclopedia Judaica*, vol. 11, p. 603.

Slonim: A city in Belorussia. Rabbi Abraham ben Isaac Mattathias Weinberg headed a yeshiva in Slonim which combined Hasidic mystical teaching and rigorous *mitnagid* (those who oppose Hasidim) Talmudic scholarship. His great-grandson Abraham emigrated to Palestine in 1935. Many Slonim Hasidim settled in Tiberias.

CHAPTER 2

Page 21
Bob Dylan: "The Times They are a Changin'," copyright © 1963, 1964 by Warner Bros. Copyright reissued 1991 by Special Rider Music.

Robert Johnson (1911–1938): Robert Johnson was a noted Delta Blues musician. He was a seminal inspiration for Son House and Muddy Waters and also for Eric Clapton and the Rolling Stones. Johnson died in Greenwood, Mississippi. See Peter Guralnick, *Searching for Robert Johnson* (New York: E. P. Dutton, 1992), p. 56; also: Stephen La Vere, *The Complete Recordings*, liner notes (New York: Columbia/Legacy Records, 1990), pp. 3–4.

Piqué: Carbon spots.

Bava Metziah: "The Middle Gate." A tractate of Mishnah and Gemarah (Talmud) dealing with objects lost and found. In Judaism, great emphasis is laid on the obligation to return lost property. If, for instance, an animal is returned and lost again, a man must return it even "100" times (31A Bava Metziah). Laws of guardianship, interest, and leasing are all dealt with. There are also legends recounted in Bava Metziah. "At one point Rabbi Eliezer called on heaven to support him in an argument. A heavenly voice, *bat kol*, 'daughter of a voice,' issued forth: 'Why do you challenge R. Eliezer for the law is according to his opinions in all matters.' But Rabbi Joshua interrupted and said, 'Since the giving of the Torah at Mount Sinai no attention is paid to a heavenly voice, but the opinion of a majority of scholars determines authentic law.'" *Encyclopedia Judaica*, vol. 4, pp. 342–43.

Page 27
Taj Mahal emerald: Perhaps the finest carved Moghul Gem emerald known. Its carved flower heads, a lotus, a meconopsis, and its combination flower represent Babur, Akbar, and Shah Jahan. In 1925, in Paris, the emerald was exhibited at the Exposition des Arts Decoratifs as Cartier's most extraordinary gem. It is currently on display at the Smithsonian's Arthur M. Sackler Gallery, Washington, D.C. (private collection).

Sir Ernest Oppenheimer: Founder of the DeBeers diamond syndicate.

Page 29
Hasid of Breslov: Quote from Elie Wiesel, *Souls on Fire: Portraits and Legends of Hasidic Masters* (Northvale, N.J.: Jason Aronson, 1993). Copyright Elie Wiesel; used by permission of Jason Aronson Publishers.

Page 31
Piqué goods: Diamonds that have visible inclusions (flaws), often black carbon spots. Diamonds without piqués are called "clean goods" in the diamond world.

Parnas: The most honored lay official in a Sephardic synagogue. The Parnas would sit to the left of the Rabbi, next to the Aron Hakodesh (the Holy Ark), where the scrolls of the Torah rested.

Page 35
Alkabetz (1505–1576): On the eve of Shavuot (the holiday celebrating the giving of the Torah) in 1528, while Solomon ben Moses Halevi Alkabetz was studying with Joseph Caro, a *maggid* (mystical preacher) came and taught him Kabbala. Alkabetz arrived in Safed in 1535 and probably initiated the custom of going out into the fields with Isaac Luria and other Kabbalists to welcome the Sabbath. The hymn he composed, "Lekhah Dodi" ("Come My Beloved"), is sung throughout the Jewish world to welcome the mystical bride of the Sabbath.

Page 37
Angels: Literally, in Hebrew, Mal'akh (messenger) or Kedoshim (holy beings). Israel has a ministering angel, Michael ("He who is like you O G-d") and his assistant, Gabriel. Along with Michael and Gabriel stand Raphael ("G-d will cure") and Uriel ("The light of G-d") at the four sides of G-d's throne.

Page 39
Shlomo Carlebach: Perhaps the greatest Jewish singer and composer of the twentieth century. Carlebach studied in Lakewood Yeshiva and was a brilliant student, extraordinary storyteller, and a Hazzan (Cantor) without equal. What a great loss to hear no longer his *niggunim* each holiday. May his songs continue to inspire the world.

Chair of Rabbi Nachman of Breslov: The wooden chair was the chair that Rabbi Nachman used in the late eighteenth century. He composed elegant mystical stories in response to questions posed to him by his Hasidic followers (see note for page 9). Before the Second World War, the chair was divided into many parts. Each Hasid who took a piece of the chair took a vow to meet in Jerusalem and reassemble it. Those Hasidim all miraculously survived the war, and the chair is now reassembled and may be seen in the prayer hall of the Breslover Hasidim in Jerusalem.

Page 41
All quotes and anecdotes on this page are from Mary Ellen Jordan, *Walks in Gertrude Stein's Paris* (New York: St. Martin's Press, 1988), pp. 10, 14–15, 39.

Page 43
Erusin and Nisuyin: In Jewish law, marriage consists of two separate acts: Kiddushin (holy or set apart), which is also called Erusin, and Nisuyin (to wed). Kiddushin can often be related to the engagement of a couple or the placement of a ring on the woman's hand with the blessing "Behold you are consecrated unto me by this ring according to the laws of Moses and Israel." Nisuyin is where the bride is brought under a *huppah* (wedding canopy) and to a private meeting, Yichud, with two competent witnesses and a reading of the *kettubah* (the marriage contract), to make the marriage proper and the ceremony complete. *Encyclopedia Judaica*, vol. 11, p. 1048.

A Gerer Hasid: A follower of the Gerer Rebbe, leader of perhaps the largest Hasidic sect in Eastern Europe in the 1920s. Abraham Mordekhai Alter (1866–1948) established youth organizations and schools throughout Central and Eastern Europe. The Gerer Rebbe received thousands of visitors who flocked from Warsaw to Ger, a small town an hour from Warsaw. Every person would say a personal shalom (peace) to the Rebbe. They would write a *kvittel* asking for his advice or blessing and upon leaving say goodbye. On a holiday there would be thousands of people. It was on such a holiday that Dora Dymant's father came to ask the Rebbe's assent to Franz Kafka's request to marry his daughter.

Milena Jesenska: Nahum N. Glatzer, *The Loves of Franz Kafka*.

Bob Dylan: "One of Us Must Know," copyright © 1966 by Dwarf Music.

Page 45
Ashkenazi, Sephardi: The entire Jewish people originate from the land of Israel but over the millennia have spread through much of the world. There are three broad categories of Jewish people. The Ashkenasic Jews are European Jews who originated from the German ("Ashkenaz" in medieval Hebrew) Rhine Valley and spread throughout Europe. Sephardic Jews originated from Spain (Sepharad) but after the expulsion in 1492 wandered

throughout northern Africa, Italy, Greece, and the Holy Land. Finally, there are the Oriental Jewish communities in Persia, India, Yemen, and other parts of northern Africa. There are variants in pronunciation of Hebrew between the various communities as well as differences in religious rites and customs. Israel today uses the Sephardic pronunciation of Hebrew. Hasidic Jews pray according to the Sephardic rite because of Isaac Luria's influence.

Zevi Hirsch ben Jacob (1660–1718): Known as the Haham Zevi. He escaped with his grandfather Ephraim ben Jacob Katz from Vilna to Moravia in 1655. At the age of sixteen, he wrote his first responsa. He studied under Sephardic rabbis in Salonica and Belgrade, 1676–1679. Zevi Hirsch adopted Sephardic manners and was given the Sephardic title for Rabbi, "Haham." His responsa, questions from other rabbis throughout the Jewish world, were widely accepted.

CHAPTER 3

Page 47
Bob Dylan: "A Hard Rain's A-Gonna Fall," copyright © 1963 by Warner Bros.; copyright reissued 1991 by Special Rider Music. "Never Say Goodbye," © 1974, 1975 by Ram's Horn Music.

Peacock flue: The fine fluffy feathers at the very center of a peacock's plumage. Often an ounce of peacock flue, according to Charles Zucker (1905–1988), noted feather dealer and the author's father, was worth more than an ounce of gold. Satinettes were long goose feathers used in ladies' hats, and ostrich feathers were strung together and dyed to make ostrich boas.

Eighteen: A lucky number in Jewish thought. Each letter has a numerical equivalent. Aleph is one, beth is two, etc. Chai (to live) is equivalent to eighteen. Hence pledges of charity are often given in amounts of eighteen: for example, one hundred eighteen dollars, eighteen hundred dollars.

Page 49
Chief Crazy Horse: Anecdote from Robert Clark, ed., *The Killing of Chief Crazy Horse* (Lincoln, Neb.: University of Nebraska Press, 1976).

Max Brod: Anecdote and quote from Nahum N. Glatzer, *The Loves of Franz Kafka* (New York: Schocken Books, 1986).

Page 51
Capablanca (1888–1942): José Raul Capablanca was the World Champion chess player, 1921–27. He watched his father and uncle play chess from the time he was two years old in Cuba. At four, he defeated both men at the chessboard after they innocently asked him whether he understood the game. Educated in the United States as an engineer, he found his studies tedious and withdrew from Columbia University. Although said to be "lazy" and unable "to learn to learn," Capablanca had an uncanny ability to immediately judge the entire sight of the board. "He wanted only to play the game and never studied books on the game." David Hooper and Kenneth Whyld, *The Oxford Companion to Chess* (New York: Oxford University Press, 1984), p. 55.

Max Brod: See his *Franz Kafka: A Biography* (New York: Schocken Books, 1963).

Rabbi Nachman of Breslov: *Likuteh Maharan.* Ostrog, p. 6.

James Joyce: Anecdote and quote from Richard Ellman, *James Joyce* (New York: Oxford University Press, 1982), p. 736.

Nora: James Joyce, *Ulysses* (New York: Random House, 1961), p. 47.

Page 55
Bob Dylan: Quote from *Tarantula*, a novel by Bob Dylan, written before 1966 (New York: Bantam Books, 1972), p. 144. It was not published until May 1971 by Macmillan. Originally, the text of the book was sold on the streets as a bootleg work. Robert Christgau notes that "Dylan borrowed techniques from literature, most prominently allusion, ambiguity, symbolism, and fantasy. And he obviously loved language, but he despised the gentility with which it was supposed to be tailored." Robert Christgau, *Bob Dylan: A Retrospective*, ed. Craig McGregor (New York: William Morrow, 1972), p. 393.

The Kotsker Rebbe (1787–1859): Menachem Mendel of Kotsk was called the Master of Silence because of his many ascetic years living in a room adjoining a synagogue. The Kotsker Rebbe has always symbolized devotion to truth and to G-d. "Where is the dwelling of G-d?" the Kotsker asked his disciples. And his disciples answered, "What a question! Is not the whole world full of His glory?" The Kotsker Rebbe answered his own question: "G-d dwells wherever man lets Him."

The Rizhiner Rebbe: Quote from Elie Wiesel, *Souls on Fire: Portraits and Legends of Hasidic Masters* (Northvale, N.J.: Jason Aronson, 1993), p. 147.

James Joyce: Quote from *Finnegan's Wake* (New York: Viking Press, 1964), p. 627.

Page 57
Delmore Schwartz: Quote from Elizabeth Pollet, ed., *Portrait of Delmore: Journals and Notes of Delmore Schwartz, 1929–1959* (New York: Farrar, Straus & Giroux, 1986), p. 341.

T. S. Eliot: "The Hollow Men," excerpt from *Collected Poems 1909–1962*, copyright © 1936 by Harcourt, Inc; © 1963, 1964 by T. S. Eliot. Reprinted by permission of the publisher.

Page 59
Mikhail Botvinnik (1911—): Quote from Hooper and Whyld, *The Oxford Companion to Chess.* "Although considered the greatest chess player in the world in the 1940s, the title fell to him only at the end of the decade. His style was characterized by good judgment, thorough adjournment analysis, excellent end-game technique, and, above all, preparation." In 1960, Botvinnik was defeated by Mikhail Nekhemyevich Tal, twenty-four years old, who became the youngest chess champion up to that time.

Mikhail Tal: World Chess Champion, 1960–1961. Born in Riga, Latvia, Tal became interested in chess when he saw it played in his doctor father's waiting room. Tal played chess constantly and obsessively, even escaping from a hospital recuperating room to play. Chess was his life. A chain-smoker and prolific writer in chess journals, he wrote just one book, *Tal-Botvinnik, 1960 Match for the World Championship.*

Boris Spassky: World Chess Champion, 1969–1972. Very much the romantic, Spassky thought of quitting chess when his first marriage faltered. "We were like Bishops of opposite colors," Spassky stated succinctly. He was the most handsome champion since Capablanca. A bon vivant, he was the polar opposite of the reclusive, ackward, and fundamentalist Bobby Fischer, who defeated Spassky at Reykjavik in 1972. Hooper and Whyld, *The Oxford Companion to Chess*.

Curious Indian Miniatures: Rembrandt, a contemporary of Shah Jahan, possessed a collection of Indian Mogul miniatures. There is a question whether his Mogul drawings are faithful copies of his miniatures or whether these Indian miniatures served as inspiration for Rembrandt's drawings. See especially Shah Jahan's drawing, c. 1654, of the Mogul ruler by Rembrandt, now in the Cleveland Museum of Art. Rembrandt sold his "curious miniatures" after his bankruptcy in 1656–57 at a public sale in Amsterdam.

James Joyce: Joyce to Arthur Power. Clive Hart, ed., *Conversations with James Joyce* (Chicago: University of Chicago Press, 1974) pp. 43, 47.

CHAPTER 4

Page 61

Yehezkel of Shinyeveh (d. 1899): Named after the Shinyeveh, Yehezkel of Shinyeveh in Eastern Europe. A renowned Hasidic Rebbe, he was utterly straightforward and devoted to the truth. "When Yehezkel of Shinyeveh was in Ujhely in Hungary, he had the town crier announce that he would preach in the House of Prayer. Yehezkel ascended to the Bimah [pulpit where the Torah is read] and said, 'My friends, once I preached here and my heart was not totally in my talk and my thoughts were not with G-d. I have come here again to confess my sin. A sin must be expiated where it was done. And I pray to you, The Holy One, to be forgiven.' And the entire congregation was moved to repentance, for the fear of G-d entered their hearts." Martin Buber, *Tales of the Hasidim* (New York: Schocken Books, 1948), p. 215. After Yehezkel of Shinyeveh's death, thousands of newborn children were named after him.

Yitzhak Bunam Zucker: Anecdote from Abraham Yaakov Finkel, *The Great Chassidic Masters* (Northvale, N.J.: Jason Aronson, 1992), p. 170; also Talmud, Rosh Hashanah 21b. All quotations copyright © Abraham Yaakov Finkel; used by permission of Jason Aronson Publishers.

Cloisons: Thin metal channels into which enamel is poured (cloisonné enameling).

Bosses: Round knobs in ornamental goldsmithing.

Page 63

Hofets Hayyim: See Jerome R. Mintz, *Legends of the Hasidim* (Chicago: University of Chicago Press, 1968), p. 360.

Bob Dylan: "All Along the Watchtower," copyright © 1968 by Dwarf Music.

J. P. Morgan: See Cass Canfield, *The Incredible Pierpont Morgan: Financier and Art Collector* (New York: Harper & Row, 1974).

Page 65

Alan Lomax: See his *The Land Where Blues Began* (New York: Delta Books, 1995), p. 17. Alan Lomax and his son traveled through the South in 1930, recording and preserving songs of southern blues musicians. In Mississippi, the work of Huddie Leadbetter, Son House, and scores of other musicians would surely have perished had it not been for Lomax's extraordinary efforts.

The Seer of Lublin (d. 1815): Jacob Yitzhak of Lublin was called a

seer because he could gaze from one end of the world to another. He could see the future and the past on his Hasidims' foreheads. "Rabbi Baer of Radushitz once said to the Seer of Lublin, 'Show me one general way to serve G-d.' The Zaddik [the righteous one] of Lublin replied: 'It is impossible to tell people what way they should take. For one, the way to serve G-d is through the teachings of the Torah. For another, through prayer. For another, fasting. And still another, through eating. Everyone should carefully observe what way their heart draws them to and choose this way with all their strength.'" Martin Buber, *Tales of the Hasidim*, p. 313.

James Joyce: Quote from *Finnegan's Wake* (New York: Viking Press, 1976), p. 627.

Zaydeh: Grandfather.

Page 67

Bomberg (d. 1553): Daniel Bomberg was one of the first and most prominent of Christian printers of the Hebrew Bible. In 1520, with the approval of Pope Leo X, he published for the first time the entire Babylonian Talmud (*Encyclopedia Judaica*, vol. 4, p. 1195; vol. 15, p. 758). The text of the Talmud is in the center and the commentary by Rashi on the inside of the page, toward the spine. On the left side and bottom are commentaries by Rashi's grandsons and other early medieval scholars.

Walker Percy: Quote is from Percy's *The Moviegoer* (New York: Noonday Press, 1962), p. 89.

Mississippi John Hurt: Lawrence Cohn, ed., *Nothing but the Blues* (New York: Abbeville Press, 1993), p. 383. Hurt was a great blues singer who recorded "Avalon's My Home Town" in 1920. He was rediscovered in 1963 and enjoyed a great renaissance in American folk music circles.

Page 69

Billie Burke (1886–1970): American actress.

Grandfather Rojko Milan: Nebojsa Bato Todasevic and Rajko Djuric, *Gypsies of the World* (New York: Henry Holt, 1988), p. 15.

A Lubliner Hasid: Hasidic devotee of the Seer of Lublin.

The Apter Rebbe (d. 1822): Abraham Joshua Heschel, the Apter Rebbe, said, "Everyone of Israel is told to consider themselves to be standing at Mount Sinai to receive the Torah. For people, there are past and future events, but not for G-d. Day in and day out, G-d gives the Torah." Martin Buber, *Tales of the Hasidim*, p. 116.

Laurence Sterne: Boswell's *Life of Johnson*, ed. George B. Hill and C. F. Powell (Oxford: The Claredon Press, 1934), quoting Boswell, March 20, 1776. Also quoting from Laurence Sterne, *The Life and Opinions of Tristram Shandy, Gentleman*, ed. Howard Anderson (New York: W. W. Norton & Co., 1980).

Niggun: A song or tune, often impromptu, composed by a Hasidic Rebbe and sung in his court, sometimes for generations after his death. "Hasidim believe that in the highest of heavens there is a gate that only music can unlock," said Rabbi Shlomo Carlebach.

Page 71

Bob Dylan: "Went to See the Gypsy," copyright © by Dwarf Music.

Albert Einstein: Quote from *The New York Times*, 13 March 1944.

Michaelangelo Besso (1873–1955): Lifelong friend of Albert Einstein. An engineer by training, Besso's intellectual friendship with Einstein, which started in Zurich in 1902, lasted their entire lives. "Now he has departed from this strange world a little ahead of me, that signifies nothing. For us believing physicists, the distinction between past, present, and future is only a stubbornly persistent illusion." From Einstein's letter of condolence to the Besso family, March 21, 1955, less than a month before his own death. Alice Calaprice, *The Quotable Einstein* (Princeton, N.J.: Princeton University Press, 1966), p. 61.

Abraham Abulafia: Born in Saragasso, Spain (1240–1291). At eighteen, he trekked to the Holy Land in search of the mystical River Sambatyon, which did not flow on the Sabbath and on whose banks the remnants of the ten tribes of Israel were said to live. In Italy and Spain, Abulafia was trained in Kabbalah. He would wrap himself in white clothing, meditate all night on a single sentence of the Bible, and in the morning through gematria (numerical association of words) and word association, decipher the true meaning of the text. In 1280, responding to an inner voice, he went to Rome with the intention of calling Pope Nicholas III to account for the suffering of the Jews. His intention to convert the Pope led Pope Nicholas to grant Abulafia an audience, listen patiently, and then, upon reflection, order that Abulafia be sent to jail to be killed by burning the following day. This sentence was not carried out because of the Pope's death that same night, August 22, 1280. Quote in commentary from Moshe Idel, *The Mystical Experience of Abraham Abulafia* (New York: State University of New York Press, 1958), p. 107.

The Vilna Gaon (1730–1797): A man of iron will, Elijah, called the Vilna Gaon (genius), reportedly knew the Talmud by heart by the time he was nine years old. After his marriage at eighteen, he retreated to a small house outside of Vilna and studied hour by hour, day by day, year by year. According to his sons, he did not stop for more than two hours a day or for more than one half hour at a time. His commentaries on the Torah, Mishnah, Talmud, and even Kabbalah are models of lucidity and inspiration. He said, "Everything that was, is, and will be is included in the Torah" (*Encyclopedia Judaica*, vol. 6, pp. 651–658). His pupil, Rabbi Chaim of Volozhin, wrote of the Vilna Gaon: "He was literally prepared to give up his life for every word of the Torah. . . . When he was unable to clarify some aspect of Torah to his complete satisfaction, the Gaon would stop eating and drinking for days and nights in a row and drive sleep from his eyes until his complexion grew dark from weariness. He gave up his very life until Hashem [G-d, literally "the Name"] enlightened him in the topic he wished to fathom." *The Gaon from Vilna* (New York: Art Scroll Messorah Publications, 1994). Quote in text from Abraham Yaakov Finkel, *The Great Torah Commentators* (Northvale, N.J.: Jason Aronson, 1996), p. 29.

Halakah: The practice of Judaism, literally "the way."

Theodor Herzl: *Encyclopedia Judaica*, vol. 6, p. 1336.

David Wolfsohn: *Encyclopedia Judaica*, vol. 6, p. 612.

Tallit (or tallis): A fringed prayer shawl worn while praying in a synagogue or a home.

Sugyia: A Talmudic section that is difficult to understand.

Page 73

Dov Ber of Mezeritch (d. 1772): One of the most important of the early Hasidic masters. The leader of Hasidim after the death of the Ba'al Shem Tov in 1760. So impressive was Dov Ber to fellow Hasidic master Reb Leb, the son of Sarah, that Reb Leb is said to have visited Dov Ber "to see how he puts on his shoelaces." The *maggid* (teacher or lecturer) of Mezeritch preached total attention and devotion to one's prayers (*devekut*) to G-d. For Dov Ber, there was no evil, only gradations of good; for there is no place not occupied by G-d.

Søren Kierkegaard: Quote is from his *Fear and Trembling*, trans. Alastair Hannay (London: Penguin Books, 1985), p. 17.

Wedding Ring: This ring is a seminal and unique piece in the development and understanding of the history of Jewish wedding rings, first shown to the author by his great friend and remarkable connoisseur of Judaica, Dr. Alfred Moldovan. (Over the years Dr. Moldovan has served as an inspiration and conscience to the author for all things Jewish). Dr. Moldovan pointed out that this single object might explain why so many Jewish wedding rings have "vestigial" gold loupes on their sides, why their great finger size seems to prevent them from being worn as rings, and finally why the interior message of the letters of "mazel tov" was hidden from view. If this pendant is one in a line of pendants that inspired each successive version, perhaps what we have here is an original pendant dating back to Spain in the time of the Marranos. Eventually the Jewish wedding ring with a pendant casing shed its outward pendant (no longer did the message "mazel tov" have to be so hidden) and went back to its original ring form. That Jewish wedding rings existed in pre-expulsion Europe is clear. For example, see a high house ring listed in a sixteenth century Munich museum inventory.

Italki: Jews who lived in Italy since the first century of the common era were called Italian, or Italki, Jews.

Page 75

Laurence Sterne: *Monthly Review*, vol. 36, 1767, p. 102, as quoted in David Thomson, *Wild Excursions: The Life and Fiction of Laurence Sterne* (New York: McGraw-Hill Book Co., 1972), p. 256.

Sanzer Rebbe (1793–1876): Chaim Halberstam of Sanz, Poland. A Hasidic Rebbe, all of his five sons became outstanding Tzaddikm (righteous rabbis), the most prominent of whom was Rabbi Yehezkel of Shinyeveh. The Sanzer Rebbe's seven daughters all married Hasidic leaders. In addition, both the current Bobover Rebbe and the Klauzenberger Rav, Yekutiel Yehudah Halberstam, descend from the Sanzer Rebbe. The Sanzer said, "Abraham was now old, advanced in years, and G-d blessed Abraham in all things" (Genesis 24:1). In *Divrei Chaim* (the words of Chaim) the Sanzer Rebbe explains, "The Talmud remarks that until Abraham appears on the scene, old age is not mentioned in the Bible. And yet the Torah records that people lived for hundreds of years (Methuselah for 969 years). To the spiritual world, days that are wasted on idle pursuits do not count. Until the advent of Abraham, people lived lives of emptiness and futility. . . . Even though they lived for many centuries, in a spiritual sense they did not reach old age. Abraham was the first to proclaim G-d's existence, making people aware of spiritual values and giving meaning to their lives. Now their days and years counted. Thus it may be said Abraham introduced the concept of old age to the world." Abraham Yaakov Finkel, *The Great Chassidic Masters*, p. 140.

Johannes Vermeer: X-radiography reveals that Vermeer changed the position of the woman while painting the portrait. This accounts for the full-faced reflection in the window. In the Dresden portrait's window reflection white tears can be discerned, while in the profile figure reddish drops of tears or a scar is visible. The red curtain is a later working addition and echoes the red on the profiled sitter's cheek. A portrait of Cupid was overpainted and is missing from the final version we have now.

Yehudah Ibn Tibbon (c. 1120–1190): Jewish Medieval scholar and translator in Grenada, Spain.

Page 77

Johannes Vermeer: There are Hapsburg eagles on this chandelier, referring to a period when The Netherlands and southern Holland were one country. Perhaps this is a reference to Antwerp. In 1654, Holland was required to cede Brazil to Portugal, and many Sephardic Jews arrived in Holland. They followed Sephardic Jews who had fled in increasing numbers from Spain and Portugal and entered Holland in the late sixteenth century from Antwerp. It was not until "half a century after 1670, the date of Spinoza's statement, that Marranos had become so intermingled with the Spaniards so as to leave of themselves no relic or remembrance before the last fires of the Inquisition here extinguished and more than another century before all search was abandoned for remnants of Marranism among candidates for office." B. Netanyahu, *The Origins of the Inquisition in 15th Century Spain* (New York: Random House, 1995), p. 1077.

Page 79

Claude Monet: Letter to Evan Charteris, 21 June 1926, from Giverny. Richard Kendal, ed., *Monet by Himself* (Boston: Little, Brown & Co., 1989), p. 265.

Babur (1483–1530): Babur was called "the tiger" for his military and personal prowess. He was the first moghul ruler to conquer parts of northern India. At the battle of Panipat in 1526, Babur, a descendant on his father's side of Timur (Tamerlaine) and on his mother's side of the Mongol emperor Ghengis Khan, routed the Rajput Hindu rulers and established Moghul dominion in Hindustan. (Moghul is a mispronunciation of the word Mongol.) Babur was a great naturalist and a keen observer of India, which he chronicled in his Turki diary, the Babur Nama. Wheeler Thackston, ed., *The Baburnama: Memoirs of Babur, Prince and Emperor* (New York: Oxford University Press, 1995).

Akbar (1542–1605): The grandson of Babur and the grandfather of Shah Jahan. "By 1592, when Shah Jahan was born, Akbar had conquered the whole of Northern India and insured the empire's continuance by providing a solid administrative infrastructure. Akbar had also become the first Muslim ruler in the country to inspire confidence and loyalty among the majority of his subjects, who were Hindus. In addition to marrying into Hindu royal families, he appointed Hindus to high offices, abolished sectarian taxes imposed only on Hindus, had Hindu epics translated, participated in Hindu festivals, and even attempted to establish a new religion that encouraged universal tolerance." Pratapaditya Pal, *Romance of the Taj Mahal* (Los Angeles: Thames & Hudson/L.A. County Museum of Art, 1989), p. 14.

Sarmad (d. 1661): Persian poet from a Kashani (Persian) rabbinical family. Although he converted to Islam, he was called the "Jewish mystic." A composer of Sufi poetry, he wrote part of *The Dabistan*, a comprehensive work in Persian on comparative religion that included a chapter on Judaism. He led the life of a dervish and was a "naked fakir, wandering through the streets of Delhi." He was chosen by Shah Jahan to be the instructor of his son Dara Shikoh, who was the crown prince apparent, only to be beheaded by his brother Aurangzeb in 1661 when Aurangzeb seized the throne.

Marcel Proust: Quoted in Ronald Hayman, *Proust: A Biography* (New York: HarperCollins, 1990), p. 12.

Page 81

James Joyce: Richard Ellman, *James Joyce* (Oxford: Oxford University Press, 1982), p. 525.

Isaac Luria: See Gershom G. Scholem, ed., *Zohar—The Book of Splendor: Basic Readings from the Kabbalah*, 5th ed. (New York: Schocken Books, 1963), p. 10.

Torah crown: "The torah scrolls are rolled, tied with a cord, encased in a fabric cover and two finials (bells or silver crowns) placed on top of the wooden rollers. One acts towards a . . . Torah scroll with additional holiness and great honor. . . . a Tik (container) that was prepared for a Torah Scroll which was laid in it, textile wrappers, and the ark and the reader's desk . . . and also the chair prepared to rest the Torah scroll on it, all are implements of holiness. . . . and the silver and gold rimmonim (finials) and the like, that are made for the beauty of the torah scrolls, are implements of holiness. . . ." Maimonides, Mishneh Torah, Hilkhot Sefer Torah, 10:44. From Rafi Grafman, *Crowning Glory: Silver Torah Ornaments of the Jewish Museum*, ed. Vivian B. Mann (Boston: David R. Godine Publishers, 1996), p. 1.

Parnas: Leader of a synagogue, an elective post. In early modern times, there were several parnasim in each community who led by rotation, each for one month, "the parnas of the month."

Darantière: The printer of James Joyce's *Ulysses*, Darantière had to meet the required deadline of Joyce's birthday. Under this immense pressure, it is altogether understandable that Darantière's typesetters, who spoke no English, made a large number of mistakes in the galley text. Some of the mistakes Joyce found amusing and kept, some he amended, which have validated Joyce's prediction that *Ulysses* will keep scholars busy "for a thousand years."

Page 83

Laurence Sterne: *Tristram Shandy* (New York: W. W. Norton & Co., 1980), p. 55.

Page 85

Simha Bunam: Martin Buber, *Tales of the Hasidim*, p. 250.

Bob Dylan: "Never Say Goodbye," copyright © 1974, 1975 by Ram's Horn Music.

Harry Bober: A professor of art history at the Institute of Fine Arts at New York University. Bober haunted antique stores in the 1950s, 1960s, and 1970s and collected medieval art, oceanic sculpture—anything he found beautiful. He encouraged his students to borrow his objects for as long as they wished so that they could write term papers on them. He was a scholar who could see arcane connections and influences between Coptic artifacts, for example, and the Book of Kells. Professor Bober was a man who saw with his eyes and taught with his heart.

Page 87

Mikhail Botvinnik: Hooper and Whyld, *The Oxford Companion to Chess* (New York: Oxford University Press, 1984), p. 46.

Jacob de Paiva (d. 1687): A Sephardic gem merchant who left London to go to Fort St. George (Madras) with money from fellow Sephardim. "He was authorized by the East India Company to travel to Madras in 1684, taking with him one man servant, one Christian maid, and one Jewish servant to attend on his wife, Hieronyma de Paiva, in his voyage to the port. He took ill on a trip to the Golconda diamond mines in 1687. Paiva was buried in the cemetery at Memorial Hall in Peddenaipetam near Madras, which had been acquired with his help. His Sephardic widow, Hieronyma de Paiva, subsequently lived with Elihu Yale, the governor of Madras, after whom the university is named." Walter J. Fischel, *Encyclopedia Judaica*, vol. 13, p. 14.

Elie Wiesel: *Souls on Fire: Portraits and Legends of Hasidic Masters* (Northvale, N.J.: Jason Aronson, 1993).

CHAPTER 5

Page 89
Bob Dylan: "A Buick 6," copyright © 1965 by Warner Bros.; copyright reissued 1993 by Special Rider Music.

Franz Kafka: Robert Alter, *Necessary Angels* (Cambridge, Mass.: Harvard University Press, 1991), p. 76.

Dylan Thomas: "In My Craft or Sullen Art" from *The Poems of Dylan Thomas* (New York: New Directions, 1971), p. 196. Copyright © 1946 by trustees for the copyrights of Dylan Thomas and New Directions Publishing Corporation; reprinted by permission of New Directions.

Page 91
Bob Dylan: "Forever Young," copyright © 1973, 1974 by Ram's Horn Music.

Reb Noson of Breslov: Chaim Kramer, *Through Fire and Water* (New York: Breslov Research Institute, 1992).

Somerset Maugham: Helen Sheehy and Leslie Stanton, *On Writers and Writing* (East Hartford, Conn.: Tide Mark, 1998), p. 9.

Page 93
Woody Guthrie: An American songwriter ("This Land Is Your Land") who sang folk music he considered as the "people's form of expression" throughout the 30s, 40s, and 50s. Riding the rails, singing at union rallies, he was the seminal influence on Bob Dylan. Dylan visited Guthrie in 1961 at Greystone Park State hospital where Guthrie was suffering from Huntington's chorea. Woody, barely audible, signed a card that read "I ain't dead yet" and gave it to an adoring Dylan.

Kurdistan: A mountainous region in the Middle East (in modern-day Iraq, Iran, and Turkey). Kurdish Jews believe themselves to be descendants of the ten tribes of Israel scattered during the Assyrian exile, eighth century B.C.E. The Jews of Kurdistan spoke an Aramaic with insertions of Hebrew, Turkish, Kurdish, Persian, and Arabic words (Lashon Ha Galut, the language of the Diaspora). The Arabs called the language Jabali (of the mountains). *Encyclopedia Judaica*, vol. 10., p. 1298.

Zakho (or Zahku): A town located near Mosul in Iraqi Kurdistan. When the Iraqi government opposed Zionism in the 1920s, the position of the Zakho Jewish community markedly deteriorated. A quarter of the town's 25,000 Jews fled, many to Jerusalem. With the establishment of the state of Israel, all remaining Jews in Zakho emigrated. *Encyclopedia Judaica*, vol. 16, p. 921. Amadiya and Sinne were also towns in Kurdistan that had a significant Jewish population.

Page 95
Sfas Emes: A book written by Yehuda Leib Alter of Ger in 1905. Its title derives from Proverbs 12:19. "Truthful speech abides forever." The Gerer Rebbe commented on Deuteronomy 6:5: "Love the Lord the Lord thy G-d with all your heart with all your soul and with all your might," asking how can the Torah command a person to love? How can feelings be dictated? The Gerer Rebbe said the fact that the Torah gives the command shows that inherently a person has an innate love of G-d. This love, lying dormant in the innermost recesses of the soul, must be aroused and actualized. It is this process of awakening that constitutes the blessing of "Thou shalt love your G-d," which means in effect, "Do all you can to awaken your latent love of G-d." Abraham Yaakov Finkel, *The Great Chassidic Masters* (Northvale, N.J.: Jason Aronson, 1992), p. 189.

Pardes Rimonim (Garden of Pomegranates): Written by Moses Cordevero (1522–1570), the outstanding Kabbalist in Safed before Isaac Luria. Cordevero was a disciple of Joseph Caro and of Solomon Alkabetz and a teacher of Isaac Luria. In *Pardes Rimonim*, Cordevero sums up past Kabbalistic thought. G-d (the Ain-Sof or "without end") is transcendent but reveals Himself to the world through the vessels of emanations (the Sephirot). The "revealing is the cause of concealment and concealment is the cause of revealing," wrote Cordevero in the *Pardes Rimonim*.

Dana Niswender: High school English teacher and author of *Elements of Style* (New York: The Horace Mann School, 1956).

Judith Barbier: Leading French feather supplier in early twentieth century. Hans Nadelhoffer, *Cartier: Jewelers Extraordinary* (New York: Harry N. Abrams, 1984), p. 82.

Page 97
Bob Dylan: Clinton Heylin, *Bob Dylan: Recording Sessions 1960–1994* (New York: St. Martin's Press, 1995), p. 15.

Page 99
Shiur: A Talmud session. Generally the Talmud is studied by pairs of students, a chavrusa. In the yeshiva (from the word for "to sit and learn"), there would also be a speech for all the students together. The head of the academy would speak twice a week to elucidate especially difficult Talmudic conundrums. There would also be several character-building lectures (Mussar) two or three times a week.

Robert Johnson: Peter Guralnick, *Searching for Robert Johnson* (New York: E. P. Dutton, 1992), p. 20. Copyright © 1989 by Toby Byron/Multiprises; text copyright © 1982, 1989 by Peter Guralnick. Used by permission of Dutton, a division of Penguin Putnam, Inc.

Page 101
Claude Monet: *Monet's Years at Giverny Beyond Impressionism* (New York: Metropolitan Museum of Art, 1978), p. 34.

Georges Clemenceau (1841–1929): Monet met Georges Clemenceau (who later became prime minister of France) when Clemenceau was a medical student in 1864. Clemenceau was a patron, a collector of Monet's paintings, and a frequent guest at Giverny. He was at Monet's bedside when he died.

Page 103
Camera Obscura: A viewing camera that catches "an image of the real world through an aperture or lens and projects the image in a darkened chamber. There were two types of camera obscura in Vermeer's time, a portable one called cubiloro or a chamber type which was stationary. Vermeer might have employed a stationary camera obscura in his studio on the top floor of the house in which he worked; or he may have traveled with the portable type, employing it to sketch indoor scenes. The image rendered in both types of camera obscura is both upside down and reversed. While the image can be traced or copied quickly, it is marked by distortion of near-term figures or objects, a characteristic of many of Vermeer's paintings." Hans Konig, *The World of Vermeer* (New York: Time Life, 1967), p. 139.

Johnny Shines: Peter Guralnick, *Searching for Robert Johnson*, p. 20.

Page 105

Franz Kafka: See Willi Haas, ed., *Letters to Milena*, trans. Tania and James Stein (New York: Schocken Books, 1965); Nahum Glatzer, *The Loves of Franz Kafka* (New York: Schocken Books, 1986), pp. 52–68.

Mechlin: A Belgian town near Antwerp. Jews lived in Mechlin as early as the twelfth century. It was the cemetery area for Antwerp Jewry (*Encyclopedia Judaica*, vol. 4, p. 416, and vol. 11, p. 826). In 1941 Belgian Jews were concentrated in Mechlin, and on 4 August 1942 the first group of Jews was transported to Auschwitz from Mechlin. In all, more than 25,000 Jews were sent to Auschwitz, with only a few hundred managing to survive until the camp was liberated by the Allies in September 1945. Today there is a Holocaust museum on the Mechlin deportation site.

Page 107

Agus: See Irving A. Agus, *The Heroic Age of Franco-German Jewry* (New York: Yeshiva University Press, 1969), p. 10. Copyright © Irving Agus; used by permission of Yeshiva University Press.

CHAPTER 6

Page 109

Isaac Cardozo: See Yosef Yerushalmi, *From the Spanish Court to Italian Ghetto: Abraham Cardozo: Study in Seventeenth Century Marranism and Jewish Apologetics* (New York: Columbia University Press, 1971), p. 381. Isaac Cardozo was born in Portugal in 1604. He studied in Spain and taught philosophy and medicine at the University of Valladolid. A physician at the royal court, he fled in 1648 to Italy. Renouncing his Marrano past, he openly proclaimed his adherence to Judaism in the Verona ghetto, writing his defense of Jews and Judaism, "Las excelencias de los Hebreos." Cardozo writes, "The election of Israel to be the people of G-d, this sacred betrothal, was neither temporary nor conditional, but eternal and absolute, for so the sacred verses confirm and reason persuades. G-d is not like earthly rulers who at one time choose a favorite minister and at another time repudiate him because of some dereliction he has committed. . . . Israel has no planet (no guiding angel or star). They are guided by G-d alone."

James Joyce: Quote from *Ulysses* (New York: Modern Library, 1961), p. 682.

Bob Dylan: "It's All Over Now, Baby Blue," copyright © 1965 by Warner Bros.; copyright reissued 1991 by Special Rider Music.

Page 111

Amedeo Modigliani: Christian Parisot, *Modigliani* (Paris: Pierre Terrail, 1992), p. 129.

Rabbi Elijah of Chelm, Poland (d. 1583): He is credited with creating a golem, a man without a soul. The legendary golem was brought to life by placing the word "truth," *emet* in Hebrew, on its forehead. The golem protected the Jewish people.

Page 113

Pa Ta Shan Jen: Pa Ta Shan Jen was of an aristocratic family. He chose to be a recluse and never joined the Manchu court.

Simha Bunam: Siach Sifrei Kodesh I, 48. Rabbi Shalom Meir Wallach, ed., *Haggadah of the Chassidic Masters* (New York: Art Scroll Messorah Publications, 1990).

Genesis: Genesis 29:20.

Spinoza (1632–1677): Dutch Sephardic philosopher who claimed G-d or nature "is the only possible substance and that everything in the world is an aspect of G-d." Baruch (Benedict) Spinoza was described by Noualis as a "G-d-intoxicated man." Spinoza knew that in the application of his critical reading of the biblical text, many difficulties existed owing to the incomplete knowledge of old Hebrew and of the "circumstances of the composition of the biblical books." Spinoza felt that these difficulties do not touch the central content of faith, that there is one G-d who demands justice and neighborly love and forgives those who repent. This faith is independent of philosophical thought and leaves complete freedom for it (Tractus Theologico-Politicus). Summarized in *Encyclopedia Judaica*, vol. 15, p. 281. See also Yirmiyahu Yovel, *Spinoza and Other Heretics* (Princeton, N.J.: Princeton University Press, 1989), p. 4.

Issachar and Zebulun: Two of the twelve tribes closely associated in terms of their birth order in the blessings of Jacob and Moses and which held land contiguous with each other in Israel. In the Talmud, Zebulun is said to have been a merchant, supporting Issachar, who was a scholar. ("Rejoice Zebulun in thy going out and Issachar in thy tents.") In modern times, business partners will make an agreement where one will study for perhaps two years, supported by the other, and then switch back to business and support his partner for an equivalent period of time.

Rosh Hashanah: The beginning of the Jewish year, "the head of the year," when a person's deeds are weighed and the totally wicked are said to be marked for punishment and the totally good are inscribed in the Book of Life for the coming year. Those "in between" have ten days to repent before Yom Kippur, the Day of Atonement.

Page 115

Shabbes Hagadol: The great Sabbath, the Sabbath before Passover. In the supplemental readings (the Haftorah) to the weekly portion in the Torah, the sentence is read, "Behold I will send you Elijah the prophet before the coming of the great and terrible day of the lord" (Malachi 4:5). The Messianic redemption for Israel, it is believed, will come on the great Sabbath.

Franz Kafka: Max Brod, ed., *Dearest Father*, trans. Ernst Kaiser and Eithne Wilkins (New York: Schocken Books, 1954).

Page 117

Monet: Letter to Duran Ruel, September 1882. Storm Coast at Belle-Île, 1806. Rachel Barnes, ed., *Monet by Monet* (New York: Alfred A. Knopf, 1990).

A Kotzker Hasid: Abraham J. Heschel, *A Passion for Truth* (New York: Farrar, Straus & Giroux, 1973), p. 78. Copyright © 1973, 1995 by Sylvia Heschel, executrix of the Estate of Abraham Joshua Heschel.

Belz: Rabbi Shalom of Belz (1779–1855), the founder of the Hasidic dynasty of Belz. When Rabbi Shalom of Belz's wife died, he said, "Lord of the world, if I had the strength to wake her, should I not have done so by now? I am simply not able to do it. But you, Lord of the world, you have the strength, and you can do it. Why don't you waken Israel?" Rabbi Shalom built a splendid Bet Medrash (house of study) in the tiny Polish town of Belz. He was reputedly a miracle worker but also stressed Talmudic learning as well as improving the great economic distress of Galician Jewry. His grandson, Issachar Dov (1854–1927), was the leader of

Belz in the 1920s. (The author's grandfather, Tuviah Gutman Gutwirth HaKohen, was a Hasid of Belz.) It was to Issachar Dov's "summer court" at Marienbad that Franz Kafka and his friend Max Brod once went; see p. 17.

Franz Kafka: Ernst Pawel, *The Nightmare of Reason: A Life of Franz Kafka* (New York: Random House, 1985), p. 360.

Page 119
Tung Ch'i-ch'ang (1555–1636): Born in Shanghai, this late Ming Chinese art theoretician and painter is cited in James Cahill's *The Distant Mountains: Chinese Painting of the Late Ming Dynasty, 1570–1644* (New York: Weatherhill, 1982), pp. 87–127; and also in Nelson Wu's study in 1962, *Tung Ch'i-Ch'ang 1555–1636: Apathy in Government and Fervor in Art.*

Vincent van Gogh: Susan Alyson Stein, *Van Gogh: A Retrospective* (New York: Beau Arts Editions, 1986), p. 64.

Echo Star Helstrom: Bob Spitz, *Dylan: A Biography* (New York: McGraw-Hill Book Co., 1989), p. 67.

Hatam Sopher (1762–1839): A leader of Orthodox Jewry in Frankfurt and Pressburg, his yeshiva was central in Orthodox Judaism's attempt to counter the German Reform Movement. It gave him no pleasure to engage in struggles: "There are no quarrels without wounds." *Encyclopedia Judaica*, vol. 15, p. 78.

Page 121
Rabbi Nachman of Breslov: Recounted from Rabbi Nachman of Breslov, *Advice* (Likutey Etzot) (New York: Breslov Research Institute, 1983).

Miantonomo, a Narragansett sachem: William Cronon, *Changes in the Land: Indians, Colonists, and the Ecology of New England* (New York: Hill & Wang, 1983), p. 97.

Page 123
Bob Dylan: Dylan to A. J. Lederman, in Craig McGregor, ed., *Bob Dylan: A Retrospective* (New York: William Morrow, 1972), p. 388.

Mette: Mette Gad was a Danish governess when she met Gauguin in 1873. He was a broker's agent in the Paris stock exchange Mette claims not to have known Gauguin was an occasional painter when she married him. They had five children together. Although Mette returned to Copenhagen in 1884, Gauguin made numerous attempts at reconciliation with her, visiting her for the last time in 1891 in Denmark before sailing in March of the same year for Tahiti.

Ephraim ben Jacob HaKohen Katz (Gutwirth family) (1616–1678): Leading rabbinical authority. Ephraim's wife, Rachel, was the daughter of Rabbi Elijah of Chelm, who created a golem. He grew up in Jerusalem, where his grandfather Ephraim was a *dayan* (judge). He served as a judge in Vilna, established yeshivot in Prague and Ofen (Buda). After receiving a call to be the chief Ashkenazic rabbi in Jerusalem, Ephraim died in the plague that ravished Ofen.

Page 125
George Sword: An Oglala Holy Man. See J. R. Walker, *The Sun Dance and Other Ceremonies of the Oglala Divisions of Teton Dakota* (American Museum of Natural History, *Anthropological Papers* 16(2), 50–221).

Akbar: *Shawwal*, October.

Max Meyer: M. L. Marks, *Jews Among the Indians* (Chicago: Benison Books, 1992), pp. 49–59.

CHAPTER 7

Page 127
Sara Lowndes: Bob Spitz, *Dylan: A Biography* (New York: McGraw-Hill Book Co., 1983), p. 278; Bob Dylan, "Mr. Tambourine Man," *Writings and Drawings* (New York: Alfred A. Knopf, 1973), p. 167.

Rabbi Irael of Stolin's Son: Jerome R. Mintz, *Legends of the Hasidim: An Introduction to Hasidic Culture and Oral Tradition in the New World* (Chicago: University of Chicago Press, 1974), pp. 70, 91.

Jean Baptiste Tavernier (1605–1689): Born in Paris of Huguenot parentage, Tavernier made six voyages to the East: Turkey, India, Ceylon. A great expert on jewels, he had entrée to the courts of Shah Jahan and Aurangzeb as well as to the French court of Louis XIV. Louis XIV was interested in meeting the famous traveler and granted him a title, Baron d'Aubonne. Tavernier retired to Geneva, where in 1676 he wrote an extraordinary account of his adventures in the seventeenth century gem trade. Convinced by his nephew to travel on one last voyage to the East, he left at the age of eighty-two, only to die en route two years later. His grave was discovered in an old Protestant cemetery near Moscow.

Page 129
Rabbi Nachman of Breslov: Quote from Avraham Greenbaum, trans., *Rabbi Nachman's Tikkun: The Comprehensive Remedy* (New York: Breslov Research Institute, 1984), p. 27.

William Moore: Blues musician, barber by trade, born in Georgia around 1894, he spent his life in Rappahannock, Virginia.

Page 131
Tishbite: A question posed in the Talmud and then left unanswered—with the phrase Tishbi Yetaretz Kushyot Ve'ibbayot, "The Tishbite will solve difficulties and problems"—is known as *teyku*. Elijah (or Eliyahu) the Tishbite was a prophet who ascended to heaven alive in a fiery chariot. It is believed that he will return in the messianic age when he will not only bring peace to our world but also the answers to irresolvable talmudic questions. See Louis Jacobs, *Teyku: The Unsolved Problems in the Babylonian Talmud* (London: Cornwall Books, 1981).

Page 133
Mosheh Futerman: Irving J. Rosenbaum, *Holocaust and Halacha* (New York: Ktav Publishing House, 1976), p. 81.

Page 135
Khurram: The princely name of Shah Jahan before he became emperor (he ruled as emperor 1627–1658). Shah Jahan built the Taj Mahal. Jahanghir wrote of Khurram: "His advent made the world joyous (Khurram) and gradually, as his years increased, so did his excellencies, and he was more attentive to my father (Akbar) than all my other children." (From *Tuzuki-i Jahangiri*, vol. I, pp. 19–20, as quoted in *Romance of the Taj Mahal* by Pratapaditya Pal [Los Angeles: Thames & Hudson/L.A. County Museum, 1989] p. 16.) Khurram wrestled and battled with his elder brothers, ascended to the throne, and named himself Ruler of the World. He ruled from a peacock throne studded with jewels that he loved, emeralds that he meditated on (see *The Taj Mahal Emerald*, Sackler Museum, Smithsonian). He fell extravagantly in love with Mumtaz Mahal

("light-of-the-palace"), had thirteen children with her, and watched her die bearing her fourteenth child. He hired 20,000 workers to build the Taj Mahal, only to have his favorite son, Dara Shikoh, killed and the throne usurped by his other son, Aurangzeb. For eight years, Shah Jahan was a prisoner of the fanatical Aurangzeb; he paced on the roof of the Red Fort, in sight of his usurped greatest creation, the Taj Mahal, meditating, dreaming, thinking, and preparing for paradise.

Julius Meyer: A Jewish merchant who settled in Omaha, Nebraska, in 1866. He traded with Indians, spoke six Indian dialects, and was a Pawnee chief. He brought a group of Pawnee to Paris for the Paris Exposition and was given the Pawnee name "Curly-headed White Chief who Speaks with One Tongue" in appreciation for his great integrity of speech and deed. *Encyclopedia Judaica,* vol. 2, p. 1374.

Eagle Chief: David Borgenicht, ed., *Native American Wisdom* (Philadelphia: Running Press, 1994), p. 24.

Page 137
Teresa Talani: A prominent Neapolitan cameo carver in the late eighteenth and early nineteenth century. There were virtually no other renowned women gem carvers in that period. Her extraordinary production includes a carving of Napoleon (Walters Art Gallery, Baltimore), Josephine and Napoleon (British Museum, Grundy collection), and George Washington, which was modeled after the life mask of Washington by Houdon. See *Context in Cameo*, the Benjamin Zucker Lecture Series, 1990, Ashmolean Museum (a study inspired by the Content family collection at the Ashmolean Museum, Oxford).

Page 139
Bob Dylan: "Simple Twist of Fate" lyrics. Michael Schumacher, *Dharma Lion: A Critical Biography of Allen Ginsberg* (New York: St. Martin's Press, 1992).

Edward Curtis: Photographer of the vanishing Native American tribes from 1904 to 1930. Virtually starving at first, he traveled from the Arctic to the southwestern American deserts, photographically recording and interviewing Cheyenne, Apache, Hopi, Oglala, Sioux, Zuni, and Alaskan tribes. His work was eventually funded by J. P. Morgan and appeared in 1907 as *The North American Indian* (Cambridge: Cambridge University Press, 1907–1930). His son, Harold Curtis, wrote of his father: "He once told me that the reason he took up photography (building his first camera from instructions printed in the *Seattle Post Intelligencer*) was that it was easier than cutting wood for a living. He was a weekend regular at the Teddy Roosevelt home at Oyster Bay, but then he could just as easily go back to a reservation and sit in a circle of Indians as one of them. He could do anything, was at home in any circle. He was the best man I ever knew." Edward Curtis, *Visions of a Vanishing Peace* (Carollton, Tex: Promontory Publications, 1976).

Page 141
Marienbad: A spa in Czechoslovakia, about a hundred miles west of Prague. People would go to Marienbad from all over Europe to "take the waters," especially in the summer. There was a group of Orthodox Jewish Kosher hotels that catered to Hasidic Rebbes who met their followers each year in Marienbad. Franz Kafka visited the Belzer Rebbe in Marienbad in 1916.

Meletz (Mielec): A town in Rzeszow province, southeast Poland. Jews lived in Meletz from the seventeenth century. "In 1765, there were 585 Jewish poll-tax payers in Mielec . . . among them 12 tailors, 3 hatters, 3 bakers, 2 goldsmiths, 5 butchers, 4 musicans

(klezmer), and 3 jesters (*badhanim*). . . . The descendants of the Zaddik of Ropczyce were Rabbis there. There were Jewish farmers in nearby villages. In 1907, a Zionist organization, B'nei Yehudah, was organized. . . . In 1917, a Jewish library and a sports club came into being. The Jewish population, 2802, was 50 percent of the population in 1920." All in all, Meletz was a typical Eastern European shtetl. The few wealthy Jews were timber or grain merchants or feather dealers (*Encyclopedia Judaica*, vol. 11, p. 1525). My father, Charles Zucker, emigrated from the town in 1914 to France and eventually to America. While I was growing up, he convinced me that perhaps half of America's Jewry descend from Meletz's feather families. At first I was incredulous but his view was confirmed in 1962 when the families of forty percent of my first-year professors at Harvard Law School originally came from Meletz and its environs (Professors Alan Dershowitz and Charles Haar).

Mem: A Hebrew letter, the first in the phrase "mazel tov."

Van Leeuwenhoek: A brilliant Dutch scientist, Antonie van Leeuwenhoek invented one of the earliest microscopes. He was curiously an executor of the estate of Vermeer, who was most probably his friend.

Jiri Langer: *bocher*, a young student.

Page 143
Samuel Sanders: Howard M. Sachar, *A History of the Jews in America* (New York: Vintage Press), p. 23. Samuel Sanders was a Jewish-American scout who accompanied Daniel Boone in his travels in Tennessee and Kentucky. Boone's contact with Jews was extensive. Cohen and Isaacs of Richmond, Virginia, employed Boone in 1781 to survey land in Kentucky. Boone was given six pounds as an advance payment. On the back of the land-warrant receipt is the Yiddish, *Resit fun Kornel Bon far 1000 akir lanit. Encyclopedia Judaica*, vol. 10, p. 909.

Black Elk (1863–1930): Black Elk was an Oglala Sioux holy man. The quote is from David Borgenicht, ed., *Native American Wisdom*, p. 20.

Page 145
Bobby Fischer: Chess moves and quote are from Hooper and Whyld, *The Oxford Companion to Chess* (New York: Oxford University Press, 1984.), p. 117

Page 147
Weingarten Gospels: A sumptuous medieval gospel bejeweled book cover that J. P. Morgan acquired. Morgan's "feeling for works of art was the outcome rather of a romantic and historical feeling for the splendor of past ages than a strictly aesthetic one. What he recognized in an object was primarily its importance, the part it had played in the evolution of history." Cass Canfield, *The Incredible Pierpont Morgan: Financier and Art Collector* (New York: Harper & Row, 1974), p. 101.

Page 149
Eliza Draper: David Thomson, *Wild Excursions: The Life and Fictions of Laurence Sterne* (New York: McGraw-Hill Book Co., 1972), p. 238.

Laurence Sterne: *Wild Excursions*, p. 262. Sterne to Liza Draper in March 1767. See also William Cutley and Arnold Wright, *Sterne's Eliza* (New York: Alfred A. Knopf, 1923). Copyright 1923 by William Cutley and Arnold Wright; used by permission of Alfred A. Knopf, a division of Random House, Inc.

Simha Bunam: Quote from Elie Wiesel, *Souls on Fire: Portraits and Legends of Hasidic Masters* (Northvale, N.J.: Jason Aronson, 1993), p. 224.

Dara Shikoh (1615–1659): Dara Shikoh was the eldest son of Shah Jahan and very much his father's heir apparent. Sensitive, perhaps overrefined, and religion-intoxicated, Dara Shikoh made significant contributions to the intellectual history of India. As the historian S. M. Ikram has observed, "In *Manna-ul-Bahrain* [the mingling of two oceans] which was completed in 1655, Dara Shikoh tried to trace parallels between Islam Sufism and Hindu Vedantism. In the introduction, he says that after a deep and prolonged study of Islamic Sufism and Hindu Vendantism, he came to the conclusion that there were not many differences except verbal in the ways in which Hindu thinkers and Muslim Sufis sought and comprehended truth. He sounded a note that was to become the hallmark of many Hindu (as well as Western) thinkers in the 19th and 20th centuries." S. M. Ikram, *Muslim Civilization in India* (New York: Columbia University Press, 1904), quoted in Pratapaditya Pal, *Romance of the Taj Mahal*, pp. 36–37. "As a political strategist, Dara Shikoh fell far short of his brother Aurangzeb. After Shah Jahan fell sick in 1657, Aurangzeb first defeated the other two brothers, Murad and Shah Shujah, and then beheaded Dara Shikoh and slowly poisoned his son Suleiman Shikoh, thus ending the reign of the Ruler of the World" (Pratapaditya Pal, *Romance of the Taj Mahal*, p. 32).

CHAPTER 8

Page 151
Daniel Guggenheim: John H. Davis, *Guggenheim* (New York: Shapolsky Publishers, 1988).

Guggenheim Exploration: Meyer Guggenheim, the father of seven sons, founded one of the largest mining fortunes America has ever produced. In 1879, Meyer acquired a one-third interest in the A.Y., an enormous but water-logged silver mine near Leadville, Colorado. What was purchased for $25,000 turned out to be valued in 1887 at $14,556,000, producing a million ounces of silver a year. Merging M. Guggenheim & Sons with Philadelphia Smelter and in turn into American Smelting and Refining Company, the Guggenheims became one of the premier American business and philanthropic family dynasties of the twentieth century. Jacqueline Bogard Weld, *Peggy: The Wayward Guggenheim* (New York: E. P. Dutton, 1986), p. 7.

Page 153
Mikhail Nekhemyevich Tal: Hooper and Whyld, *The Oxford Companion to Chess* (New York: Oxford University Press, 1984).

Jahanghir: A. Rogers, ed., *The Jahanghir Nama*, trans. H. Beveridge (Delhi, 1968), vol. 2, pp. 143–144.

Page 155
Claude Monet: Hereward Lester Cooke, *Painting Techniques of the Masters* (New York: Watson-Guptill Publications, 1972), p. 186.

Johannes Vermeer: John Nash, *Vermeer* (Amsterdam: Scala Books, 1991).

Neesk cushion: According to John Nash in *Vermeer* (p. 113), "her diligence preserves her virtue. Of that, there is little doubt. Within easy reach of her right hand lies a book which is surely The Book, the Bible. But what is the work box doing there, so prominently placed? . . . The work box was known in Vermeer's day as

naaikussen, which is literally a needle cushion. But *naaien* means, vulgarly and metaphorically, to copulate, and though the noun *kussen* means cushion, the verb *kussen* also means to kiss."

Subrahmandan Chandrasekhar: A brilliant Indian astronomer who posited astronomical laws explaining the collapse of stars.

Page 157
Peggy Guggenheim: Deborah Solomon, *Jackson Pollock* (New York: Simon & Schuster, 1987), pp. 109, 157.

Page 159
Dr. Paul-Ferdinand Gachet: A French doctor and expert on melancholia who opened a clinic in Auvers-sur-Oise, where he treated van Gogh. Letter to Vincent van Gogh, Auvers, July 1890; Susan Alyson Stein, *Van Gogh: A Retrospective* (New York: Beaux Arts Editions, 1986). A painter himself, Gachet totally identified with van Gogh. He seemed to think, however, that van Gogh's problems were less than serious. Van Gogh noted about Gachet, "I have seen Dr. Gachet, who gives me the impression of being rather eccentric, but his experience as a doctor must keep him balanced enough to combat the nervous trouble from which he certainly seems to be suffering as seriously as I." David Sweetman, *Van Gogh* (New York: Crown, 1990), p. 326.

Sonny Boy Williamson II: Sonny Boy, a prominent Delta Blues musician, was with Robert Johnson, the greatest Delta Blues singer, when Johnson was poisoned on Saturday night, August 13, 1938. Stephen C. LaVere, *Robert Johnson: The Complete Recordings*, liner notes (New York: Columbia/Legacy, 1990), p. 20

Vincent van Gogh: John Russell, *The Meaning of Modern Art* (New York: Harper & Row, 1984).

Theo van Gogh: In a letter to Wil van Gogh, 27 September 1890. Susan Alyson Stein, *Van Gogh: A Retrospective*.

Page 161
Shas: The printed multivolume edition of the Talmud.

Yischar Dor of Belz (1854–1926): Hasidic Rebbe, leader of the Dynasty of Belz.

Mitnagdim: Those Jews who oppose the Hasidim.

Page 163
Jacob ben Joseph Abendana (1630–1685): A member of a Sephardic family widely dispersed among northern European countries. The name is originally from the Arabic: Ibn-Dina. Jacob was the elder brother of Isaac Abendana. He was born in Spain and grew up in Hamburg. In 1655, he became principal of a yeshiva in Amsterdam, and in 1681 he was the Haham (rabbi) of the Spanish-Portuguese synagogue in London. A polemicist, he translated Hebrew books into Spanish to make them understandable to fellow Marranos and Christian theologians. *Encyclopedia Judaica*, vol. 2, p. 66.

Isaac Sardo Abendana: A Dutch Sephardic diamond merchant who lived in Fort St. George, Madras, he served as diamond consultant and adviser to Thomas Pitt. Litigation followed Isaac Abendana's last will and testament, described in Madras court records as "written in certain characters and other numerous abbreviations unknown to all of us." This was probably a reference to Hebrew. Abendana asked his widow only to remarry in "a city where there is a synagogue."

Bob Dylan: See Bob Dylan, *Bob Dylan: Writings and Drawings* (New York: Alfred A. Knopf, 1973).

Page 165
Paul Gauguin: Michael Howard, *Gauguin* (London: Dorling Kindersley, 1992), p. 6. Clovis and Aline were Gauguin's parents. Clovis, his father, was a revolutionary newspaper reporter.

Kaddish: A prayer in Aramaic (meaning "holy") recited with congregational responses at the close of individual sections of the public synagogue prayer service. The heart of the prayer is the congregational response, "May his G-d's great name be blessed forever and to all eternity. . . ." It is recited as a prayer for the soul of the departed but is really an expression of the justification of divine judgment (*zidduk ha-din*).

CHAPTER 9

Page 167
Jacques Derrida: An Algerian Jew, and founder of the deconstructionist critical movement in France, Derrida stressed examining a text in and of itself. He is fascinated by interplay of the written and oral texts, much given to hermeneutics (close reading of the text). He believes in no fixed canon and in an infinity of meaning. Norman Cantor, *Twentieth Century Culture* (New York: Peter Lang Publishing, 1988), pp. 359–360. Quote from Jeff Collins and Bill Mayblin, *Introducing Derrida* (New York: Totem Books, 1997), pp. 100–101.

Hayyim Vital: Lawrence Fine and Louis Jacobs, *Safed Spirituality* (New York: Paulist Press, 1984), p. 67.

Page 169
Remez: Literally, in Hebrew, "hint": there are four levels to interpret the Torah. The acronym Pardes (Paradise) sums them up: Pshat (the literal meaning), Remez (the allegorical meaning), Derash (Haggadic storytelling meanings), and Sod (the secret meaning). Thus the Torah was to be read and understood, each word, on at least four different levels.

Rashi: Galut in Hebrew means "exile."

Samuel ben Meir: See Chaim Pearl, *Rashi* (London: Weidenfeld & Nicholson, 1998), p. 32.

Vincent van Gogh: From John Russell, *Meaning of Modern Art* (New York: Harper & Row, 1974).

Bimah: A raised pulpit in a synagogue from which the Torah is read; also, the stand on which the Torah is placed. In an Ashkenazic synagogue, the pulpit tends to be in the center. In a Sephardic synagogue, the bimah is often at the opposite end of the synagogue from the arch.

Page 171
Isaac Luria: Jacob Neusner, *Judaism's Theological Voice* (Chicago: University of Chicago Press, 1985).

Vincent van Gogh: Bruce Bernard, ed., *Vincent by Himself* (New York: New York Graphic Society, 1985), p. 185.

Page 173
Milena Jesenska: Ernst Pawel, *The Nightmare of Reason: A Life of Franz Kafka* (New York: Farrar, Straus & Giroux, 1983). See note for page 7.

Page 175
Vincent van Gogh: Hans Konig, *The World of Vermeer* (New York: Time Life Books, 1967), p. 160.

Page 177
Michael Ventris: In 1952 Ventris, an architect, deciphered the Minoan language (linear B), the earliest European script. The language predates the Greek alphabet by five hundred years. Andrew Robinson, *The Story of Writing* (London: Thames & Hudson, 1995), p. 109. Linear B Syllabic Grids, p. 117, Decipherment of Linear B by Michael Ventris.

Seer of Lublin: See note for page 65.

Page 179
F. Scott Fitzgerald: Quote from Zelda Sayre Fitzgerald, *Save Me the Last Waltz* (New York: Charles Scribner's Sons, 1932); vignette from Jeffrey Meyer, *Married to Genius* (New York: Barnes & Noble Books, Harper & Row, 1977), pp. 190, 192.

Ernest Hemingway: Morley Callaghan, quoted in Jeffrey Meyer, *Married to Genius*, p. 174.

Zelda Sayre Fitzgerald: F. Scott Fitzgerald, *Tender Is the Night* (New York: Charles Scribner's Sons, 1934).

Page 181
Yidden: Jews.

Rebbe Mendel of Rymanov: Abraham Joshua Heschel, *A Passion for Truth* (New York: Farrar, Straus & Giroux, 1973), p. 64. Copyright © 1973, 1995 by Sylvia Heschel, executrix of the Estate of Abraham Joshua Heschel.

Yo'etz Rakatz: Polish rabbinical text, nineteenth century. Quote from Abraham Yaakov Finkel, *The Great Chassidic Masters* (Northvale, N.J.: Jason Aronson, 1992), p. 109.

Max Brod (1884–1968): Franz Kafka's boyhood companion in Prague. A novelist and a Zionist, he left Prague in 1939 for Palestine, where he directed the Habima Theater. Brod was a precocious writer, already published while in high school. Part of the "Prague Circle" (with Kafka, Hugo Bergman, Franz Werfel), Brod introduced Kafka to the writings of Plato, encouraged him as a writer, was Kafka's literary and personal confidant, and eventually became his biographer. "Many were the nights we spent together in theaters, cabarets, or in wine taverns in the company of pretty girls. For as it happens, the picture of Kafka as some sort of desert monk or anchorite is totally misleading. At least it most certainly does not apply to his student years. And later on, what he wanted out of life was too much rather than too little—either perfection or nothing at all. . . . His whole being was a quest for purity." Ernst Pawel, *The Nightmare of Reason: A Life of Franz Kafka* (New York: Farrar, Straus & Giroux, 1984), p. 133. Max Brod, *Franz Kafka* (New York: Schocken Books, 1963).

Mendel of Rymanov (d. 1815): An ascetic Hasidic rebbe, he prayed for Napoleon to be victorious because he saw the Napoleonic wars as a struggle between Gog and Magog—heralding the coming of the Messiah. His student, Naftali of Ropshitz, told the tale that the Rymaner had blessed a man who became richer and richer each day. The Ropshitzer inquired of his master, Menahem Mendel, why this man deserved to receive a blessing of such magnitude. The Rymaner replied, "I merely blessed him that he might enjoy a comfortable living. But the man gives away so much to charity that his fortune must be increased abundantly by Heaven, so that he may have sufficient for his personal comforts." Ohel Naftali, quoted in Louis Newman, *The Hasidic Anthology* (New York: Schocken Books, 1963), p. 38.

Apikoras: A non-believing Jew. From the Greek for "epicurean."

Page 183
Hibbing: Hibbing, Minnesota, is situated at the center of the Mesabi Iron Range. In 1893, a German prospector, Frank Dietrich van Ahlen, discovered the vein; he later changed his name to Hibbing. Bob Dylan spent his youth (1947–1959) in Hibbing.

Caitlin Thomas: Wife of Dylan Thomas. See Paul Ferris, *Caitlin: The Life of Caitlin Thomas* (London: Pimlico Books/Random House, 1995).

Page 185
Vincent van Gogh: Meyer Shapiro, *Van Gogh* (New York: Harry N. Abrams, 1983), p. 60.

Messiah: "From the Aramaic *meshiha* or king (the anointed king). A charismatically endowed descendant of David who the Jews of the Roman period believed would be caused by G-d to break the yoke of the heathen and to reign over a restored Kingdom of Israel to which all Jews of the exile would return. This is a strictly postbiblical concept." (*Encyclopedia Judaica,* vol. 11, pp. 1407–8.) Maimonides felt that a Messiah would be a man whose teaching would change the world. This simple human would provide a political deliverance of the Jews from the rule of the Gentiles. A Messiah would be born in a human fashion, and no cataclysmic effect would occur during the Messiah's lifetime. This minimized the medieval apocalyptic approach to the days of the Messiah.

Page 187
Sir Alfred Beit: Partner to Cecil Rhodes in developing mines in South Africa, he was the last private owner of a Vermeer painting. Arthur K. Wheelock, *Johannes Vermeer* (Washington, D.C.: National Gallery of Art, 1995).

Sir Ernest Oppenheimer: Sir Theodore Gregory, *Ernest Oppenheimer and the Economic Development of South Africa* (London: Oxford University Press, 1962), p. 49.

Nathan Oppenheim: Ron Chernow, *The Warburgs* (New York: Random House, 1993), p. 45.

Page 189
Academy on High (Yeshiva Shel Ma'lah): In this academy, Torah is studied each day. As in the Academy Below (Yeshiva Shel Matah), what occurs on earth influences what occurs above. According to the Talmud, "Greetings are sent from the Academy on High to people still alive. Abbaye received these greetings once a week on the eve of the Sabbath." (*Encyclopedia Judaica,* vol. 2, p. 208.) Nothing suggests this academy is identical to paradise. There is a belief that admission to the academy on high is automatic for scholars. The rest may enjoy the privilege by performing deeds or by assisting scholars to study by supporting houses of learning (Talmud: Pes. 53b).

Isaac Luria: Quote from Daniel C. Matt, *The Essential Kaballah, the Heart of Jewish Mysticism* (New York: HarperCollins, 1995), p. 14.

James Joyce: From Richard Ellman, *James Joyce* (Oxford: Oxford University Press, 1982), p. 466.

Page 191
Black Elk: At thirteen, Black Elk, an Oglala Sioux, watched Chief Crazy Horse fight Custer in July 1876. See Alvin M. Josephy, *Five Hundred Nations* (New York: Alfred A. Knopf, 1994), pp. 401, 442. Black Elk was present at the Wounded Knee massacre of Indians in Pine Ridge in 1890 and recorded it in his memoir, *Black Elk Speaks: The Mystic Warriors of the Plains* (Thomas E. Mails, Marlowe & Co.).

Sephiroth: Kabbalists regarded the world as being influenced by ten Sephiroth (from the Greek for "sphere"). The Sephiroth are aspects of G-d. The Sephiroth interact with one another in harmonic and dynamic fashion, linking heaven and earth.

Page 193
Aurangzeb (1618–1707): The Moghul emperor of India from 1658 to 1707, Aurangzeb defied the credo of his great-great-great-grand-father, Babur, who believed "that defeated enemies must be conciliated rather than antagonized if they are to be ruled effectively afterwards, and that one's own followers must be prevented by rigid discipline from victimizing the local population." Bamber Gascoigne, *The Great Moghuls* (New York: Harper & Row, 1971), p. 42. Aurangzeb's reign was marked by intense religiosity and generally unbending antagonism to the Hindu majority of India. After ascending the throne as emperor in 1660, Aurangzeb held prisoner "at one and the same time his father (Shah Jahan), in the fort at Agra, and his eldest son (Mohammed Sultan), in the fort at Gwalior." Aurangzeb, as emperor, appointed a censor of morals. "Hostilities between Muslims and Hindus undeniably increased," which many feel led, two-and-a-half centuries later, to the partition of the subcontinent into India and Pakistan (Gascoigne, *The Great Moghuls*).

Max Brod: Max Brod, ed., *The Blue Octavo Notebooks of Franz Kafka* (Cambridge: Exact Change, 1991), p. 1.

Louis Ginsberg: *Legends of the Bible* (Philadelphia: Jewish Publications Society, 1992).

Franz Kafka: See Max Brod, ed., *The Blue Octavo Notebooks of Franz Kafka*, p. 1.

Page 195
Yehezkel Shraga Zucker: Story adapted from Abraham Yaakov Finkel, *The Great Chassidic Masters*, p. 171.

CHAPTER 10

Page 197
Bob Dylan: Craig McGregor, ed., *Bob Dylan: A Retrospective*, p. 141.

Ushpizin: Patriarchal/matriarchal guests.

Søren Kierkegaard (1813–1855): Danish philosopher of faith. See his *Philosophical Fragment*, trans. David Swenson and Howard V. Hong (Princeton, N.J.: Princeton University Press, 1941), pp. 57–58; also, *Unscientific Postscript*, trans. David Swenson and Walter Lowrie (Princeton, N.J.: Princeton University Press, 1941), p. 483. The youngest child of a large family, Kierkegaard's spiritual abode was the same melancholy that had haunted his father. "What the English say about my sadness, my sadness is my castle." William Hubben, *Dostoyevsky, Kierkegaard, Nietzsche, and Kafka* (New York: Simon & Schuster, 1980), p. 16. Kierkegaard broke his two-year engagement to seventeen-year-old Regine Olsen, who was "light as a bird and as bold as a thought," sending his engagement ring back to her with the following words: "In the Orient it means death to receive a silken cord but in this case to mail the ring is death to the sender" (Hubben, p. 15). He transformed himself from an ironic bound-up dreamlike figure in a world of pleasure (*Diary of a Seducer*) into a lonely knight of faith. In *Fear and Trembling*, Kierkegaard describes the lonely knight of faith's sense of the absurd: "The fact that with G-d all things are possible. The absurd is not one of the factors which can be discriminated within the proper compass of understanding. It is not identical with the improbable, the unexpected, the unforeseen. Faith is the highest passion known to man." *Fear and Trembling*, trans. Alastair Hannay (London: Penguin Books, 1985).

Page 199
Nathanael West: Quote is from Jay Martin, *Nathanael West: The Art of His Life* (New York: Carroll & Graf Publishers, 1970), p. 388. Nathanael West is a pseudonym for Nathaniel Weinstein. Born in 1903, he published his first novel while at Brown University, where he obtained his admission by substituting his application for that of another (successful) applicant also named Nathan Weinstein. West's experiences as a hotel manager from 1927 to 1933 in New York formed the background for *Miss Lonelyhearts*, which he wrote in 1933. From 1935 until his death in 1940 he lived in Hollywood. He was a great friend of F. Scott Fitzgerald, who considered West the most promising of American novelists. West died in an automobile accident while rushing back to Hollywood after hearing of Fitzgerald's death.

F. Scott Fitzgerald: Quote from *The Crackup* (New York: New Directions), p. 171.

Rabbi Barukh of Mezbozh: A grandson of the Baal Shem Tov. Rebbe Zvi Hersh of Zhidachov so yearned to hear Rebbe Barukh sing songs that he hid himself in Rebbe Barukh's study. Zvi Hersh later confided to his friends, "The master was in ecstasy, his entire being a flame, evolving in another world; and when he came to the verse *Ani ledodi* ("I belong to my beloved as my beloved belongs to me"), he repeated each word with such fervor that I too found myself thrust into another world." Elie Wiesel, *Somewhere a Master* (New York: Simon & Schuster, 1993), p. 75.

Page 201
Cohanim: Members of the priestly class of Jews. They comprise approximately five percent of the Jewish male population. Recent studies have disclosed a common genetic map in Cohanic males.

Page 205
Franz Kafka: Quote from Nahum N. Glatzer, ed., *Franz Kafka: Parables and Paradoxes* (New York: Schocken Books, 1961), p. 81.

Claude Monet: Vignette is from Edward Lucie Smith, *Impressionist Women* (New York: Abbeville Press/Artabras, 1993), p. 40.

Aryeh Judah Leib ben Ephraim HaKohen (Gutwirth family) (1658–1720): A Moravian rabbinic authority and Fisher's ancestor. In the introduction to the book of responsa Sha'ar Ephraim, published in 1688 by Aryeh Leib, he described how his father, Ephraim HaKohen, prayed that his own life be taken and that of Aryeh Leib—who had succumbed to the plague in Ofen in 1678—be spared. His father charged Aryeh with the responsibility of publishing his rabbinic manuscripts. Aryeh went to Jerusalem, published his father's responsa on the Shulhan Arukh, Sha'ar Ephraim. After returning to Prague, Aryeh Leib headed a yeshiva. Subsequently, Aryeh returned to Eretz Israel, where he died in Safed. *Encyclopedia Judaica*, vol. 3, p. 667.

Page 207
Kippah: Hebrew for head covering, A *yarmulke* or other covering

that Orthodox Jews today wear while praying or eating to show fear of G-d.

Sambatyon: A legendary river that rested (did not flow) on the Sabbath.

Rembrandt: He married in 1634 and lost a child, Rombartus, in 1635. See "The Angel Stopping Abraham from Sacrificing Isaac to G-d" (Genesis 22:10–12), 1635, the Hermitage, St. Petersburg. See also Gary Schwartz, *Rembrandt: His Life, His Paintings* (New York: Penguin Books, 1985), p. 171.

Rabbi Yitzhak Meir of Ger (1789–1866): Great-great-grandfather of Abraham Mordechai Leib of Ger; the quote is from Abraham Yaakov Finkel, *The Great Chassidic Masters* (Northvale, N.J.: Jason Aronson, 1922). Gur, or "Ger" in Yiddish, was a Hasidic dynasty that flourished in Poland from 1859 until 1939, when it moved to Jerusalem. Yitzhak Meir was its founder. A student of Simha Bunam of Pshiskhe and of the Kotzker Rebbe, Yitzhak Meir wrote Hiddushei HaRim: "Every Jew possesses some good trait pleasing unto the Lord, but no one of us is able to diagnose himself adequately to discover which trait it is. You may be sure that the qualities which bring you satisfaction are not those which the Lord approves in you." Yo'etz Rakatz, *Siah Sifrei Kodesh* (Lodz, Poland: 1929), p. 104.

Abraham Mordechai Leib (1866–1948): The most prominent figure of early twentieth century European Jewish Orthodoxy. He is also called the Imre Emet (Speaker of Truth). He escaped from Ger to Warsaw and finally to Israel in 1940. He died on Shavuot at the height of the siege of Jerusalem in 1948.

Sfas Emet: Literally, in Hebrew, "the true language." Name of the Ger yeshiva founded after the Holocaust. "Six days shall you do your work but on the seventh day you shall stop, in order that your ox and your donkey may rest and your maid's son and the foreigner may be refreshed" *(Exodus 23:12)*. Commenting on this passage in Exodus, Mordechai Leib said: "In order that your ox and your donkey may rest—could this really be the reason for resting on Shabbat? This is what the scripture means. Your rest on Shabbat must be ushered in with feverish preparation and accompanied by fiery ecstasy, purity, and intense joy, so that you inject a hallowed Shabbat atmosphere into your environment, into nature, and into the animals around you. Create an aura of holiness that influences everything that encompasses you. For example, we read in the Midrash [commentary on the Torah] that Rabbi Yochanan ben Torta's ox was so strongly affected by his master's Shabbat atmosphere that it refused to do work on the Shabbat even for a non-Jew." Abraham Yaakov Finkel, *Contemporary Sages* (Northvale, N.J.: Jason Aronson, 1994), pp. 187–190.

Page 211
Yehezkel Shraga Zucker (1905–1982): See Jerome Mintz, *Legends of Hassidim* (Chicago: University of Chicago Press), p. 195.

Sanzer Rebbe (1793–1876): Hayyim Halberstam of Sanz was a Hasidic leader who believed in the ecstasy of prayer and composed and sang many Hasidic melodies. See *Encyclopedia Judaica*, vol. 7, p. 1176. The Sanzer Rebbe could never spare the money for the purchase of a new book. He used to say, "I must use this money to supply the poor who depend upon me for aid." Louis I. Newman, *Hassidic Anthology* (New York: Schocken Books, 1963), p. 24. Among the Sanzer's sons was Yehezkel of Shinyever (1811–1899). The Sanzer's grandsons included Solomon ben Mayer of Bobov and Jekutiel Judah, the Klausenburger Rebbe.

Hayyim: "Life" in Hebrew.

Page 213

Menachem Mendel Schneerson (b. in 1902): Perhaps the greatest Hasidic Rabbi of the past century. Based in the Crown Heights section of Brooklyn (770 Eastern Parkway), the Lubavitcher Rebbe, as he was known, lived through many of the greatest political cataclysms of the twentieth century. From an early Czarist Russian childhood onward, Menachem Mendel displayed enormous learning. Reared under communism, he married Yoseph Yitzhak Schneerson's daughter, Chaya Mushka (1901–1988), his cousin. He moved to Warsaw and later to Berlin to study mathematics and science at the University of Berlin. Leaving in 1933 because of the rise of Nazism, Menachem Mendel again moved, this time to Paris. In June 1941 he escaped to New York, where in 1951 he was chosen to be the Lubavitcher Rebbe. Each year the numbers of his Hasidim and those who came to draw religious inspiration grew. Because of his dedicated Lubavitch emissaries, through more than 1,500 Habad Lubavitch centers and institutions, the words of the Rebbe girdle the globe. Even in the largest of crowds, one always felt a direct connection to him. See Simon Jacobson, *Towards a Meaningful Life: The Wisdom of the Rebbe Menachem Mendel Schneerson* (New York: Morrow Press, 1995), pp. xxiii–xxv.

Especially successful were the Rebbe's efforts to keep alive the embers of Judaism in the Soviet Union before and after the Second World War. Professor Yirmiyahu Branover, an observant Jew and prominent Israeli scientist who emigrated from Russia to Israel in 1977, made a startling revelation. He disclosed that when former Soviet President Mikhail Gorbachev came to power in 1985, the Lubavitcher Rebbe instructed Branover to notify the authorities that the Soviet Union would soon change its policy toward Soviet Jewish emigration and Israel should begin making preparations for their absorption. "Everyone laughed," said Branover, "but in the end, his prophecy, just like other prophecies uttered by the Rebbe, materialized." Branover said that when Gorbachev and his wife Raisa were visiting Israel in 1992, Branover met with them and told them of the Rebbe's prediction. "They were shocked," Branover said. "They told me that in April 1985 they themselves were not even thinking of changing." Abraham Yaakov Finkel, *Contemporary Sages* (Northvale, N.J.: Jason Aronson, 1994), p. 159.

Rembrandt: See Rembrandt's sale catalog in Christopher White, *Rembrandt* (London: Thames & Hudson, 1984), p. 176.

Mansur: Court painter to Jahanghir. Called Nizam-al-Dor (the wonder of the age), Mansur traveled throughout Kashmir, painting both flora and fauna with an exactness and vivacity that revolutionized Moghul miniature painting.

Page 215

Pinchas Ehrenberg: Retold from Finkel's *The Great Chassidic Masters*, pp. 37, 38. Pinchas Ehrenberg was a survivor of the Holocaust. He miraculously found an original handwritten manuscript by Pinchas Shapiro of Korets (noted Hasidic Rebbe, 1728–1790) seven years after the war ended. Accompanying the manuscript were handwritten commentaries by Pinchas Chodorov, a twentieth century Polish scholar. Ehrenberg was the publisher of Rebbe Pinchas Shapiro's work, *Imrei Pinchas* (*Pinchas Spoke*), as well as the learned commentaries of the twentieth century scholar Pinchas Chodorov.

Korets Rebbe, Pinchas of Korets (1728–1790): Born in Shklov, Russia, and died in Shipitovka, Russia. The Baal Shem Tov said of his follower, Pinchas of Korets, "A soul such as that of Rabbi

Pinchas comes down to this world only once in five hundred years." Rabbi Pinchas once explained: "At the time of creation, the light of G-d flowed from the sphere of the spiritual down to the physical world through a series of vessels or emanations, but the vessels proved unable to contain the divine light. They broke. This primordial catastrophe is called the 'Shevirat Hakelim,' the breaking of the vessels. You can better understand it with an analogy. Think of a man who is deeply troubled and depressed. Suddenly he receives an exhilarating piece of good news. His troubles are over. Instead of jumping for joy, the man will break down crying. The bright light of the good news is too much for him. Similarly, the 'Shevirat Hakelim' meant that the vessels broke because they could not encompass the brilliant splendor of the luminescent light." Abraham Yaakov Finkel, *The Great Chassidic Masters*, p. 34.

Rabbi Leib: From Martin Buber, *Tales of the Hasidim*, p. 126. Martin Buber (1878–1965) was a Jewish theologian and philosopher. Born in Vienna, Buber lived in Lemberg with his very learned grandfather, Solomon Buber. A Zionist and humanist, at the age of twenty-six Buber began his studies of Hasidic tales and philosophy. *I and thou* is his interpretation of Hasidic ideas of relationship between G-d and Man and Man and G-d. *Tales of Rabbi Nachman* (1906) and *Tales of Hasidim I and II* as well as *I and Thou* (1957) and *Knowledge of Man* (1965) are among his best-known texts. In 1935, Buber was prohibited by the Nazis to speak at Jewish gatherings. He then spoke at Quaker meetings until the Gestapo forbade him from speaking there as well. In 1938, Buber emigrated to Palestine, where he taught at the Hebrew University. He was active in Berit Shalom, which favored a joint Arab–Israel state. He was a great influence on Christian and Jewish theologians. See *Encyclopedia Judaica*, vol. 4, pp. 1429–1433.

Page 217

George C. Williamson: Cataloger of the J. Pierpont Morgan collection. See Andrew Sinclair, *Corsair: The Life of J. Pierpont Morgan* (Boston: Little, Brown & Co., 1981), p. 201.

Max Brod: Johann Bauer. *Kafka and Prague* (Prague Publishers, 1971).

Page 219

Vincent van Gogh: Bruce Bernard, ed., *Vincent by Himself* (Boston: Little, Brown & Co., 1985), p. 214.

Marcel Proust: *Swann's Way* (New York: Random House, 1981), p. 14.

Page 221

Rabbi Nathan: Disciple of Rabbi Nachman of Breslov. Quote is from Marc-Alain Ouaknin, *The Burnt Book* (Princeton, N.J.: Princeton University Press, 1995), p. 265.

Page 222

Johannes Vermeer, *Young Woman with a Water Jug*: "The painting was bought by Henry Marquand for $800 in 1887 and given by him to the Metropolitan Museum of Art the following year. It is the first Vermeer painting to enter an American collection." Arthur Wheelock, Jr., *Vermeer* (New York: Harry N. Abrams, 1988), p. 88.

Page 223

Rabbi Akiva Eiger (1761–1837): A great Talmudist and halachic authority. At the age of thirteen he wrote a learned text on a tractate of the Talmud (Chullin); at fifteen was already known for his devout piety and soaring knowledge. His yeshiva in Friedland attracted hundreds of students. He was the outstanding Torah personality of his generation and the author of a Talmic gloss (Gilayon Hashas) as well as numerous responsa. Abraham Yaakov Finkel, *The Great Torah Commentators* (Northvale, N.J.: Jason Aronson, 1996), p. 71.

Chief Seattle: Quote is from Kent Nerburn, *Wisdom of the Great Chiefs* (San Rafael, Calif.: New World Library, 1994), pp. 73–76.

Author's note: Many years have passed since this novel was begun, and many books were read. Some of these books were lent to friends and, as happens, found new homes in other people's libraries. Trying to check some of my quotations and references and trying to remember what Kafka, Joyce, and van Gogh did or did not say have proved to be difficult, if not impossible. I apologize to author and reader for any misquotations or incorrect references, but all should keep in mind that mistakes were made in the hallowed name of fiction.

ACKNOWLEDGMENTS

On a marvelous day at an Allen Ginsberg concert I met Peter Mayer. His enthusiasm and extraordinary energy have shepherded this novel into print.

Blue owes much to all at The Overlook Press: Tracy Carns, Albert DePetrillo, John Siciliano, Janet Hotson Baker, and Hermann Lademann have been wonderful to work with. Bernie Schleifer is a miracle.

The manuscript has been expertly edited and prepared, over and over, by Cindy Cordes Ross, Tasha Blaine, George Blecher, and Rachel Zucker. Alison Jasonides has beautifully shaped the art work. Mary Flower graciously gathered permissions.

Long time friends have helped immensely: John Flattau, David Birnbaum, Lee Grove, Milton Ginsberg, Alfred Moldovan, Daniel Friedenberg, Bill Gross, Jim Traub, David Jaffe, Jan Mitchell, Caroline Alexander, Derek J. Content, William Hamilton, Eden Collingsworth Hamilton, Emil Kleinhaus. All at the Golden Notebook (Woodstock), Manning and Jane Rubin have all tirelessly discussed aspects of the work. Elie Wiesel and Jay Margolis have been an inspiration.

Over the years my family has given me the loving confidence to persevere. Finally, always, the charms and wisdom of Barbara made all this possible.

To everyone, my deepest thanks.

ART SOURCES

Frontispiece (Opposite Title Page)
Photograph of Jewish wedding ring, Venice, late sixteenth century. The blue enameled roof on this ring opens to disclose a compartment and a gold plaque engraved with the initials of the words "mazel tov." An almost identical ring is in the British Museum (London, catalog no. 1337-9), and a similar one was sold in the Melvin Gutman jewelry sale (May 15, 1970, no. 111). Private Collection (RCZ), New York. Courtesy Peter Schaaf.

(Opposite Guide to the Reader)
Johannes Vermeer (Johannes van der Meer van Delft, 1632–1675), *The Kitchenmaid*. Credit: Rijksmuseum, Amsterdam.

CHAPTER 1

Page viii
Franz Kafka at about thirteen. Photo: Archive Klaus Wagenbach, Berlin.

Page 2
Johannes Vermeer, *The Lacemaker*, detail (c. 1669–1670), oil on wood. The Louvre, Paris. Credit: Erich Lessing/Art Resource (N.Y.).

Page 4
Julie Löwy, mother of Franz Kafka. Photo: Archive Klaus Wagenbach, Berlin.

Page 6
Passport photograph of Franz Kafka at the time he worked for the Worker's Accident Insurance Company. Credit: Archive Klaus Wagenbach, Berlin.

Page 8
James Joyce setting out for a walk, 1938. Credit: © Gisele Freund/Agency Nina Beskow.

Page 10
Bob Dylan performs at the Nassau Coliseum in Uniondale, Long Island, January 29, 1974. Credit: Amalie Rothschild/Corbis-Bettmann.

Page 12
Vincent van Gogh (1853–1890), *Cafe Terrace at Night* (1885), oil on canvas. Rijksmuseum Kroller-Muller, Otterlo, Netherlands. Credit: Erich Lessing/Art Resource (N.Y.).

Page 14
Photograph of Tuviah Gutman Gutwirth, Raphael Fisher's mother's father.

Page 16
Joan Baez and Bob Dylan, along with entertainers Joni Mitchell and Richie Havens, performing at Madison Square Garden, December 8, 1975. Credit: UPI/Corbis-Bettmann.

Page 18
Yeshiva student looking at a page from the Talmud in Slonim, 1937. Gelatin silver print. Credit: Roman Vishniac; © Mara Vishniac Kohn. Courtesy International Center of Photography.

CHAPTER 2

Page 20
Claude Monet (1840–1926) in his garden in Giverny. Credit: Corbis/Underwood & Underwood.

Page 22
Photograph of sixteenth century Venetian ring set with uncut diamond crystals of the purest white water from Golconda, India. Courtesy Peter Schaaf.

Page 24
Prague. Credit: Archive Klaus Wagenbach, Berlin.

Page 26
The Taj Mahal Emerald, 1630–1640, 114 carats. © Michael Freeman, Arthur M. Sackler Gallery, Smithsonian (private collection).

Page 28
Photograph of Rabbi Ezra Dangoor with his family in Iraqi dress in Rangoon, 1895. Credit: The Exilarch Foundation, London.

Page 30
Golconda diamond, purest white "D" color, weighing 3.22 carats, cut in India, c. 1780. Courtesy Peter Schaaf.

Page 32
Albert Einstein with Dr. Charles St. John. Credit: UPI/Corbis-Bettmann.

Page 34
Johannes Vermeer, *The Art of Painting*, detail. Kunsthistorisches Museum, Vienna. Credit: Erich Lessing/Art Resource (N.Y.).

Page 36
Rough (uncut) diamond crystals separated by color. Courtesy DeBeers Diamond Information Council.

Page 38
Ceremonial crown of Rabbi Israel of Ruzhin. Courtesy Sotheby's.

Page 40
Photograph of Magen David Synagogue in Calcutta. Credit: The Israel Museum, Jerusalem. Photo by Richard Lobell.

Page 42
Photograph of Franz Kafka at the time he received a doctorate of law, c. 1906. Credit: Archive Klaus Wagenbach, Berlin.

Page 44
Rembrandt van Rijn (1606–1669), *The Jewish Bride (Isaac and Rebecca)*, detail. Credit: Rijksmuseum, Amsterdam.

CHAPTER 3

Page 46
Enoch Zeeman, *Governor Elihu Yale*. Credit: Yale University Art Gallery. Gift of Dudley Long North, M.P., in 1789.

Page 48

Raphael, *La Velata* (1516). Palazzo Pitti, Florence. Credit: Alinari/Art Resource (N.Y.).

Page 50

Bobby Fischer. Credit: Keystone Press Agency.

Page 52

Johannes Vermeer, *The Geographer* (c. 1668–1669). Stadelscher Kunstinstitut, Frankfurt.

Page 54

Johannes Vermeer, *The Art of Painting*. The way the curtain is drawn back "is reminiscent of the theater, and indeed the curtain as a theatrical prop has a long tradition in painting. By introducing painting in this way, Vermeer emphasized that he was staging a scene." (Arthur Wheelock Jr., *Vermeer* [New York: Harry N. Abrams, 1988]; and "Proof," H. Miedema's Johannes Vermeer Schilderkunst, Amsterdam, 1972). Kunsthistorisches Museum, Vienna. Credit: Erich Lessing/Art Resource (N.Y.).

Page 56

Johannes Vermeer, *The Art of Painting,* detail. Kunsthistorisches Museum, Vienna. Credit: Erich Lessing/Art Resource (N.Y.).

Page 58

Norbert Goeneutte (1854–1894), *Dr. Paul Gachet*, art collector, doctor to Vincent van Gogh. Credit: Art Resource (N.Y.).

CHAPTER 4

Page 60

Jewish wedding ring, Venice, seventeenth century. Engraved with "mem" and "tav," the abbreviation for mazel tov, "Good Luck" in Hebrew. The plaque reveals the Hebrew initials M.T. for mazel tov, engraved in square Italian script. A variant reading in Hebrew, "morid tal," or "bestowing heavenly dew." Also the initials of a prayer for dew and precipitation in the winter time. Dew is always a blessing in Kabbalistic thought, as it, unlike rain, can never inconvenience or harm. See frontispiece photograph. Courtesy Peter Schaaf.

Page 62

Same as above.

Page 64

Page from the manuscript of James Joyce's *Finnegan's Wake*. Credit: © Gisele Freund/Agency Nina Beskow.

Page 66

The Bomberg Talmud, printed in Venice, 1520–23: the first page of the Talmud tractate Ketubbah. Courtesy Jewish Theological Seminary Library. Photo: Suzanne Kaufman.

Page 68

The three younger sons of Shah Jahan, moghul. Victoria and Albert Museum, London/Art Resource (N.Y.).

Page 70

Jewish wedding ring, southern Germany, c. 1620. Courtesy Peter Schaaf.

Page 72

Pendant Jewish wedding ring brooch, seventeenth century. The roof of the ring opens to reveal a plaque with letters abbreviating the words "mazel tov." The letters are hidden by the crystal inserted into the ring shank when it is worn as a brooch. Courtesy Peter Schaaf.

Page 74

Johannes Vermeer, *Lady Writing a Letter with Her Maid*. National Gallery of Ireland, Dublin. Credit: Giraudon/Art Resource (N.Y.).

Page 76

Johannes Vermeer. *The Art of Painting* (c. 1665–66), detail. Courtesy Kunsthistorisches Museum, Vienna. Credit: Erich Lessing/Art Resource (N.Y.).

Page 78

Claude Monet, *Waterlilies at Giverny* (1908). Private collection, Zurich. Credit: Giraudon/Art Resource (N.Y.).

Page 80

James Joyce's hands. Note the ring containing a cabochon sapphire on Joyce's finger, probably of a Ceylon (Sri Lankan) origin. The stone's blue color was emblematic to Joyce of both mystery and the sky of Greece. It was this sapphire's color that Joyce wished to use as a printer's color guide for the cover of *Ulysses*. Credit: © Gisele Freund/Agency Nina Beskow.

Page 82

Leon Bonnat, *Portrait of William T. Walters*, 1883. William Walters, a railroad magnate, was the richest man in the south in the late nineteenth century. His son, Henry Walters, continued and greatly enlarged his father's collection in all areas of art. The collection of art in the Walters Art Gallery in Baltimore is characterized by a remarkable level of taste and catholicity. It is widely regarded as possessing one of the finest collections of jewelry from all periods. Courtesy The Walters Art Gallery, Baltimore.

Page 84

Jewish marriage ring brooch, seventeenth century. Courtesy Peter Schaaf.

Page 86

Johannes Vermeer, detail of Cleo, from *The Art of Painting* (c. 1665–66). Note the signature of Johannes Vermeer placed directly next to the royal blue neck band of the dress worn by the sitter for the portrait. One feels the presence of Vermeer almost physically pulling at her dress. The model, representing the muse Cleo, with the instrument of Fame and a book of History, will trumpet Vermeer's fame long after his death. Kunsthistoriches Museum, Vienna. Credit: Erich Lessing/Art Resource (N.Y.).

CHAPTER 5

Page 88

First page of the Talmud Berakot. Gutman Gutwirth's study volume. Printed Vienna, 1871. In the center of the page (shaded) is the mishnah. Directly below it is the gemorah, itself a commentary and an expansion of the mishnah. The inner column (to the left of the mishnah and gemorah) is the commentary of Rashi, written in "Rashi script." The commentary on the extreme right of the page is the tosfot, by twelfth and thirteenth century master scholars largely of the family of Rashi. "Further still in the margins there are yet other commentaries, often taking the form of simple references: a sort of inter-textual concordance . . . the Ayin Mishpat-Ner Mitzvah of Rabbi Joshua Boaz: concordance between passages of the Talmud and the text of Halakhah by Maimonides. Also in the margins, we find parallel texts in the Talmud: Masoret Hashas as well as the references of Biblical verses quoted in the Talmudic text (Torah Or)." Marc-Alain Ouakin, *The Burnt Book: Reading the Torah* (Princeton, N.J.: Princeton University Press, 1995), p. 35.

Page 90
Rembrandt van Rijn, *The Sacrifice of Abraham.* The Hermitage, St. Petersburg, Russia. Credit: Giraudon/Art Resource (N.Y.).

Page 92
Bob Dylan and Joan Baez, April 27, 1965, Savoy Hotel, London. Credit: UPI/Corbis-Bettmann.

Page 94
Marc Chagall (1884–1920), *The Ari Synagogue, Safed,* 1931. Israel Museum, Jerusalem. Courtesy The Israel Museum, Jerusalem/ARS (N.Y.).

Page 96
Amedeo Modigliani, *Gypsy with Baby* (1919). Credit: National Gallery of Art, Washington, D.C., Chester Dale Collection.

Page 98
Amedeo Modigliani, *Woman with Blue Eyes* (1918). Musée d'Art Moderne de la Ville de Paris, Paris. Credit: Giraudon/Art Resource (N.Y.).

Page 100
Claude Monet, *The Waterlily Pond* (1899). Musée d'Orsay, Paris. Credit: Erich Lessing/Art Resource (N.Y.).

Page 102
Johannes Vermeer, *The Little Street* (c. 1657–58). This painting is dated in the 1650s partly because the signature matches the signature of another painting of the 1650s and is different from the later "I Ver Meer" signatures of the 1660s. Credit: Rijksmuseum, Amsterdam.

Page 104
Johannes Vermeer, *Allegory of Faith* (c. 1671–74), detail. Credit: The Metropolitan Museum of Art, New York, the Friedsam Collection. Bequest of Michael Friedsam, 1931.

Page 106
Claude Monet, *Poplars on the Epte* (1891). Tate Gallery, London. Credit: Tate Gallery, London/Art Resource (N.Y.).

CHAPTER 6

Page 108
Photograph of Bob Dylan. Courtesy Waring Abbot.

Page 110
Amedeo Modigliani, *Portrait de Jeanne Hébuterne (au Foulard).* Credit: Christie's Images, Ltd., 1999.

Page 112
Rembrandt van Rijn, *Etching of Saskia.* Private collection.

Page 114
James Joyce's daughter, Lucia. Photo: Berenice Abbott/Yale University Library.

Page 116
Claude Monet, *The Rocks of Belle-Île* (1886). Musée d'Orsay, Paris. Credit: Erich Lessing/Art Resource (N.Y.).

Page 118
Haham Zevi (1660–1718), grandson of the Sha'ar Ephraim (Fisher's ancestor). Courtesy The Jewish Museum, London.

Page 120
Ketubbah (Jewish wedding contract), Verona, 1695, with a picture of the walled city of Jerusalem. Credit: The Jewish Theological Seminary. Photo: Suzanne Kaufman.

Page 122
Bob Dylan in Jerusalem, 1983. Credit: AP/Wide World Photos.

Page 124
Old Horn Weasel signing at Fort Belknap, 1909. Credit: The Milwaukee Public Museum, Milwaukee.

CHAPTER 7

Page 126
The Taj Mahal, India, built 1640. Courtesy Catherine E. Asher.

Page 128
Siddur (prayer book) of the Rabbi of Ruzhin. A famous Hasidic Rebbe, Israel Friedman of Rizhin, who lived in great splendor, c. 1850, once owned this Siddur of the German Rite, illuminated in southeastern Germany in 1460. Although the Ruzhiner Rebbe was served on golden dishes, and the splendor of his court was meant to remind his Hasidim of the temple in Jerusalem, he himself was said to be ascetic. With no soles on his shoes, his feet often froze on the bare ground. A tortured visionary, he proclaimed: "Why is the Messiah so late in coming? Does he think the next generation will be better? More deserving? I tell him here and now that he is wrong. They will be worse, much worse." Elie Wiesel, *Souls on Fire: Portraits and Legends of Hasidic Masters* (Northvale, N.J.: Jason Aronson, 1993), p. 158. And further on p. 159: "A day will come when man will stop hating others and hate himself; a day will come when all things will lose their coherence, when there will be no relation between man and his face, desire and its object, question and its answer." Credit: The Israel Museum, Jerusalem.

Page 130
Franz Kafka in front of the Oppelt House where his family lived in Prague, 1922. Credit: Archive Klaus Wagenbach, Berlin.

Page 132
Gravestones of Vincent and Théodore van Gogh at Auvers. Credit: Van Gogh Museum, Amsterdam.

Page 134
Sitting Bull, 1885. Credit: Corbis/Bettmann.

Page 136
Johannes Vermeer, *Woman with a Lute,* oil on canvas. The Metropolitan Museum of Art, New York. Bequest of Collis P. Huntington, 1900.

Page 138
Bob Dylan and Allen Ginsberg, along with Joan Baez and Roberta Flack, in New Jersey's Clinton State Prison giving a benefit concert for Rubin "Hurricane" Carter. Credit: UPI/Corbis-Bettmann.

Page 140
Johannes Vermeer, *View of Delft,* detail. Mauritshuis, The Hague. Credit: Scala/Art Resource (N.Y.).

Page 142

Floral pattern of a poppy and lotus carved on the Taj Mahal emerald, 141 carats. Courtesy Peter Shaaf.

Page 144

Jackson Pollack. Credit: Rudi Burckhardt.

Page 146

Photograph of James Joyce before a bookcase. Credit: © Gisele Freund/ Agency Nina Beskow.

Page 148

Staircase at Worker's Accident Insurance building in Prague. Credit: Archive Klaus Wagenbach, Berlin.

CHAPTER 8

Page 150

Sapphire suite. Courtesy Peter Schaaf.

Page 152

Mikhail Tal. Credit: *British Chess* magazine.

Page 154

Johannes Vermeer, *The Lacemaker*, oil on wood. The Louvre, Paris. Credit: Erich Lessing/Art Resource (N.Y.).

Page 156

Jackson Pollock painting, 1950. Courtesy Rudi Burckhardt.

Page 158

Vincent van Gogh, *Portrait of Dr. Gachet*. Credit: Christie's Images, Ltd., 1999.

Page 160

The Books of Rabbi Hayyim Eleazar Shapira. Gelatin silver print. Credit: Roman Vishniac; © Mara Vishniac Kohn. Courtesy International Center of Photography.

Page 162

Isaac Sardo Abendana's tombstone in Madras, 1632–1709. Courtesy *Encyclopedia Judaica*, Macmillan.

Page 164

Paul Gauguin (1848–1903), *Where do we come from? What are we? Where are we going?*, oil on canvas. Credit: The Museum of Fine Arts, Boston.

CHAPTER 9

Page 166

Johannes Vermeer, *Lady with a Turban*. Maruitshuis, The Hague. Credit: Scala/Art Resource (N.Y.).

Page 168

Amedeo Modigliani. Courtesy Corbis/Bettmann.

Page 170

Juhanghir with portrait of his father, Akbar. From a portrait album of the Moghul Rulers of Dehli. Bibliothèque Nationale, Paris. Credit: Giraudon/Art Resource (N.Y.).

Page 172

Johannes Vermeer, *Woman in Blue Reading Letter*. Credit: The Rijksmuseum, Amsterdam.

Page 174

Johannes Vermeer, *Woman in Blue Reading Letter*, detail. Credit: The Rijksmuseum, Amsterdam.

Page 176

Vaster's copy of a Renaissance pendant, detail. Courtesy Peter Shaaf.

Page 178

Amedeo Modigliani, *Head of a Woman*. Courtesy: Christie's Images, Ltd., 1999.

Page 180

Raphael, *Lady and a Unicorn*. Galleria Borghese, Rome. Credit: Scala/Art Resource (N.Y.).

Page 182

Johannes Vermeer, *The Astronomer*. The Louvre, Paris. Credit: Erich Lessing/Art Resource (N.Y.).

Page 184

Vincent van Gogh, *Self-portrait at the Easel*. Credit Amsterdam, van Gogh Museum (Vincent van Gogh Foundation).

Page 186

Johannes Vermeer. *Girl Reading a Letter at an Open Window* (1659). Staatliche Kunstsammlungen Gemaldegalerie, Dresden. Credit: Erich Lessing/Art Resource (N.Y.).

Page 188

Vincent van Gogh, *Vincent's Bedroom*, 1889, oil on canvas. Musée d'Orsay, Paris. Credit: Erich Lessing/Art Resource (N.Y.).

Page 190

Tao-chi, called Shih-t'ao, *Mountain Landscapes after Huang Kung-Wang*, Qing dynasty, 1671, Musée Guinet, Paris. Credit: Giraudon/ Art Resource (N.Y.).

Page 192

Franz Kafka's father, Hermann. Credit: Archive Klaus Wagenbach, Berlin.

Page 194

Rabbi Leibel Eisenberg and his gabbai, 1936. Gelatin silver print. Credit: Roman Vishniac; © Mara Vishniac Kohn. Courtesy International Center of Photography.

CHAPTER 10

Page 196

Abdul Hassan (Nadir al-Zaman), Shah Jahan holding a turban jewel, 1616–17. Moghul dynasty. Gouache and gold on paper. Inscribed by Shah Jahan, "A good portrait of me in my twenty-fifth year." Credit: Victoria and Albert Museum/Art Resource (N.Y.).

Page 198

Claude Monet, *Vetheuil*, 1879, oil on canvas. Músee des Beaux-Arts, Rouen. Credit: Giraudon/Art Resource (N.Y.).

Page 200

Johannes Vermeer, *View of Delft*. Mauritshuis, The Hague. Credit: Scala/Art Resource (N.Y.).

Page 202

Sassoon family ketubbah, 1765, from Baghdad, Iraq. The earliest known illuminated Iraqi Ketubbah. Zucker family collection (RCZ). Credit: The Jewish Theological Seminary. Photo: Suzanne Kaufman.

Page 204

Claude Monet, *Self Portrait*, 1917, oil on canvas. Musée d'Orsay, Paris. Credit: Giraudon/Art Resource (N.Y.).

Page 206

Rembrandt van Rijn, *Ephraim Bonus*, Rembrandt's physician and neighbor. Private collection.

Page 208

204-carat Gem Star Sapphire. Credit: American Gemological Laboratory and Precious Stones Company, New York.

Page 210

Rabbi Chuna Halberstam leaving the court of Rabbi Rabinowitz in Munkacevo, 1938. Gelatin silver print. Credit: Roman Vishniac; © Mara Vishniac Kohn. Courtesy International Center of Photography.

Page 212

Ustad Mansur, *Emperor Jahangir's Zebra*, 1621, gouache on paper. Moghul. Credit: The Victoria & Albert Museum/Art Resource (N.Y.).

Page 214

Students studying in Trnava, 1937. Gelatin silver print. Credit: Roman Vishniac; © Mara Vishniac Kohn. Courtesy International Center of Photography.

Page 216

Cabochon Sapphire. Courtesy Peter Schaaf.

Page 218

Jewish wedding ring, Venice, c. 1600. Courtesy Peter Schaaf.

Page 220

Johannes Vermeer, *The Art of Painting* (c. 1665–66), detail. Kunsthistorisches Museum, Vienna. Credit: Erich Lessing/Art Resource (N.Y.).

Page 222

Johannes Vermeer, *Woman with a Water Jug* (c. 1664–65). Credit: Metropolitan Museum of Art, New York, Marquand Collection. Gift of Henry G. Marquand, 1889.